UNBURIED

NICHOLAI CONLIFF

SECOND EDITION
10 9 8 7 6 5 4 3 2 / 16 15 14 13

Cover Photograph: Cassaundra Eck
Cover Model: Dylan McKay

ISBN-10: 0989076024
ISBN-13: 978-0-9890760-2-9

Library of Congress Control Number: 2013904456

For my father,
Steven E. Conliff

Chapter 1

A record spun silence into the air; the needle of its player was held captive by two pale fingers. Watching the vinyl reel about the spindle was a set of eyes—one red and one blue—unblinking for what could have been moments or a lifetime.

Ashley's thoughts were of a face without form, a voice without sound, and the embrace of flesh without texture. Yet no matter how vivid the ghost—no matter how close Ashley came to a dream—he remained aware as ever of the empty space in the bed beside him.

He turned his head to examine an antiquated clock:

5:21 a.m.

Four walls, a roof, and boarded-up windows would spare him—as they had for twenty years—from the creeping morning light.

The record needle slipped from Ashley's hand as he sat upright and perched on the bedside. The old iron frame groaned with each subtle movement of his body.

There were times, such as now, when he would have to take a look around and remind himself that *this* was home. This small house in northern Ohio with pink shag carpet from time immemorial was where he lived—where he would live forever, at this rate.

All night in his head, two lovers had lazily drifted along a narrow dirt road dividing two desolate moors. A broken sign lay in the dirt, pointing the way to a nameless village. Their arms were draped softly across one another's shoulders while their hands tenderly entwined. In time, the older of the two asked his friend if he in any way feared the future.

"I'm afraid of a lot of things," answered the younger, *"but that isn't one of them."*

What more was said meant little; Ashley instead clung to the fleeting feeling of the older boy leaning in to kiss the younger's forehead. The younger could in no way resist the urge to kiss back. They soon slowed to a stop while they indulged in the moment; their fingers untangled and they moved to hold one another. The older's eyes closed—the younger's did not. Soon, the older brought his hand up and let his fingers slide through the soft, short blonde hair of his lover….

Ashley stood. He took the record player under his arm, and after a few steps, found himself across the room in front of a chest-high stack of unsorted record singles waiting to be alphabetized. On top was a curled, dusty, yellowing newspaper, which he picked up and carefully unrolled. "Vampire Slay" read the front page headline. Even the passage of time had yet to make it true; not one word in the decaying British rag was worth reading. Instead, he was drawn to the image: an old photograph of three young men lying battered and dead in the dirt. One in particular held Ashley's attention as his fingertips pawed gently across the body. He stood entranced by the photo, and then considered the publication date for what must have been the thousandth time over the years: *7th July, 1958.*

With his hands full, Ashley strode through the kitchen where a dizzying pattern in the linoleum further betrayed his old house's age. When he reached the living room, he found a place for the record player atop a wrought iron coffee table, and then glanced to the walls where milk crates and metal shelves housed a seemingly limitless collection of vinyl.

He started toward them, only to be stopped when a sharp squawk tore through the silence. *"Brawwwwk. Wanna die!"*

He shot a harsh look toward a blue and yellow macaw perched on a small stand nearby. "Sydney, that's a horrible thing to say. You're a bad bird."

"Good bird!" Sydney snapped back, seemingly amused by himself.

Ashley rolled his eyes as he made his selection from the meticulously organized albums. He blew dust off the sleeve of a fragile forty-five and carried it back to the old player where, before he could place the disc down, a knock at the door interrupted him.

Sydney squawked again, *"Aurelio,"* and Ashley glanced at a clock:

5:29 a.m.

He left the record waiting and approached the door. It was unlocked, and a weak tug was all it needed to open. "Hey." He smiled at his visitor. "Come in."

He headed toward the kitchen as Aurelio, an older teenager with a few years on Ashley, stepped inside.

"There was a letter stuck on your door." He held it up as he turned the lock. "It's from the city—it says you'll be fined if you don't cut your grass."

Ashley was unmoved. "Would you like something to eat?"

He laughed, "Sure, thanks," and dropped the notice on the coffee table as he approached Sydney. "Hey, buddy."

"I love you," Sydney squawked back.

He began to scratch the bird's neck. "So," he called to Ashley. "I didn't get the part—any part."

"I'm sorry to hear that," said Ashley. "You said you didn't do so well in the audition."

"Botched it. I'd probably be more disappointed if

they *had* wanted me." He paused. "Okay, that's not true at all."

Ashley chuckled.

"I'm just bummed because there won't be many other commercials shooting until after Christmas," he added while Ashley prepared two sunny-side-up eggs.

"We'll keep you busy." Ashley sprinkled salt over the sizzling pan. "For instance, my lawn apparently needs mowing — and I'm sure Stam will be up for some movies."

Aurelio smiled and glanced about the room. "I guess she's not home yet?"

"No." An oat fell from a bag as Ashley slid two slices of bread into a toaster. "She works late in the winter." He reached down, swiftly, to pluck the fleck of grain from the floor.

"She's over at that church like, *every* night."

"There's nowhere Stam would rather be —" Ashley gestured to the record player. "Can you hit the music?"

"Sure." Aurelio crossed the room to the player and lifted the needle. "Who's this?" he asked as he set it onto the vinyl and — through crackles and popping — a rich, crooning voice began to sing of cloudy skies and dreams.

"Crosby," replied Ashley.

As the song played, Aurelio's gaze wandered the shelves upon shelves filled with records of all shapes and sizes, in cases and slips of all colors and textures. Atop one particular stack, he noticed a picture frame laying face-down, and turned it upright to expose a photograph of Ashley with a young girl.

"Who is this?" He held the picture out to Ashley. "A friend from back in New York?"

Ashley glanced over to see what Aurelio meant, and quickly — though subtly — recoiled at the sight. "No, no...." His teeth had gritted, but he soon smiled and even laughed softly as he returned to cooking. "I don't remember her name."

"Was it taken in an antique shop or something?" There was an old record player — not unlike Ashley's — in the foreground of the shot.

"A music shop." Ashley kept his reply terse, not that

there was all that much more to the story.

Eventually, Aurelio turned away from the records and photograph and noticed the newspaper on the coffee table. He picked it up so he could examine the front page and its sinister headline.

"You sure collect a lot of weird stuff."

"You're one to talk," said Ashley. "I've seen your movie library."

Aurelio couldn't argue, and shrugged in agreement as Ashley pulled his skillet from the stove and observed the time:

5:36 a.m.

Bing Crosby continued to croon, and the clouds in his song soon gave way to sunshine.

* * *

A girl's pale fingers reached out to pluck a single grain of rice from frosted grass beneath her feet. She gently placed it into a small plastic bag before seeking out another, and then another. The scattered remnants of a rare December wedding kept her unusually occupied and stuck outside through the night and into a bitter cold morning.

She did not mind.

At last, with one final grain dropped safely into the bag and the monotonous task complete, she took hold of a large, rusted metal case at her side; it was roughly two feet long and a little less than half that in width and depth. She carried it with her across the frozen earth toward the entrance of a nearby church, searching the ground as she walked, and eventually sighted a small stone which she paused to pick up. When she reached the church's thick wooden door, she rapped on its surface with the rock.

After no answer, she tried again.

The door soon creaked open and a girl's head poked out. "It wasn't locked, Stam," she said, making no effort to hide her perplexity.

"May I come in?"

The girl stepped aside, "Whatever," and Stam quickly

slid through, avoiding contact with the door as it fell shut.

Inside, the church was quiet; the morning mass had not yet begun, and only a handful of tired students had begun to assemble in the vestibule. Stam appeared noticeably different from the others: her skin, chilled from the winter air, was the color and texture of flour, and her pale blonde—almost white—chin-length hair set her far apart from the primped, tan preteen girls beginning to experiment with foundation. Her simple sweaters and jeans always stood her out against the blue jumper uniform of Saint Elia's Academy for Girls, and several students watched with their usual skepticism as Stam passed by and entered the nave.

She busied herself placing a few scattered Bibles, very carefully, into their proper places in the back of the pews. She then glanced at her wrist, from habit, before reaching into a pocket to remove a cell phone. She took note of the time:

6:21 a.m.

From a janitor's closet, she procured a broom and began dutifully sweeping the floor, pausing every now and then to retrieve her metal case so it was seldom more than a few feet from reach.

The idling students had begun to grow in numbers, and now, a few had moved into the nave and were fluttering about. Stam continued as though unaware of their chatter—even after a voice called out to her.

"Hey."

It was a boy's voice, one that was commonly heard on Sunday mornings.

"Hello," Stam replied, unfaltering in her task.

A group of girls abruptly shifted their attention to this exchange.

"I wanted to ask you something," the boy said, with all the confidence expected from the deacon's son and top athlete of the nearby public school.

"What?"

The boy grasped the plastic handle of Stam's broom, stopping her and successfully bringing her eyes to his.

"I was wondering if you'd wanna go with me to the

Christmas Dance this weekend."

"No."

He was shocked, more by the fact that she'd turned him down than the terseness of her response.

"Why not?" he asked, ego unwavering. "It'd be fun."

"I don't think so," she replied, with no intended rudeness.

"Come on." He took the broom from her.

"I'd rather not."

"That sucks." He handed it back. "Oh well...."

As quickly as he'd come, he left. Stam went on sweeping, hardly noticing that in under a minute, the boy had been replaced by the group of girls who had been watching. They surrounded Stam on one side.

"Hey, Stam," blurted one particularly abrasive voice.

"Hello."

"What's *wrong* with you?" the tallest asked, harshly.

"What do you mean?"

The tallest girl reached out and took hold of Stam's broom, just as the boy had. "You just blew off *David Boylan*." She said it as though he was a celebrity or household name. "You know he doesn't really like you — he just feels sorry for you."

"Why would he feel sorry for me?"

The tall girl started laughing and was joined immediately by her two counterparts.

"Do you think she's a lesbian?" the tall girl suggested to the blonde girl on her left.

The blonde girl feigned tremendous shock and covered her mouth. "Oh my God, she *is*."

The tall girl focused again on Stam. "I'll bet you like girls." She moved in close and mimicked seduction as legitimately as a twelve-year-old could, batted her eyelashes, and puckered-up. "Do you wanna kiss me, Stam?"

"No."

"She's totally a lesbian," laughed the blonde girl.

Stam produced her cell phone once more and examined the time:

6:37 a.m.

Her eyes lifted from the screen to the tall girl.

"I need the broom back. I have to go home."

"Not until you kiss Samantha." The tall girl pushed the third girl forward, who had been silent until this point.

"Eww!" Samantha balked.

Stam glanced at her, and then back to the tall girl. "I don't want to."

"Yeah, well, she wants to kiss you," the tall girl claimed.

"No I *don't*," Samantha insisted.

Stam had lost interest. She raised her hand to take the broom, but the tall girl quickly pulled it back.

Again, Stam checked the time:

6:39 a.m.

Taking full advantage of Stam's distraction, the girl plucked the metal case up from the floor. It was heavier than expected, and forced the girl to struggle enough that Stam was immediately able to grab hold of one end in an attempt to retrieve it.

The tall girl jeered, "You're short, ugly, *and* a lesbian." She laughed as she pulled the case free from Stam's hands. With some effort, she raised it high, out of Stam's reach.

"I need that," Stam said flatly.

"What's in here, anyway?" the girl demanded as she rattled its small, rusted padlock. "Is this like your gross lunchbox or something?"

Stam took hold of the tall girl's arm, but not before a pass had been coordinated, and the case was maneuvered to the blonde girl.

"Why are you touching *me?* Sarah's the one who has it."

Stam quickly let go and moved on to Sarah, unfamiliar with the childish game.

"You just wanted to *touch* me." The tall girl feigned disgust.

"Give it back," Stam requested, her patience waning.

The game of keep-away persisted until the case wound up in Samantha's hands. David's voice then interrupted, "Stop being so mean, Hannah."

The three looked in David's direction as he approached. The tall girl, Hannah, acted quickly and grabbed the case from Samantha, offering it back to Stam.

"They were just being immature," Hannah claimed, sounding annoyed.

Stam did not hesitate. With the metal case now retrieved, she pushed past the girls and David, and went straight toward the door. On the inside was a crash bar which she quickly — though carefully — pressed down. Outside, she hurried through the dark down a stone path, across a section of the school's track, past a small field, and into a parking lot empty but for one car: a beat-up, maroon sedan of what might have been — twenty years prior — a nondescript make and model which now stood out as newly vintage. She tossed her phone and the metal case onto the passenger's seat as she dropped into the driver's and slid a key into the ignition. With some strain, the engine started, and Stam immediately observed the time on the car radio:

6:43 a.m.

Quickly, she moved the metal case from its precarious position and slid it into a snug resting place behind her own seat. With her hand on the shift, she glanced at the clock as it changed:

6:44 a.m.

With a sigh, she turned off the car.

* * *

Ashley pressed a button on his cell phone where it sat on the table in front of him:

6:59 a.m.

He glanced at a note on the refrigerator which had several sequential dates scribbled on it, each one preceding a time. Each date's time was close to the others — just a few minutes' difference at most. Many of them were crossed-off, but the first in the list that was not was: *Sunday, 12/02/2001 — 7:01 a.m.*

Aurelio was still sitting at the table with the plate he had cleaned almost an hour prior. "It's just that Kent,

Ohio, isn't really the place to be if you wanna be an actor, you know?"

"I certainly believe that." Ashley nodded. "Would you move if you could?"

"I dunno. I *want* to."

"Where would you go?"

"New York or L.A., I guess."

"I strongly advise Los Angeles," Ashley replied. "New York is a pigsty."

He pressed the button on his phone once more:

7:01 a.m.

He grabbed the cell, flipped it open, and brought it to his ear as though he had been waiting all night to make the call.

"Sorry, hold on," he said to Aurelio with a hint of nervousness in his voice.

"Sure." Aurelio stood and took his plate to the sink to wash it.

A few moments passed and Ashley pulled the phone away from his head, looked for a button, and then put it back to his ear. He repeated this two more times before finally giving up. He set the phone on the table. The small time display soon faded:

7:03 a.m.

He stood up and moved to the refrigerator where he struck off the date and time that had just passed.

"Anyway," Aurelio glanced over to him, "yeah, I mean, I think L.A. would be the place to go, but New York City always seemed cool though."

"I never liked it."

"Yeah," Aurelio laughed, friendly as ever. "I think the suburbs suit you better—"

A thump outside broke their conversation. Taking note of it, Aurelio dried his hands and started for the door. Ashley excused himself around a corner as Aurelio stepped outside where the morning twilight had imperceptibly begun to overtake the night. He retrieved a bundled newspaper and re-entered the house quickly, shutting out the cold. He untied the string around the thick Sunday publication and folded it open as he scanned the front page. "Oh, wow," he said. "George Harrison died."

"Mm," Ashley grumbled as though this news was somewhat expected. "He had cancer." He moved to pick up his cell phone again.

"Oh yeah, that's what it says." Aurelio noted as he read. "He wasn't... the *last* one, was he?"

"The last *Beatle*?" Ashley chuckled. "No — there are still two more." He put his phone to his ear and made another call. No answer.

Aurelio finished looking over the paper and handed it off to Ashley. He glanced at the headline: "Enron Scandal Deepens." His brow furrowed slightly as he noticed the dead musician was only a blurb toward the bottom of the page.

Aurelio examined the clock on Ashley's wall:

7:07 a.m.

"When do you think Stam'll get back?" he asked.

Ashley could only glance nervously back to his phone.

Chapter 2

A blond boy, maybe twelve years of age, clutched a pamphlet tightly in his hand as he rushed down a dirt road toward home. He hopped over an old wooden fence and hurried through a field in a desperate attempt to catch up with his brother who, being the more athletic of the two, had left him in the dust at the sound of the school bell.

"Hallo, Gunther." An old man waved to the boy as he fled past.

"Hallo, Herr Petersen." Gunther waved back.

He reached the other side of the field, went right over the fence, and back onto the streets, but then began to slow his pace. It was difficult to keep up such a speed for so long; Luther had outrun him again. His run became a jog, his jog became a walk, and his walk became a shuffle. He covered his eyes as he passed the corner drugstore where, about a year prior, the owner had placed an anti-Bolshevik poster in the window with a strange illustration on it. Gunther could hardly remember what the caption was—something like "So ist das Sowjetparadies"—but recalled vividly the image of an emaciated caricature with a contorted expression, deep hollow eyes, and a trickle of blood escaping its mouth. He wasn't entirely clear on what a Bolshevik was, but he knew not to like them, and he didn't like looking at the picture even in the daylight.

He was almost home. He had regained some wind and had better paced himself for this last leg of the journey. His family lived in a dense but small village, and it always felt very isolated in Gunther's opinion; it was a humble cluster of homes surrounded by a sea of derelict farmlands. Their residence, like many others, was packed tightly between two neighbors: The Mohns, whom he didn't care for much, and the Müllers who had a son, Jens, of whom Gunther was tremendously fond. Jens was two years older, but had always treated him like an equal— more of an equal than Gunther's own twin brother ever did.

Upon arriving home, he submerged himself all evening in the pamphlet, reading and re-reading line after line, and just before suppertime, Gunther's father requested he read aloud the closing verse:

"Those words it was that first awakened us,
From dull brooding, hollow death —
We can no longer perish,
A light burns for us in the night!"

Luther scoffed at Gunther's enthusiasm. "You just want to join since I did."

Gunther balked at this, but their father interjected, "Well, I think it's a fine idea. Gunther, I'm glad to see you actually showing some initiative."

"This is stupid," shouted Luther. "Every time I do anything, *he* has to tag along."

Their mother joined in as she set dinner on the table, "Bayerischer Mit Spargel," she called.

"Hm," Luther mumbled, "Gunther's favorite, of course." He climbed to his feet and moved to the table. Gunther followed humbly behind, bringing the pamphlet with him.

"Gunther, please say the prayer," his mother instructed to his surprise. It was something of a rarity that he, with his unassuming character, was ever asked to do anything of the sort. He cleared his throat—he had already pushed himself by reading the pamphlet, but he did his best. "Father, bless this meal, for our strengthening and to your praise. Help us, God, today and at all times, make us prepared for... *eternity*."

He had never liked the concept of eternity, and shuddered at the word. The idea of living forever, in God's graces or otherwise, wasn't a comforting notion, but that was how the prayer went.

"God bless Germany, and God bless the Führer," added his Father.

Everyone began to eat while Gunther picked nervously at his veal rather than diving right in as would have been typical for him. He felt dejected, as was often the case, by his brother's comments. He looked across the table as Luther eyed some asparagus with great skepticism. To an observer, watching the two of them might have been like seeing double, but Gunther was perfectly able to pick out the negligible differences between himself and Luther only their parents might notice. Meanwhile, Luther simply insisted he and Gunther looked nothing alike at all, scorning the very notion.

Eventually, Luther noticed he was being watched and reacted with a kick to Gunther's shin.

"Ouch! Mom," squealed Gunther. "He kicked me."

"You're such a baby," said Luther. "You wouldn't last ten seconds in the Hitlerjugend."

"Luther," their mother chastised him. "Leave your brother alone."

"But you're gonna let him do it. You're gonna let him do it and he's gonna tag along with me and he's gonna embarrass—"

"I will not," Gunther insisted. On a normal day, he would sit and suffer silently through Luther's torments, but for some reason, he felt aggressive, and Luther wasn't backing down.

"—I'm gonna be the kid with the *schwul* running

arou—"

"That's enough," their father shouted. "Luther, go to your room."

Luther furiously pushed away from the table and stormed off without a word. Their father turned to their mother. "Where the *hell* did he learn a word like that?"

Gunther stared down at his plate, looking pathetic.

"And you stop being such a baby," his father added.

"Yes, Father," Gunther replied.

Silence fell over the table; the only sounds were the clinking of utensils as the three worked on their meals. After a few minutes, their father spoke up once more, "You're going to learn real skills, real survival techniques, and you're going to learn how to be a proud German citizen in the HJ."

Gunther nodded. It had all been a ruse; his fate had already been decided, and feigning excitement was all he could do. If he lied to himself long enough, maybe even *he* would believe the pamphlet—maybe the HJ wouldn't be so bad.

The next day—Sunday—his mood deteriorated as a result of the cold scorn he had received from his brother the remainder of the previous night *and* all morning as they prepared for church. Gunther's family always seemed to wind up in the same spot in the pews—never too close to the front, never rudely far back—always right in the middle and close to the aisle. Today, Gunther was on the outside. He hardly listened during the usual speeches and prayers, and instead counted the minutes as he waited for the service to end. Then someone caught his eye as he looked over his shoulder.

It was Jens, across the aisle and back two rows. Jens made an exaggerated expression, betraying his own boredom, and then pantomimed blowing his brains out using his fingers as a gun. Gunther snickered quietly and was promptly whacked in the arm by his brother. He turned his attention back to the sermon.

Jens was tall and gawky, but outgoing and well-liked around town by everyone. Gunther, not being terribly popular, felt fortunate he had a next door neighbor of such notoriety; Jens served as a buffer of sorts between Gunther and the teenage bullies. He recalled an afternoon earlier that spring when he was too afraid to try a cigarette some of the older boys had found. They'd mocked him mercilessly until Jens shut them up with an issue of *Reine Luft,* convincing them within minutes that not only would they all die of cancer, but it was decidedly un-German to smoke. If anyone other than Jens had tried that, they'd have been laughed out of town. He had a way with people, and always seemed to be aware of some big secret far before anyone else was — even the adults. *Nobody* could pull one over on him.

Before too long, church ended and the families began to filter outside. Gunther took extra care to make sure he wound up beside Jens as the crowd squeezed down the aisle.

"That was unbearable," Jens whispered.

"Yeah," Gunther replied. He often didn't know what to say to Jens; he always wanted to be clever, but that was not his strong suit. Oddly, Jens always laughed at his jokes, and so he tried one, "I wasn't sure eternity would *last* long enough for him to finish."

It met with success; Jens smiled and laughed, and whether he really thought it was funny or not, it was still genuine.

As the two finally made it outside into the bright, late morning sun, Gunther's father patted Jens on the shoulder. "You staying outta trouble?"

"Always, Herr Gruenwold."

"Good," he replied. "You know, Gunther is starting up with the HJ later this week."

"Yeah?" asked Jens, with a glance at Gunther. He anticipated what the man's instructions might be. "I'll keep an eye on him, sir." Jens threw up his right hand in salute. "Heil Hitler!"

Gunther's father returned the gesture, "Heil Hitler," before moving on to mingle with the crowd.

Jens mumbled quietly to Gunther, "*Heal* Hitler? Why? Is he *sick*?" playing off the similarities between the words.

Gunther laughed, but stopped when Luther whacked Jens in the arm. "Don't be stupid," he said as he walked past.

Jens pursed his lips.

"He's being a bastard," Gunther murmured.

"Nah," Jens replied. "He's right. I could probably get my ass kicked for saying something like that." He turned to Gunther. "So, you're gonna do it?"

"I guess so, yeah," said Gunther. "Do you think it's a good idea?"

"Has Luther been trying to scare you out of it? It's just the boy scouts, plus a bunch of Nazi stuff. You can handle it."

"He doesn't want me around, I guess." Gunther slumped a little. He and his brother had never had a perfect relationship, but he had been acting unusually hostile toward him in the last year or so, and Gunther couldn't peg a reason why.

"He'll get over it," Jens replied, seeming to read Gunther's thoughts. "This sort of thing happens. A few years ago — before my cousin Manfred moved to America — he just stopped talking to me one day...." He started to trail off.

"At least you don't have to share a bedroom."

"True." He smiled at Gunther, trying to cheer him up, and then began to run. "Come on, let's get out of here."

The two hurried down the street.

The pair had met at church three years prior, when the parish met after mass to discuss the newly-passed Nuremberg Laws. Gunther was nine, Jens eleven, and the two had been left in the nave to play with some other boys. One of them thought it would be funny, for no real reason at all, to try and spit on Gunther from several pews away. After a few failed attempts, with Gunther doing his best to avoid it, another boy crept up behind him and let a huge wad of saliva drop on Gunther's head. Shocked and disgusted, Gunther might have cried were it not for Jens who, at some point, had visited the church's stoup.

Jens tapped the shoulder of the boy above Gunther

and made a muffled sound, "Mhrm."

He looked over just as Jens spat a mouthful of Holy Water onto his face with such force, the boy toppled backward. He *did* cry, and Gunther laughed.

Jens was always sticking up for Gunther, and no matter how awkward or embarrassing he acted, Jens never seemed to notice or care. He didn't even laugh when Gunther told him about being afraid of the Bolshevik poster at the drugstore. Instead, whenever they passed by, Jens would distract and captivate Gunther with conversation until they were safely out of its sight. When they were alone, he'd talk about music: often about swing and, to a lesser extent, jazz, both of which were decidedly non-German things. Bad influences. When they were in public or around adults, Jens was careful to discuss tough-sounding, nationalistic things like how he wanted to be a soldier or how much he admired the Führer's strength and conviction.

That was how conversation went that evening; Jens and his family came over for Sunday dinner, and Jens, being the oldest child present, was the focus of what little attention the adults gave the children. Gunther sat quietly as Jens effortlessly kept them placated with his stories of learning to use a Karabiner 98 Kurz just like soldiers in the Wehrmacht, going to Nuremburg for rallies, and so on. Gunther's father proclaimed proudly at one point, "Children are the future of Germany. They shall be the ones to realize the dreams of the Führer. Gunther, Luther, you both could learn a lot from this fine young man."

The brothers nodded politely, but afterward, nearly imperceptibly, Jens rolled his eyes at Gunther.

That night, as Gunther lay in bed staring at the ceiling, he wondered what it would be like to go to Nuremberg, or Munich, or Berlin—those big cities that seemed so unbelievably far away. He wondered if he'd have to learn to use a gun like Jens had. He didn't really *want* to do that. He didn't want to join the HJ *at all....*

"It's dangerous, Gunther."

His attention was pulled to his brother, who lay in the bed next to his.

"What?" he asked, surprised Luther was speaking to him again.

"How long do you think you can hide it from everyone? What do you think's going to happen to you when somebody finds out?" Luther asked.

He wasn't sure what to say.

"Mother and Father don't know, but *I* do. I *know*."

"... What are you talking about?"

"Gunther," Luther replied harshly. "It's obvious, and it's gonna get you or him in a lot of trouble."

He shifted nervously. "You're being weird."

"Gunthe—"

"Leave me alone." Gunther turned away and shut his eyes, forcing the world to disappear. The last sound he heard before sleep was a heavy sigh from his brother.

* * *

Stam stood with her back to a mirrored wall. A long time—a *very* long time—had passed since her last look at herself. It was moments like those from earlier that would start her wondering what it was that made her so different; she would wonder what made her face so unlike anyone else's. In her time at the church and among the students, she was always held in strange regard; her behavior, it seemed, accounted for much of it, but she could never shake the feeling her two eyes, two ears, one nose and mouth somehow also set her apart. She wondered, with the idlest of curiosities, what her own face looked like.

In time, a girl entered the restroom in which Stam had taken up refuge. The girl proceeded to a stall and ignored Stam until, after flushing and moving toward the sink, she eyed the pale figure with some skepticism. Stam remained where she was as the girl dried her hands and left, seeming unnerved by Stam's statue-like poise.

This was how the day went on. Now and then, a girl would stop by briefly, more or less ignoring Stam, and then be on their way. One girl entered and walked right back out. Another stepped into the room and used the mirror to apply lip gloss with trembling fingers.

Stam was a poor judge of time, and having left her phone in the car, was unsure how long she had been waiting—until suddenly, the room was overtaken by almost a dozen women and girls of all ages chattering back and forth about the day's sermon. They stood with Stam, some of them seeming to wonder about her as they waited for their turns in a stall. A few more trickled in over time, but before too long, they had all gone. Mass was over, and so by Stam's estimate, it must have been around 11:45 a.m.

Not long after, there was a knock at the door and David peeked inside. "Uh, Stam? You in here?"

Stam was out of sight around a wall, but she replied, "Yes?"

"Are you okay? What are you still doing here?"

"I'm fine." She fell back on a lie rehearsed long-ago. "My ride is late."

David seemed dissatisfied by this answer. "Is anyone in there?"

"Just me."

He entered and stepped around the corner where Stam stood still avoiding her reflection.

"That was like, five *hours* ago."

She said nothing.

"I didn't know you were still here. You should come and hang out—I'm stuck at the church until three."

His father was a Deacon at the parish, and thus, David often wound up at the church every Sunday more or less performing the same duties Stam took care of at night—cleaning, straightening, and so on—though he did so less willfully than she. Prior to today, they had had few notable interactions; his sudden fascination with her was mysterious.

"I'd rather not," she replied.

David seemed unsure how to react. He stood watching her for a bit, and then glanced at the reflection of the back of her head.

"Hey." He pointed to it. "You should turn around—there's a really hot girl in the mirror."

Stam made no move. Her eyes remained on him, and her expression showed no hint of amusement, but David recovered quickly. "Okay, you're too smart to fall for that." He laughed, and again waited for some kind of reaction, but when she had none, he was forced to continue. "So... why won't you go to the dance with me?

"I'm not interested," she reiterated.

"Do you *like* me at all?"

"Yes."

"You do?" He let his excitement show.

"You stood up for me. I appreciate that."

David laughed. "Is that the only reason?"

"Yes."

Excitement was traded for disappointment. "Oh. Well, I guess it's obvious *I* like *you*...."

"It's not."

"It isn't?"

Stam was silent. She had already answered once.

"Well, I *do*," David insisted.

"That's nice of you," she replied.

He looked uncomfortable. "I guess I'm bothering you."

"Not really."

Silence took over between them. David was unclear how to move on—smoothly, anyway—at this point, and decided not to try. "So," he said, "are you going with somebody else?"

"To the dance?" Stam raised an eyebrow. "No."

"You just don't want to go at all?"

"It's not something I'd find enjoyable. I don't have romantic feelings for anyone. I can't dance." She answered with a laundry list.

"Well, the dancing thing doesn't matter. I can hardly dance either." He realized what he'd said was unlikely to elicit much of a response. "So... why don't you like anyone?"

"I like some people."

"Okay, but like—like *romantically*, as you put it."

"... I don't know."

"How could I get you to like *me* that way?" His

confidence seemed to be returning.

"Hannah likes you," Stam replied. "She and I aren't so different—maybe she would go with you."

David scoffed. "Hannah's a bitch. You're nothing like her. I like *you*."

"You said that." Stam had a vague impulse to look in the mirror, as if it might provide some clue as to what distinguished her from Hannah, Sarah or Samantha, but did not indulge. "What is it you like about me?"

"It's like, your personality. You're *different* from everyone else."

"How so?"

"Stam—you've been hanging out in a bathroom for five hours. Most girls who do that are usually doing their makeup."

"I don't own any makeup."

"Yeah, 'cause you're pretty without it."

Stam, once again, did not have the anticipated reaction. David did his best to hide his shock that several of his best lines had now fallen flat. "You're just... really unique." He approached her and let his voice drop to the point of almost begging, "*Come on.* I wanna get to know you better." He smiled. "Will you go with me, please?"

She looked at him. Her voice lacked even a hint of malice, but the reply seemed set in stone. "No."

* * *

The day was one like so many others: an endless grind of grueling exercises. In the early weeks, it was just like Jens said it would be: they collected firewood and built camps and occasionally wrote poems praising the Führer. Recently though, things were changing: Gunther had been up since before sunrise running around a track while Rudolf, an older boy closer to Jens' age, barked commands at the ten boys grouped with him. When that was over, they learned to dig trenches, how to put on gas masks, sat through a lecture about the dilution of racial purity in Germany, ate lunch, and after some more running, sometime in the late afternoon, Rudolf handed

Gunther a rifle.

"How's it feel?" he asked.

"Heavy."

"Go on and hold it up."

Gunther cautiously brought the rifle into what he believed was a readied position. Some of the other boys chuckled as Rudolf moved Gunther's left hand to its proper placement and raised his right elbow and shoulder. "Like that," he said.

Gunther nodded, more than ready to hand off the weapon. He looked over at Luther, who had gone well out of his way to make sure he was *never* standing beside his brother.

"Go ahead and squeeze the trigger," Rudolf instructed. "Get a feel for it."

Gunther resisted at first, then pulled it and —

BAM!

He felt himself thrown backward several times his own height. He landed flat on his back with the rifle lying on his chest. His arm ached horribly; he clutched it, wincing and doing his very best not to whine or moan. He focused on this rather than the laughing faces that appeared above him. Rudolf was laughing the hardest. "That was quite a scream." Gunther didn't remember screaming; he only remembered feeling like a horse had kicked him in the chest.

Rudolf picked the rifle up off of him. "Oh, come on...."

"Hey, Luther, hope you're not as much of a wuss as him," jeered one of the other boys. Luther ignored him, avoiding any display of sympathy or embarrassment.

"It hurts," Gunther groaned.

"Let's go." Rudolf took hold of Gunther's arm and pulled him up.

Once on his feet, Gunther pulled the collar of his shirt away to look at the front of his shoulder, which was already a bright purple color. Luther caught sight of it and winced. With some reservation, he turned to Rudolf who was handing the gun off to another boy. "Rottenführer, he should go to the medic."

Rudolf glanced over and saw the bruise on Gunther's arm. He shrugged. "Ain't always gonna be a medic around, you know."

Luther looked at Gunther and gestured toward the nearby infirmary with a cock of his head. Gunther didn't really want to embarrass his brother further, and he wasn't sure which would be worse: staying or going. He stood with the group another minute or so, but finally gave in and took off toward the building. Luther kept his attention on the training.

Gunther remembered how thrilled his father had been when he'd found out the local HJ met and trained on a Wehrmacht boot camp. *"It'll be just like the army, boys,"* he'd said, excitedly. Gunther had feigned appropriate joy about the matter, as the last thing he needed was his father thinking there was anything unusual about him, but in reality he didn't *want* to be in an army, and that was what this felt like. As he walked, he passed several groups of other boys from other villages; there were boys even younger than him going through the same rigorous exercises. And then there were the older teenagers—older than Jens or Rudolf—who had guns of their own, marching in formation. Gunther *hated* marching. He hated everything about this.

As he sat in the infirmary waiting for a nurse—alone but for an older woman tapping away on a typewriter on the other side of the room—he wished that something, *anything*, would distract him from all of it... and then something did. The door creaked open and Jens walked in. He smirked at Gunther, immediately causing his face to light up with an almost embarrassing glow—it *would* have been embarrassing to anyone other than Jens. He walked past Gunther and took a roll of gauze from a cabinet. The woman at the typewriter glanced up and Jens simply waved dismissively. "I'm all right."

He dropped down beside Gunther and began wrapping a cut on his hand.

"Ouch," Gunther offered sympathetically. "You okay?"

"It's not even a scratch—did it on purpose," he said.

"What about you? Are *you* okay?"

"Yeah—it's nothing."

"Let me see." Jens reached up to take a look. Gunther's instinct was to resist, but he allowed it.

"Shit. Rudolf is an asshole," he grumbled, his hand still on Gunther's shoulder. "He thinks that fucking gag is funny."

"I'll be okay."

"He's *still* an asshole. I'll deal with him."

"Don't...." Gunther shook his head, pulling away.

Jens raised an eyebrow and leaned down, trying to make eye-contact with him. Gunther obliged, though just for a moment, before looking down at the floor.

"Gunther," Jens was very serious, "are you *sure* you want to be here?"

"... Yeah."

"You're *sure* you're sure?"

He couldn't seem to lie twice.

"Listen—life is a lot simpler than all these pamphlets and doctrines make it seem." He looked Gunther deep in the eyes. "You shouldn't ever do anything you don't want to do. *Nobody* can *make* you. If things get too bad, there's always a way out."

Gunther looked at him quizzically. Jens smiled and pantomimed shooting himself in the head as he had done in the past. Gunther smiled back, not at what Jens was saying, but simply because he cared enough to try and cheer him up.

"In fact," continued Jens, "I'll go one better than that: not only should you not do what you don't want to do... you *should* do what you *do* want. You can't live your life running from fears—you've gotta chase your desires."

Gunther nodded, understanding this, but he still felt dreary. It was a nice sentiment that Jens was expressing, but not entirely realistic. Still, Gunther was curious. "What do *you* want?" he asked. "Why are *you* still doing this?"

Jens wrinkled his face a bit, balking and not really wanting to answer, but he did. "Well, I guess this probably sounds contradictory, but... sometimes it's appropriate to suppress what you want in the interest of not hurting anyone."

"Huh?" Gunther didn't understand, so he asked a more specific question. "Do you mean you *don't* want to be in the HJ?"

"That's part of it."

"*I* don't want to be," said Gunther, "but I guess you do a better job of faking it. If my father wasn't, well, the way that he is, he'd have noticed by now." He sighed. "I have to stay here."

"Why? Who cares if you disappoint your father?"

"I just...." Gunther was beginning to tremble as he searched for the right words. "It's more than *that*...."

Jens put his arm around Gunther, "It's okay," and swallowed nervously as he looked up at the ceiling. He let out a breath and gave Gunther a comforting, gentle shake. There was silence between them for a time, until Jens said, "In two years, I'll move up into the *Schutzstaffel* and maybe I can get out of here," he said. "It's not really what I want, but...."

He trailed off. Gunther looked at him, hoping for a continuation, but a medic finally appeared and offered Gunther an ice pack for his shoulder. "There you go, lad," he said as friendly as could be. "Now, back outside with you."

The medic brought Gunther to his feet, out from under Jens' arm, and scooted him toward the door. Jens followed, and they found themselves outside, feet sinking back into the mud while groups of children shouted and struggled in their training exercises.

* * *

Time had left Stam weary of standing, and now she sat on the cold, tile floor of the restroom with her arm resting lazily across her metal case. Her would-be suitor had left hours ago, not bothering to hide a feeling of harsh dejection, and in the time that had passed, Stam had not had a single visitor.

"Stam?"

Though she hadn't heard the door open, he was back.

David stepped around the corner, now wearing a heavy winter coat which rustled loudly when he moved. "Hey."

"Hello."

He came and sat next to her.

"I was gonna ask somebody else, but, I couldn't think of anyone."

"What about?" asked Stam. "The dance?"

"Yeah," he answered. Stam said nothing more, and so it was up to David once again to move things along. "Are you upset about something? You've been in here all day," he said. "Do you need a ride?"

"I'm fine."

He didn't bother asking her again. Hearing something once from Stam, he was learning, was enough. He had been working at the church once a week for as long as he could remember, and it had taken him the last two years, since he'd first met Stam, to work up the courage to ask for a date. He had never encountered anyone so beautiful.

That's what he said, anyway, before planting a kiss in some awkward place between her lips and cheek. Stam's eyes turned to him, while her head failed to move until David's hand pulled her face to his.

His kiss stopped only long enough to speak. "I really like you." He placed his mouth onto her immobile lips once more.

She made no attempt reciprocate, but she wasn't stopping him, either. A short time passed before he pulled away and smiled, hopefully. The look on Stam's face was cold and dispassionate, at least relative to what would be expected in reaction to the wild display of affection David had just offered. He looked into her eyes. "Have you ever kissed anyone before?"

"I just did."

"I mean, like, *before* right now."

"Yes."

"Oh," he said, hiding disappointment with amusement. "So I'm not your first?"

"No."

"Oh well." He laughed and moved in close. "So,

like," he took a chance, "what have you done before?"

"What do you mean?"

"Like, with a guy?"

Stam stared at him. "You want a list?"

He laughed. "Is it a *long* list?"

"That depends."

He laughed again. "Okay, well, you're a virgin, right?" he asked, rhetorically.

"No."

That shut him up. "Really? *You?*"

Stam saw no reason to answer. She stood, no longer comfortable in a seated position against the wall. David hurried to stand beside her.

"Your coat is on," she observed. "Are you leaving?"

"I've got time." He wasn't interested in changing the subject yet. "So, wait…." Her last statement had taken him so off guard, he wasn't really sure how to proceed, and so instead, he laughed nervously. "I guess a kiss isn't a very big deal then, huh?"

"I suppose not," she said. "But—"

She was cut off as David kissed her full on the lips once more. In an awkward attempt to move things forward, his hand found its way to her stomach, and then under her shirt, where it gravitated to her belly button. Meanwhile, his tongue began reservedly pushing its way into her mouth. When his attempts failed, he instead kissed her cheek, then moved toward her ear and as far down as the neck of Stam's thick wool sweater would allow. As he went on with this, Stam eventually looked down at his head. She watched his lips drift in an inexperienced but determined manner across her, and then she took note of the taught, stretched skin of his craned neck.

"David Boylan," scolded a shrill voice, almost knocking him over. He broke away from Stam and looked toward the woman who had just come around the corner. She was in her early forties, though her hair had grayed early, and despite her small frame, she had a strangely authoritative presence. David stammered, unsure how to save face, while Stam pulled down the bottom of her shirt, covering her exposed stomach.

The woman's tone shifted to one more confused. *"Stam?"*

"Yes?"

The woman focused her attention on David. "Young man, you get out of here this instant and wait for me outside."

"Sister Carroll, it's not—"

"Outside!"

He marched out of the room, head down, his coat rustling noisily as he walked. She watched him until he was gone, and then turned to Stam. Before Sister Carroll could get out a word, Stam gestured to the woman's watch. "Do you know what time it is?"

Sister Carroll did not even entertain the idea of answering; her tone only grew more furious. "Stam Miller, what do you have to say for yourself?"

"What do you mean?"

"You know what I mean, young lady." She approached Stam. "You're a fifteen-year-old girl, and you know better than to be doing something like this."

Stam generally found she didn't like it when people yelled at her, and did her best to assuage it. She nodded in agreement with Sister Carroll. "Yes, sister."

"I'm going to be calling *both* of your parents about this."

Stam was genuinely skeptical about the idea, but said nothing as she leaned down to pick up her metal case.

"Are you giving me attitude, young lady?"

"What?" Stam was confused. "No."

Sister Carroll reached out and took Stam's arm, leading her toward the door, "You come with me this instant."

As she was pulled, Stam glanced at Sister Carroll's watch:

4:54 p.m.

"No," she said, resisting.

"Excuse me?"

"I'll come with you in..." she made a quick calculation, "... twenty-two minutes."

* * *

Ashley moved gracefully about his expansive collection with a stack of records in one arm. He examined the cover of one—Joni James' "Have You Heard?"—as he searched for its proper place among the thousands of sleeves. He found it with ease and slid it between at least a dozen other Joni James singles and LPs.

Chet Baker's breathy voice and a sparse piano haunted the room as he wistfully sang of an unphotographable valentine. After only a verse, Chet's words were interrupted by another song—not from the record player, but from Ashley's phone. He set down the sleeves and hurried to the table. There, he glanced at the time—5:12 p.m.—before silencing a digitized rendition which surely only he would recognize of "You Belong to Me" when he answered an unfamiliar number.

"... Hello?"

* * *

16th July, 1940
Dear Jens,

It's really great to hear from you! Gosh, it's been months! I have been trying to get your address from one of the commanders or from Rudolf, but nobody seems to know anything. I'm so glad you found mine!

To answer your question, I've been training in a place called Larosbach all summer, which is right on the edge of Austria. Ever since the war started, all we have been doing is combat training and marching. I can't stand it. I wish I had listened to you that day two years ago and gotten out of here, but even now, I still do not know where I would go.

Speaking of wishes: Luther got his. He's in Munich right now, which means he won't have to be around me anymore. I sent him a letter last month, but I have not heard back. I don't think he's going to reply.

Do you think they're going to make us fight in the war? I

worry about that a lot. Some of the oldest kids already went off to fight in France, but I guess they already won. I guess it will all be over by the time we're old enough.

What is it like in the Schutzstaffel division? What do you do? Rudolf was transferred into the SS a few weeks ago, and the new Rottenführer, Martin, is even worse. I never thought I'd miss Rudolf.

But who I really miss is you. I miss the way things used to be. That probably sounds silly, but it's true.

I'm really happy you wrote to me. I think about you a lot and I'm glad I have a friend out there somewh —

"Hey, whatcha writing there, *Heulsuse?*" a voice called from behind Gunther as a hand snatched away the letter he was in the middle of writing. Gunther immediately grabbed for it and in trying to reach, awkwardly fell out of his cot, bringing his coarse blanket with him.

"Give it back," he cried.

A few other boys in the room snickered. "What's it say, Heinz?"

Gunther managed to get up and made another unsuccessful attempt at grabbing the paper away from him. Heinz, his bunkmate, was not only taller, but much thicker than Gunther, and easily deflected him with his free arm while scanning the letter.

He laughed as he read through it. "You're a real pussy, Heulsuse. Who're you writing this shit to, anyway? Your mommy and daddy?"

In that moment, a young officer opened the door to the room, "Shut up in there!" He looked at Heinz and Gunther. "What are you doing, Heulsuse?"

Gunther had somehow retained this terrible nickname since the day Rudolf had so embarrassingly had him unintentionally fire off a rifle. How the name had stuck, he wasn't sure. He didn't remember crying or screaming, and yet that was his reputation now: a *crybaby.* Truthfully, he rarely ever cried, but his father had done the same thing: he always accused him of being on the verge of tears. It was very strange.

"He stole my letter, Rottenführ—"

"Shit, Heulsuse, I don't care. Get back in bed, both of you."

Heinz crumpled the letter and shoved it into Gunther's chest. He took it and climbed back into his bed.

"God, you're like a bunch of fucking children," the Rottenführer, Martin, grumbled as he shut the door.

In his cot, Gunther could feel a hard kick in his back from Heinz beneath him. He did his best to ignore it as he sat in the dark and attempted to flatten out the letter against his legs. He searched his person before noticing the pen had rolled away in the struggle and now lay on the floor. He decided not to retrieve it.

Instead, he laid his head down and waited for morning. He counted seventeen more kicks from Heinz before sleep was upon him.

Before the sun had even threatened to rise, Gunther found himself outside and marching for what seemed like the thousandth time. At this point, he wasn't sure any of them could actually improve their marching skills, and so he wondered why they had to keep doing it.

The boys all sang words that had grown to mean nothing:

> "Hell erklinget deutscher Sang;
> unser ganzes Leben lang;
> Treue frohe Lieder;
> klingen immer wiede;
> durch die ganze Welt!"

They spent an awful lot of time marching, but it didn't seem like either this *or* singing would be very practical in combat. Gunther found that questioning these things—and continuing to ask himself why he was doing this—was one of the easiest ways to pass the time and, for a moment anyway, forget that Heinz was periodically trying to trip him. Another skill Gunther had mastered was ignoring the other boys' attempts to heckle him. It was only at times like the night before—when he couldn't finish his letter — that he reacted to them at all.

"Heulsuse was writing to his mommy last night," he heard Heinz whisper to someone while the Rottenführer's attention was elsewhere. "I guess he's scared. You *scared*, Heulsuse?"

Gunther heard a snicker from at least one boy behind him.

"Or were you writing to your girlfriend, huh?" Heinz stifled a laugh. "You got a little *girlfriend?*"

Every word from Heinz's mouth had a sickening sneer to it — it wasn't just when he was mocking someone. It was as though he was incapable of sounding any other way. Then again, insults were about all that ever came from his mouth, so it was hard to truly gauge.

The whispering and snickering went on until the march was over. As they took their final step, Gunther felt the all too familiar feeling of Heinz's foot catching his and, being unprepared, toppled forward into several boys. Martin screamed at them, "Dammit, Gunther!"

"I'm sorry, Rottenführer, sir."

Gunther was starting to hope Heinz might eventually find a way to get him expelled from the whole thing, although he had heard membership in the HJ was now compulsory for all boys his age. Instead, as usual, the only immediate effect of the blunder Heinz had inflicted was that Martin was upset and Gunther was sure to have extra laundry duties.

The day wore on, and like so many others, the boys slowly marched it away.

* * *

Ashley carefully grasped a narrow iron handle and pulled, opening one of the church's thick doors. As it shut behind him, he took a brief look around the empty vestibule before wandering into the nave, where he let his eyes roam across the stained glass icons of Saints. It wasn't often Ashley found himself inside churches — he had been to this one once or twice in the past — but typically, he avoided it. He walked the center aisle, up toward the

Sanctuary, as his mind seemed to drift to a distant dream. Soon his gaze fell upon a small stoup, half-full of stale sanctified water. He approached it thoughtfully and placed his hands on the stone rim of the bowl, letting his fingertips rest in the dusty soup until footsteps out in the vestibule interrupted his silence. He left and followed them.

"Excuse me," he called. Sister Carroll stopped and turned to him as he continued, "Hello. I'm here to pick up my sister."

"Your sister? Oh, we just spoke on the phone, correct?" She asked. "You're here for Stam?"

"Yes." He smiled again.

"... I don't suppose your parents are here?" she asked.

"Afraid not."

Sister Carroll pursed her lips, disappointed by the answer, but she then motioned for Ashley to follow her toward a walkway connecting the church to the school proper. As they neared it, Sister Carroll confessed, "I was hoping I might be able to talk to them—your parents—about some things."

"Such as?"

"Well," she began, only to stop when she could see Stam waiting for them on the opposite side of a glass door leading to the connecting hallway. The pale girl tapped softly against the clear pane.

"It's open," Sister Carroll called to her.

"May I come in?" she asked, still on the other side with one hand grasping the handle.

There was a trace of annoyance in Sister Carroll's voice. "Stam, this is a *church*."

Ashley winced discretely at the phrasing, knowing its ineffectuality, while Stam made no further move and remained expectant.

Sister Carroll, in a voice no longer simply hinting at irritation, instructed, "Come in, Stam."

Upon stepping inside, her eyes quickly met Ashley's.

"You all right?" he asked.

She nodded.

"Stam," Sister Carroll spoke up. "We need to have a talk with your parents."

Ashley smirked. "What'd you do?"

"A boy kissed me," she answered flatly.

He raised an eyebrow. "Was he cute?"

"Excuse me," interrupted Sister Carroll, turning away from Ashley. "Stam," she said, "maybe you and I should talk alone for now. Would you come with me?" She glanced at Ashley. "We'll just be a moment, if you don't mind."

He shrugged politely.

Sister Carroll's windowless office was dim and quiet. The room was out of another era, furnished only in hues of brown, salmon, yellow, and another kind of brown. It reminded Stam of the outdated décor in Ashley's home. Stam sat with her metal case on her lap, across a desk from Sister Carroll, who seemed to be choosing her words carefully. It was unclear if she was succeeding in saying what she wished to say.

"Now, Stam, you know the Father, Deacon Boylan, and myself all really appreciate the work you've done with us over the last few years — we would never take you for granted. But it's my concern that maybe you're not..." she stopped, trying to phrase things just right, "... fitting in, as would be proper."

"How so?"

"You were thirteen-years-old when you came here, about the same age as the seventh and eighth graders, and I know a lot of them picked on you for being different."

"How am I different?" Stam asked, quite genuinely, having been wondering about it more than usual today. "Is there something wrong with me?"

"No, no, Stam, honey, not like that...." Sister Carroll faltered.

"David said that he liked me *because* I'm different."

"Yes, well, David is a young man, and he's just starting to be interested in girls. Things can be very confusing for a boy his age, as they can be for a girl your age," she said. "But, Stam, you have to understand you are getting to be older than the other children here. David is only thirteen-years-old, and it isn't appropriate for you to be indulging in your or his curiosities this way."

"You mean I shouldn't let him kiss me because I'm too old?"

"Stam, he may be the one who kissed you, but you have to ask yourself what you may have done to encourage that, and as always, think about how God would feel about what you two were doing in that bathroom."

Stam obliged her and thought about it.

"I already talked to David," said Sister Carroll. "But were you, perhaps, taking advantage of his feelings? You look much younger than you are, and it's easy not to be aware of how a boy his age might see things."

"I didn't want to kiss him."

"Did you say no?"

"It happened quickly—I didn't expect it." She paused. "I'd tell him to stop if it I suspected it would happen again, though that might not be enough to stop him."

Sister Carroll became very quiet. She unfolded her hands and used them to push herself up in her seat. She leaned deeper into the table between them and kept her eyes on Stam's. "Are you *worried* about that? Do you not feel comfortable?"

"I'm not afraid. The most he wants is to have sex with me."

"Stam!" Sister Carroll was shocked.

"It's a normal desire."

"You know that's a very serious matter and not something a girl your age should even be considering." Sister Carroll seemed appalled. "You know better than that. And certainly David does too—"

"I wasn't going to permit it."

"Listen." Sister Carroll was unsettlingly serious. "It's normal for a girl your age to be curious, but that's not the sort of thing you should be exploring this way, nor should you be making yourself so open—so confusing—to a boy like David. You should look to God to help you overcome temptation."

Stam nodded, seeing no reason to argue.

"You agree?" Sister Carroll asked.

"Yes," she answered. "I have some things to think about."

"Well, that's good." Her voice sounded satisfied before turning serious once more. "Something else I'm worried about is your relationship to some of the other girls here...."

Stam said nothing.

"I know there are a lot of pressures on a young girl, and it can be hard if you're not as..." she acted as though her next words were random, "... you know, as tall or tan or feel as though you're not as pretty as others, or, anything else."

"God makes everyone beautiful."

This gave Sister Carroll pause. "Yes, he does, but I know sometimes you can see other girls developing at different times, or see made-up women in magazines...."

"I have never read a magazine."

"Well, that's not my point. I know you're very mature and very quiet, Stam, but everybody feels self-conscious sometimes."

Stam nodded.

"I want you to think about what happened in the restroom, and think about the fact that God was watching. I'm going to have another talk with David and Deacon Boylan tomorrow—you know he and I only want the best for both of you."

Stam nodded once more.

In the vestibule, Ashley idly paged through a small Bible. He had never really read one before, though he had certainly held one up and pretended to when forced as a young child. Ashley was unlikely to read something he was actually interested in, and today was not the day to break old habits. He set the book down after skimming two and a half Psalms.

Stam and Sister Carroll then reappeared. Sister Carroll nodded to Ashley. "We had a good talk, I think."

"Good, good." He glanced at Stam. "Everything all right?"

"Yes," Stam replied quietly.

Ashley turned to Sister Carroll. "Well, thank you very much."

He started toward the exit and Stam followed. As the two headed outside and down the stone steps, Sister Carroll came to the door and watched them for a few moments before the icy air sent a shiver through her and she disappeared inside.

The pair crossed the track and field and moved through the parking lot, exchanging no words until Stam slowed to a stop. Ashley did the same.

"Where's my car?" he asked, seeming to pick up on Stam's concern.

She was quiet as she looked around.

"Stam?"

"It was right over there."

Ashley's eyes narrowed, not at Stam, but at the situation. The maroon sedan was nowhere to be seen.

"Was there anything... *in* it?"

The question seemed to make sense to Stam. "No," she shook her head. "My phone," she added.

"Did it get towed? Stolen?"

"I always park here," Stam answered, finding the keys in her pocket.

"Cars don't get stolen in this neighborhood," Ashley mused wearily.

Stam nodded, agreeing.

"I've had that car for over twenty years," he grumbled before folding his arms. "This is going to be a long night."

Chapter 3

18th October, 1943
Dear Gunther,

I hope this letter finds you before they send you out.

I can't believe how much time has passed! The accident turned out to be a sort of blessing – working in an office is very preferable to marching in the mud all day. The work itself is boring: I just push papers around. They send in documents from the work camps and I either file them or burn them, depending on what the big guys tell me to do.

I work on the seventh floor. I've got a great view of the plaza below. It's always so full of activity during the day.

You know, my doctor said I could probably return to the Waffen division in a few more weeks, but here's hoping the war is over by then, eh?

I noticed that everybody here in the office – the men, anyway – keep growing mustaches like the Führer's. Don't tell anyone, but I think it looks really ridiculous.

So they shipped you to Romania? Gosh, I'm shocked! You have to wonder what they want you out there for, or what kind of assignment it must be. That's really far away, on the other side of Hungary, right? Oh, I just checked on a map. It's south of Slovakia. Wow! I hope for your sake it's something glamorous, but I wouldn't hold your breath. Maybe that's what all those years of marching were for, yeah? Just joking!

I hope that bastard of a bunkmate of yours has been laying off of you lately. I'd show him a thing or two if I were there.

Does it say anything peculiar about me that I've used the word "hope" at least three or four times in this letter? I have a lot of hopes lately, a lot of optimism about the future. I think it helps that I don't have to carry a gun anymore.

I always have more I want to say to you, ~~and feel as though I should write something right now that's~~

Nevermind! I really have to get this sent out to you as fast as possible, so you get this before you leave. I know I might not hear back from you for a while, but just know I'll be looking forward to our next exchange.

By the way, happy 16th birthday! I know it's not for another few months, but I may not get to send another letter before then with you being out on the front lines and all. Spending the winter in Romania hardly sounds like a good present. I wish I could take you out to tear up the town! When we get the chance, I'll give you a night you'll never forget!

It's weird looking over this map and being able to touch where you're standing. It must feel like a million miles are between us, but remember, the world is not as big as it seems. I'll see you again soon!

"Heal" Hitler,
Jens Müller

Gunther had re-examined the letter at least a dozen times so far that morning while pushing all afternoon through rugged, densely forested hills toward the distant snowcapped Carpathians, which never seemed to get any closer. He would look up from the paper every now and then to reassure himself that nothing at all had happened in front of him. He brought up the tail of the squad; the only task he had been entrusted with was guarding their rear, and it didn't seem too likely an ambush would come from Hungary. Their orders, outlined very lengthily — but vaguely—were to join up with a division currently advancing on the Soviet border... or something. He couldn't remember. It wasn't his job to remember. Martin had told him, "Don't think, just shoot," and that was all he intended to do if it came to it.

If asked, he couldn't have said where the last several years had gone. It was a new decade, but it felt like no time had passed at all—like he hadn't even grown. He didn't feel like a sixteen-year-old man, if that's what he really was: a *man* now and not a boy, enough of a man, anyway, that he'd been given a rifle and sent off to a foreign country. His memories of the last four years were of nothing but a string of drills, uncomfortable nights with Heinz, and the occasional visit with his parents that only served to further convince him he had no place to go. Try as he had on a few occasions to contact Luther, no replies ever came, but Jens, on the other hand, was always prompt. In fact, the only things he *could* remember that brought him the slightest joy in ages were letters from Jens.

Thinking about Jens was what kept him occupied throughout most the day. Jens' excitement about the future and how, when all this was over—regardless of the conflict's victors—it would all be forgotten and the two of them could spend time together like in the old days.

"Heulsuse," shouted a voice. "Move it."

He looked up from Jens' letter and hurried to catch up with the others.

As the afternoon wore into the evening, they passed through a village. It was the first one they had seen in days, but Martin neglected to have them stop, not even long enough to learn its name. Gunther kept an eye out behind them as curious townspeople came to their windows and doors to watch the soldiers. As they pushed on, the rough land flattened out into forested plains, and by the time night fell, the squad was more than ready to set up camp by a small stream in a relatively open area that was a welcome change from the thickly packed trees with which they were growing so familiar.

Gunther lay on his back staring up at the stars—they were vibrant and innumerable. Out here, it seemed, the sky was much bigger than it ever was in Germany. Gunther knew this to not be true, but still, he couldn't shake the feeling this sky was somehow different than the one he remembered. Not far away, he could hear the running stream; it was perhaps the most comforting sound he had heard in weeks. As he listened to it, a cold October wind blew and, shivering, he pulled himself deeper into his sleeping bag.

His mind drifted once more to Jens, who was probably sleeping in a warm bed somewhere, but if Gunther was at all jealous, it was only because of the circumstances surrounding this particular night. Abstractly, it was nice being under the stars. He wished Jens could be there to enjoy it with him. That would be nice. He pulled a few of Jens' letters out of their hiding place inside a case of ammunition. He could barely read them in the darkness, but he had more or less memorized all of them anyway. He thought about what he would say to Jens right now, if he were here.

"Ew! Gross! Heulsuse is masturbating."

"What?" Gunther was doing no such thing. "No, I'm not."

There was a mixture of laughter and repulsion amongst the others.

"Shut the hell up, all of you," screamed Martin, though the snickering continued. "I don't give a shit what any of you are doing, but I want to fucking sleep!" He crawled out from his sleeping bag, picked up his belongings, dragged them a few feet, and hopped back to the other side of the narrow stream they had crossed.

"You're like a bunch of fucking children," he mumbled for the hundredth time over the years before lying back down. "I swear, if anyone wakes me up again...." He trailed off, not needing to make an explicit threat.

Silence came over the group once more. Heinz had found yet another way to embarrass and ostracize Gunther despite him having not done anything at all: the mark of a typical evening.

As was also typical, Gunther was the first to awake the next morning, and he lay there awkwardly waiting for someone else to make a move. This happened all the time, and while it was uncomfortable and boring, he was somewhat pleased that Heinz, being a late sleeper, never had the opportunity to wake him up.

The sun was beginning to peek out from over the distant mountain range and the sky was alight with more colors than Gunther could ever have imagined. For all the grim nature of what they were doing there, it was a beautiful place; he hoped he'd have reason to come back someday under less miserable circumstances. As minutes and then almost an hour crept along painfully slowly, Gunther finally felt the urge to stand up and take care of some morning business. He crawled out of his bag and cautiously stepped through the other still-sleeping bodies around him before reaching the stream, where he stood, quietly unbuttoned, and answered nature's call. It had taken most of the journey for him to desensitize himself to the idea of peeing in front of so many people right out in the open. It was one of many skills acquired in this whole experience that he wished he had never needed.

As he finished, he took a look around. There was a heavy autumn mist hanging low over the area, and in the morning twilight he could see—even more so than last night—the open area really was unusual in comparison to the dense forestation they'd seen the past few days. The stream ran off in either direction, with no hint of a spring or source, and in several directions were almost impenetrable walls of trees. It seemed the way they had come was nearly the only one into the strange clearing; he wondered if they'd have to double-back a bit.

He was about to return to his sleeping bag when he noticed Martin's was empty. Martin often woke up early, like Gunther, but not *this* early. Gunther hopped across the stream and looked around; in the distance and behind a hill he noticed the top of a structure—it resembled a church's steeple but was made entirely of wood. There were a few dozen trees in between him and it, preventing a good view, and with curiosity setting in, he started toward it.

... And then stopped when he noticed something strange.

A few feet from Martin's sleeping bag was a crudely constructed wooden cross, maybe two feet high and driven into the ground. The dirt around it had recently been disturbed and by all appearances, it looked like a fresh grave. Gunther furrowed his brow, trying to remember if this marker had been here the previous night.

An uneasy feeling crept over him. He looked around once more and called out, "Rottenführer?"

His voice echoed through the misty valley, disturbing a tranquility that seemed as though it had not been in centuries.

There was no reply. He tried again. "Rottenführer?"

This stirred some of the other soldiers, Heinz among them. As soon as he realized the ruckus was coming from Gunther, he beamed with malicious intent.

"Hey, Heulsuse," he called, but Gunther snapped back at him.

"Martin is missing."

"Whatever, pussy. He's probably off taking a shit." Heinz rolled back over.

Gunther looked down at the little grave once more. Lying next to it was Martin's first aid kit, and the only disturbed item was a roll of twine. Gunther quickly noted it had been used to bind the two pieces of wood together, and then, he noticed something entangled with it on the cross.

Martin's dog tags.

"Guys, I'm serious," he said nervously. "I think something's wrong."

Heinz made an exasperated sound, but soon, one of the soldiers spoke up. "What is it?"

"I don't really know...."

The soldier rose and looked over at Gunther, seeing both him and the cross.

"The hell is that?"

"Okay, seriously, go back to sleep." Heinz flipped over angrily and sat up. "It's hardly even morni—" He, too, noticed the marker. The soldier had approached it and now stood next to Gunther, who reached down to show him the dog tags.

"When did you find this?"

"Just a minute ago."

"Oh my god, it's a grave. Scary," Heinz spat with mock fright as he hopped over the stream. "It's gonna get you."

"Shut up for a minute, Heinz," the soldier instructed.

Heinz rolled his eyes and walked away from the group, looking for privacy for his own morning business. The soldier with Gunther worked the dog tag out of the twine and examined it. A few of the other boys' attentions had been caught as well.

"This is fucking weird," one of them commented. Nobody seemed to know what to make of it until, finally, the soldier who had first joined Gunther squatted down and began to dig at the dirt with his hands.

"What are you doing?" asked somebody—but everyone shared the morbid curiosity. Gunther swallowed and stepped back as two others began digging as well. The dirt was loose and easy to move, and within minutes they had gone down two feet, where someone hit something.

"Oh, shit," he gasped, almost falling backward. One of the others reached over with a stick and began pushing away at where the other had been digging, and it became clear what was under them: a bright red Swastika—on the Rottenführer's armband.

Nobody knew how to react. They stood in uncomfortable silence for several minutes, trying to work out what had happened overnight, but no one could recall anything unusual. They might not ever have moved were it not for a sudden sound overhead: a smoking fighter plane struggling to stay in the air above them.

"American," observed one of the soldiers. A few other planes could then be seen coming over the trees, most in much better shape than the first one. They watched, most having never seen American planes before.

Gunther remained focused on the grave, still trying to understand, when suddenly he heard another new sound, something much more horrifying: gunfire.

Two of the soldiers next to him toppled over instantly, their blood splattering on Gunther and the others. He heard a voice in the distance shout, "Krauts!" while somebody right next to him shouted, "Ivans!"

The group rushed back across the stream, evading bullets with only their hope and luck. Gunther grabbed his rifle, and with nothing but instinct and Martin's old instructions guiding him, fired back at their aggressors before even seeing them clearly. It was loud. He couldn't tell if he was actually hitting anyone at all—and it only seemed like *more* appeared each moment. The other members of Gunther's squad did their best to take cover behind trees or other objects, and even with their grey jackets, proud swastikas, large guns and well-trained aim, they looked like scared children.

The enemy did not. They were adults—hardened Soviet soldiers—and they were *beyond* terrifying.

Gunther fled from his open position to behind a hill with three other boys. His face was still wet from the blood that had splashed him—he wiped it away, hands trembling.

"What do we do?" called one of the boys over the roar of bullets and the airplane engines above.

"Retreat!"

Retreat? What the hell did that even *mean*? Where would they retreat to? Gunther started to hope somebody would say "surrender," but he couldn't possibly be the one to do it—*nobody* wanted to do that. Soviet POW camps were of worse repute than death.

He had never once imagined even thinking these things. He'd never imagined seeing Soviet soldiers. It hadn't even sunk in yet that he'd watched two boys shot right in front of him and now wore their blood on his face and shirt. He had no idea what to do, and so, he ran. He shot away from the hill and fled back in the direction they had come the night before, as far away from the advancing enemy as he could. The boys with him followed suit, and after a minute of running, they passed Heinz, who stood with his rifle looking bewildered. "What's happening?"

"Soviets," yelled one of the boys without stopping.

"You're not supposed to fucking run," shouted Heinz, though hesitation gripped him when he saw their bloodied clothes. He looked in the direction they had come from and spotted another frantic boy trailing behind. With a grumble, Heinz started after Gunther and the others.

They ran for what seemed like hours; nobody wanted to be the one to stop and listen to what was happening behind them. The occasional backward glance suggested it might only be the five of them who had escaped, and between them, they had only three guns.

They ran and ran, all the way back to the village from the day before, which had fallen eerily silent. Once safely in the town square, the group took their first real break, catching breath for the first time since morning. Gunther felt like his lungs had long since withered away. He was flushed and cold and dirty, as were the others. The whole way back, Heinz had called out to the four of them, questioning their cowardly behavior — especially Gunther's — but this time, Gunther had support.

As they all panted, one of the boys spoke up, "What do we do now…?"

"You think those fucking crazy Ivans killed the Rottenführer?"

"Why the hell would they bury him like that?" came a harsh response.

"I don't fucking know — they're fucking Ivans."

Tensions were high among the group, but they all fell silent when a solitary gunshot rang out from behind a nearby wall of rickety wooden houses. They all stood, petrified, until Heinz shrugged. "You guys are a bunch of babies."

He took off to find the source of the noise. The others followed cautiously, and Gunther brought up the rear.

Heinz carefully pressed up to the wall of one of the houses and peered around. Whatever he saw comforted him, and he quickly shouted out, "Hey," as he took off toward it. The others looked at one another and ran after him.

As Gunther stepped around the corner, he too saw the unusually refreshing sight: about twenty German soldiers from the *Schutzstaffel Einsatzgruppen*. The commanding *Hauptscharführer* watched the five of them skeptically as they approached.

"Heil Hitl—" Heinz had thrown his hand out in salute, but wavered as he saw the scene around the soldiers. " —Hitler!" He managed to finish strong.

"Heil Hitler," replied the Hauptscharführer.

Gunther and the others had come to a nervous stop— around them were not just the Einsatzgruppen, but almost a hundred bodies. Most killed, it appeared, from single headshots. One body, very fresh, with blood still seeping into the dirt, was right by the Hauptscharführer. Gunther felt ill: he had never really seen a dead body before, let alone dozens. It didn't help that he was still queasy from the running. He sat down, and one of the other boys, who didn't look much better off, did the same.

Gunther could hardly hear what Heinz was saying, but he seemed to be explaining who they were, what division they were part of, and so on. Gunther passed a few minutes with his face buried into his knees until he heard a scuffle nearby. Looking up, he saw a tall officer dragging a handcuffed boy—maybe Jens' age—through the dirt. He was putting up a violent struggle, but it looked as though he might be injured, with a broken arm or wrist. The officer easily overpowered him, and then tripped him at the Hauptscharführer's feet. He looked familiar to Gunther; he had seen the boy when they'd passed through the village the day before. He had watched with curiosity as the unfamiliar soldiers marched through his home. Now the boy looked terrified—the fear he wore on his face far outweighed anything Gunther had felt earlier while running from the Soviets, yet it was tempered by rage. The boy did his best to lunge at the Hauptscharführer, and with no luck whatsoever—by the sound of a gunshot—fell to the earth.

Gunther tried to avoid looking at the body, instead reading the expression on the Hauptscharführer's face. It was indecipherable to him in the short time before the other officer leaned down and removed the handcuffs from the boy's body and another wave of illness brought Gunther's face back to his knees. He clenched his eyes shut like he had when he was a kid, in vain hopes of blocking out the world.

By early evening, Gunther was feeling a little better after spending most of the day lying down. The Einsatzgruppen officers had taken some pity on him, being the youngest of the boys, and let him rest while the others dug a hole and, one by one, made all the bodies disappear. The only evidence of what had taken place was the earth itself, blackened with dried blood. Gunther looked away from the scene and saw several of the officers standing nearby and decided to climb to his feet and join them where they were crowded around a map. The Hauptscharführer was pointing and speaking.

"… Got maybe a day's lead on them. The American bombings are still isolated to the south—odds are they're targeting oil fields, not civilian locations. Tomorrow evening we'll push into former Slovakian territory, here…." He pointed to a place on the map. "There is a MASH along this river, here, where we'll meet with group C and divert back toward Poland."

Gunther's attention was caught by a sound not far away: Heinz had dropped a huge crate of potatoes beside a few other crates, boxes and barrels. Gunther swallowed and approached him, and Heinz noticed. "Oh, look who's up."

"What are you doing?" asked Gunther.

"The Hauptscharführer said to gather stuff from the town, so I'm doing it," he said in his typical tone of condescension. "What are *you* doing?"

"They're giving their food to you?"

"You fuckin' stupid, Heulsuse? Everybody here is dead."

Gunther swallowed, looking around. "Everyone?"

"Oh, man…. What'd you *think?* They were *all* fuckin' Romanis." Heinz shook his head. "Why don't you make yourself useful or something? God…."

"Hey, you there," called one of the Einsatzgruppe officers. "Check these houses." He gestured to a small collection of dilapidated shacks. Gunther nodded and hesitantly started toward one of them. He was evidently going to go be useful.

Heinz let out an exaggerated sigh as Gunther walked away. "Ivans couldn't have fucking killed you?" he murmured under his breath.

Gunther found the door had already been broken in. He was hesitant about entering, even though he knew it was empty. He looked around the modest room: there were a few simple wooden chairs, a tiny stove in the corner, a table which had been upturned…. The little home did not appear to have electricity, but light streamed in through the dusty windows and illuminated the faces in photographs on the wall. Gunther looked them over before finding that doing so made him tremendously uneasy. He turned his attention to the stove and small kitchen; he dug through cabinets and drawers, finding little other than wooden utensils and crumbs, and so moved on to a bedroom.

…Empty. The sheets had been ripped from the bed and a bookshelf had been toppled over, but there was nothing of interest.

He left the home and repeated his scavenging. In the next one, he found a loaf of bread and a basket of apples. Four plates were set out on the table, with half-eaten breakfasts turned stone cold. He shuddered and left.

He dug through the cabinets of the third house, finding absolutely nothing. He wondered whether or not to bother with the bedrooms, but decided, against his conscience, to continue prying farther into the stranger's home. The wood floor beneath each footstep creaked agonizingly as he cautiously moved toward the rooms. The eyes of another family of photographs gazed upon him, and even in broad daylight, he had to look away. He

opened one door and saw a stripped and defiled bed
much like in the other homes—nothing of interest. He
moved on to the second—the wooden door groaned
hideously and Gunther found another identically ravaged
room. He turned to leave, and between the squeaking of
the door and his own footsteps, heard something
unexpected. He scanned the room once more as he
stepped farther in. It was a small room; there was hardly
any space at all not occupied by a tiny bed and dresser,
but the silence around him now felt somehow backed by
intent. Gunther nervously raised his rifle. First he leaned
down and checked below the bed, behind the door, the
floor beneath a rug…. He was about to shrug it off before
noticing the huge dresser nearby: the bottom drawer was
open just a few inches, with bed sheets blooming out of
the gap as though it had already been searched. Gunther
approached it slowly and kneeled down. He knew he was
being paranoid, and ripped the sheets away, exposing the
empty drawer.

… Empty, but for a small girl. She was facing away,
cowering. All Gunther could see was her arm,
uncomfortably crammed with the rest of her trembling
body into the undersized space.

He didn't know what to do. He kneeled, petrified,
before standing up and glancing out a nearby window.
Heinz was outside, still moving boxes of food, and he
could see a few of the Einsatzgruppe officers milling
about. Gunther went to the door and shut it; the hinges
squealed. He hurried back to the dresser and knelt by the
girl.

"*Hallo — sind Sie ok?*"

She had no discernible reaction.

"*Ich werde Ihnen nicht wehtun.*" He paused. "*Sie
verstehen kein Deutsch, oder?*"

Nothing.

Gunther did not know one single Romanian word.
One of the Einsatzgruppen surely did, but that was hardly
an option.

"*Warten Sie mal,*" he said, knowing it meant nothing,
as he started stuffing the blanket back into the drawer.

Once finished, he hurried over to the second house where he had left the apples and bread. He carefully hid two of the fruits and the whole loaf of bread in the pockets of his jacket, stepped outside, and ran right into Heinz.

"What're you doing now, Heulsuse?" he asked with his permanent disdain.

"Nothing."

"Uh-huh," he said, suspiciously. "What'd you find?"

"There are some apples in that house, there."

"Why don't you bring 'em out then, you idiot?" Heinz was exasperated by him, as usual.

"I'm just checking the other house for something...."

"God damn, Heulsuse, you don't make any sense at all." Heinz stormed past him and into the house containing the fruit. Gunther hurried quickly into the other home. He opened a small corner of the blanket in the drawer and set the bread, two apples and his own small canteen of water in with the girl, making sure one of them touched her. She tensed up violently.

"*Schon gut. Das ist für Sie,*" he whispered before covering her up. He had just enough time to get out of the bedroom and into the main living area before Heinz barged in.

"You're such an idiot, Heulsuse, God. You've got to take the silver and shit, too." In his hands were a few items he'd obtained at the previous house, including the apples. He started looting the drawers, finding candles and a few metal utensils amongst the wooden ones. On the floor, he found a pair of leather shoes and snatched those up as well.

Heinz pushed open the door into the first, empty bedroom, and Gunther hurried to the second, with the girl, looking around for anything he could take to show Heinz and prevent him from digging around. Gunther began opening and closing the other drawers of the dresser, loudly enough that Heinz could hear, unfortunately causing the whole thing to shake. He winced as he was sure he heard the girl whimper, and glanced over to Heinz, who was piling up clothing in the other room. Gunther sighed and started removing the clothes from his dresser. A few minutes later, Heinz joined Gunther to give the room his inspection. He pulled the drawers open, angrily checking Gunther's work. The top drawer... the second... the *third*....

Gunther swallowed as the fourth caught on the bed sheet crammed into the final, bottom drawer. Heinz gave it a strong tug, shaking the whole dresser once again and also tearing the bed sheets from the drawer below.

A voice outside interrupted them. "Attention."

Gunther peered through the window, and Heinz stood up to join him. They could see the Einsatzgruppen hurrying to group together. Gunther thought quickly and immediately exited the room. Not to be one-upped, Heinz shot after him, pushing him aside to be the first out the door. Gunther shut it as he stepped into the street and let his hand linger on the knob. From where he was, he could hear the group.

"Heil Hitler," saluted the Hauptscharführer to the soldiers, and the soldiers back to him. "Heil Hitler!"

He announced their plans and next course of action to the group once more. Gunther figured all he was going to have to do was follow orders when they were given, and so elected to not pay particular attention. He sat down against the wall and began digging through his bag, hoping writing something to Jens, even if it might not be sent for a long time, would help him forget what he'd found inside the house.

The air outside was warmer than it had been the previous day, but when the wind blew, it sent a shiver through his body. The sun had nearly set, and Gunther sat for a while looking over Jens' most recent letter and thinking — taking the occasional break to watch the colors in the sky — before putting a pen to paper.

30th November, 1943
Dear Jens,

I'm very happy to know you're doing better. When you sent that letter a while back saying you had been shot, I think my heart stopped! I don't think I could have gone on if I couldn't look forward to seeing you again.

Today was a really bad day. We were attacked by the Soviets and I think Martin is dead. I have never been too good at imagining the future, but I never realized until today I might not make it out of this. It feels like I'm never going to come home.

I don't want to write about all of this again — I know I've mentioned it before — but as time passes, it keeps crossing my mind I should have listened to you all those years ago in training. I should have run away. Why should I give up my life jus —

"Whatcha got there, Heulsuse?" asked Heinz, looming over Gunther. One of the other boys from their group, Lutz, was with him.

"Nothing."

"Writin' *another* love letter to your mommy? Or your little girlfriend?"

"No."

"Don't lie to me." He reached down to grab the letter, but Gunther managed to keep it away.

"Leave 'em alone, Heinz," mumbled Lutz as he pushed open the door to the house and entered it. Worried, Gunther turned to watch him. During the distraction, Heinz snatched the letter, and Gunther immediately sprung to his feet, attempting to wrestle it back.

"Dear Jens," read Heinz. "Ohhh, you're writing to a *boy* now, huh?"

"Give it back." Gunther struggled with him, but was still no match in terms of size and strength.

"Oh, it feels like I'll *never* come home," Heinz read a line aloud melodramatically. "You're such a pussy."

"Stop calling me that," Gunther growled.

"You two," came a harsh order from someone nearby. "Stop fucking around."

Heinz sneered hideously at Gunther, and spit onto the page before shoving it, spit-side-first, into Gunther's chest. He marched off toward the house where Lutz had gone.

Gunther tore off the afflicted portion of the paper,

which fortunately had not yet been used—he could finish on a separate sheet. Then, against his better judgment, he followed the two into the house. His heart pounded almost audibly as he approached the second bedroom and pushed the door open. Heinz was lying on the bed; his foot was hanging over the side and hovering just inches from the large dresser. The squeal of the hinges immediately caught Heinz's attention and he looked over.

"*Now* what the hell do you want?"

Gunther swallowed. "I was gonna sleep in this room."

"Yeah, well, so much for *that*."

"There's a nicer bed in the house next door."

"Yeah? You take a shit in it or something? Fuck off, Heulsuse."

Gunther remained in the room. Heinz slowly became more and more incredulous, yet some sinister part of him seemed to enjoy—almost revel in—the opportunity to have another fight.

"I said get out, you shit," he hissed.

Gunther could still feel the beating in his own chest and his hands trembling nervously at his sides. He wasn't about to leave the girl alone in the room with Heinz, and the result of his stubbornness would inevitably be ugly.

Lutz stepped in. "Hey, Heinz, you got some extra shee—" he cut himself off momentarily. "Oh, yeah...." He started to lift the sheet that had been shoved into the bottom drawer but had been pulled out by Heinz's earlier rummaging. "Can I take this? Haven't had a real fuckin' bed sheet in months."

"Fine with me." Heinz shrugged.

The boy pulled the sheets up and started to leave the room. All that obscured the contents of the half-opened bottom drawer now were the four drawers pulled out above it.

"Unless you're gonna stay and watch me jerk off tonight, Heulsuse, you better get the fuck out of here."

Gunther decided to try a long shot, and invoke a bit of Heinz's brand of crassness. He shrugged. "You're already lying in mine from earlier."

"In your—" it took Heinz a moment to process what had been implied, "—oh, ew! Fuck!" He rolled out of the bed and rubbed his hands on the back of his shirt, disgustedly, as though trying to clean himself off. The opened drawers of the dresser stood between the two of them, and could easily be disturbed if anyone tried squeezing past them, but leaving the room to draw Heinz out remained the best—and only—option at this point.

"Don't run away from me, pussy." Heinz immediately lunged after him, bumping, in his aggression, the dresser and causing it to shake. A hollow metallic rattle could be heard, and Heinz stopped.

Gunther tried his previous tactic again, "Come on, you fuckin' schwule."

That did it.

Heinz froze. "The *hell* did you just call me?"

Heinz rushed after Gunther and gave him a hard shove, knocking him into a table, which flipped it onto its side. "Don't you fucking call me that."

"I'm not gonna fight with you." Gunther stood up. "I just figured you wouldn't want that room. I was trying to be nice—"

Heinz swung at Gunther, who managed to block it, though not painlessly. He held his arm where Heinz had struck him.

"Hit me back, schwule," Heinz turned the accusation around onto Gunther.

"No."

Heinz grabbed him and the two grappled. Lutz stepped out of the other bedroom. "Hey," he shouted. "What's wrong with you two? Knock it off."

Heinz landed a strong punch in Gunther's stomach, buckling him over, and then, with every apparent ounce of his strength, grabbed Gunther's shoulders and slammed him into the wall so hard that the weak plaster and wood cracked. He nearly fell through the wall, and may have, were it not for the dresser on the opposite side stopping him. Gunther heard a bad sound: the weight of the drawers, coupled with the force of Heinz's throw, caused the thick piece of furniture to tip forward and several drawers to slide right out. Lutz had started toward Gunther and Heinz to break them up, but stopped when he saw something in the bedroom.

"What the hell...?"

Gunther winced and tried to pull himself out of the crumbled plaster.

"Heinz, Heulsuse. Come here—now."

Heinz seemed to want to ignore him, but stepped over anyway. "What?"

And then he saw the girl.

Gunther hobbled over as well, horrified and unsure of what to do as Lutz pulled away the extra drawers and exposed the girl who, even in the dark room, Gunther could see was older than he had expected, maybe eleven or twelve. Her skin was dark and her hair black. She had literally crammed herself into the drawer and it looked as though some of her pressured points had begun to swell. One of the apples had been partially eaten, as had some of the bread, and the water canteen was open and empty. She was quivering in terror. Heinz and Lutz seemed paralyzed as well, until Heinz turned to Gunther. "Did you know about this?"

Gunther stammered, "N-No."

"I'll go tell the Hauptscharführer." Lutz started to hurry away.

"Wait," called Heinz. He leaned down and spoke to the girl—she couldn't understand a word, but Gunther did.

"Hey, what's your name?"

No response.

"My name is Heinz. You hurt?"

No response.

"Hey." He reached out and touched her arm. She tensed up, refusing to open her eyes. "I said, you hurt?"

"She's not gonna speak German, Heinz." Lutz said, annoyed. Heinz might have snapped back with some kind of retort if he hadn't spotted the empty, very recognizable Wehrmacht canteen. He picked it up and turned to Gunther.

"Oh, you're fuckin' in for it."

Lutz looked at Gunther as well.

"That's not mine," Gunther replied.

"You're a liar," Heinz snickered with amusement before turning his attention back to the girl. "Hey, so you don't understand me, huh?"

No response.

"Alright, come on...." Heinz started to pull her out.

She resisted and whimpered, "*Te rog nu mă omorâ.*"

"Come on," Heinz said again, as gently as he could manage. He carried the softly crying girl to the bed and sat her down. She was stiff and appeared to be in substantial pain along with her terror. Her arms fell from her dirty, tear-stained face while her eyes opened only long enough to briefly glimpse the three German soldiers before she crawled, sniffling, to the farthest point on the bed. Heinz sat at the foot of it, watching her, while Gunther and Lutz stayed by the door.

He turned to the two of them and wrinkled his face. "Little bitch smells like piss."

"Gross," replied Lutz. "She's probably been hiding in that thing all day."

"You think you were gonna keep her somehow, Heulsuse?" Heinz asked as he stood up and threw the canteen at Gunther. He deflected it with his arm.

"I didn't know about her," Gunther lied with tremendous conviction. "It must have been one of the others."

"Yeah, right," Heinz saw through it. "Hey... you keeping her to fuck her, Heulsuse? Maybe you've got nuts after all."

"What?" Gunther was appalled. "That's disgusting."

Heinz sneered. "Huh, you don't like girls?"

Gunther scoffed, "Let's just leave her alone, guys... Come on."

"Oh no, you've got me curious now, Heulsuse. I'll bet you *are* a fuckin' schwule."

Lutz spoke up again. "That's not even funny, Heinz. That's sick. Heulsuse isn't like that."

"Yeah?" Heinz ignored him and turned to Gunther. "Who you been writing letters to? What was his name?

Jens? Is that your little boyfriend?"

Gunther knew what to say in the face of such an accusation. "That's sick, Heinz. You want me to kick your ass?"

"No, here." He reached over to the little girl. She yelped and resisted as Heinz pulled her up and held her by her shoulders. "Come on," he commanded. "Give her a kiss."

"What in the hell is wrong with you?" Gunther was still horrified by all of it, but was trying to let disgust at Heinz's insult—not genuine concern for the girl—be his most apparent reaction.

"Come on." He was holding her like she was little more than a ragdoll. "Do it." The girl started crying more audibly, and Heinz quickly put his hand over her mouth to keep her quiet. "You better at least touch her tits or something so I know you're not a homo." Heinz demonstrated by grabbing one of the girl's breasts. She cried out, though it was muffled.

Gunther felt wretched, but maintained his composure. "I don't need to prove anything to you."

"Heulsuse, I swear to God. Get over here or I'm gonna tell the Hauptscharführer you're a fuckin' homo," he demanded. "Lutz will tell him, too."

Gunther looked at Lutz.

"Just do it so he'll shut up," he said.

Gunther sighed. He wanted to grind Heinz's face into the dirt, and it took every ounce of acting and deception he could summon to have his actions not betray what he was feeling. He did his best not to look at the girl as he stepped up to the two of them and planted a kiss on her forehead. She squirmed violently, but Heinz held her fast. Gunther didn't want to press his luck, so he didn't wait for a response from Heinz. He turned and started to walk away.

"Not so fast," said Heinz. "That's was nothing."

Gunther, still trying his best to operate on Heinz's level, responded, "What do you want? I'm not gonna rape some dirty Romani for you."

"God," Heinz said. "It all makes sense now. You're a

schwule. A fuckin' schwule." He had been idly caressing the girl's chest, but now drifted down to her stomach and under the waistband of her skirt.

Gunther tried not to watch. "No, I'm not."

The girl whimpered again, saying something, but her mouth was still covered, her voice muted by Heinz.

"She's just a little kid. *You're* the sick one." Gunther turned to Lutz. "Right?"

Lutz swallowed, but offered no response.

Gunther looked back at Heinz. "I'm gonna tell the Hauptscharführer."

"The Hauptscharführer's just gonna kill her. Might as well get a good feel of pussy first."

A sudden bright light shining into the room and a loud rapping on the window interrupted them. It was accompanied by a voice. "Hey—what's going on in there?"

The three boys turned, stunned, as the light disappeared and they heard the door to the house open. Heinz shoved the little girl onto the bed and stood as though he had hardly even noticed her when one of the Einsatzgruppe officers barged into the room. He shined the flashlight on the three of them and then the girl.

"What the hell is this?"

"Sir," Heinz spoke up. "We found one hiding."

The Einsatzgruppe seemed suspicious, but ignored the boys and approached the girl. She was still shaking as the man knelt by the bedside and spoke gently. "*Eşti bine?*"

In between sniffles, shock could be detected—she understood the officer's Romanian.

"*Locuieşti aici, da?*" he asked.

"*Da…. Te rog nu mă omorâ,*" she whimpered, her voice and body quivering.

Gunther watched, oblivious to what was happening. He hoped she would rat out Heinz, but he wasn't sure that would make any difference.

"*Eşti în siguranţă acum,*" the Einsatzgruppe replied, standing up. He turned away from her and discretely removed a Walther P38 from inside his jacket. He looked at the boys who all stood motionless, watching. Gunther felt more ill than ever before.

* * *

Ashley lay on his back in his bed, sunken down into the silk sheets with a thick goose-feather duvet pulled halfway over him. His eyes stayed stuck on the ceiling as the voices of The Chordettes rang out from the player in the living room.

"And so he kissed you, just like that?"

Stam, who was lying beside him, responded, "Yes."

"How rude."

"He's not a courteous person," she replied. "He's ignored me until very recently. I don't really understand."

"Eh, puberty," Ashley responded dismissively.

"Boys have crushes before puberty," Stam countered.

"Yeah, but it's like that nun said: you're weird and ostracized, and potentially, a normal girl could compensate for that by being more outwardly sexual to anyone receptive to it or easily taken-advantage of, such as a younger boy," Ashley mused. "David was banking on more or less the same idea: that you'd be more susceptible to his advances *because* you're an outcast."

"That's very calculated."

"He's a teenage boy," Ashley answered flatly.

Stam considered this while the music continued; the girls beckoned to "Mister Sandman," and Ashley paused to listen.

"Anyway, I never had the opportunity to go to a dance when I was young. That wasn't the sort of thing we did back then." He said. "I used to *love* to dance—but that was a different time." Ashley moved to get out of bed; the iron frame creaked like always as he sat on the side. Stam remained fixated, as Ashley had been, on the ceiling.

Ashley looked at the nightstand clock out of habit. Whatever the time was, it didn't appear to matter to him greatly.

"All he wants is to have sex with me," Stam continued. "Does he think going to a dance would make it happen?"

"Of course." Ashley snickered. "It's romantic, and romance works. They *all* think that way." He stood up and started to leave the room, but stopped by the door. "Ahh, I guess I shouldn't say that." His voice sounded guilty. He turned back to Stam and she glanced over to him. "*Most* teenage boys are that way," he corrected himself.

"Not *you*, though." Stam smiled.

Ashley laughed, knowing Stam's dry tone had obscured a joke. He chuckled. "Yes, except me," he said as he passed through the doorway and into the kitchen. Stam heard the music stop as Ashley removed the vinyl record from the player. The silence was followed by a squawk from Sydney: "*Never Sunday!*"

"You're a good bird," she heard Ashley reply.

"*Good bird.*"

"And you're so clever."

"*Clever!*" Sydney's pride was palpable even from two rooms away.

* * *

Next door to Gunther's home—the opposite side from Jens' family—lived the Mohns. They had replaced the Fischers, a Jewish family of which all Gunther's memories were fond. Though he saw them regularly until he was six or seven years old, it was made clear one day by Gunther's father that he was never to associate with them again. Not long after, the family up and vanished, and hardly a day had passed before the Mohns moved in. At the time, it failed to seem as sinister as perhaps it should have.

Jens and Gunther discussed the Fischers at one point during training, only to be overheard by Heinz, whose assertion was that they had surely been exterminated. It was the first occasion on which Gunther had heard the word used in such a way, and naively, he dismissed it as Heinz simply being crass and cruel, but now he had to wonder.

Gunther's eyes followed a patrolling guard as he

passed. Regardless of how used to sleeping on the hard dirt he was, the evening's events—and the dying yelp of the Romani girl—were enough to keep Gunther awake through the night. His thoughts jumped from recalling the Fischers, to Martin's bizarre death, to Jens, and to the terror he'd felt at the sight of the Soviets. Though it seemed to take a small eternity, the sun at last began to creep into the sky above. It was a relief, despite the quick onset of activity and shouted orders. Gunther shambled about, feeling corpse-like between the stress and sleeplessness, but he managed to force the occasional "Heil Hitler" or salute as necessary. Before long, it was another full-fledged morning quickly dissolving into an afternoon as the troops began packing their possessions and spoils.

Gunther came to a stop as he noticed a discarded pamphlet lying in the dirt. On the cover was a grimy illustration of a hulking, hook-nosed, hardly-human creature with wild, curly hair and sharp fangs standing in an inferno captioned with the words *"The Jew: the inciter of war, the prolonger of war!"*

It looked nothing like Herr Fischer. *Nobody* looked like the monster on the pamphlet.

He looked over to Heinz, whose head shot back and forth with attention and fascination between each speaking Einsatzgruppe officer. He hung on the Hauptscharführer's every word, and for the first time, the boy ceased to seem like merely a nuisance; he had become terrifying. It was sickeningly clear how far Heinz would have gone had that girl not been killed. Heinz was scarier than a Jew or a Bolshevik.

Gunther examined his rifle—he had grown so used to holding it, it felt like an extension of his hands. The day before, when he'd fired it at his unseen aggressors, it wasn't impossible that he had shot one of them. It wasn't impossible he had *killed* someone. He hadn't done it because he was ordered to, but simply because he was scared. Maybe that's what it was all about: the Germans— his countrymen—and their fear.

As his thoughts wandered to darker places, he

considered what it would mean to shoot Heinz. If ever he had known someone who might deserve such a fate, it was him. Gunther didn't need a pamphlet to explain why he needed to be afraid of Heinz, but he knew the truth in his heart: it was neither right nor reasonable to kill him. There was no one who deserved to die.

Gunther could see the Einsatzgruppen gathering for their departure from the village. He started toward them, fighting a sick feeling in the pit of his stomach as he counted the four remaining boys from his squad. Trying to ignore his illness, he bent down to pluck up his few belongings, but paused when he heard a strange noise from the east. He couldn't say exactly what it was, but no one else had seemed to notice.

He shrugged it off and started toward the clustered group. He gave a cursory glance back to the dense woods from which the sound had come and only felt more unsettled. He was almost sure he had seen something, but it must have been an animal.

Then, with all the suddenness of the first ambush, a horrible sound tore through the trees: a deafening series of rapid bangs, ricocheting bullets, splintered wood, and finally, screams.

"Over there!"

"*Ostorozhno!*"

"Fire!"

Both sides were shouting orders which could only barely be heard over the gunfire. Somebody nearby was howling in agony, but he couldn't say whether it was a German or Soviet. All Gunther could think to do was dive to the earth.

"*Bystryeĭ!*"

He was too terrified to look up—he kept his face planted in the dirt.

"*Fuckin' Ivans!*"

That voice sounded like Heinz.

"*Granata! Lozhis'!*"

The shots subsided noticeably, abruptly followed by a loud explosion—a mine or maybe a grenade. It was far off, but Gunther still felt a ringing in his ear afterward, which only worsened with the renewed gunfire. He couldn't tell if it had only been seconds or if it had already stretched to minutes, but he finally brought his eyes up to look around. At least five of his own were sprawled in the dirt or bent over logs. Lutz was on the ground, and so was the Hauptscharführer; they weren't moving, but Gunther couldn't see if they were hurt.

He lay there, petrified, while the fighting went on.

"Ne ostanavlivaĭtes'!"

Someone dropped beside Gunther. He winced with fright, afraid for the worst, when he felt a hand pat him on the back.

"Hey, you okay?"

Gunther glanced up to see it was one of the Einsatz-gruppen.

"Hurt?"

Gunther shook his head. The officer grabbed his hand, "Get up—hurry," and pulled Gunther to his feet. He dragged him for a short distance, and then, using the momentum, Gunther managed to keep up with the officer as they ran together out of the village and into the woods. Bullets followed, whizzing through the air all around them, and though it soon seemed they might escape the mayhem, Gunther jerked to a stop and toppled into a tree trunk. There was a feeling in his stomach—kind of in his side—unlike any he had ever felt before. It was wet... and warm.

He slid to the ground.

He couldn't breathe, and he couldn't stand up.

He felt sick and his skin was flushed. His vision washed away just as he witnessed the Einsatzgruppe beside him reach to pull the pin from a grenade, unsuccessfully, before buckling over amid a red spray from his chest. He fell onto his back across a stump with his arm outstretched and the bomb still dangling from his finger.

The world flickered and phased in and out. Gunther couldn't think clearly enough to be scared anymore.

In one last wave of semi-conscious energy, Gunther turned over on his back and clutched his hands against the wound in his abdomen. He could feel blood not trickling, but *gushing* through his fingers, running down his stomach, seeping into his sleeves, into his gloves, and into the dirt beneath him.

He couldn't see. He couldn't hear. His body was numb. He thought he was screaming—or crying—but he wasn't sure. Reality was more than half gone; all was dark and the world had muted.

This was it. Just like that, he was to meet death.

Chapter 4

A city bus pulled to a stop, hissed, and opened its doors for Ashley, Stam, and Aurelio to disembark. They stepped out onto cold, empty, suburban streets, and as the bus pulled away, dousing the trio in thick black smoke, Ashley was the first to speak.

"I'm too old to be taking a bus around."

"Still haven't heard anything about your car?" Aurelio asked, coughing as he waved the exhaust cloud away. "Maybe you should call the impound lot, or —"

"It wasn't in a tow zone." He glanced to Stam, who nodded in agreement. "It wasn't doing anyone any harm."

"Maybe you had an old ticket, or maybe —"

"My plates were expired," Ashley interrupted. "Very expired."

"That could be it."

"Well, then, the DMV should consider expanding its hours."

Aurelio laughed. "Maybe you should start going to bed at a more reasonable time."

"The DMV, banks, the post office," he mused,

ignoring him. "Nine-to-fivers...."

"I know what you mean," Aurelio offered. "When I used to work overnight, I'd usually fall asleep at nine in the morning."

"Mm-hmm."

"You know, in New York City they supposedly have a twenty-four-hour post office?" Aurelio commented.

"They do." Ashley nodded. "Never used it, though. I don't send a lot of mail—it's just the principle of the thing." He held up a full two-gallon tank of gasoline in his hand. "At least the petrol station keeps respectable hours."

The streets around them were as silent as ever—the small town was always asleep by sunset—and no one spoke for another minute or so, until Stam at last opened her mouth.

"What did you buy?"

"Oh," Aurelio reached into the bag he was holding and produced a DVD case. "It's called 'The Petrified Forest.'"

"What is it about?"

"A washed-up writer who meets a girl in a diner in Arizona. It's also one of Humphrey Bogart's first major roles. It's embarrassing that it was just sitting in a gas station bargain bin."

"Who?"

"He was in..." Aurelio tried to think of a title she'd know, "oh, remember when we watched 'Across the Pacific?'"

Ashley interrupted. "Was that that ridiculous war movie with the terrible ending?"

"Yeah," he confessed before turning back to Stam. "Anyway, he was the lead in that."

Stam nodded as she brushed a strand of hair from her face.

"Hey." Ashley placed a hand on her head. "You need a haircut." He ruffled her hair.

"Already?" She made no move to escape his touch.

He said nothing, and slowed to let Aurelio take a slight lead.

"I've... had a ghost on my mind." Ashley's voice had

grown suddenly very somber.

Stam said nothing, but listened.

He sighed. "And I need a distraction."

* * *

There was no sound. No sight. No discernible feeling at all.

Gunther lay flat in the snow. A wide swath around him was stained bright red, while the grey wool of his uniform was turning a deep brown and his fair skin blued from the cold. To him, the world had disappeared, but in reality there was still the occasional spat of gunfire or a distant shout from the direction into which the battle had moved. The immediate area was host only to a few dozen sprawled bodies slowly being buried beneath snow.

As the gunshots faded further, the area reclaimed serenity, forgotten by whoever still lived and fought in the distance. Meaning nothing to the dead, night fell upon the woods, and only one figure still crept through the darkness....

It moved carefully, giving calculated thought to each and every step as it surveyed both the land and the bodies. Each object was treated with suspicion, until it last came upon one of the Einsatzgruppe officers. It knelt and felt his face, then his neck, before moving on.

The figure's cautious search continued, determined but now skeptical, before seeing Gunther. It approached and touched his face, then his neck, this time not dissatisfied. From Gunther's throat came the weakest whimper a voice could ever make.

The figure gently wrapped its arms around him, and with some strain, lifted part of him from the snow, exposing a dirt silhouette beneath his head. It folded back the collar of his jacket—snowflakes landed on Gunther's skin without melting as two small hands worked his dog tags off and slid them carefully into a pocket.

While it continued searching his person, Gunther's eyes flickered open for but a moment. Somehow, through his haze, he made out the form of a girl, paler than a corpse, with colorless hair that was wet and frozen where it dangled in long, stringy clumps from beneath an ill-fitting Soviet soldier's cap. She was swaddled in a thick Russian jacket—many sizes too large—adorned with bloodstains and bullet holes.

Then, he saw nothing.

As the girl examined Gunther's neck once more, a reluctant expression crossed her face. She took a deep breath, which deeply contrasted against the short, inaudible ones coming from the body in her arms. Her face moved in slowly, until the tip of her nose met and lingered on his jaw. With one more uncomfortable breath, she opened her lips and rested two pointed teeth on Gunther's cold, sickly skin.

In a flash, Gunther awoke in a lifeless body. His eyes opened wide; the treetops above became clearer than ever. He felt wispy, icy fingers holding his head and something piercing his throat. Through what pain and terror he could manage to feel, he did nothing more than try and fail to scream. His mind fought to flail his body out from death's paralysis, but soon, just as darkness had come over him before, he felt it coming again. While his vision remained crisp and vivid, there was a sense he couldn't describe, but knew to be his own final fading from the world.

It was then the sound of a soft thud took the girl's gaze away. Not pulling her mouth from Gunther's throat, she tilted her eyes to its source. The frozen body of a man dangling an iron ring from his finger had not moved, but on the ground, like a fallen fruit from his hand, a snow-coated sphere trembled as it hissed a thin wisp of smoke. It held the girl's attention, but did nothing to interrupt her further—

—Until, in a flash, the device shed its skin and an explosion tore through the air and earth. The girl's tiny body was catapulted violently away; her head slammed into a tree, cracking her skull. Her previously flawless face was burned and dirty—splattered in a mix of her own blood and Gunther's.

Gunther had flown only a few feet; the explosion had

rolled and contorted him across the ground. Much of the blast had hit his torso, and a hundred tiny shards of shrapnel had eaten into his chest and stomach. The dull nothingness that had consumed him was replaced by pain in every corner of his body: his neck, the earlier bullet-wound, the shrapnel, broad swaths of scorched skin, bruises and broken bones, and strangely, his muscles, which had been so unresponsive to his attempts to move now worked, however painfully. He winced and writhed in agony in the snow where he lay while his burning eyes refused to shut; they remained open wide, taking in all around him.

He knew he lacked the strength to do so, and yet, he still succeeded in a struggle to hold himself up. From there, he completed the impossible task of climbing to his knees. He felt little more alive than he had before, and yet he began to crawl, toward what, he couldn't say. His head hung limp and all he could see was the ground beneath him; it jaggedly moved just inches at a time as his entire frame lurched and trembled. His mind was a thick fog; everything felt like a dream. Where he was, what had happened — life itself — it was all lost in a haze.

And then something felt real: a piercing fear. He ripped his hand away from something it had rested on and painfully lifted his head to look at what had crippled him with such terror. He already somehow *knew* what it was, though he was bereft of reasoning for *why* it, of all things, terrified him: it was only a small, fallen tree branch. He searched carefully for an alternate place to rest his hand, and though he was still filled with inexplicable dread at the sight of the little twig, Gunther pressed on while avoiding any contact whatsoever. He was no more alert than before, but some part of him beamed with an overwhelming urgency to *watch out* for any other wood. A horrifying fear surged through his body — beyond the fear of death or any possible loss — that he could not possibly, ever — no matter what — willfully touch it.

The forest around him closed in. Each tree was more terrifying than a Soviet, and every log or broken limb was like an exposed landmine. All he could do was crawl, stricken with a childlike panic and desperation, to flee somewhere — anywhere — from the surrounding wood.

Dazed and weak, the ghostly girl strained to lift her head and watch Gunther. Utter terror had crossed her face not unlike it had his, and as urgently as she could, she called out after him, "*Opreşte-te!*"

Her soft, breathy whisper of a voice went unheard. Some part of her frail body vital to movement had been shattered against the tree, and she could not follow Gunther as he vanished into the darkness.

Gunther shambled toward the dwindling sounds of gunfire. At some point, he had begun to hobble on two feet. The earth was peppered with bodies completely submerged beneath the snow, but as he pushed on, there were ones more exposed — more freshly dead.

In time, he reached a clearing. The guns and rifles had fallen silent in the last few minutes and the nearest bodies had yet to develop a coating of snow — one still had a red pool expanding slowly beneath him. Gunther trudged past, still delirious — oblivious to the carnage around him — and continued moving until a hand grasped at his foot.

"Heulsuse…" came a gurgling call.

He looked down at bloodstained fingers creeping their way up his leg, pulling desperately at the fabric of his pants. Dazed as he was, he managed to recognize the dirty face beneath him: it was Heinz. He looked bad — not as bad as Gunther — but still bad.

"Help… me…." Heinz's weak voice quivered while his hand feebly twisted against Gunther in pain.

He knelt down beside Heinz and took his hand, but he had no idea what to do; he couldn't tell from where Heinz was bleeding. Gunther's trembling head slowly twisted in one direction and then another, seeking any kind of first aid kit or materials. In the darkness, he could make nothing out, and performing even the little first aid he did know seemed an impossible task. His mind raced as best as it could, and he did the only thing he could think to: he took hold of Heinz.

"Come on," Gunther managed to whisper.

As he struggled to lift Heinz from the ground, the boy let out a hideous, agonizing scream. Gunther winced at the sound, but still got Heinz up. He threw the boy's arm around his neck and put an arm around his torso. He was bigger and taller than Gunther and his feet were limp and useless, but with tremendous strain, Gunther was able to take short, labored steps and drag him along.

Heinz whimpered softly, mumbling unintelligible words and possibly even prayers. The small piece of Gunther which didn't feel like a lifeless corpse stumbling in terror at the sight of the wood tried to comfort him, "It's okay, Heinz. It's gonna be okay."

* * *

"Brazil was beautiful, and a welcome change from dull, drab New York," Ashley explained to Stam as his fingers and scissors slid through her hair, "but it was hard to pay much mind to things like that."

Stam listened, but kept her head in place.

"The car belonged to this old couple, the Bosserts. They —"

"I thought you wanted to be distracted," Stam interrupted him.

He took a breath, silenced as he remembered his initial intention. He said nothing more as he snipped a few final strands of hair and backed away. He framed Stam's face with his fingers in the air, winking one eye as best as he could. He nodded as he turned his attention to the counter and began cleaning up.

"Hey, Ash," Aurelio called as he approached from down the hall. "It's almost noon. I was gonna get started on the lawn for you."

Stam climbed out of her seat and removed a towel from over her shoulders only to be stopped by Ashley.

"Shirt?" he asked, offering a loose-fitting black T-shirt to cover her unclothed torso.

With no motivation beyond habit, she slid it on just

before Aurelio's head peeked around the door.

"Do you want me to—hey, nice hair."

"Thank you."

"You kind of look like... Edie Sedgwick."

"She does?" Ashley, busy shaking a comb dry, examined his work on Stam's head.

"Who's that?" she asked.

"She was, well, an actress, I guess," Aurelio replied, glancing at Ashley.

"Sort of." Ashley couldn't offer a better description, and was still struggling to come to the same conclusion as Aurelio about Stam's hair.

Aurelio noticed his confusion and offered help, "Did you ever see 'Vinyl?'"

"I don't really like Andy Warhol." Ashley shrugged helplessly.

Aurelio laughed. "Yeah, me neither, but in 'Vinyl,' her hair was like... well, kind of like that."

The meaning of it all was still obscure and bewildering to Stam. Ashley instinctively took note and looked at her. "It's a compliment," he said, smiling. "She's often touted as one of the most beautiful women of the 1960s."

"Yeah, but, eh," Aurelio fumbled in his attempt to compliment Stam further, "you look, well, even *better*."

"Thank you," Stam replied.

Ashley politely excused himself from the room, patting Aurelio on the shoulder as he passed. "Want some lunch before you go out?"

"Sure." Aurelio waited for Stam to join them. She followed at her own pace, idly stroking her hair as she walked. She looked uncertain.

"It looks really good," Aurelio reassured her. "Ahh, but... you always look good."

Stam smiled and reiterated, "Thank you," before having her attention quickly pulled away by a loud squawk.

"Out!" Sydney flapped his wings furiously. *"Out!"*

She started toward the bird. Aurelio watched her for a moment before finally breaking his gaze away and approaching a door in the kitchen. Nearby, Ashley was busy stripping the husks from a few ears of corn.

"The mower is up and running?" Aurelio asked with his hand on the doorknob.

"Yeah, I filled it up."

"You know, I can give you a ride to the gas station next time if you don't get your car back soon and don't want to take the bus."

"You do enough as it is."

"Well, it's no problem, just let me know," Aurelio responded as he opened the door. He noticed Stam approaching with Sydney perched on her forearm.

"*Out*," the bird squawked again.

"Can you take him with you?" Stam asked, offering him to Aurelio.

"He could use some sunlight," Ashley added.

"Oh yeah." Aurelio smiled and took Sydney. "*Vamos, amigo.*"

"*Aurelio!*" Sydney screeched, hopping onto his arm.

"*Buen pajaro,*" Aurelio praised him as he shut the door to the garage behind him.

In the kitchen, Ashley and Stam heard Sydney's proud reply outside disappearing beneath the loud cranking sound of the garage door opening. "*Good bird!*"

Ashley went back to shucking corn while Stam locked the kitchen door and then took a seat on their couch in the living room. She began paging through a newspaper. The two focused on their activities in silence until Ashley finished the last ear of corn and plunked it into a pot of boiling water.

"I need a distraction," Ashley eventually said, referring to their earlier conversation. "It has nothing to do with what I want."

Stam said nothing. She seemed to understand what he meant.

"Sorry about the hair," he added.

"Perhaps you should take it all off," she suggested. "It would take more time to grow out."

He rolled his eyes. "I'm not trying to butcher you," he said. "And besides...." He hesitated once more, failing to hide frustration in his voice. "What is *time* to you or me?"

Again, Stam said nothing.

"Aurelio likes it," Ashley added.

"Does it make such a difference?"

"To him? Probably not. It doesn't really for me anymore either — it's just a habit now."

Silence resumed.

"By the way," Ashley spoke up once more as he threw a dash of salt into the pot. "I got some bus tickets to Cleveland for us for this weekend... to eat."

* * *

Gunther's feet shuffled painfully through the snow. Every step felt like his last, like the next would be impossible to take. Heinz's soft whimpers had dulled, and all Gunther could do was shake him weakly. "Stay with me. Wake up." His body was limp, but warm to Gunther's touch. "Stay with me...."

They followed the river the Hauptscharführer had pointed out on the map. Gunther couldn't count the miles, but it seemed like they might wind up walking forever. He could feel Heinz getting heavier on his shoulder, his own strength dwindling, and all hope fading. The wind howled and bit at Gunther's ears, and each new snowflake felt like a tiny shard of glass cutting his frost-coated face. He pulled Heinz closer, burying the bully's face in the folds of his coat and doing what he could to block the wind. "It can't be much farther."

The night wore on and Gunther's morale waned. Each bend of the river looked just like the last and the forest grew ever thicker. Each short movement required careful calculation lest he scrape a tree branch or stumble on a log, and through his thick haze of thoughts and frantic emotions, it infuriated him. *What was wrong with him?*

He couldn't press on any farther.

He'd been taxed beyond mortal limits. He couldn't move Heinz another inch. With a stumble — though he could hardly feel it—he knew Heinz was slipping from his arms, and he dropped to help bring him down gently. As Heinz hit the dirt and snow below, Gunther sank down beside him. The two lay on the ground by the river, and too weak to say a word, Gunther reached out to his tormenter's dark, frostbitten hand.

There was no change around them. Gunther had expected things to fade as they had before—for darkness and silence to engulf him—but they did not. His eyes felt frozen in every sense of the word, and try as he might to shut out the world, it was impossible. He watched, immobilized by the cold and pain, as snow began to cover Heinz as it had the dead.

"Hey—"

There was a sound: words.

"Wer ist da?"

The words were German, but Gunther could hardly make them out.

Then, a light suddenly shined across the two bodies. Gunther heard another word shouted, and then responses. He tried to twist and look toward the commotion, but before he could mount the strength, he felt strong arms grasp him and turn him facing upward. Above him, a man looked down, and then another. They were saying something.

"Er ist tot…."

He knew the words. "He's dead."

Gunther tried to make a sound, and the two faces above him looked startled, even horrified.

"Oh, Gott…."

Gunther heard the men talking back and forth again. One of them checked Heinz.

"He. Lebst Du noch?"

Another pair of strong arms took hold of Gunther. He felt himself lifted upward—it hurt, just as everything else had. He tried to scream, or at least gurgle, but had no success. He could hear German voices, but found it hard to process their words.

"Er sieht nicht gut aus…."

"Die Pfleger werden ihn ruhigstellen."

Gunther struggled to speak, "Help... me."

In response, he heard shouting—more words he had to struggle to comprehend with his tired mind.

"Oh, shit. Is he conscious?"

"Medic, over here. Quick."

Gunther was placed on a soft surface. Above him was a canvas covering. Faces buzzed around him and voices called out orders while hands and arms holding needles and bandages passed over his body.

"I don't even know where to start."

"Got that injection yet?"

He was numb from the cold, and much of him was coated in ice and frost, but from the corner of his vision as his eyes darted about, he saw two medics stripping away his bloody, frozen clothes and someone sticking a thick needle into his arm. Another man's face appeared above Gunther's suddenly, looking down at him and speaking urgently, "Can you hear me, son?"

"Yeah," Gunther managed to painfully cough out.

"We're gonna give you morphine for the pain—I need you stay awake for me. Can you do that?"

He could only groan.

"Son? Stay with me."

The man clasped Gunther's cheeks; the warm hands felt like fire on his cold, brittle skin. He shook violently and felt his body restrained by the figures around him.

"Doc, I dunno about this," someone said.

Words drifted about.

"There's a lot of tissue damage down here. Look at this shrapnel."

"This kid hardly has a stomach left."

"Look at this."

The face above him was scanning his body, and eventually looked back at Gunther's peeled eyes. "Can you feel this, son?"

He felt nothing.

"This?" the man asked again.

There was a tiny point of pressure somewhere on his left arm. Gunther nodded, and one of the other men looked at another, shocked.

"Can you move your foot?"

Gunther struggled and folded his toes, however minutely.

"We might be able to save the limb."

"There's no way. Look at this."

The face above him disappeared amid more heated, urgent discussion. Gunther could only pick out pieces of the conversation, but nobody seemed quite sure what to do with him.

"Help… me," he pled again. Some of the numbness in his fingertips, ears, and nose was disappearing, and in their place was a burning, *itching* sensation. He could feel something warm and wet on one arm, both arms, on most of his body. As agonizing hours passed, feeling was returning and there was pressure all across his skin. The scrapes and bruises from earlier, his raw flesh blistered from the cold, his shredded midsection, and the sharp stabbing of the bite mark on his neck all resurfaced, and Gunther felt panic rising with them.

"Help me."

He shook violently, needing to be restrained once again. Tears began to well in his eyes as they unfroze and a whimper formed in his throat, graduating to a moan. The pain of his injuries was winning over every ounce of his self control. He began to thrash about wildly, bashing one of the medics near him.

"Hold him down."

They pinned him to the bed, and a needle jammed into his arm — whatever it was proved ineffective.

"Please, help me," Gunther cried, begging they do something to dull the feeling.

"What else can you give this guy?"

"He's had almost ninety milligrams of morphine already — he can't handle much more."

"Well, it's obviously not working."

The squabbling continued, and Gunther's efforts to writhe and free himself continued to be fruitless. As the pain came on stronger, he gave up, settling into a fetal position, crying — oscillating from a weak sniffle to agonized howl every few minutes. A sheet was wrapped across his mouth, only marginally deadening the sound of his screams. Now and then one of the doctors would inject him with something else, or bandage another wound, but all Gunther could do was lie on the bed, shaking uncontrollably in short, rapid bursts. In between his cries, a name occasionally crossed his muffled lips as his mind fired off in desperation.

"… Luther… Heinz… Martin…."

"… Jens…."

The night wore on. Gunther's throat had grown raspy and raw from the cold, dry air and his own constant wailing; the only sounds he still made were gritty and pathetic. His mind was dark and muddled, and hardly a conscious thought had crossed him since being taken in, but his eyes stayed wide open, catching medics and soldiers moving about from cot to cot, tending to other wounded men. Voices crossed his ears now and again.

"Bad storm last night."

"Yeah, got a lot of guys with frostbite."

Gunther looked over to a man lying a few feet away in the cot next to his own. His arm was blackened and cracked. It didn't look real.

"Hey, kid…."

A voice was directed at Gunther. He moaned in acknowledgement.

"Close your eyes and get some sleep—it's almost morning."

He struggled to utter any comprehensible sounds. "Can't…."

He heard only a sympathetic sigh in response. More time passed, and as Gunther watched some of the men from the night shift disappearing and being replaced by new medics and soldiers, he grew nervous.

His body shifted. Only minutely—almost imperceptibly at first—his discomfort grew.

The mysterious apprehension inside was expanding. It morphed into worry, then to alarm, then fear, then terror, and something beyond, until the sensation was so overwhelming, Gunther couldn't bear immobility any longer.

"Help," his dim, scratchy voice brimmed with whatever urgency it could.

No one noticed.

"Help," he forced out a little louder.

"What's wrong?" asked one of the new medics.

Gunther's voice was panic-stricken. "I don't know... I don't know... *I don't know....*"

He had only once felt anything like this: it was the fear that had gripped him when he touched the fallen branch in the forest, but he couldn't tell where it came from now. Something about the entire world, or being uncovered, or outside, or *something*, was so horrifying he thought he might vomit, and did. The medic drew back. "Ah, shit. Get me a rag over here—"

Gunther couldn't hold back any longer; he ripped himself from the bed, toppling the medic over. Gunther dove to the ground, knocking instruments and pulling sheets down with him in a tangled mess to the dirt floor of the tent. He scrambled like an injured animal, flailing wildly about the earth and screaming like never before in between violent coughing fits which splattered bloody phlegm around him.

"Hey, what the hell?"

Amid the ensuing commotion, he grasped desperately beneath his own canvas cot, crawling under and curling up with his face buried into his knees. He didn't know what he was hiding from: the air itself, or perhaps the sky. He couldn't understand, but something horrified him.

"Get out here, you."

A hand grasped Gunther's foot to pull him out. He kicked violently as another arm took his wrist.

He screamed tearfully, "Stop, please," as someone ripped the canvas cot away, exposing him. Gunther flailed and began to wrestle and crawl again like a frightened, cornered beast. A clenched fist drove another syringe into Gunther's neck with no effect. Another medic caught hold of his arm and drove one more needle in, this one breaking as Gunther spun away.

"Please! Help!" he screamed.

The more conscious patients were watching in terror as the medics and three soldiers scrambled to contain the frenzied boy. Gunther broke away from his captors once again and collapsed against a heavy metal crate. With desperation, he threw open the lid and began to rip out medical supplies, throwing them away until enough room had been made inside that he could slip in. The soldiers grasped him once more and a medic thrust another syringe into Gunther's spine with a massive dosage of morphine, but Gunther wrestled them away again. He wasn't any stronger than the soldiers — far from it — but his ferocity was shocking — almost carnal — and their grips weakened long enough for Gunther to bury himself in the crate. He slammed the lid down and held it fast; the sound of his tearful panting echoed inside.

The soldiers, medics and patients looked around now that the chaos had subsided. Nobody understood what they had just seen.

In the darkness of the crate, Gunther's perception of time disappeared once again. He could hear commotion outside and around him from occasionally, but no one tried to open it. His fingers were pressed readily against the latch though, prepared to forcefully pull it closed should anyone expose him to whatever it was he was so scared of.

A single panicked thought boomed through his mind repeatedly: *don't let the light in… don't let the light in….*

* * *

Aurelio leaned downward to pull a branch out of the path of Ashley's push lawnmower. He took a deep breath of cold air as he prepared to continue onward — it wasn't the right time of year to be mowing the lawn, but Ashley had been putting it off for weeks, and it needed to get done before the worst part of winter set in.

"Hello —"

Aurelio turned to Sydney, who was nesting in a nearby tree.

"Excuse me—"

It wasn't the bird who was talking. Realizing it, Aurelio turned to the voice's actual source—a woman and younger girl approaching from the driveway. He shut down the roaring mower.

"Sorry to bother you," the woman began. "Is this the Miller residence?"

He nodded. "Yes, ma'am."

"Do you know if Mr. or Mrs. Miller are at home?" she asked. "I'm Sister Carroll, from Saint Elia's academy—this is Hannah."

"Oh, uh, sure." He pulled off his gloves and started toward the front door of the house.

"Sorry to be a bother—"

"It's no trouble," he assured her as he rapped his knuckles against the door in a distinct pattern.

There was a short silence, followed by a muted, "Come in."

Aurelio pushed the door open, letting Sister Carroll and Hannah step inside, and without following, shut it behind them.

The pair briefly stood all alone in the living room, but Ashley soon emerged from around a corner into his steam-filled kitchen. He was taken aback. "Well." His tone was pleasant enough. "This is a surprise. How are you, Sister?" He switched off a burner on the stove and moved a pot away.

"Oh, just fine. Good afternoon," she said. "*Ashley*, right?"

"Yes, ma'am." He nodded. "What can I do for you?"

Behind Ashley, Stam appeared from some hidden location and slowed as she noticed the two visitors.

"Hi there, Stam, dear." Sister Carroll greeted her before replying to Ashley. "I thought maybe I'd be able to have that conversation with your parents."

Ashley stepped away, carefully balancing a plate on one hand and two tea cups in the other. "Aw, gee." He feigned dismay, having already anticipated and prepared. "They're out of town right now—I'm sorry."

"…Oh." Sister Carroll was put off. "I see."

Ashley placed the plate, cups, and additional utensils on the kitchen table. "Yeah—I'm sorry."

"When do you expect them home?"

"It's hard to expect anything around here," he said. "We sort of had a… family emergency."

"Oh no, nothing bad, I hope." Sister Carroll's concern was genuine.

Hannah, in silence, feeling out-of-place, scanned Ashley's dusty, record-filled living room as the conversation went on. She appeared to be deliberately avoiding eye contact with Stam, who stood by Ashley, also unsure of how to conduct herself in this strange scenario.

"No, not at all." Ashley smiled. "It's just a long story—nothing to be concerned about." He gestured to the kitchen table, set for three people. "Would the two of you like to join us for lunch? I always make more food than Stam and I can eat."

"Oh, no, we couldn't possibly," Sister Carroll declined while Hannah shook her head, politely indicating no interest on her end either. Outside, the sound of a closing garage door could be heard.

"Some tea, then," Ashley suggested, holding up a pot. "I insist. You came all this way for nothing—I feel terrible."

"Well, I tried calling ahead, but maybe I didn't have the right number?" Sister Carroll looked at Stam. "I couldn't get through on either your cell or the other I had for your house."

"I'm so sorry to have troubled you," Ashley offered, answering for Stam. "I don't often answer the phone. We weren't expecting any calls."

The kitchen door squeaked open as Aurelio and Sydney appeared through it. Sydney squawked, emulating the sound, as Aurelio smiled to the group and headed to the sink to wash his hands.

"Oh, my," Sister Carroll gasped. "What a beautiful bird."

"*Beauti-ful*," Sydney clacked.

Ashley chuckled. "You have no shame." He took the

bird from Aurelio.

"What's her name?" Sister Carroll asked.

"His," Ashley corrected her. "It's Sydney." He motioned to the set table. "Anyway, why don't you stay for a few minutes and at least have some tea?"

Seeing that Ashley was hardly giving them an option and had already begun to move over an extra chair, Sister Carroll and Hannah approached the table. Aurelio and Stam took their seats while Ashley pulled up a second chair for Hannah. "And what's your name?" he asked, smiling.

"Hannah," she said, quietly taking her seat. "Thanks."

"I thought it might be good to have Hannah here to talk with Stam and your parents. She volunteered to share some of her story and talk about some of the issues she faces as a teenager and how she deals with them through God, extracurricular activities, and so on. I think she could be a good role model for Stam." Sister Carroll smiled at Hannah. Hannah smiled back, a bit bashfully, a bit more uncomfortable.

Stam's eyebrow was raised in perplexity and had been for several minutes now. Aurelio glanced at her, and to Hannah, and to Ashley, and then Sister Carroll, feeling mystified by the whole scene—like an outsider. He picked at his food. His was the only plate on the table aside from a small dish holding a corn cob in front of Ashley.

"You think so?" Ashley's fascination with Sister Carroll's offer seemed genuine. He directed his attention to Stam and Hannah as he lifted his tea cup to his mouth. "You two know each other at all?"

"Yes," replied Stam.

"Kind of," Hannah agreed.

Ashley inhaled a lush, lavender scent from the cup and then set it back down.

"Hannah's been picked as the soloist for our Christmas concert tomorrow," Sister Carroll explained. "The choir still has openings, and there's even still time to practice—obviously not for tomorrow—but for some of the spring concerts."

Her suggestion was lost on Stam. Ashley had to

nudge her. "You interested in choir?"

"No," Stam replied.

"I think it would be good if you got involved with more activities around the school—straightening up the church is one thing, but we're about community; just attending mass now and then doesn't really allow you to meet other kids and make friends, does it?"

"No, I suppose not," Stam offered, with little emotion.

"Hannah has a lot of friends. I'm sure she could introduce you to some of the other girls who you might have things in common with. You know, shopping, movies, even boys." She winked, pleased by her own wit.

Ashley stifled a laugh, though Sister Carroll failed to notice.

"You could all hang out, right?" she urged Hannah.

"Of course, Sister." Hannah played up her charm and then spoke defensively, "I mean, we always *try* to include Stam."

Ashley smirked. "She's a little shy sometimes."

Sister Carroll nodded. "Well, we're all friends at Saint Elia's, Stam. Maybe you could start staying after mass for some of the bible studies? Hannah is part of the afternoon Small Group—maybe you could join that."

"I could," Stam replied, noncommittally.

"Well, it's definitely something to consider." Ashley held up the small piece of corn cob to Sydney, who quickly began to gnaw away at it. "Maybe you should have gone to that dance with that kid after all."

"You're not going?" Hannah feigned shock.

"No," Stam replied.

"I think it's best you and David keep your distance," Sister Carroll interjected before glancing to her wrist watch.

"Sister," Ashley said, letting Sydney wrestle the corn cob from his hand—the bird clutched it with one claw and continued gnawing away. "Stam's a good kid—she really means no harm to anyone." He shot a surreptitious glance at Hannah, which only she noticed.

"Oh, I would *never* think that," Sister Carroll insisted. "I'm just worried about you, honey." She offered a hopeful smile to Stam. "I really do think it would be great for you to get involved with one of the Small Groups or one of our other activities, right, Hannah?"

"Oh, absolutely," Hannah agreed.

Sister Carroll looked to Stam, who only nodded, and then the woman examined her watch once more. Ashley noticed and glanced to his own clock:

5:14 p.m.

"Well, listen," Sister Carroll began, "we have choir practice tonight—we really need to be going, but thank you so much, Ashley, for your hospitality."

"Oh, no trouble at all." He stood and motioned to the front door.

"I still need to have another talk with David," Sister Carroll spoke firmly to Stam. "I know you're both good kids."

Stam nodded again, and Sister Carroll turned to Ashley as he politely ushered them toward the door. "Thank you again for the tea."

"Yeah, thanks," Hannah joined in.

"You're quite welcome," Ashley smiled and turned to Hannah, "and thank you. Stam could really use more nice friends like you." His eyes narrowed imperceptibly to anyone but Hannah. "It's not easy to move to a new town, not know anyone, be a little different, you know. It's really nice when people are willing to accept others who aren't just like them."

Hannah nodded, unnerved by his tone. As the group reached the door, and Sister Carroll grasped onto the knob, Ashley shot out a hand out to hold it shut and glanced at the clock once more:

5:16 p.m.

He turned to the confused pair, and then smiled again as his hand pulled away. As though nothing had happened, he motioned for Sister Carroll to open it. After one last brief goodbye, she and Hannah disappeared down the steps and into the darkness of a new night.

As the door shut, Ashley let out a heavy sigh.

* * *

Gunther had gone undisturbed for several hours. Inside the box, his trembling hands clutched a small flashlight which kept things dimly illuminated. There was still commotion outside periodically—a scream from a patient or a medic calling for morphine—but it seemed they had forgotten about him.

His mind struggled to form lucid thoughts through the biting, intense pain of his injuries and the fear that somebody might open the crate.

Was Heinz okay? He had never liked Heinz a day in his life—he hated him, in fact, but he hadn't wanted him to die.

Had anyone else survived? *What was going to happen now?*

His mind wandered to Jens—a distant memory he always tried to keep close. He hadn't seen him in years, and their interactions had been reduced to nothing more than letters, but Jens seldom left Gunther's th—*the letters!* They'd been in his jacket, but he couldn't think of what had happened to that after the medics stripped it off him. Realizing it, Gunther wanted desperately to burst out of the crate and find them, but... he couldn't. Every ounce of his being compelled him to suppress whatever nonsensical fear he had about the outside world and go find the letters, but it was impossible: his will was incapable of conquering it.

Footsteps suddenly shuffled to a stop outside the crate. Hearing them, Gunther put his fingers on the latch again, ready to force it back down, and felt fear welling up inside again that trumped all other thoughts: *don't open it... don't open it....*

He heard someone speaking.

"This is the one."

"In here?"

The top of the crate pushed down slightly as someone put weight on it.

"Don't open it, please," he screamed, hardly meaning to.

There was silence, but the weight disappeared.

Gunther listened, worried still, and then a man's delicate, gentle voice called out, "What's your name, son?"

He hesitated, still nervous, and had to wait a moment for his trembling to subside. "Gunther."

"I see, Gunther." The man said the name as if intending to remember it well. "Why are you in this box?"

"I don't know." It was the light, but what did that *mean?*

"You know you gave everyone here quite a scare."

"I'm sorry."

"Oh, no, they'll all be fine, but we're worried about you."

Gunther winced, giving no response

"Your injuries are pretty severe, and I hear you're in a lot of pain. I'd like to help you."

He said nothing.

"To do that, I'd need to open this box," he said. "Gunther, coul—"

"No," Gunther replied loudly.

"Is there something out here you're afraid of?"

"I don't know."

The man hesitated. "I see. Then we'll find another way to help. No one wants to hurt you."

There was talking outside the crate for few seconds, and then the voice spoke to him once more, "The body you were found with was another Wehrmacht soldier—what happened to the rest of your unit?"

Gunther was quiet. "Is he okay?"

"Pardon me?" the voice asked.

"Heinz."

There was talking among the voices outside once more.

"I apologize, but he didn't make it."

Gunther was silent.

"Gunther?"

Still no response.

"Gunther, by all rights, you shouldn't have survived either: it's a miracle that you did, but you still need proper medical attention." The man waited for a reply which never came. "Gunther?"

Someone pressed down on the lid again.

"Don't open it," he screamed.

The weight disappeared. The man started speaking again, but his voice was directed to others, and he couldn't make out the conversation. Before long, the men were gone, and the only sounds were the idle ones he had heard all day.

The flashlight in his hand began to dim and flicker, until finally, it went out. It was tremendously uncomfortable in the box, but he was careful not to move, lest he bump open the lid. He continued to moan painfully now and then from his injuries, but no one else approached the crate. It wasn't until much later, and quite suddenly, that he felt the whole thing lifted upward. It jostled him and he immediately grabbed the latch, holding it fast.

"What's happening?" he tried to shout, urgently.

There was no response. Two people were carrying the crate unevenly, and one of them said something to the other, "Guess the Hauptsturmführer has a new project."

Gunther shook around a bit, and called out again, "What's happening?"

"Hey—hey!"

Gunther heard the voice from earlier—no longer gentle as it had been with him—aggressively calling out, "What the hell are you doing? Be careful."

The crate suddenly plunked down; the lid shook, but didn't open.

"Move," the voice demanded, harshly, before addressing him. "Are you alright, Gunther?"

"What's happening?"

"This is a war zone," the voice answered. "I'd like to transport you somewhere safe."

Was there anywhere safe left?

"We have to get you somewhere where nothing can harm you, so perhaps you could safely leave your box, right?"

Gunther said nothing.

"Trust me, Gunther, I won't do anything to hurt you."

Again, he only offered silence.

"Here, in fact, I'll put a lock on your box. Only I have the key, okay?"

"Okay." Gunther gave a weak reply. He heard the lock click on the latch of the crate, and while the idea of being locked in such a small space was disconcerting, it paled next to his inexplicable fear of exposure.

"See now?" The man shook the latch of the lid, rattling it.

Gunther squirmed, frightened, "No—" but stopped as he realized it was held shut. After a moment, an engine started and the box began to shake with it.

"We're headed up north, Gunther, away from all of this madness and bloodshed."

* * *

"That's good. Wait, no...." Aurelio instructed from a seat on the couch while Ashley stood by an antiquated television, fiddling with the rabbit ears. Static hissed on the screen, disappearing for only moments at a time as Ashley's hands swiveled about.

"Like tha—no... wait, okay—okay... *there.*"

Ashley froze and then carefully backed away as Aurelio literally perched on the edge of his seat. Ashley dropped down beside him as two newscasters bantered idly before throwing to a weatherman.

"Thanks, guys. Well, we've still got clear skies through the weekend. We're following a winter storm pattern up in Michigan, but we aren't expecting to see any of that down here in the northern Ohio or Pennsylvania area—maybe a few flurries as that storm dissipates over Lake Erie. But storm or no storm, bundle up this weekend as temperatures in the area hover in the single digits. Saturday low in Cleveland is nine degrees, over in Kent and Akron it'll be down to six and seven...."

Aurelio smirked. "You know, Ash, you're the only person I know who waits until the middle of December to mow the grass."

Ashley only grumbled in reply; he was withdrawn from conversation as he poked through a small stack of records on the coffee table.

Aurelio then spoke up again, "Hey Stam—we should take a picture of your new 'do."

"My what?" Stam raised an eyebrow.

"Haircut," Ashley clarified for Aurelio.

"Why?"

"So we can remember it." He produced a small camera from his coat pocket.

"Just indulge him—and go ahead and put down that box."

She did as she was instructed, setting her metal case on the carpet by Ashley's feet, and turned so Aurelio could snap a photograph.

"We should take one together," he insisted, placing a hand on Ashley's back and urging him to stand up. "Come on."

Once they were together, the flash spat a burst of light and the three were free to pull apart.

"See?" Ashley dropped back into his seat. "*Aurelio* likes the haircut. Maybe you should have gone to that dance after all and wowed all the boys."

"I don't know that that would have happened," she replied.

"Whatever," Aurelio interrupted. "They would have been fighting over you."

"Mm." Stam remained unconvinced.

"By the way, who's this David guy?" Aurelio asked.

Ashley laughed, raising his feet up and dropping them onto Stam's metal case to use it as a rest. Stam ignored him and responded, "A boy from the public school. He's the Deacon's son."

"So he's a nice guy?" Aurelio asked, cautiously.

"He's a total jackass," Ashley interjected. "Stam's a poor judge of character."

"What do you mean?" he asked. "What's wrong with him?"

"People like him are why teenage boys carry such a poor reputation, that's all." Ashley offered his opinion again.

"Huh?"

"We had an unpleasant encounter," Stam answered.

Ashley smirked and cocked his head at Stam while speaking to Aurelio, "If you catch her drift."

"What?" Aurelio still struggled to follow.

"Don't worry about it." Ashley stood, patting Aurelio on the shoulder. "She can take care of herself."

Aurelio was hardly satisfied by Ashley's response, but said nothing as the news continued in the background. For several minutes, it had gone unnoticed by the three —

"... *Now onto the developing story of the unusual automobile mystery here on the north side....*"

—Until it caught Ashley's attention. He drew back from the television and watched it intently.

"*Authorities say a 1972 Chevy Chevelle found abandoned in a parking lot outside a private school on Sherwood Road may have been involved in a twenty-year-old theft case. What first seemed like a routine find occurred early Sunday morning when a patrol officer took note of the suspicious vehicle....*"

Ashley's eyes narrowed. The screen cut away to a police officer speaking.

"*Well, we don't see a lot of vintage cars in this neighborhood — definitely not left in parking lots overnight. Just routine, you know, we checked the plates and they didn't match the vehicle....*"

The screen jumped to a shot of the maroon sedan.

"*Authorities say those plates were reported stolen from a car of a similar make and model twenty years ago in 1981, while the mysterious vehicle itself — according to records — is unregistered. Police say as of yet, no one has come forward to the impound lot to claim the mysterious automobile, and they are asking anyone with information to please call the local —*"

Ashley stood motionless, eyes fixated on the screen, with his mind seemingly elsewhere. Aurelio glanced between him and Stam. "That looked like *your* car — '72 Chevelle, right?"

"It *is* my car," Ashley said flatly.

* * *

There was a knocking sound on the lid of the box.

"Gunther? The sun set out here," a voice called. "You're safe now."

He was still uncomfortable. He said nothing.

"You said it was the light that was bothering you?"

"… Yes." Gunther's voice quivered nervously.

"I'm going to unlock this box," the voice replied. "You try coming out when you're ready, okay?"

"…Okay."

The lock clicked open and slid away, but Gunther still lacked sufficient courage to try the lid. In time, as they drove along, the truck hit a rough patch in the road, jostling the crate in such a way that for but a moment, the top bounced open… and it was fine.

Hesitantly, Gunther reached upward. He was stiff from being crammed in the tiny space for so long, but he managed to lift the lid one cautious inch at a time. The fresh air was a welcome change from the stale, wet breaths he had been taking all day. Slowly, he adjusted his position to where he could lift his head from the crate, and in doing so — with a fairly wide opening to peer from — he could see where he was. It was indeed on the back of a truck; he could see out the back that wherever they were, it was still snowing. He pushed up more, and then caught sight of the man bearing the gentle voice.

"Hello, Gunther." The man grinned, exposing a small gap between his two front teeth. He had a wide face and exuded a palpable warmth. His pleasant demeanor was a welcome change from the hostile, abrasive teenagers and gruff Einsatzgruppe officers.

The man shot a quick Nazi salute to Gunther and then reached out a hand. "My name is Doctor Josef Mengele — you can call me Josef."

Gunther struggled to raise his arm in salute, knowing it to be the proper response, but failed. Josef took his arm, gently. "Don't strain yourself —" He seemed to notice something upon feeling Gunther's skin, and waivered before continuing, "Come, let's get you out of there."

He lifted Gunther carefully from the crate. Gunther stumbled weakly in Josef's arms a few feet over to a sleeping bag that had been laid out. Josef helped Gunther to lie down and then pulled a thick canvas blanket over him.

"Gunther," Josef said after a time—he was looking over some of the exposed parts of Gunther's body. "What on earth *happened* to you?"

"I was shot," he struggled to answer.

"Yes, it looks like they got that bandaged up, and you took some heavy shrapnel over here," he observed. After a pause, he asked, "Are you cold, Gunther?"

"Yes."

"I'm worried about your temperature—you may have hypothermia." He pulled another canvas blanket onto Gunther and then laid his own coat on top of that. "Do you mind if I take it?"

"Okay."

Josef dug through a bag, eventually producing a small thermometer. He wiped it down. "Open, please."

Gunther obliged.

With the thermometer waiting in Gunther's mouth, Josef took hold of his wrist. He held it briefly, looking more confused each moment, and then reached two fingers to Gunther's neck before stopping at the sight of a bloody bandage.

"What's that?" Josef asked.

"I don't know."

"Hmm...." Josef replied, moving on and touching Gunther's throat. He felt around a bit, still looking worried and dissatisfied. He pulled away and murmured again, "Hmm," while scribbling something onto a notepad.

Gunther shifted. The extra covers seemed to be doing some good with the cold, though when he moved, pain ripped through his body all over again. He winced in agony.

"Gunther?" Josef asked urgently. "Are you all right?"

Gunther grumbled painfully. The thermometer fell from his mouth—Josef was quick to catch it. He looked it over.

"Hmm," he said for a third time, making another note on his pad before checking on Gunther again. "Gunther...." Josef pursued his lips, trying to think on how to word his next remark. "I think I know why you're not responding to morphine."

* * *

"Brawwwwwk." Sydney squawked. *"Watsrong?"*

Ashley was buried in a mess of cardboard boxes and old files, digging through crinkled, yellowed papers.

"Watsrong?" Sydney repeated. He was perched on Aurelio's shoulder.

"What are you looking for, Ash?" Aurelio squatted down beside him, offering to help.

Ashley was visibly frustrated; he stopped his digging and let his head hang.

"Ash?"

"Shut up, will you?" Ashley snapped angrily and glared at him. "What are you even still doing here?"

It left Aurelio shocked, speechless even. "Uhh," he drew back, "I was just offering…."

"I knew it," Ashley interrupted, standing up, having found whatever it was he was looking for. "I fucking *knew* this would happen someday."

Stam turned to Aurelio, who was still squatted down and looking very dejected. "You should go."

"Both of you should go," Ashley hissed. "I need people to leave me alone for five fucking minutes." He began studying a piece of paper while Stam and Aurelio stood behind him in silence. Only Sydney was brave enough to make a sound.

"Braaaaaawk."

"… What do you wanna do?" Aurelio whispered to Stam, lest he somehow further enrage Ashley.

She was quiet until she looked over to her metal case by the couch. "We should leave him alone. Can you wait outside?"

"Uh, I guess, yeah." He was still baffled by his friend's uncharacteristic outburst, but seemed to grasp that whatever the issue was at present, it was private. He tapped on Sydney's perch and the bird carefully shuffled down his arm and onto the stand before squawking again as he settled.

"I'll go get my car started." Aurelio headed toward the door and disappeared through it.

"He was upset," Stam pointed out to Ashley, who had yet to look up from whatever he was examining.

"*I'm* upset," Ashley growled back, tossing the document to the table and turning to Stam. "I've had that car for over twenty years. Never had a problem. I got one parking ticket—*one*—in 1980."

"I'm sorry," Stam replied. "But we can get a new one."

Ashley sighed and fished in his pocket for his cell phone. It was set to a silent mode, and incidentally, receiving an incoming call. He tossed it onto the kitchen table, where it began to vibrate and shake across the surface. "All day," he grumbled, watching it. "The police called earlier, and after I hung up, they've been calling back *all* day." He sighed. "Your phone was in the car. If they look up the provider and the plan...."

"Then they have *my* name." Stam was beginning to follow him.

"And our address," Ashley finished, mournfully shaking his head. "Attached to a stolen car."

Stam seemed to understand the severity of the situation. "What do you want to do?"

"I know I don't want to move," Ashley grumbled, looking at his records, the metal and plastic fixtures and cabinets, the inconspicuously-blocked windows—all the things which made the home so uniquely his. He had yet to finish when the phone, which had stopped rumbling, began once more, and a look of both defeat and disgust crossed his face.

"And I'm not very good with police."

Chapter 5

To Gunther, sleepless and wide-eyed, the days crawled by with an agony only outdone by the pain throughout his body. He had been in a room carefully combed over by Josef to be rid of any wooden objects, and across the only window, a metal plate had been bolted to the brick wall. The floorboards had been pulled up, exposing the dry earth beneath them; the only things now saving the room from feeling like a large, empty coffin were two metal tables stacked high with instruments and medications, as well as the several daily visits from Josef and other doctors. Gunther had not been expressly confined to the dank, stale space, but in his weakened state, which only seemed to bear down harder each day, he could scarcely move a muscle. In addition, he was buried beneath a dozen blankets—it was the only thing able to warm his body to any level of comfort, and the idea of leaving them had no appeal.

Josef would always greet him, "Good morning," and say "Good night," when he left. For the longest while, aside from directly asking, this was the only context he had for the passing of time. He hadn't seen the sky or felt a breeze since the first night they arrived, when Josef had wheeled him along a broad swath of barren dirt, past row after row of cold, ugly brick houses that reminded Gunther of the barracks he had trained on. Eventually, Josef brought a calendar into the room, affixing it to the wall where Gunther could see.

Through December, Josef spent all the time he could by Gunther's side, asking questions and trying various medications and small operations. He examined every injury on Gunther's body, continuously baffled, though he tried his hardest to hide the full extent of his amazement from the boy. He also asked a nearly endless list of questions. Speaking was a difficult task, but no matter how drained Gunther became, it always seemed he could be drained a little further. However close to death he felt, it always seemed he had a little more dying to go. He talked about his family, about growing up, about joining the HJ and being conscripted into the Wehrmacht. As he grew more comfortable, he talked about his experiences with Heinz and about Martin's mysterious death. He even talked about the little Romanian girl he had found hiding in the village.

"Compassion is a virtue, even when it's misguided," Josef responded. "There's no need to be ashamed about trying to save the girl, even if it *was* just a Romani—I understand."

He talked about Jens some—not everything, but certain things, mostly what a good friend he had always been.

And then there was Luther. *Nothing* captivated Josef more than Luther. Even in Gunther's haze, it had struck him as odd, but Josef explained, "On a fundamental level, you and your twin are identical, and yet you're exhibiting behavior unlike *anyone* else in medical history. If your brother is like you, then think of the implications. And if he's *not*? Think of the implications."

Josef marked off each day on the calendar for Gunther, telling him each night, "We're a little closer to solving your mystery."

Each waking moment—as all moments were, now—Gunther's injuries pulsed brutally as ever, and his constant groaning and wincing went ignored by both Josef *and* himself—what could they do? In a more lucid state, Gunther may have pressed Josef as to the details of his condition, but all he could do was lay quietly and trust him. Josef seldom offered information. "I'd like not to frighten you," he'd say. "It's best if you just try and rest."

On Christmas morning, Gunther heard a train somewhere in the distance, and before the day was out, Josef brought Gunther a small radio.

"It's not brand new, but it works, and here," he showed Gunther that on the back, he had glued a piece of paper with two frequencies written on it, "these are the German stations we get out here."

Josef placed the radio near Gunther's fingertips and then slid a glove onto his cold hand.

"I'll get you new batteries whenever you need them." Josef grinned and then gestured to the radio dial. "Go ahead, try it."

Gunther struggled a bit, but managed to twist his fingers enough to turn the dial. Static rolled in and out as he approached one of the stations Josef had listed. When he found it, there was a Christmas song playing, and as they listened, Josef moved his hand to Gunther's shoulder.

When the song ended, Josef stood up. He said the same thing he always did before leaving, "You'll make it through this, Gunther."

The next few days went on like any other, until a harsh and unusual scream pulled Gunther away from the Christmas songs. It sounded like a child. It was the first of many. Sometimes Gunther felt like he could hear soft whimpering from the other sides of the wall. Occasionally they might have been adults, but most often, it sounded like one or two children. He asked Josef about it.

"Well, this *is* a children's ward," Josef replied while treating some of Gunther's injuries with an alcohol rub. "War is a brutal thing—I think it's best if I don't tell you what's been going on out there lately."

With the Christmas songs disappearing from the radio, news was the most frequently available option, but the last thing Gunther cared to hear about was the war or another of the Führer's speeches. He scanned the radio for other stations, finding several, all in Polish, of which his understanding was extremely limited.

All winter, Gunther heard trains, sometimes one each day. He wondered where they were going—where they came from—but never asked.

Each night Josef seemed convinced they were on the brink of curing him.

"It won't be long now, Gunther."

January passed.

February... He felt like little more than a corpse. His injuries, still unhealed, were dried and hard. They never seemed to fester. Nothing ever seemed to change, and he was *never* hungry. In three months, all that Josef had offered him—from breads to fruits to candy to water—if it went in Gunther's mouth, it came right back up. It was the only reaction his body seemed to have to *anything*: violently expelling food.

For the first few weeks, Josef had kept a bed pan on hand which went unused.

He felt lifeless but for the pain which bit through him in constant waves. The whole world felt impossibly far away. Everything he had ever known seemed too distant and out of reach to ever be had again, and so often now, he could hear a voice inside himself praying for death.

* * *

Stam's footsteps echoed as she crept into the church. The young girl who had welcomed her inside had already disappeared, leaving Stam all alone as she passed into the silent and empty nave. She wouldn't typically have come on this particular night, but Ashley deserved the solitude he demanded, and she knew there was little else she could do for him.

A few bibles were strewn about on the pews. Dutifully as ever, she began to gather them, but had only managed to cover one side of the room before a voice called out to her.

"Hey, Stam."

She turned to David, who had materialized by the entrance with a few friends at his side. He bade them a quick goodbye and started toward Stam as his friends disappeared down the hall.

"Hello," she replied, returning to her task.

"Hey," he repeated. "How are you?"

"Fine."

"I didn't know you'd be here tonight," he said, fetching one of the bibles in an effort to assist her.

"I wasn't expecting it."

"So you came just to see me?" He grinned as he handed the book to her.

"No," she answered.

"No?" He laughed, feigning disbelief. "You mean you didn't reconsider going to the dance with me this weekend?"

"No."

Her manner tonight was terse, even by Stam's standards, and David seemed to notice. He moved to the end of a row she was in. "Hey, listen, Stam...."

She glanced to him, though it may have been because he was in her way.

"I just want to get to know you better, you know? I want to be your friend."

"That's not necessary."

"Well sure, but," he began, "why won't you give me a chance?"

"It has nothing to do with you."

"What does it have to do with, then?" He still stood in her path, and it became clear he had no intention of moving. Stam turned away.

"Me."

"Come on, that's not an answer."

Stam said nothing as she moved to a cart where extra bibles were stored and began unloading her arms' contents. Her belated reply came with a hint of resignation in her voice. "What do you want?"

"I just want to get to know you better," he repeated. "I just want to know about you, stuff like that."

She said nothing.

"Like, okay, that big metal trunk or whatever that you're always carrying around — that's not normal."

"So?"

"So it's interesting," he explained. "In fact, this is like the first time I've *ever* seen you without that thing."

"Hmm," she replied dismissively.

"What's in it?" he asked pointedly.

As she finished placing the last book on the cart, she replied, "It's something of Ashley's which he asked me to watch."

"Ashley?"

"My… friend."

"So, your friend Ashley asked you to carry that thing around?" He raised an eyebrow. "All the time?"

"No," she replied.

Dissatisfied, but knowing it was the best answer he'd get, he moved on. "So, what is it?" He pressed her.

"It's a German ammunition case from the second world war."

"So, is it like, valuable or something?"

"Not particularly," she answered, unsatisfactorily.

"Is there anything in it?"

Stam shook her head, fed up with the conversation, "I have things to do." She began walking away, but David quickly reached after her, clutching hold of her arm.

"Wait," he pled. "If you won't go out with me, will you just give me a few minutes? I mean, you've got all night to clean this place."

She glanced at David's hand, where it was clenched about her tiny wrist, and then at his face, which wore a hopeful smile.

* * *

April.

Spring had come with no discernible change; the names of months and each passing day struck from the calendar had shed all of their meaning.

For at least a week, Josef had been working on a project outside of where Gunther could comfortably watch. He talked less often to Gunther than he used to, but still explained things now and then. "You wouldn't believe how difficult it is for me to get supplies out here, Gunther. I've been putting in requests for this equipment for ages." The sound of clanking glass and metal briefly punctuated Josef's words. "Your condition, however inexplicable it appears, still maintains some degree of logic. There's a reason your wounds aren't healing."

Gunther, at best, could only ever mumble in acknowledgement.

One day, Josef approached him with a small glass cup.

"I need you to try drinking this for me, if you could."

Gunther groaned. "I'll just throw it up."

"Anything is possible, Gunther, but I think we're getting closer." He held the cup to Gunther's lips. "Please, I don't want to see you like this any longer than I must."

Gunther winced as Josef lifted his head. He poured the contents of the cup into his mouth, and Gunther grimaced with disgust, swallowing a little, but messily spitting what remained in his mouth. He gurgled hideously, "Urgh, what the hell...."

He spit again.

"Bad taste?" Josef expressed concern. "I'm sorry."

"Tastes... like blood," Gunther grumbled.

"Hmm," Josef responded, taking a rag to the thick red liquid dripping down Gunther's chin. "Do you feel anything?"

"No," Gunther started, and then, he hesitated.

Josef noticed, and a hint of excitement spread across his face. "Gunther?"

Gunther shuddered and turned; he vomited just as he had with anything and everything else Josef had ever tried giving him. The little bit of blood he had swallowed trickled from inside his throat, to his mouth, dripping from his lips to the floor. Josef shook his head, dropped back, and sighed with defeat.

May.

It was hard to form cohesive memories when everything felt so similar day-to-day, but since the incident with the blood, there was a change in Josef's demeanor. The doctor seemed increasingly stressed, less considerate, and always agitated.

"It just doesn't make any sense," he shouted, tossing one of the dozens of notepads he had filled with theories and thoughts on his subject before standing up and pacing around angrily.

"Your wounds don't heal because your body has no blood in it," he mused out loud. "That is the key to all this."

He dropped down by Gunther's side. "You defy all conventions of life itself," he growled. "Absolutely nothing about you, other than the fact that you're speaking to me, even suggests you're alive."

Gunther could offer no response.

"What in the hell is keeping you here?" he demanded. "They say you came stumbling out of that storm looking more dead than the frozen corpse in your arms."

The doctor's rage was unnerving—frightening even. He had never before displayed such callous frustration.

"If you're not going to get better, then why don't you just die?" In a fury, Josef took hold of Gunther's shoulders, lifting his head. Gunther was powerless to fight back.

"Those absurd fangs, those red eyes. You're like some folkloric monster."

Red eyes? He knew about his fangs—he could feel them in his mouth—and wasn't sure when they had appeared. They'd grown in slowly, and he was used to them now, but... red eyes?

"My eyes are blue." Gunther coughed, still held up by Josef.

"Don't be ridiculous." Josef angrily grabbed a mirror nearby and thrust it into Gunther's face. Gunther caught a glimpse of his own visage, and immediately, the same shock and terror that had held him when the sun rose and when he stepped on the twig hit him all over again. His whole body flailed and an uncontrollable scream ripped from his throat. His head smashed into the mirror, casting it from Josef's hand to the dirt, where it shattered. Gunther shook wildly, breath heaving, as Josef watched, alarmed but fascinated. Ultimately the boy's gasps and convulsions shortened, and despite a few trailing whimpers, he resumed his normal, limp state.

Josef sighed, also seeming to calm down. He picked up his notepad and made a new entry, scribbling almost half a page before finishing, at which point he offered a sympathetic half-smile in Gunther's direction.

"We're going to figure you out."

* * *

A single tiny flurry drifted down from the sky, dancing and swirling in the air before landing on Stam's cheek, where it stuck like the body of an insect caught in a spider's web, neither melting nor escaping as the wind blew across her face. Beside her, David shivered from the icy breeze and seemed wrapped in thought as he stared at Stam, who in turn, was staring off across the football field shared between Saint Elia's and David's own school. She had indulged David and allowed him to coax her to the bleachers; Ashley would no doubt be laughing about the whole situation if he knew.

"It's snowing," David commented, brushing a few flakes from the cold metal where they sat.

"Yes," Stam replied, taking note of a dot of ice which had landed on her wrist.

Silence persisted between them, as it had for a few minutes now, until David shifted uncomfortably and spoke again. "Listen, Stam," he started. "I'm sorry about, you know, in the bathroom the other day."

"It's fine," she replied. "I'd appreciate it if you didn't do it again."

It wasn't exactly what he was hoping to hear. He took

an audible breath. "Why not? Don't tell me it's because of that old bitch. She was talking to my dad like you and I were *fucking* in there."

Stam was quiet, and considered that if she explained her reasoning to David, he would only then attempt to mislead her — convince her she was wrong. That was what Ashley had said, anyway, and she instead decided to try what he had suggested.

"I'm not ready," she replied, hardly even sure what it meant.

"Oh," David responded as though he had heard it a thousand times. He too, was silent in thought before he continued, "But you said, like... that you've done stuff before...."

"It wasn't by choice," Stam explained, watching the snowflakes fluttering around them.

David was uncomfortable. "So, wait, you mean like...." He waited to see if Stam would clarify. When she didn't, he continued, "You mean like, somebody forced you?"

"I suppose that's accurate enough," she replied, turning to him. "I don't understand. Why do you want to have sex with me?"

David just about choked with shock at the accusation. He stumbled over his words. "Whoa, whoa, it's not like... I mean, I like you, but... like...."

Stam raised an eyebrow at his fumbling.

"I just really like you. Do you think that's all I want?" He paused. "I mean, that's not it."

"What is it, then?"

"I want to go out with you and hang out and stuff, and like, I dunno, like I said the other day: your personality and stuff... I just like you."

"You also said you find me physically appealing."

David laughed, trying to mask his nervousness. "Physically appealing...." He repeated Stam's words. "Even the way you talk is like, so weird. It's cool." Stam was silent, and so David continued. "I mean yeah, I think you're really beautiful, but that's not why I like you. It's not like, about sex...."

He took her hand. "Jeez, you're always so freezing," he remarked at her icy skin. He played with it idly and then added, "I guess we don't have to do anything. I mean, I want to, but I'd really be okay if we could just be friends."

Stam looked down at her hand in his, and then at his face. He smiled meekly at her, but neither of them said anything until David shook his head. "You have the craziest eyes. They're so beautiful."

"Thank you," she replied, out of habit more than genuine appreciation. She was unsure of how genuine David was being, but her mind had ceased to focus on that; it had become preoccupied with a sick sensation she was feeling—something small pervading her thoughts.

"What color are they without the contacts?" he asked, still examining her eyes. "I don't think I've ever seen you without them—everyone was joking when you first came to the church that you had like, monster eyes and stuff."

Stam's attention was still distracted. Her reply was cursory, "They're real."

David laughed. "Uh-huh."

She placed her free hand on her stomach and looked down. David was oblivious.

"Okay, okay." He still chuckled. "You have red eyes—whatever. I guess it's like, a Goth thing?"

"What?"

"Your whole like, thing you do, it's like, Goth, right? Being all sad and wearing black shirts and stuff?"

"I don't understand," Stam replied as she glanced at him, failing even to feign that he still held her attention.

"No, like, I'm not making fun of it—I think it's cool. Like, I'm a Jock or whatever, and you're Goth."

Stam said nothing; her focus was captured by what she was trying discretely to fight.

"Nevermind." He laughed, "It's not important," and then he trailed off, unsure what to say next.

Stam had no reply on the matter. She lifted her head, watching the snow, and then turned to David.

"I'm cold." Her voice was weaker than her usual whisper.

"Oh," David sighed, "yeah, I guess it is cold. We can go in...."

Stam stood up abruptly. Her hand slipped from his and took hold of her stomach, while David remained on the metal seat, totally unaware of her preoccupations.

"Could we just like, kiss once?" he asked.

"You already did that," Stam replied, taking a step down to the next row of seats to pass him.

He reached out to her. "Can I try, like, just one more time?"

She broke away. "No." She hurried down from the bleachers. Her shoes clanked loudly on the metal with each step, steadily growing more rapid until she was almost running as she hit the gravel path leading back to the church.

"Wait, Stam." David hurried after. "I'm sorry."

She trudged through the tiny stones, feet dragging as she stumbled to a stop. Her hand came to her face as she struggled to endure and restrain the sensation that had overcome her. Her lips parted, tiny fangs peeking out as she strained to breathe normally while standing half buckled over. Unlike the nearly opaque steam bursting from David's mouth as he hurried after, Stam's breath was invisible, no different in temperature from the cold air around them.

David slowed to a stop. "Stam?" He put an arm on her hunched back. "What's wrong? Are you okay?"

She was unable or unwilling to explain.

"Should I get somebody?" he asked urgently.

Stam struggled to lift her head. She looked David over, and soon, her eyes came to rest on his neck.

"Stam?" he asked, kneeling down so he was staring up at her.

She shuddered and shook with each breath, but finally conjured the strength needed to ask, "May I borrow your phone?"

* * *

July.

There had been screams all day—far worse than usual. When Josef came to check on him, Gunther heard a little boy's voice calling, begging and pleading through tears. Josef hurriedly shut the door behind himself, muffling the cries, and was quick to start digging through the instruments on the table near Gunther.

"What is that?" he asked.

"What's what?" Josef replied, annoyed, not looking up.

"Screaming...." Gunther coughed out.

"A particularly bad case. Poor kid," Josef explained. "You really don't need to know the details."

After more digging, he turned to Gunther. "We've got a new experiment to try today. I've got a good feeling about this one." Josef brought a thick, long needle to Gunther's chest. "But it's probably going to hurt."

Gunther groaned. He was used to it all now.

Josef drove the needle in under his sternum, carefully angling it directly into Gunther's heart. He shook in pain.

"Careful, *careful*...." Josef put a hand on his chest in an attempt to sooth him. He had made no effort to anesthetize anything, as it had always proved futile in the past. Gunther struggled a bit longer, before settling into his typical quiet, obedient anguish. Josef often worked this way now: quickly and without any consultation with his patient beforehand.

Gunther lay motionless, while in the other room, the cries of the little boy grew weaker and weaker. When they fell silent, Josef excused himself. "I'll return in a moment," he said and disappeared, leaving Gunther to lie there with the needle in his chest. His eyes followed a long tube which ran from the end of it and hooked to a small reservoir.

A few minutes passed and Josef returned. Two doctors in aprons and masks splattered with blood were carrying a large vat which they sat on one of the tables near the container at the end of the needle. The two men looked like butchers.

He could hear some urgency in Josef's voice. "Come

on, now."

The two doctors stepped aside as Josef took the container and attached a small pump hose to it. He flipped a switch and the pump began to vibrate and hum as he donned thick rubber gloves. With that, he dipped his whole project into the vat.

Gunther watched, feeling ill as a thick red liquid began to work its way up the tube and toward the needle in his chest. Josef, on the other hand, watched with wild fascination as he excitedly scribbled in his notepad.

Gunther's chest felt heavy; he could almost feel the liquid settling inside him. It felt *awful*. He groaned and began to writhe.

"Just another moment, Gunther," Josef assured him. "Just hold on."

For another agonizing minute, the machine hummed, until finally, it fell silent. Josef hurried to remove the needle from Gunther's chest and then moved to the opposite side of the table where a large machine was waiting. He pulled a pad away from it, attached to a thick cord, and flipped another switch. It buzzed loudly.

"This may hurt a bit," Josef explained, "but we need to get your heart pumping."

Gunther whimpered unintelligibly in response. With that, Josef pushed the pad onto Gunther's chest. An electric shock ripped through him; his body lurched and flailed where it lay, burning and stinging all over. He let out a harsh but stunted scream while Josef watched, seeming dissatisfied.

He tried again... again... and again.

August.

Gunther thought it *must* be August by now. Josef had stormed away after the last failed experiment and the calendar had gone unmarked for some length of time.

In desperation, at some point, Gunther had writhed and flung himself from the table. All the while, the thought remained that maybe he could escape—run away—or at least kill himself. Now he lay on the dirt ground, not far from the metal door. Over several brutal hours, he had crawled toward the exit, only to find upon reaching it that it had been locked tight. He pounded on it as best as he could, crying out to Josef—to anyone—but there was nothing.

He had no idea to where he would possibly run away, or what he could possibly do to end his suffering. There hadn't been anything outside but rows and rows of dismal brick shelters. He tried to remember back to the night they had arrived: he'd been brought into one particular building and wheeled through a few rooms not vastly dissimilar from the one he was in now that had become his prison. He pictured himself inside a labyrinth of cold, empty rooms filled with nothing but stale air and the echoes of distant screams. It was a prison from which even death seemed unable release him, and he was all alone.

* * *

Sister Carroll was already shivering as she placed a bag of salt on the ground by her feet. With a small shovel in hand, she began taking spade-fulls from it to sprinkle on the church's front walk, but only a few minutes passed before a shouting voice caught her ear.

"*Stam.*"

Stam, trailed by David, shambled toward the street out front.

"Stam, what's the matter?" he asked for the tenth time. "I told you—I'm sorry."

She said nothing as she started toward an idling car waiting nearby. She had nearly made it to the door when Sister Carroll intercepted the pair.

"Stam," Sister Carroll called as she reached out to catch her. "What are you doing here? What's the matter?"

Stam glanced at Sister Carroll's hand, then to her face. "Let go."

Sister Carroll was hesitant, but did accede to the demand. Stam immediately turned away and continued to the car.

"Stam," Sister Carroll began. "Will you talk to me,

please?"

"No."

Sister Carroll turned to David and folded her arms. "David?" she asked expectantly.

Stam grasped hold of the passenger door handle and opened it, revealing Aurelio in the driver's seat. She winced with pain as she climbed in beside him and slammed the door.

"What's going on?" Aurelio asked, alarmed. "Are you okay?"

"Just drive, please," Stam instructed, putting her hand to her forehead.

The car started moving. A bewildered and angry Sister Carroll could do little but watch as the vehicle pulled away and disappear down the street into the darkness.

"What was all *that* about?"

"It doesn't matter," Stam replied. It was avoidant, even by her standards.

"Are you okay?" He couldn't get a clear look at her, but simply by the urgency of her earlier phone call summoning him, he knew that something was wrong.

"I'll be fine," Stam answered with her face still hidden by her own hand. "Thank you for coming. You didn't have to."

He shrugged. "I was just sitting at home watching movies," he answered. "I was trying out the DVD player Ash got me."

Stam said nothing in response.

"You sure you're okay?" he asked, worried.

"I don't feel well," she answered, revealing a pained expression on her face as she moved her hand to her midsection.

"You can put the seat back, if you want."

Stam made a sound of acknowledgment as her hand felt for the lever. The seat dipped back, taking her with it; she stared upward, taking long breaths as she attempted to calm herself.

There was silence between the two. Stam was fixated

on the ceiling of the car; one hand rested somewhere between her chest and stomach and the other slowly loosened its rigid grip on the seat as she tried to recover. Aurelio continued to periodically check on her, but said nothing until red and blue lights began to flash in the rear-view mirror.

"Oh, what the *hell*?" he moaned, pulling over and coming to a slow stop. He reached over Stam's legs and into the glove box, digging through a few pieces of paper until he found what he needed. Stam was uninterested in the event, and remained focused on herself. Aurelio glanced at her one more time before rolling his window open and waiting patiently.

"Come *on...*" he grumbled to himself. "I know my stupid headlight is out—can't get it fixed on a Friday evening. Jeez...."

There was a sudden light shining in from the passenger's side, coupled with a swift rapping on the window which caught him by surprise. He leaned over Stam and fiddled with the handle on the door, lowering the glass.

"Uh, hi." Aurelio tried to sound as friendly as possible, closing his eyes at the harsh brightness of a flashlight.

"License, registration, and insurance?" the stocky police officer requested.

"Uh, yeah. Here you go." He handed the stack of papers to the officer, who noticed Stam as he took the items. He shined the bright light down on her; she moved a hand to cover her eyes as the officer looked her over and then gave a quick scan to the cluttered backseat.

"You know you've got a headlight out. You look like a Cyclops comin' down the road in the snow there."

"I know." Aurelio let his voice stress excessive remorse. "It just went out today... I couldn't ge—"

"How do you pronounce this?" the officer cut him off. "Arell-yo?"

"*Aurelio.*"

"Mm," the officer responded. "Where are you both going so late?"

"Just picking her up from church," Aurelio replied.

"Yeah? Which church?"

"Saint Elia's."

"Mm-hmm." The Officer seemed to accept it, but then took another look at Stam. "You all right?"

Stam said nothing.

"She got sick," Aurelio answered for her. "I was taking her home"

"You two related?"

"No, sir," he responded. "Just a family friend."

"Hmm...." He thought it over. "All right, sit tight."

"Sure, sure." Aurelio nodded. The officer headed back to his cruiser and Aurelio watched until he was certain the officer was inside. "Man, I'm sorry, Stam, I've never been pulled over before."

"How long does this take?" Stam murmured.

"I dunno. Not long, I don't think," he grumbled. "Man, this would happen now."

Stam shifted, wincing more. "It's okay."

Aurelio sighed as they waited several more minutes. Snowflakes drifted into the car and a light coating was forming on the inside of the door before the officer re-approached and handed a small piece of yellow paper to him. "I'm not giving you a ticket for the light, but I've got to give you something for not having all front seat passengers wearing seatbelts." He motioned to Stam. "She's gotta buckle up."

Stam's eyes narrowed as best as she could at the Officer's request. She shifted slightly. "I'll be fine."

"No, no, he's right. I just didn't even realize...." Aurelio insisted. "You gotta put it on, Stam."

"Buckle up for safety, there," the officer repeated.

Stam glanced to Aurelio, seeing the urging look on his face, and then struggled to reach her seatbelt. "This isn't necessary." She pulled it across herself.

"Hey now," the officer was put off by her words. "What if you two were in an accident?"

Stam almost replied with a simple answer, but caught herself, responding instead with a half hearted, "Oh," as she clicked the buckle into the latch.

The Officer continued to eye the two of them with suspicion, and then asked, "Two of you got anything illegal in here?"

"What?" Aurelio asked, baffled as to what he meant.

"You know, like pot?"

"Oh, *no*," Aurelio replied, understanding. "No, sir."

"All right, well, you need to get that light fixed or you're just gonna get pulled over again."

"Yes, sir, thanks." Aurelio nodded.

"Drive safe—be careful in this weather."

"Yes, sir."

The officer walked away from the window and Aurelio rolled it up. With it closed, he grumbled, looking at the ticket, and then murmured some string of curse words under his breath in Spanish before taking note of Stam again.

"I'm sorry about this, Stam. Let's get you home."

Carefully, he pulled back into the street and continued driving. The officer's cruiser trailed behind him, awkwardly, making every second more uncomfortable. They made two turns before finally parting ways, and Aurelio let out an annoyed sigh. "This is just not a good day."

"I'm sorry," Stam replied.

"Oh, no, it's not your fault." He quickly glanced at her. "It's just Ashley being so upset earlier, and you getting sick, and then *this*...."

"Ashley didn't mean to yell at you," Stam pointed out, struggling to get comfortable with the belt now across her.

"Yeah, I know. I just feel bad he's so stressed out."

"I do too," Stam replied, giving up and sitting up straight. She pulled the lever and returned the seat to its upright position.

Aurelio looked at her again as they waited at a light. "Are you feeling any better?"

"A little, yes," Stam lied, but she was at least suppressing her reactions to her feeling more successfully.

"You just got a nausea thing?"

"I don't know," Stam replied.

Aurelio wasn't satisfied by the answer, but he let it go. As they resumed moving, he turned to watch the road again. "Who was that kid with you?"

Stam said nothing.

"At the school," he clarified.

"David."

"Mm," he nodded, expecting as much. "What was he doing there?"

"His father is the deacon. He's been there a lot lately."

"Is everything okay between you two?"

"Ashley was right about him," she replied. "Not that I didn't believe it."

"So he tried something?"

"Yes."

"Did you tell him 'no?'"

"His desires remained the same."

"Well," Aurelio mused, "I guess he likes you—can't say I blame him." He smirked at Stam, who had turned to look out the window. He continued, more seriously, "If he's really bothering you, you should talk to that lady, Sister Carroll."

Stam was quiet, until, struggling to speak through her pain, she replied, "I suppose sometimes I'm curious about what it would be like to...."

Aurelio raised his eyebrow, worried by what she might say next.

"... Live life that way," she finished.

"Huh?" He was unsure what Stam meant.

She remained quiet—it wasn't clear whether she was simply too ill to go on, or if her explanation still required more consideration, but after a moment, she continued. "To be satisfied by something so simple. To be content just because you have someone—*anyone*—in bed with you. To have such a narrow desire."

"Don't say that," Aurelio scoffed. "I mean, he might be a normal jerk and just like you because you're cute, but there's a lot to like about *you*, specifically."

"That's what he said," Stam replied. "He talked about my personality, the way I speak, my eyes...."

"Yeah, okay, that sounds pretty fake to me," Aurelio

agreed. "But it's still true, I mean, you *are* really different from most girls, and your eyes *are* awesome."

Stam was quiet. She continued to simply stare out the window until Aurelio picked things up again.

"When I first met you, last year, when you came into the store," Aurelio reminisced, "and you were buying fruit and nuts for Sydney—Ashley had him on his shoulder and he was showing him every single brand, letting him pick which one he wanted, and you were wearing that huge overcoat even though it was the middle of the summer." He chuckled. "The three of you were such a trio."

"Hmm," Stam responded, idly.

"But when we started talking, I knew there was something really cool and special about you. I dunno—I think what I want to say is, *any* guy would be really lucky to get to hang out with you, or go to a dance with you, or whatever."

She had no reply.

"So if this kid screwed it up by only being interested in one thing, well, that's his loss," Aurelio said, harshly, seeming appalled by the very idea. "It actually really makes me mad somebody could do that to a girl as sweet and nice as you. It's so messed up."

"It's okay," she responded. "I'm not upset about it."

"I am." He laughed a little, only partially hiding his genuine irritation toward the subject at hand.

She smiled, however subtly, but it was enough that Aurelio noticed. He smiled as well. "Are you feeling any better?"

Stam raised a hand to her forehead, letting it fall as she dropped back against the seat once more.

"No."

* * *

A brutal scream tore through the walls; it was a violent, anguished voice that surpassed and muted the whimpering of children so often heard in Doctor Mengele's facility. In this particular room, there were hard wooden floors and cabinets—amenities that had long since been removed from Gunther's crypt-like chamber. Josef looked up from his notations and gazed down at the slab in the center of the room. Two doctors beside him worked quickly, but carefully, on something inside the mouth—held wide open by a speculum—of the squirming German boy on the table held down tightly by leather straps. Josef reached out to him to brush away an errant strand of blonde hair from watering eyes, opened to their widest by two smaller speculums.

The boy gurgled, shook, and tried to scream, but every inch of him was immobilized by straps and vices. Josef watched a pair of pliers in the hand of one of the doctors as it left the mouth and dropped a bloody canine onto an already-stained tray. He then reached out, examining it with brimming fascination as he scribbled wildly onto his notepad. The unbearable sounds coming from his subject tangled and echoed with the wailing from some nearby room while the doctors continued their work.

Josef remained quiet and only set the tooth down as a nearby door opened with a creak. A head poked in. "Doctor?"

"There you are." Josef stood up. "Where the hell have you been?"

"I'm so sorry, Hauptsturmführer, sir, there was an emergency in—"

"Shut the hell up," Josef snapped. "You want me to waste time with your Poles and cripples? I have *serious* patients here."

Josef motioned to the sorry sight on the slab. The man who had entered balked at the sight. "Are you not ready for me yet?"

"Are you mad?" Josef grumbled as he picked up a tray full of sharp, unsettling tools and instruments and shoved it into the man's hands. "You're fucking late. Get to work."

The man looked at the quivering body. "I can't—I can't operate while they're doing oral surgery; the anesthetics will—"

"There's no need," Josef spat, angrily. "Now get to

work."

"But your patient this morning—"

"Are you listening to me?" Josef slammed his fist on a table. "You miserable fucking kike—why do I keep you around?"

The two busy doctors ignored the exchange while the man stood nervously enduring Josef's berating. Josef grabbed a small metal box sitting beside the slab and popped the top; it was filled with ice, and a cold mist billowed from inside.

"Now," he commanded, motioning to the container.

The man swallowed again as he approached the body on the slab. He sat the tray of tools down by the boy's head and tried to ignore the bloodshot eyes as they darted around in a panic. As the man donned a pair of gloves, he asked Josef, "How long have his eyes been open like this?"

"Who cares how long his eyes have been open? Get started."

He slowly moved his hands to pick up a small scalpel. He shivered, terrified at what he was about to do.

He whispered to the boy, "I'm sorry."

Oh God, oh god, my fucking God.... Gunther's mind was a swirling haze empty of coherent thought; what he had previously devoted to emotions or feelings was replaced by pain that dwarfed even what he had already experienced.

My eye... my fucking eye... Oh my God.... The words in his head made no sense; they failed to form any meaning. His body flailed as it had so often before, but unlike in the past, his torso and extremities were now held down tight; he could only barely shake his head as he screamed more loudly than ever before.

It hurts. Oh fuck... fuck... fuck. Hideous sounds escaped his dry lips, rivaling the worst he had ever made previously.

"Gunther," a voice said, going unheard by him. "Gunther."

Some part of him recognized it, but could take no notice.

"You really need to quiet down," the voice scolded. "It's getting excessive."

Josef reached up to Gunther's face with both hands, using one to subdue his violent shakes and the other to pull away a small eye patch.

"Hmm," Josef jotted down a note and then took hold of Gunther's jaw, prying it open. He examined a raw, dry socket where a long fang had once protruded, only getting a brief look before the jaw snapped shut. Josef drew back quickly.

"I know it hurts — don't be angry." He started writing something again. "I'm trying to help you."

Gunther struggled to lash out in rage, fruitlessly, as Josef turned his attention back to the boy's face. He watched curiously and then held a hand toward Gunther while closing one eye.

"It's really fascinating," he mused out loud. "Like a mirror image."

Gunther could hardly discern a word of the doctor's nonsense or what it meant. Josef patted him on the shoulder — seeming completely oblivious to the enduring screams — and started toward the door. As he reached it, he took note of the calendar — the last crossed-off date was in early December.

"Hmm." Josef considered it before reaching up and taking it down. "I suppose it's time to replace this."

January.

Some minute scrap of sanity had somehow persisted and stayed with Gunther through the worst of the pain; it waxed now, slowly as the agony waned, and his thoughts became more coherent. *My eye…. What did he do…?*

He lay motionless, giving his newest injuries — places where he had rubbed his flesh raw against the straps restraining him — time to rest. He tried to remember the sequence of events: Josef had appeared, along with two doctors, and they started to work on his teeth. The pain had been absolutely unbearable; the operation culminated in them removing one of his odd fangs. He was already reticent to recall the details of the event, but he remembered it getting worse from there. There had been a man — he didn't look like a doctor or one of Josef's men — and Josef kept yelling at him, almost forcing him. Gunther's thoughts hesitated. He could hardly believe what it was he was remembering.

... The man *cut out my eye.*

February.

The screams continued — he could hear them echoing through the walls more clearly than ever. Sometimes, he thought he heard his own voice screaming even when he was certain he wasn't — like he was *truly* going mad now.

His injuries were so innumerable, it was impossible to feel all the pain at once. Sometimes it was the eye socket beneath the patch, or his missing tooth, or his broken arms, or the rope-burnt marks from his straps, the shrapnel, the bullet wound, the burns, the unhealed bruises... even the hole in his neck... and something else: it was an ill feeling, some sickly craving that was not the same as — but had taken the place of — any hunger or fatigue. It was perhaps the worst of all his pain: some insatiable need for something unknown. It had been there since the very beginning, vague and indistinguishable from everything else. He didn't know what it was. Food couldn't cure it and sleep was impossible. Josef had long ago speculated it might be related to Gunther's lack of blood, but several attempts had been made to address that possibility.

In the midst of his cloudy thoughts, the door creaked open.

"Well, Gunther," Josef began. "Let's see how we're doing." He reached down to Gunther's eye. Like always now, the prisoner fought angrily, screaming and hissing at his captor, but Josef seemed content to ignore it as he peeled the eye patch away.

"Oh, this is good." His voice almost trembled with excitement. "Gunther, this is really good." He stepped away, appearing oblivious to Gunther's violent rage and, holding a fresh notepad in his bandaged right hand, used his left to record his latest observations.

"You really do look *just like* your brother now."

Gunther could hardly discern a word, but he recognized one.

"How the hell... would you... know...?" Gunther gurgled.

Josef only grinned his toothy grin. "Don't worry yourself about that," he replied. "You need to keep focusing on recovery."

March.

Josef moved Gunther out of the room and into a hallway. A passerby asked someone for the date at one point, and it was the only context Gunther had for what month it was. A constant stream of people buzzed about— mostly Schutzstaffel soldiers and medics, but occasionally Gunther would see dirty, ragged men and women being led through by armed guards. They weren't soldiers and hardly *any* of them were German.

Gunther had been turned onto his stomach, and had been gagged at some point, deadening his screams which initially had made him an even more hideous spectacle in the crowded area. He whimpered—softly and constantly—to anyone who passed by. *Please... please....* His thoughts always fought to become words.

... Please....

It was all to no avail. Most who looked at him turned their heads in disgust or horror. Sometimes children would gasp or cry at the sight of his battered face and crippled, dirty body.

There was a daytime and nighttime now. There was no sunlight, but the stream of people would quiet periodically, and Josef, who now passed by Gunther nearly every day on his way from one place to another, resumed "Good morning" and "Good night" routine from what seemed so long ago.

Nothing felt real. None of the people around him seemed human. It was all an endless, waking nightmare. The soldiers and medics seemed stressed or even worried; they were all short-tempered and afraid of something. He heard them talking about the Bolsheviks sometimes in hushed, urgent tones.

It just dragged on, day in and day out, and then Josef appeared once more. He was holding something in a gloved hand: it was small and dark and fleshy, like a piece of putrid meat.

"What a fucking disaster," he grumbled, looking at the rotten lump, and then to Gunther. With his free hand, he held Gunther's face, focusing specifically on the eye socket that had once been covered by a patch. It was swollen now, often quite itchy, and Gunther could only imagine what the hole must have looked like, but Josef didn't seem distressed. In fact, a smile crossed his face. "But one out of two isn't the end of the world." He smiled. "It's just another testament to you, another day in our adventure, Luther."

Luther…? Gunther thought but couldn't find the strength to say.

"Gunther, rather," Josef corrected himself, laughing. "Like I said, you're the spitting image. I've never seen two people so alike, yet so different."

It hit Gunther then—was Luther there? He shook, trying with all his might to break free. The gurney rattled loudly, briefly catching the attention of a one-armed boy being lead down the dank hallway.

"Oh well," Josef mused to himself, looking over the thing in his hand once more. "I don't really think there's anything I can do with this anymore. If we had the time, I might give it back to you," He examined Gunther's eye socket again, "but you don't look like you need it."

April.
The halls were empty now.

Days would pass without a soul walking by, but somewhere in the distance he heard a radio. If he strained, he could make out the words: constant, urgent, patriotic declarations.

"You are the fighters of the Third Reich. You are the future of Germany. To arms — for the preservation of our people."

Each morning, he heard the date announced. The 16th, 17th, 18th, 19th….

On the 20th, a booming voice urged everyone to celebrate the Führer's 56th birthday, and a short while later, a weather report dissolved into static.

The signal returned a few minutes later, and before the transmission fell dead for the last time, Gunther heard a poem, read aloud by a triumphant young boy's voice:

"Those words it was that first awakened us,
From dull brooding, hollow death —
We can no longer perish,
A light bur — "

The hissing of the static went on until, after many hours, it fell silent as the hallway fell dark — power to the building had been lost. There were no more screams, no more trains; there was nothing.

"Gunther."

A hand appeared on his shoulder. "Thank goodness you're still here."

The rage Gunther had felt toward Josef was gone; his will was lost. He was still tied down, but even if he were free, there seemed no way he could overpower the doctor.

Josef pulled the gag from Gunther's mouth and knelt down beside him. "It's over," he said in a voice as soft and gentle as they day they had met. "The Soviets took Berlin yesterday — there is no Germany anymore," he stood, "and no such thing as a German."

Gunther's eye followed Josef as he took a few steps away and stared down the dark, empty hall. He picked up a flashlight and flipped it on, casting a dim beam through the dusty air.

"We're all like you now — totally helpless." He sighed. "Our brightest future is death at the hands of Stalin."

"Luther," Gunther managed to whisper.

Josef was silent before he turned to Gunther. "I might never see you again. The future world may not ever know what a miracle was born in this German boy." He placed a hand on Gunther's head. "They'll never know what *could* have been." Josef seemed genuine in his hurt. "They won't know you. At your best, you'll just be as much of a monster as they see the rest of us." He took hold of the gurney. "The life you wanted to live is over, and the future we all wanted is dead."

Gunther was wheeled across the floor, through the hall, then into a room, and another, where they stopped. To his shock, he saw his own face staring back at him—a reflection hardly recognizable now. His cheeks were sunken and his skin was blotched and dark. One hollow eye socket festered and oozed, and the other was... shut.

Something stirred in Gunther, like a quickening pulse. His body began to shake as reality sunk in. An unrivaled despair gripped him as words and thoughts failed.

"He's alive, though I don't expect for much longer since the power went out," Josef observed. "He lost a lot of blood from infection. He's in a pretty delicate state."

It wasn't a mirror. It wasn't Gunther.

"He's not like you," Josef commented, shuffling through some tools nearby, out of Gunther's sight. "But for as bad as he looks, he at least responds to morphine."

Gunther stared at his brother's ghastly, disfigured face.

"He's drugged right now, shouldn't be awake for a few hours yet."

Gunther was immobilized—by rage, horror, shock— no reaction could manifest itself. His thoughts were stunted and chaotic.

"In any event, he's been very supportive," he explained. "He wanted to help you, just like I do. You should be proud of him." Josef stepped away from his instruments, up beside Gunther, but still out of his range of vision. Gunther heard him removing the straps which bound Luther. "What can we still learn now?" Josef asked, expecting no response. "Your life and mine are dissolved. Even if you live a hundred—five hundred years—where you have been and what you have known is gone. You and I are dead, Gunther."

He lifted Luther's limp, emaciated body from the

table and moved him on top of Gunther so they were back-to-back. Luther's limp head dropped beside his, lips brushing Gunther's ear.

Josef let his hand rest on Gunther's broken arm. "When you erase the past, you erase the essence of humanity," Josef continued. "Germany and its plight have been washed from the annals of history, and we can *never* have it back. The victors of this war will paint us as monsters and criminals, when it was we who sought to rid the world of such vermin."

Gunther felt something cold against his back, somewhere between himself and Luther.

"What I wanted to learn was *why* people are what they are and what makes us that way. What makes a Pole or a Romani or a Jew or even some lowly *schwule* inferior to you and me? What makes you and me different? What makes you and your identical brother so different?" He paused once more. "All that being said: I believe with all my heart, Gunther, that if there might be one soul who can transcend the destruction of Germany and bring to the future some remnant of our age, it's you."

Something pressed down onto Gunther's skin.

"… This may hurt a bit."

* * *

"Graaargh," Ashley let out a growl as he clasped his phone shut and threw it across the floor. It rolled and flipped across the deep carpeting until coming to a stop by Stam's bare feet. He continued to stare at it before looking up at her. "Canceled," he grumbled.

A song rang out from the record player: a "Moon River" rendition by Andy Williams.

"I'm thirsty," Stam whispered, clutching herself and shivering.

"I know." Ashley put a hand on his chest as he walked over to Sydney, who had been pulled out of sleep by his outburst. He cocked his head sharply.

"Watsrong?" he squawked.

Ashley raised a quivering hand with a single

raspberry in it to Sydney's mouth. It was quickly grabbed and crushed; Sydney enjoyed every moment of it.

"*Yummy.*"

Ashley turned away, drifted across the room to the front door, and pulled it open to reveal a soft and silent world coated in several inches of snow. Andy Williams' voice continued to sing his gentle cover.

"There's no reason a bus shouldn't be able to drive in this," he murmured angrily in the doorway. Stam said nothing as she watched him, and eventually Ashley pulled his eyes away, to her. "I'm sorry about this." He sighed. "I guess I misjudged pretty bad."

"It not your fault," Stam replied, seeming to understand what he meant. She dropped to the couch. "You could borrow Aurelio's car?"

"The thought crossed my mind, but I'm not sure how well I could drive right now, and you factor in the weather, and that missing headlight.... *He* already got pulled over once. I don't have a driver license, though—well, except that old phony one. If they tried to pull *me* over, this could become ugly."

Stam nodded, accepting this answer.

"What a nuisance, everything in this whole fucking world." He shoved shut the door and looked around the room, taking in his familiar comforts before musing out loud, "We'll have to...." He didn't want to say whatever words were going to come naturally. "... *Do it* in town."

It was morning—almost afternoon now—and the record on the player continued to spin silently.

Stam lay curled on the couch, holding herself tightly. Ashley's discomfort was similar as he hobbled through the kitchen with Sydney on his shoulder and a plate in hand, which he set on the table. On the plate was a small pile of shredded chicken and a few nuts, which he offered to the bird.

"*Mmm,*" Sydney chirped after each bite.

"Seems weird to me," Ashley, sounding almost delirious in his thoughts, raised an eyebrow, "to feed a bird to a bird, but I suppose mammals eat mammals."

The rumble of his vibrating phone interrupted him. Stam reached from her position on the couch to where the phone still lay on the carpet, resting where Ashley had thrown it. She didn't even need to show him before he slammed a fist onto the table, startling Sydney.

"Brawwwk!"

"Sorry, Sydney...." Ashley calmed himself and offered a small piece of chicken to the bird. "I just want to—"

A loud, aggressive, and unfamiliar knock came from the front door and echoed through the room. Ashley's looked toward it while Sydney cocked his head in perplexity and Stam wearily lifted her face from where it was buried into a couch cushion.

Whoever it was knocked once more.

"Do you think it's that nun again?" Ashley called out in hushed tones to Stam.

"It could be," Stam replied, as the knocking continued.

"Hello?" an authoritative male voice called out. "Anyone in there?"

"Nope. Great, here we go," Ashley growled, dropping the fork from his hand. As it clanked against the ceramic plate, he pushed back from the table, standing up quickly from his seat. The metal of his chair legs bumped against another's, and the noise caused Sydney to release another loud squawk.

"Someone in there?" the voice demanded again, seeming to notice the noise. "This is the police."

Ashley moved toward the door, realizing in his delirious state it had remained unlocked after Stam's return the previous night. He trudged through the thick shag carpet as Stam struggled to stand up, using the coffee table as a brace.

There came one more knock, and just as Ashley reached out, the door gently cracked open and a narrow sliver of the afternoon sun cut across the room. In an instant, the throats of the home's inhabitants spewed a sound of irrepressible terror. Ashley and Stam's screams ripped through the house—the whole neighborhood—as each one's composure dissolved. Stam threw herself to the floor, flailing wildly and toppling the coffee table stacked high with delicate records. She scrambled along the carpet, clawing her way toward the sofa, while Ashley dove in a furious panic toward the bedroom.

"Shut the door! *Shut the door!*" Stam screamed with inhuman, tearful urgency as she stuffed herself beneath the couch. "*Shut it!*"

Their screams were more than enough to shock and startle the portly officer who stood in the doorway. Instinctively, he placed a hand onto his holstered gun and shouted after Ashley as he disappeared behind the bedroom door. "Hey. *Stop.*"

The officer hurried toward him, only to have his attention caught by Stam's kicking foot protruding from her hiding place.

"Shut the door," she continued to howl frantically.

All the commotion had sent Sydney into a frenzy. He flapped around the room wildly, knocking objects from the shelves and only making the scene more disorienting to the officer. "Okay, *okay.*" He closed the door behind him.

With the sound of the latch, Stam's screams dwindled to a hyperventilating pant. It took Sydney another moment to calm down and land on his perch; he angrily fluttered a few more times, making clear his disapproval of the whole situation.

In the relative quiet, the officer remained where he was with one hand on the knob and the other ready to draw his weapon. With trepidation, he took a few steps toward the legs poking out from under the couch. As he did so, the bedroom door opened slightly, redirecting the officer's gaze and potential aim.

"Show me your hands," he demanded.

There was a pause, but one by one, Ashley's hands slipped out from behind the door, one of them grasping it for balance as he slowly opened it wider. The other then moved to the door frame, where he held himself up as though hardly able to stand on his own. His heaving breaths were not dissimilar to Stam's as his head rose to observe the intruder.

"It's rude," he began, voice straining to be heard over his own panting, "to barge into someone's home uninvited."

"What's going on in here?" The officer stepped toward him.

"My bird and I were eating dinner." Ashley gestured to Stam's legs. "She was trying to rest."

"Why were you screaming?"

Ashley put a hand on his forehead and took a weak step forward, moving into the kitchen but still using the door as a brace. "You surprised us."

"Bullshit," the officer growled. "What are you hiding from?"

Stam's arm inched out from her hiding place; her fingers grasped hold of the long carpeting as she slowly pulled herself out. Her breaths—like Ashley's—were still sharp and labored.

"Can we... help you?" Ashley asked, not bothering to answer the question.

"I said: what are you two hiding from?"

With difficulty, Ashley let go of the door and took a few steps across the kitchen. He watched Sydney, who was huffily side-stepping back and forth on his perch, and then he looked at Stam; she had made it onto the couch and was lying in a heap.

"The sun," he replied, finally looking at the officer. Ashley's grim expression gave way to a smile. "My sister read some Bram Stoker the other day—we were playing vampires."

"That was some pretty intense acting for a *game*."

Ashley shrugged helplessly as his tone changed. "I didn't realize you were a policeman. I thought maybe the wind had blown the door open. We didn't mean to startle anyone."

"It sounded like somebody was running away when I knocked."

"I didn't even hear that—I'm sorry. What can we do for you, officer?"

Whether the officer believed him or not, he at least

answered the question. "I'm looking for a Stam Miller. Is this her residence?"

"Oh...." Ashley's face dropped. "Um...." He glanced at Stam before continuing. "It *was*...."

"What do you mean, *it was?*"

Ashley wore a pained expression. "Stam was my — *our* — mother." He looked down. "She passed away."

The news took the officer by surprise. "I'm sorry to hear that." Then, seeming to think of something else, he asked, "Do you live here alone?"

"Yes," Ashley replied, still feigning sorrow.

"Just the two of you?"

"Yes, sir."

"How old are you?" There was an element of skepticism in his voice.

"Nineteen."

The skepticism remained as he looked Ashley over. "I'd peg you at fifteen or sixteen, tops. You got an ID?"

Ashley's eyes narrowed before he fished around in a basket sitting on the kitchen table. He found and offered a driver license to the officer for examination.

"You know this expired when you turned eighteen," he said.

"Did it?" Ashley tried his best to sound interested.

The officer made an affirmative sound and continued reading the plastic card. His attention briefly deviated as he looked over to Stam, but he soon turned back to Ashley and asked, "This isn't fake, is it?"

"Kids give false identification to bartenders, not cops. I would hardly be so naïve."

"So if I run this, it's going to be legitimate?" he asked. "What year were you born?"

"Nineteen twenty-seven."

The officer looked unamused.

"Nineteen eighty-two," Ashley replied. "Believe me, if I could look my age, I would."

He considered the ID a little longer, and then handed it back to Ashley. "You know anything about a maroon Chevrolet Chevelle?"

"My car?"

"*Your* car?" The officer folded his arms.

"It went missing earlier this week. I assumed it was towed or something, but I didn't know who to call. Plus, my phone was in there. It's been a big mess."

"You just let your car disappear and didn't go find out what happened to it?"

"I didn't know what to do."

The officer thought about it, and then explained, "That cell phone is how we tracked that car to your address. You don't happen to have the title, do you?"

"Title?" Ashley furrowed his brow. "Oh, I think I know what you mean. It was in the glove box."

A hint of exasperation could be detected in the officer's voice. "You kept your title *in* the car?"

"I think so." He appeared completely bewildered. "Should I not have?"

Embarrassed for Ashley, the officer sighed. "And how long have you had the car?" he asked.

Ashley produced another lie. "Three years—I think we got it in 1998—my mum found it in the newspaper."

He nodded. "And you wouldn't have any reason to believe that whoever you purchased it from may not have been the real owner?"

Ashley's expression was concerned. "Of course not."

"It's worth mentioning that your license plates have been expired since the early eighties. Your car was reported stolen almost twenty years ago."

"I don't know what to say," Ashley replied after a short silence. "I had no idea. If I had known—"

"You're not in trouble," the officer assured him. "What's your name, son?"

"Ashley," he replied. He could sense yet more skepticism on the officer's end, and so elaborated. "It's a boy's name in Britain."

"That where you're from?" he asked.

"No, sir. Spent some time there, though. Still losing the accent."

"Hmm...." The officer removed a notepad from his pocket and scribbled some things across a blank page. Stam looked at Ashley, who made clear in his expression his disdain for the situation at hand, but offered no suggestion as to what they should do.

"Do you mind if I take a look around, Ashley?"

"Mm," he murmured. "Feel free."

As the officer began to poke through the living room, Ashley took Sydney's plate and approached the bird, who refused a single bite and let out an irritated squawk, clearly still upset about the earlier ruckus.

"Come on," Ashley instructed, holding out his arm so Sydney could step onto it. Again the bird refused, hissing as he bobbed his head up and down.

"You're being grumpy today, Sydney," Ashley chastised him.

"It looks like you're pretty into music," the officer commented as he eyed the vast collection of vinyl around them.

"Not particularly," Ashley replied.

"No?" He shrugged. "Who do the records belong to, then?"

"Sydney."

He puzzled for a moment, having heard the name before. "Your parrot?"

"He's a macaw," Ashley answered.

"Mr. Miller," the officer sighed, "why are you giving me attitude?"

Ashley shrugged. "Well, he *is* a macaw."

The officer rolled his eyes and continued looking around before approaching Stam.

"Haven't I seen you before?"

She looked up at him weakly.

"You were in the car with that kid last night, right?"

Stam lay like a deflated balloon, unmoving, but answered, "Yes."

"You still don't look very good—have you been to the doctor?"

"No," she replied. "I'll be fine."

The officer seemed dissatisfied by this response, but let it go as he turned to Ashley.

"So it's really just you two here, huh?"

"Yes."

He wiped his forehead. "It's awfully hot in here, isn't it?"

Ashley glanced to the thermostat, which was set to somewhere in the nineties. "I suppose." He shook his head. "Listen, officer...."

"Wilson."

"Officer Wilson. Do you need anything else, or...?"

"You eager to get rid of me?"

"Honestly?" Ashley raised an eyebrow and shrugged helplessly. "Well, yes."

"And why's that?"

"Believe it or not, I don't just hang out here all day waiting to entertain unexpected guests," Ashley answered. His veneer of courtesy had worn quite thin. "You have a home of your own, don't you? Do you like to be bothered there?"

"Wouldn't you like to resolve this issue with your car?" Officer Wilson countered.

He shrugged. "You said it was stolen. Why not return it to its owner? Wouldn't that be the proper thing to do? One way or another, I doubt you intend to give it back to me."

The officer smiled, and after some hesitation said, "You seem like a sharp kid. Let's just say there's more to that car's history than I'm at liberty to tell you about."

"I see," he replied. "If you already know so much then, what can I do to help you?"

Officer Wilson fished a card from his pocket and handed it to Ashley. "I'll be in touch about that. There're some unusual things going on here—I may have more questions for you soon."

Ashley smiled and took the card. Officer Wilson turned to Stam, who had resumed a fetal position and looked very weak and frail.

"You need to take her to the doctor." He glanced to Ashley.

He pursed his lips, and with a cock of his head, motioned for the officer to approach him. He obliged, and Ashley whispered, "She's got cramps. She just started having her period—she's kind of embarrassed about it."

Officer Wilson hesitantly gave an exaggerated nod, indicating he understood the issue now. "Oh, I see."

"She's a bit of a drama queen, but I mean, her mom just died, you know?"

That explanation seemed to be enough. The officer nodded sympathetically as Ashley motioned to the side door. "Could you leave through here?" He smiled. "*Vampires*, you know?"

* * *

Josef glanced at his own wrist, trying to discern the time through a watch face coated—like his own hands—in blood.

"Just a few more now, Gunther."

Gunther had worn his throat too raw to scream any longer, and thrashing only made things worse. He lay there with fury seething—it felt as though the sheer power of his rage toward Josef should be enough to kill the man. Gunther felt a sharp prick, just one out of dozens before it, and then the sickening feeling of thread sliding through his skin. There was another... and another....

He couldn't do anything now. He was trapped: forced to lay as motionless as possible and endure Josef's torture, all the while knowing what the man was doing to Luther. Gunther had run out of threats to level and words with which to plead. His mind raced as futilely as always.

It went on for an unbearable length of time.

"There we are, then." Josef took a step back, admiring his work as he cleaned his bloody hands with a dirty rag. "This makes more sense."

Gunther couldn't move his head enough to see for himself what Josef had done, but he could *feel* it. Luther still lay on top of him, unconscious and silent. Another minute passed as Josef continued cleaning up, and then from somewhere far away, a quiet voice echoed through the hallways.

"Mengele."

Josef ignored it, pausing to write something in his notepad.

"Mengele, let's go."

His pen scribbled a few final notes, and when his fingers stopped, he sighed and looked down at Gunther, whose face was contorted with a thousand hideous emotions, his thoughts still straining to murder Josef.

"I know you don't believe me, Gunther." He knelt close to his face. "But I wanted to see you pull through this—see who you'd *become*." He closed the notepad and put it away. "I wanted to help you and see why you are what you are. Who knows—maybe someday I'll see you again."

Josef stood up and moved away from Gunther, toward the door, which creaked open. "Good night, Gunther."

The door was shut and locked, and Josef's footsteps echoed outside, growing fainter and fainter until there was silence.

With the distractions gone, Gunther detected subtle breaths from Luther—he was still alive. The realization at once relieved and terrified him. He wanted to scream Luther's name, wake him up, keep him conscious and make certain he was okay, but it was obvious that he was not.

Gunther felt his skin pulling with each tiny expansion and contraction of Luther's weak lungs. The two were linked by a bloody mess of stitches, and Gunther's cold shell of a body was sucking the warmth from his brother. With each passing moment, the breaths grew weaker, but faster. Every option filled him with dread.

"Luther?"

No response.

"Luther?" He strained what remained of his voice to call out louder.

At first there was nothing, but then there came a dead and desolate sound like so many Gunther had made over the months.

"Luther, can you hear me?"

"Unngh," came an unintelligible response.

Gunther's voice and strength were battered and

weak, but he tried again. "Luther, it's Gunther—listen to me."

Luther's head rocked beside Gunther's as another slurred sound trickled from his lips, "*Gunh.*"

"Can you move anything?"

No response.

"Luther, please." His gut reaction was to shake Luther, but he stopped himself. "Luther."

"*Unnnnterrr.*"

Luther shifted; the stitches in their backs pulled.

"Luther." He struggled to speak. "Luther. *Stop.*"

Luther fell motionless once more.

"Luther, you're drugged on morphine," Gunther managed to gurgle. "Can you hear me?" He couldn't get a reaction; a few more sounds slurred from Luther's throat as the seconds wore on, until suddenly a word surfaced.

"*Hurts.*"

Gunther's attention focused sharply. "Luther?"

The word slipped out again, slowly, "*Unnn…hurr…tts.*"

"Luther, listen." An idea was coming to him. "Can you move your arms?"

"*Hurts.*"

"Luther."

"*Hurts. Hurts. Hurts.*" The word repeated again and again, slipping from Luther's mouth like a recording.

Gunther continued to plead with him, eliciting no other response. Luther's head continued to rock while his body periodically writhed, only incensing Gunther's pain. "Luther."

After another brutal stretch of indecipherable replies came, "*Gun… unn… unther.*"

"Luther?"

"*Hurts. Gunther.*"

"I know, Luther," Gunther tried his best to speak clearly. "Can you move your arms? You need to untie me," he begged, hoping Luther would understand.

"*Hurts.*" Luther's head wobbled vacantly.

"Please, Luther. Listen."

"*Hurts. It hurts. Gunther. It hurts.*"

Gunther felt sicker than ever as he listened to his brother's hazy, drug-induced mumbling. It was one more horrible thing that was impossible to bear, and yet he had to. "Luther, can you move your arms?"

"Hurts. Back. Hurts. Eye."

"I know, Luther." Gunther tried to offer some kind of comfort, unsure that it was getting through. "I know."

"Hurts. It hurts. Gunther. Back. It hurts."

"My arm is tied — at the wrist." Gunther struggled to explain. "It's by yours — can you feel it?"

Luther's arm shifted slightly.

"It hurts. It hurts. Josef. Please."

"Luther —"

"Josef. Morphine. Morphine. Josef. It hurts."

"Luther...." Gunther crumbled, listening to his brother's pleas, but tried again, "Please, Luther."

"Gunther. Josef. Josef. It hurts. It hurts. It hurts."

"Luther, my arm. Can you feel my arm? There's a buckle on it."

Luther's hand fumbled before finding the strap which bound Gunther's right arm.

"There. Right there."

"It hurts. Josef. Morphine. Morphine. Josef."

"Luther, you need to —"

Luther's body lurched violently — Gunther felt some of the stitches in their backs pull and a small section tear. Gunther screamed while Luther made a horrible sound of his own.

"Uuunnnnnnuurrrr. Urrrnnn. Unnhnn." Luther's sounds dwindled to a whining whimper before his voice resurfaced, this time pleading faster. *"Unn. It hurts. It hurts. It hurts."*

"Luther, my wrist —"

"Gunther. Hurts. Gunther. Gunther." Luther's hand fumbled once more with the strap.

"Just pull the strap out." Gunther instructed desperately.

"Gunther. Gunther." Luther's face drifted to make eye contact with Gunther.

Down by his wrist, Luther was making progress. His

hand shook, trying to wriggle free. "Just focus on the strap. Just pull a little—"

"Gunther. I… I… I know."

The new word caught Gunther's attention, giving him pause as Luther's weak hand still feebly tugged at Gunther's bound wrist.

"Luther?"

Luther's eye darted across a few points on Gunther's face, finally settling back to eye contact. *"Gunther. Gunther. It hurts. It hurts. I know. I know. I know."*

"I know it hurts, Luther, but it's going to be okay. Just work on the strap—just pull it."

For the first time, Luther seemed to be hearing the words and listening. On his face, Gunther could read a desire to say something that in his current state was impossible. When Luther opened his mouth, the words were inaccurate, or at least not as clear as he intended, and his frustration showed.

"It hurts. Back. Hurts. I know. I know though. Gunther. Gunther. Gunther." Luther's body began to tremble, only increasing the pain for both of them.

Gunther gasped. "Luther, hold still."

The buckle on the strap gave way; Gunther wrestled his hand out of the leather binding and immediately reached for his other, struggling to figure out the best way with Luther on his back.

"Gunther. Gunther. Gunther."

He tried not to move his torso in the slightest as he slid his hand beneath himself, under both their weights, and toward his other wrist. His hand dragged through the tattered, dry shrapnel wounds of his midsection and he winced harshly. Luther's weight and the angle made it nearly impossible to do on his own, but with a few feeble yet determined pulls, he managed to push the leather strap out of the buckle, freeing himself.

"Gunther. Gunther."

Now his legs—his brother couldn't help with those, and he couldn't reach them without contorting in a way made impossible by the way they were attached.

"Gunther. Gunther. Gunther. Gunther. I know. I know."

"Luther, this is really going to hurt, but it's all I can do...."

"It hurts. It hurts."

Gunther struggled to bend to the left and bring Luther with him at the same angle. He reached down as far as he possibly could while trying to ignore a low, horrific groan now sounding from Luther's throat. Gunther's own grumbling and gasping only stopped when he realized the strap was too far out of reach.

"Unnnnannnngnnnnnhhh. It hurts. Unnnnn. It hurts. It hurts."

Gunther lay limp, defeated. He didn't know what to do now.

"It hurts. It hurts. It really hurts. Gunther. Gunther."

Luther's wails became louder — too much for Gunther to bear. He winced once more, knowing he had to take some sort of action, and brought both elbows around to where they could lift him. He feared what he was about to try.

"Luther, just hold on."

"Gunther. Gunther. Gunther. Gunther."

Gunther raised himself and Luther on his elbows, as best as he could. The stitching pulled, and Luther's haunting groan returned.

"Unnnaaaaaaaaaahhhhh."

Gunther took hold of Luther's shoulders, holding him up.

"This is all I can do."

Gunther forced his own body down while holding Luther up above. Hundreds of stitches between them tore and snapped while their flesh ripped and shredded. The brothers wailed in anguish; Luther began to writhe and shake and pull and flail while Gunther reached down to the binding at his ankles once more. Their backs were still connected toward the lower end, and he felt the stitching pull and tear as he bent, but he finally reached the strap.

"Unnn. Ghh... unnnther."

Gunther managed to get the strap undone and quickly moved on to the other; the second contortion to get at the final binding sent Luther moaning loudly once more, but with it removed, Gunther's movement was only inhibited by his brother's weight and flailing. He tried his best to slide off the gurney; the task seemed impossible, but he knew he had to be quick. With a brutal struggle and Luther's moans making each moment more horrifying than the last, it seemed Gunther might actually succeed before he crumpled to the floor, unable to support either of their weights. As they fell, Gunther's hand caught the corner of one of Josef's trays, launching the contents around the room, and just a few feet away from the two of them, he saw a small morphine bottle roll to a stop.

"*Gunnnnn. Thhherr.*"

He reached for it, still connected to Luther by a few stitches, but managed to brush it with his fingertips. He pulled it toward him; it was nearly empty, but it was something.

"Luther, drin—"

"*Guuunnnthhherrr.*"

"—Drink this." Gunther reached around with the bottle, feeling for Luther's limp, gaping mouth, and poured the tiny bit of fluid into it.

"*Gunn. Ggghhghh…aagh. Gghunther.*" Luther's sounds gurgled as the morphine trickled down his throat.

Gunther scanned the dirt floor and spotted a scalpel. As he reached for it, the room dimmed around them. He turned to see the weak bulb in Josef's lantern darkening to little more than a faint glow. Gunther looked away and felt for the scalpel, soon catching it and moving it carefully to his back; he couldn't see what he was doing, and so, moved slowly… slowly… to a thread not far from the base of their spines. Wincing, Gunther pulled away from Luther. The thread pulled taught, and Luther's sounds grew anguished again.

Gunther slit the stitches, one at a time. The operation grew more painful with each cut.

"*Gunntherr. It hurts. It hurts.*"

"Hold on." Gunther struggled to concentrate, staring into the darkness with his hands between their backs, trying not to let Luther's wails distract him.

"*Gunther. Gunth—*"

Luther slumped to the floor, pulling the last few stitches out with his weight. Now free, Gunther pushed himself through all the pains in his own body and spun around to Luther. It was the first time in years — since they were kids — that he had seen him. He looked at once just the same as ever and completely unfamiliar; anyone else might not have even known it was him. Gunther took hold of Luther, doing his best to avoid touching the raw, bloody swath on his back.

"It's gonna be okay —"

"*Gunther. Gunther. Gunther.*"

He lacked the strength to stand. Clutching Luther with a battered arm, he began to pull his brother across the dirt.

Luther whimpered — occasional urgent words still slurring from his mouth — as Gunther reached the door, which was still locked as Josef had left it. Gunther carefully laid Luther down on his side before reaching up to the knob and pulling himself up with it. Once he could reach a counter, he pulled himself up higher. As he struggled, the last light from the dim lantern bulb faded away, leaving the two of them in total darkness.

Gunther raised his arm, and with only a brief pause, slammed it downward on the doorknob to no avail; he couldn't summon enough force to break it.

He shifted, letting his body lean against the wall. The weak leg on which he struggled to balance trembled beneath him as he brought his arm up once more. Like a club, he bashed it against the knob once, twice... a third time....

"*Gunther. Gunther. Gunther.*"

Luther's voice went on as Gunther's fist cracked against the knob.

A fourth strike — a fifth....

On the sixth, the knob broke away, and as it tumbled to the floor, so did Gunther, in part because his balance gave way, but also from a sudden, indescribable impulse: the hole where the knob had been was small — perhaps two inches in diameter — and through it streamed a tiny beam of sunlight. It was enough to paralyze Gunther in fear; he rolled on the floor in terror from a little ray illuminating the cell no better than Josef's lantern had. Drowning Luther's moans, Gunther let out a hideous cry as he scrambled in a disfigured heap across the dirt, seeking some way to hide himself.

Two voices—two impulses—wrestled in his mind, but the conviction to save Luther was crippled and ultimately erased by an uncontrollable, overwhelming fear of the light. It trumped and abolished any concern for either of their suffering, and as Gunther flailed about, screaming, the corner of his being still possessed with some sense of reason—pleading that he overcome this unfounded fear—fell silent.

He had no reaction, hardly a comprehension, as Luther's words continued to slur, *"Gunther. Gunther. Gunther. Gunther. Gunther. I knew. I know."*

"I know. I know."

"You."

"I know. I know. I know...."

Chapter 6

A week's neglect had allowed the floor to grow unusually dirty.

The janitors at Saint Elia's Academy for Girls used to tend to the adjoining church quite regularly. It was only with the arrival of the new, quiet volunteer that they had abandoned the task. The overall cleanliness had improved, not to any discredit toward the previous caretakers, but more as a testament to Stam's meticulous, dutiful nature.

She moved delicately through the aisles, mop swaying in her wake, erasing muddy prints left by dozens of snow-covered boots. In contrast with her usual manner, however, she seemed to struggle; her hand drifted to her stomach at every opportunity as she forced herself to push through obvious pain.

The nave around her, which had been empty for the last half hour or so, was now beginning to fill with girls. Stam glanced at a watch on her trembling wrist:

6:02 p.m.

By the door, Sister Carroll had been observing for at

least five minutes. She was studying Stam, trying not for the first time to understand the odd girl who had first appeared on a balmy evening two summers ago. She had no parents, no ride—just herself, clad in a heavy wool coat, carrying a large metal box under one arm. Her first request was to come inside, and the second was to pray. It was odd, being visited in the dead of night by the young girl, and hours later, as Sister Carroll prepared to go home, there she remained—not in a pew, but with her knees on the floor, head bowed and hands folded, softly speaking indecipherable words.

"God speaks every language," Stam later advised, after explaining she had been praying in Romanian.

If pressed, Stam relayed what she believed God said to her, and did so with such placid conviction and calm certainty, it sometimes caused the hairs on Sister Carroll's neck to perk. Belief and faith were concepts so many girls her age seemed to struggle with, but there was never any question with Stam. However astray she sometimes wandered—such as the incident with David—it was indisputable that her *faith* was cemented.

It had already occurred to Sister Carroll that approaching Stam the way she had with troubled girls in the past was doomed to ineffectuality. The conversation in the office and the visit to Stam's house were attempts at getting through to her parents, who in two years had never been to a single service, while Stam made it to every one she could when not occupied with her homeschooling during the daytime hours.

She had always been a bewildering case, but watching Stam go down this dangerous and self-destructive road was not something Sister Carroll was about to allow. She knew well it wasn't easy to be like Stam, who at age fifteen hardly even passed for twelve. She had rarely—if ever—been seen with a friend by her side, and had only just very recently begun talking with the other girls, like Hannah. Stam was older than everyone else, and though emotionally mature, she was socially infantile.

"Stam, honey?" Sister Carroll asked, stopping a few

feet from where Stam lay with one skinny arm stuck into a small opening to the church organ's pipe chamber.

She was busy—always undisturbed from her task—but responded, "Yes?"

Sister Carroll considered her words carefully. She didn't want to sound like a broken record, yet she wound up starting as she always did. "I'd like to talk to you about what happened the other night."

As she watched Stam, Sister Carroll noticed that, while she was still as diligent as ever with her cleaning, something *did* appear to be distracting Stam, and after an unusually long hesitation from her came an even more unusual reply. "Not right now, please."

Sister Carroll was perplexed. Aside from the other night, Stam was always willing to talk, or at least listen. She pursed her lips before trying again. "I think the organ pipes can wait, Stam. We should really have a talk."

Stam hesitated, trying to obscure a wince before pulling out of the organ chamber. She moved slowly—carefully—as she acceded to Sister Carroll's request and stood upright, holding her stomach. Even measured against Stam's cold, pallid norm, she looked sickly.

"Are you okay?" Sister Carroll asked as Stam shivered and placed a hand onto the organ to brace herself.

"I think I caught something," she swallowed, "from the cold."

"You don't look well—maybe you should go home." Sister Carroll suggested earnestly, looking Stam over.

"I'll be fine soon." Stam pulled her coat tighter around herself as she let out a shaky breath and looked up at Sister Carroll, expectantly. "What do you want?"

Sister Carroll motioned to one of the pews. "Why don't you sit down?"

Reluctantly, Stam slid to the floor, where she held her knees to her chest and looked up at Sister Carroll. "May we be brief?"

At this point, Sister Carroll had come to expect anything but normal behavior. She took a seat on the pew nearby and folded her hands, looking down at Stam. "I'm worried about you...." She searched Stam's face for a reaction. "It's mostly the things I talked to you about last time, but I'm worried too about your situation at home. You know, Stam, you can talk to me about anything, right?"

"Not *anything*."

"Why not?" Sister Carroll asked. "I know I'm not the world's greatest nun and can't answer or help with everything, but still I feel like you and I have a good relationship, and anything you say would remain between us and God."

"Why involve you at all, then?" Stam replied, her curious tone incongruous with the harsh words.

"Well, sometimes it's easier to speak to a person, don't you think?"

Stam did think about it, and replied, "No."

Sister Carroll sighed lightly, having exhausted her approaches on the matter. She tried something else instead. "Are you a happy person, Stam?"

Her reply was hesitant. "Genuine happiness can only come from God. So long as you welcome Him, He will fulfill you."

"That *is* true, but do you mean it? Or are you just saying it?"

"God makes things more difficult for some people. Life," Stam paused after the word, "is a more brutal thing for some, and faith is a more distant goal."

The nave was beginning to fill with more students, each louder than the last.

"Not so, Stam," Sister Carroll replied over the increasing noise. "Anyone can have faith—God tests some people more than others, but never more than they can bear. There's a famous quote that goes something like: 'the reason birds can fly and we can't is simply that they have perfect faith, for to have faith is to have wings.'"

She watched Stam, whose eyes were focused on the increasing flow of students, but whose mind seemed to be considering the quotation.

"That's not true." Stam furrowed her brow. "Faith isn't a reasonable means to an end. Faith is the result of observation...."

As the students moved closer, not paying either of them any mind but still crowding the two a bit, Stam stood up.

"Birds can fly because they have hollow bones," she thought about Sydney, "and because they *have wings*. I don't think there's sense in believing in what one hasn't seen to be true."

"But that's part of faith, Stam — God isn't always flesh and blood, but he's still here, right? That's why I thought it might be easier for you to talk to me about things."

"You don't need blood to be alive — or real."

Sister Carroll sighed dejectedly, disappointed at the morbid tone she read from the response. "Stam, honey, I just wish you'd be more open with me."

"I'm as open as I know how to be. It's not my strength." She looked at her watch:

6:19 p.m.

"What would you say *is* your strength?" Sister Carroll asked, curiously.

Stam was quiet. While she was thinking, Sister Carroll tried a different question, "What do you wish was your greatest strength? What do you strive toward?"

"... Closeness to God," she replied. However true it may have been, it was a bottled answer and Sister Carroll noticed.

"What does that mean to you though?"

Stam looked out at all the students around them, talking and laughing and carrying on together.

"... Self-control."

Sister Carroll opened her mouth to ask what Stam meant when a student appeared. "Sister." She tugged her arm. "Sister."

While Sister Carroll's attention was distracted, Stam excused herself. She made her way to a closet just off the nave where she returned the long cleaner she had been using on the organ pipes and also poured out the dirty water from the mop bucket. She located a thick, heavy mat which she dragged toward the main church door. There were already a few fresh footprints tracking snowy dirt into the vestibule, but she ignored them and laid down the mat. In the time all this took, Sister Carroll had been pulled away, and Stam, now alone in the bustling crowd of students dressed — unusual for a Friday — in their Sunday best, took a moment to relax. She leaned against the stone wall and let her unblinking eyes drift upward to the beautifully vaulted ceiling. She felt relatively peaceful.

"Hey, Stam."

... And then she was torn back to reality. Stam looked toward the familiar voice.

"We heard about you and David." Hannah sneered, concurrent with the giggling of her two cohorts.

Stam had nothing to say to such a remark. She looked away, still holding her stomach; the interlopers were more difficult to bear when she was already in such discomfort.

"Don't ignore me," Hannah spat, moving closer and folding her arms authoritatively. "Everybody knows what happened in the bathroom." Her voice quieted so that no one else but Stam and the surrounding gang might hear. "You're a slut."

Stam failed to have any strong reaction, but in her own time, glanced first to Sarah and Samantha at Hannah's side before stopping on her. "I don't think that's true."

"Yeah," Hannah went on, ignoring Stam's remark but agreeing with herself. "He only asked you to the dance because you're a slut."

Stam removed herself from the conversation, looking away again. She prepared to straighten and walk away, which was growing more and more difficult each moment, as Hannah jeered to Sarah, "She's probably got, like, a hundred STDs and that's why she's so pale and gross."

"Eww." Sarah laughed. "I'll bet she's got herpes."

Hannah laughed right back before turning to Sarah again. "You know, Sister Carroll went to her house to tell her parents and they weren't even there. And her house was like, all creepy and weird and gross, and her brother has a girl's name."

Stam swallowed, some degree of frustration setting in.

"What?" Sarah laughed. "What is it?"

"I don't know, Amy or Abby or something. It was so gay, whatever it was, and they have all these animals—like birds and stuff—and there's bird shit everywhere."

"Gross," Sarah exclaimed.

Stam raised an eyebrow at the two of them, but not before noticing that most of the students were now filing out of the nave. She felt a vague compulsion to explain. "There's only one animal: a bird—he's very clean.…"

"Whatever," Hannah replied quickly, "I'll bet that's why you always smell so bad."

"Do I?" Stam asked, having never been accused of such before. The two girls laughed while Samantha nervously followed suit behind them.

"You're such a fucking loser." Hannah giggled.

Stam turned to walk away, but Hannah moved closer, allowing for no easy escape.

"You know David only hangs out with you because he knows you're a slut, too."

"You said before it was because he felt sorry for me."

"Yeah, well, all it really is is that he wants to fuck you. I don't know why anyone would.…"

"Girls," Sister Carroll's friendly voice called from across the room.

It pulled Hannah's attention away, but before leaving, she hissed one last jab at Stam, "You're just an ugly slut."

The three wandered away from Stam, leaving her in the now completely empty nave. Out in the vestibule, she could still hear everyone chattering, though it was growing dimmer as they disappeared through the glass doors of the school. Her breaths, which had become labored from the stress of Hannah's presence, quieted as she tried to stable herself.

She looked at her watch:

6:26 p.m.

As the door shut behind the last student, Stam was left in silence, staring after them.

"I'm not sure how God sees it," a voice said with quaint matter-of-factness. It failed to disturb Stam in any way—she didn't even look to the source, Ashley, as he sat up straight from a position lying on his back in the pews. Beneath his head had been a bible, and his heavily winter-bundled body had run no risk of making any contact with the wooden seat.

"... But I think some people deserve to die."

* * *

"Luther!"

Gunther screamed the name for the hundredth time as he shook the body, dragging it through the empty halls.

Luther was dead.

Gunther had lain in the corner, howling from the sunlight and drowning out the sounds of his brother's terrified moans until the last pale glow from the tiny hole in the door had disappeared. When it did, there was silence. Just when Luther had quieted—when he had died—Gunther couldn't say, and the last words he'd heard were a stream of urgent pleas he could neither understand nor fulfill.

"Someone, help," he screamed to no ears. Everyone was long gone. Gunther was alone.

He wrapped his arms around Luther as best as he could in his crippled state.

"Why?" Gunther screamed, writhing beside his brother. He couldn't ignore the sunlight—even a tiny beam—and had listened to Luther die because of it. A meaningless fear had overpowered every last ounce of his will.

Gunther lay on the ground for minutes, crying and gasping into his brother's chest until suddenly there was a noise from outside; it sounded like an engine. He struggled to lift himself, and from there, still clutching Luther's body, crawled toward a pair of double doors. After minutes of agonized struggle, he pushed against them. Outside in the darkness of the night, he saw little more than an expanse of dirt fields and ugly brick houses, but above him, there were airplanes flying through the sky. He couldn't make out whose they were.

As he lay beside Luther, half inside the building and half sprawled out on the two short stone steps leading to the dirt, another sound, mostly obscured by the buzzing engines above, came from closer by. Gunther looked over to investigate, and there he saw a man who looked somehow familiar, laying on the ground and moaning desperately. He hadn't seen many faces clearly or for very long—other than Josef's—in years. The moans were words, but not ones Gunther could understand.

"*Panie Boże, błagam Cię.*" The man coughed hideously, interrupting himself.

Soon, it hit him: it was the surgeon—the *eye* surgeon who had performed the horrible extraction on Gunther. He was weak and emaciated, abandoned at some point weeks—maybe even months—ago to whatever neglect and cruelty had befallen so many others whose cries Gunther had heard while in his prison. The man was close to death; his eyes stared with hardly any spark of consciousness, but as his body shivered on the ground, crawling helplessly, he suddenly caught sight of the disfigured brothers and a look of horror spread on his face. He had enough presence of mind to whisper a few terrified prayers in Polish.

Gunther crawled toward him, letting go of Luther. The man tried to squirm away, but with no success once Gunther caught his foot.

"*Proszę o łaskę smierci,*" the man begged, looking at the sky.

Gunther had grabbed him, but wasn't even sure why. He didn't know what he was doing. He looked at the battered man, realizing at some point—and not very long ago—his hands had been amputated. Gunther shuddered at the sight, letting his grip weaken as the sorry-looking shell of a man coughed once more. A string of bloody phlegm escaped from his mouth as he begged once again, "*Zabierz Proszę o łaskę smierci.*"

The man's delirious eyes drifted to Gunther, and with desperation, he said two recognizable words: "Kill me."

Disturbed, Gunther tried to slide away, but the man, pulling himself along by the elbows, pursued him. The festered stumps at the end of his arms fumbled for Gunther.

"*Kill me….*"

Gunther continued to resist while his mind raced. He heard the despair in the man's voice, and if that was insufficient, it was written clearly on his tortured face.

"*… Kill me….*"

Gunther managed to balance himself, and with a kick, he knocked the man away like some sort of offensive vermin. He let out a whimper, and though Gunther continued to shudder, he suddenly stopped. He listened to the old man's soft, hopeless cries; his face now lay planted in the dirt as he wept. "*Zabij mnie….*" The ghastly figure continued whimpering — pleading — to what Gunther could only assume was God. The same God he himself had once cried to. The same God who, if real at all, had no stake in or compassion for anyone. He swallowed as something stirred within himself, and with hesitation, took hold of the muttering man.

"Zabij mnie…."

He looked around, but there was nothing he could use, and his own arms were too weak to end anyone's life.

… It was then he remembered his teeth; one of the long fangs had been removed, but the other still remained. Long ago, as he lay dying in Romania, death had embraced him before a stray grenade launched him back into hellish, screaming life.

Fighting all trepidation, he moved to the man's dry, bony neck and — conjuring the will from somewhere he couldn't possibly fathom — bit down. The man screamed and flailed as Gunther held on tight. The sensation was far fouler than he had expected: the blood gushing from the wound was hot, smelled terrible, and tasted even worse.

Within a few seconds, the man's convulsions slowed, then stopped.

Only when the blood flow dried completely did Gunther break away, immediately spitting out the disgusting, iron taste in his mouth. He looked down at the man's face: it was pale and stripped of life, his open eyes staring vacantly toward the sky. Still trembling, Gunther sat back. He continued to spit, sickened by the little bit of blood he had unintentionally swallowed, until he noticed something: he felt *different*. Somewhere inside himself, a sort of a pain or longing he couldn't quite explain had faded in some small way.

It was the first feeling of comfort he had felt in over a year.

He couldn't be sure what he felt was real, but with caution, he licked the blood still on his lips, and that, too, seemed to help. It seemed to help everything; each agonizing injury diminished, and the inexplicable yearning he had felt for ages now felt—however minutely—satiated.

He looked down at the man he had just killed. His blood had tasted exactly like what it was; it was disgusting, but like a medicine. However mortifying he found the smell, texture, flavor, and origin, it was in some small way *relieving*. That alone was enough to set aside his feelings of disgust for what he was about to do. He leaned in close to the man's body and placed his tongue upon the punctured throat from which blood was still trickling.

He swallowed, but felt nothing. There was no change in his condition, even as he tried swallowing more.

Gunther's mind was working more logically now than it had in many months, and it occurred to him that Josef had given him blood on a few occasions—once even pumping it straight into Gunther's heart. None of it had an effect, so something about this man's blood had been special, at least for a moment. He already had a sinking fear about what the answer might be.

He considered the origin of his curse: the creature in the woods. She had chosen him out of all the corpses— perhaps because he'd still been alive.

He shuddered, horrified by the thought, but then was interrupted by someone shouting an order in the distance. Gunther looked around and then crawled to a nearby pile of abandoned supplies where he managed to wrestle a small tripod—probably for a machine gun—from a heap of discarded metal. Struggling, he lifted himself to a standing position using it as a cane. He hobbled across the dirt toward the sounds.

He heard voices calling out commands, but they weren't in German. It was English.

The fear Gunther had once had about the "Enemies of Germany" dissolved; he didn't care who was out there. He pressed on until he heard someone shout again, this time in German, but with an English inflection. "Get down—lay there," was the harsh, authoritative command.

Gunther wondered if the base, or hospital, or whatever it was, was being captured, and as he peered around a corner to where a mass of American soldiers stood with half a dozen Germans face-down on the dirt with their hands on their heads, that seemed to be the case. There were also dozens of bodies strewn about, curled up or twisted in some way; they didn't look like military. He scanned the area for any sign of Josef, but he was nowhere in sight.

Suddenly, gunfire broke out—just a small spattering of bullets from a single weapon. The Americans shouted to each other, scrambling, and as a few of them pointed toward something, the bullets stopped. A handful of the Americans charged in the direction from where the sound had come, which wasn't that far from Gunther. He pulled back, slinking away into the shadows.

"Get out here, fucking Kraut," one of them called out in German.

He hurried to Luther's body, not sure what he was going to do, but began trying to move him once again. It was slightly less difficult now, but still not an easy feat. He dragged the lifeless body maybe fifteen yards before reaching one of the squat brick houses. It was unlocked. He carefully reached up, avoiding any contact with the wooden door, and as his hand grasped the knob, he stopped. Something ethereal was holding him back; he suddenly didn't want to go inside.

… But he *did* want it. He wanted to hide and collect his thoughts.

He stopped again with his hand hanging by the knob, utterly sickened by the notion of entering, as if to do so would be a commission of the most heinous crime imaginable. The dread wasn't unlike his fear of the sun, and made absolutely no sense.

He growled a bit, trying to reach out again, but once more, his willingness to enter dissolved.

He gave up, dispirited and defeated by his inexplicable nuances. He left Luther's body on the ground as he stood with the tripod and looked around. He took a few steps, and then heard a hushed voice.

"Stop right there."

Gunther froze, and then slowly turned to a figure standing behind him wielding a readied pistol. In the darkness, the man tried to scan Gunther's face and seemed to notice something unusual, but his horror failed to rival the reactions Gunther was used to from those who had seen him in the hallway. All Gunther could tell about the man came from his uniform: he was a Schutzstaffel.

Gunther whispered hopefully in his pathetic, raspy voice, "I'm German...."

The Schutzstaffel guard narrowed his eyes, trying to better make Gunther out in the darkness. If nothing else, it was obvious he was battered to the point of not possibly being a threat, and so he made his decision. He motioned with his gun to Gunther. "Come on," and began to hurry away. Gunther picked up Luther and began to follow, much to the Schutzstaffel's dismay. He stopped, hurrying back. "Is he alive?"

"I don't know," Gunther lied.

"Come on." The Schutzstaffel took hold of Gunther, trying to raise him up. "There's no time for that."

Gunther resisted but could in no way overpower the man. Luther slipped from his hands as the man pulled Gunther away. He, watched helplessly as Luther's body disappeared from view.

They made their way toward a wall where, hidden, they could see the American troops. Gunther had once heard that if you had to surrender, you surrendered to anyone but the Soviets and ideally the Americans.

One of them — some sort of commander — was yelling and cursing in English, and then grabbed a Schutzstaffel officer from the ground, screaming at him in German,

"What in the hell is this fucking nightmare? You sick piece of Nazi shit." He bashed the guard across the face, knocking him back to the ground.

"What is all this?" He kicked the guard in the head, rolling him a few feet and eliciting a loud whimper.

"What were you doing when all these people were dying, huh?" The American commander made a sweeping gesture to the emaciated bodies littering the area. There was no answer.

"Fucking Nazi scum." He raised his gun and sent a single bullet through the cowering officer, who screamed, and over the next few agonizing seconds, fell silent. The commander called out to the other prisoners, "Get up."

The Schutzstaffel beside Gunther drew back around the corner, bringing Gunther with him.

"What's ha—" Gunther began to ask as quietly as he could.

"Shh," the Schutzstaffel hushed him and checked around the corner once more. He turned to Gunther and whispered, "They caught the last truck heading out."

Another gunshot was heard, then two more in rapid succession. There was angry screaming, and somewhere beneath it, desperate pleading.

The Schutzstaffel swallowed, panic setting in. "We gotta get out of here—they're gonna kill us...."

The man helped Gunther as they moved away from the mass of troops, only to nearly run right into the soldiers out looking for him. They hurried in another direction, but soon discovered they were completely surrounded. The Schutzstaffel guard grew more and more on edge, and finally, pushed open the door of one of the squat structures. It creaked loudly, but he didn't seem to care any longer. He stepped in, trying to drag Gunther who, by no will of his own, resisted.

"What are you doing?" the Schutzstaffel hissed.

Gunther grabbed the dirt outside, clawing so as not to be pulled inside.

"Get in here," he commanded urgently, voice still hushed.

"... I can't," Gunther whispered, not understanding

why.

"What do you mean you can't? Yes you can."

With those words, Gunther's unwitting resistance weakened and the Schutzstaffel pulled him forcefully through the doorway and into the empty husk of a building. It wasn't unlike Gunther's cell: there was no furniture whatsoever and the floor was nothing more than gritty dirt. The guard was shaking now, overcome with terror. The two sat together, listening, as the man's trembling hands held a pistol in his lap.

"Where are you, you fucking Kraut?"

They heard the door of a nearby shack being kicked in. The guard shook with the sound and clutched his pistol tighter, trying to hold himself steady.

"Get out here."

They heard another crash—this one was right next to them. The Schutzstaffel guard shuddered again while Gunther looked up at the window to see an American pass by. The Schutzstaffel's breaths grew sharp.

As Gunther looked over, he froze, witnessing the Schutzstaffel place his gun to his own head. His eyes shut, and with a deep wince, he started to pull the trigger—

Gunther grabbed the man's wrist, pulling the gun away. "Stop."

The Schutzstaffel tried to pull it back—his voice was panicked, "It's over."

He easily overpowered Gunther's weak arms and brought the gun back to his head, whispering through frightened panting, "They're just gonna kill us."

Gunther grabbed again for the gun, catching it just as it went off. Gunther's interference disrupted the angle of the bullet; instead of killing the man, it merely took a chunk from his face. He screamed and fell to the floor, flailing wildly.

Gunther was speechless—horrified by the sight. Outside somebody shouted, "Over there."

His panic grew. He looked down at the Schutzstaffel, who was fumbling about in desperation for the gun and screaming louder and louder. Paralyzed, unsure of what to do, he watched the Schutzstaffel guard begin to slow and his screams dwindle to softer, quieter whimpers as his consciousness steadily drained.

Mind racing as he heard the Americans coming, Gunther made a choice: he reached out, taking hold of the Schutzstaffel guard who only barely reacted. Gunther felt no more able to believe what he was doing this time than the last, but he moved in close to the soldier's neck, took a deep breath, and bit. The man moaned, but it was hardly audible. Gunther winced and fought off the urge to vomit while he swallowed as much of the warm, viscous blood as he could bear. He only managed a little before the sharp, metallic taste and the sickening reality of what he was doing caught up with him. He pulled away. He couldn't tell how much he had consumed, but it felt like a lot.

"There!" The Americans were right outside now.

Shocked by sudden clarity, Gunther thought quickly and grabbed the Schutzstaffel's gun and fired off another solitary shot for the Americans to hear.

The door was flung open. Three American soldiers rushed into the tiny house, guns raised and flashlights beaming. They saw Gunther and the Schutzstaffel guard lying on the ground in a single messy pool of blood. They approached cautiously, and one reached out to touch Gunther.

"Jesus." The American drew back, horrified. "Kid feels like he's been dead for a week."

Next he touched the Schutzstaffel guard and analyzed the bullet wound. He seemed dissatisfied as he searched the scene, until he noticed Gunther's wide-eyed stare. He shuddered at the sight, looked away, and stood, motioning for the other soldiers to follow him. They disappeared through the door and their footsteps soon faded.

Minutes passed before Gunther allowed himself to move. He had been fixated on a growing sensation within himself: recovery.

* * *

A choir was assembled; three dozen girls stood together on an auditorium stage singing "O Come All Ye Faithful" in a rehearsed—but hardly flawless—chorus. Sister Carroll stood before them, conducting, with an expression of some concern on her face. She glanced to a digital clock just barely in her field of vision backstage:

7:43 p.m.

As the song finished and applause from the parent and faculty-packed audience rang out, Sister Carroll's eyes were met by a school official who shrugged helplessly, only fueling her discomfort.

"Hannah?" David asked, poking his head through a restroom door. There was no answer. He stepped back and moved farther down the locker-lined hallway as a clock changed:

7:51 p.m....

7:52 p.m.

He made his way to another restroom—one he remembered from earlier in the week. A little smile crept across his face just before he peeked inside.

"Hannah?" he called out, to no reply. He stepped back and let the door fall shut. As he turned away, he suddenly let out a yelp, startled by an unexpected figure standing motionless behind him.

Ashley smiled, remaining silent longer than was comfortable before speaking. "Excuse me."

"Oh, uh, yeah—" David stammered—still out of breath from the shock—as he stepped aside. Ashley stumbled past him and into the restroom without a word. A bit taken aback, David stepped in after him. "Hey man," he said. "This is the girl's restroom."

Ashley took weary look around the room. "So it is," he mused. Without another word, he slowly moved to a paper towel dispenser and began pulling the lever over and over, causing a bundle to slowly grow in his hand.

David watched, mystified until, when the dispenser was nearly empty, he asked, "Hey, uh, have you seen a girl around anywhere?"

"This would be the place... to meet girls... wouldn't

it?" Ashley replied, carrying the paper towels to the center of the room. His breaths were weak and labored.

David was unsure what to make of the response, but could tell there was something wrong with the boy in front of him. "You okay, man?"

Ashley said nothing as he began to lay out the paper in generous rows to protect the tile floor. He had covered a broad swath before stopping, retaining one last wad of paper towels in his hand.

"What are you doing?" David asked, bewildered, as Ashley began fishing in the pocket of his coat. Still unresponsive, he pulled a small package of breath mints from his pocket which he placed on the edge of one of the sinks.

"Okay, well," David shrugged, "whatever...."

"Wait," Ashley commanded, not looking at him. David obeyed, with growing apprehension as he watched Ashley, who seemed absorbed in some private thought. It appeared as though he might say something, but whatever it was, it was soon abandoned. In the silence, his eyes — somehow sad and hollow — lifted to meet David's.

He sighed. "I hate this."

In the auditorium, Sister Carroll found herself conducting the final song of the evening. The choir sang the words loudly and clearly; it was their best performance so far:

"Oh, there is a holy wonder;
from Bethlehem rising, sudden;
for today was born, as has been foretold;
the One with no ending...."

Stam listened to them sing the final verse. Applause erupted, and shortly afterward, audience members trickled out into the school lobby where Stam stood nestled into a corner. She kept her head up, seeking out Ashley in the crowd, but had yet to spot him by the time the whole lobby had filled with parents and faculty. Minutes passed until she was distracted by a voice.

"Stam," Sister Carroll called. Stam turned to her as she proceeded, "Stam, honey, have you seen your friend Hannah anywhere?"

"No."

"She was supposed to be the soloist tonight, but she was just *gone*," Sister Carroll whimpered. "She was so excited at the rehearsal earlier...."

Stam replied with a slight shake of her head. "I don't know."

"Maybe she got nervous. Oh, Stam...." She was helplessly flustered and somehow disappointed in herself as much as anything else.

"I have to go." Stam walked away before all the words made it out, leaving Sister Carroll alone with her grief. She watched Stam disappear into the crowd, but made no attempt to follow.

After nearly two minutes of pushing and dodging through those around her, Stam found herself outside, with the toes of her boots sinking into freshly fallen snow. A short walk took her away from the busy school entrance to a clear, quiet part of the lawn where she stopped and looked up into the cloudy sky. Subtly, her hand rose and drew the shape of a cross before her chest as she spoke very softly, "*Mărturisesc Domnului Dumnezeului meu și în fața ta, sfinte părinte, numeroasele-mi păcate. Azi am,*" she hesitated before continuing, "*azi am ucis* Hannah Knotts...." Stam lowered her head. "*Sper ca Dumnezeu să mă ierte.*"

Chapter 7

A city lay in ruins; rubble and dust littered the jagged remnants of roads in every direction. Once-proud Swastikas hung like rags from flagpoles, dripping lifelessly down the facades of war-torn buildings. Discarded pamphlets pressed into the mud by wheels and footprints called out in vain for action and one last heroic feat of patriotism while somewhere far in the distance, brief spats of gunfire echoed through the mazes of desolate alleys and deserted streets.

Gunther moved slowly, and with each step, reached out a hand to brace himself on the crumbling walls. The city of newsreels, pride and propaganda was now just a derelict husk. It had once been the most powerful thing — the *only* thing, really — he had ever known. It had been the seat of a tremendous and awesome force — so determined and alive — hailed as the birthplace of a new Germany and new way of life, and was now little more than a stale stone corpse.

Josef was right: it was all gone.

The feeling sank in for Gunther as he pressed on

through the debris. In the days—maybe a week at this point—since he had escaped, it was only now that lucidity had returned to him sufficiently to briefly take his mind away from the past year and a half. He thought about his whole life; nearly everything he had ever known had been dissolved and that which might have not—his parents— seemed too distant and alien to mean anything now. He wondered whether his hometown had survived the wave of destruction brought by the Americans and Soviets. He wondered if his parents were still alive.

His father had always been abrasive and cruel. Gunther had sought to please him, but the stress of his work and the dizzying conviction of the National Socialist German Worker's Party had swallowed him whole since as far back as Gunther could remember. He didn't *hate* his father—he had never really known him—and now the only side of the man Gunther had ever seen was rendered invalid. He couldn't imagine him as anything more than a stranger, living in a strange town in a strange country.

His mother, he remembered, had always been kind, but quick to relent in any conflict with her husband on what was best for Gunther. Who she was had been lost amid her husband's barked assertions. Gunther loved her, but wondered now if she'd ever particularly cared for him beyond obligation—or if she still would now that Gunther was no longer an instrument of the Führer's dream for Germany. What basis for a relationship did they have beyond being related?

The idea of home as a physical place was not something he had been brought up to understand. "Home" was never anything more than the ethereal concept of "Germany" and a nationalistic ideal.

He could still remember his house... his childhood bedroom... his school... his church... the shop with the scary poster in the window... the field where Herr Petersen waved to him each day... but more vividly, he recalled the cold, smelly barracks and muddy fields in which he'd spent his adolescence. He remembered sharing a bunk with Heinz more than he remembered lying in bed beside his own brother....

"You're older than him by four minutes. You gonna let him beat you?" their father used to jeer, attempting to rile up the same athletic prowess in Gunther that Luther had always exhibited.

Gunther would never have thought on his own to be embarrassed when next to Luther. He was in awe, and at worst slightly jealous of Luther's comparative strength, speed and ability to fit in; it was their father's insistence that there was some kind of fault in Gunther which caused him shame.

In their childhood, he and Luther had been as close as, well, as twins, but when Luther began to easily make friends and even—Gunther heard later—kiss a girl one day after school, there began a shift. At that time, Gunther and Jens had been friends for a few years even though Jens' natural charm and charisma should have made him more compatible with someone like Luther. It was something Gunther never questioned, though; he liked Jens and liked listening to him talk about his passions. Jens would go on and on about singers and pop music and—as soon as the adults left the room—roll his eyes at the notion of German supremacy. He, unlike anyone else Gunther had ever met, took the Nazis in stride and regarded them as little more than a nuisance distracting him and everyone else from better, more interesting things. It wasn't *just* that it was refreshing to Gunther—though it certainly was that—but it really did captivate him. He always wanted to know what Jens was going say or think of next.

"One day, I'll go to New York City, or London, you know, one of those places that actually has a real concept of culture—and see Bing Crosby, or Glenn Miller or Billie Holiday…."

The names went over Gunther's head. Most western music was banned, or at least regarded as highly suspect. It was another way that Jens snubbed his nose to the ideologies around them. If an adult had ever known, it would have been the end of the world; behavior like Jens' was perverse and shocking, but it was only with him Gunther ever felt normalcy or anything decent.

The nostalgia he had for home and his childhood was, really, for those moments with Jens... and that had brought him to where he now was: not to his unfamiliar hometown, but to an unfamiliar metropolis.

An illegible street sign coated in ash and twisted to the ground marked the huge square where Gunther came to a stop. Somewhere far, far away, an air raid siren howled helplessly into the night. Eyes wide in the darkness, Gunther tried to make out the words above the door of a huge, half crumbled building standing across the plaza. He was seeking an address he knew by heart—he had read it a thousand times, just as he had every portion of Jens' letters years ago. He'd always imagined finding the place, meeting Jens in Munich, and celebrating the end of the war together.

"Stop," a German voice commanded, accompanied by the bright glare of a flashlight. Gunther turned, wearily. In the light, one could make out a bloodstained swath in the fabric near the neck of his stolen Wehrmacht uniform.

"What are you doing over there? Come this way."

It was a teenage girl's voice, tremulous and hushed. The flashlight flipped off. "Come on."

Before the light had shone on him, Gunther's eyes had had the whole night to adjust to the darkness. Not one electric light was left in the dilapidated city, and were it not for the stars in the sky and the occasional smoldering rubble, it might be impossible to see anything at all. Gunther barely made out the silhouette of the girl dropping back down behind an overturned jeep. In between them was a body lying on the pavement.

He ignored the girl's plea and moved on toward the building. She called out once more, "Where are you going?"

As she spoke, the distant air raid siren cut off. Gunther imagined the Americans somewhere—wherever it was—silencing the alarm as if to silence the last wails of a fighting city—as if to say it was *over*.

There was no sound now aside from Gunther's footsteps in the gritty soot beneath him. The last of the gunfire had died, and the creak as he pulled open the door of the crumbling building was like the cry of a ghost haunting the empty streets.

"What are you —"

Gunther let the door close behind him, shutting out the girl's voice. He stood alone in blackness until a flashlight of his own came on. He pointed it around, observing nothing but a plain lobby. There was a receptionist's desk littered with a mess of scattered papers, and a few chairs were piled in one corner opposite a healthy-looking plant in the other.

Gunther moved to the stairs, remembering Jens' letter: *"... I work on the seventh floor...."*

The wooden stairs groaned with each step while Gunther fought the terror that welled in him. The texture of the oak banister was more frightening than wandering the dead city — for a reason he still could not explain.

With each completed staircase, Gunther traveled farther and farther into the world that had been lost with the war. The abandoned rooms where clerks signed endless forms, filed endless reports, and propagated the infrastructure of the failed regime were like empty crypts. Gunther wondered where they all could have gone — if they had been killed or if they had run.

There were two rooms off the main hallway when he reached the seventh, top floor. One door stood open; he peered through it, shining the light in on a row of desks and a wall of opened filing cabinets. The individual drawers looked as though they had been haphazardly rummaged through, and at the base were piles of folders with papers spilling out onto the floor.

He moved to the other room. It was no different aside from being only half the size; the far end of the office had been carved away by an explosion and the remaining space was open to the air. There were more desks, more cabinets — nothing which stood out in the slightest way. Nothing to offer a clue... but at one time, Jens had sat at one of these desks.

"I push papers around; they send in documents from the work camps and I either file them or burn 'em...."

Gunther wandered through the rows, hoping he might be able to feel which desk had been Jens' by touching the wooden surface, but he couldn't, and he knew it was pointless. It had been over two years since the last letter — Jens could be anywhere. He could have gone back into the Waffen combat brigades; he could be a thousand miles away; he could have been captured.

He could be dead.

Gunther moved to the edge of the room where the linoleum floor tiles were peeled and torn and fell away into void. From where he stood, he could see out over the plaza and even make out the overturned jeep below; at least two people were huddled behind it. He scanned the ragged, bomb-torn skyline; it was a far cry from the proud ideological epicenter he'd heard of as a boy.

He had been brought up to believe in two things: the Führer and God. The Führer, Gunther now saw more vividly than ever — perhaps the way Jens had always seen it — was nothing more than a man. For all the poems and songs they had to read and sing in the HJ, their former leader had simply been the chosen. Gunther and Jens both wanted the best for Germany, but post-war depression and desperation had bore many with Hitler's convictions; they, too, wanted the best for Germany. What followed — invasion, war, and oppression — were hardly logical factors in a better life for *anyone*.

As for God: he had made himself scarce during this whole nightmare. Gunther knew well it was the nature of God to test faith through hardship and strife, but *no one* deserved what was happening around him. The things he had seen and felt were sufficient to remove the idea of a compassionate or loving lord from reason. If God was real, he had forgotten Germany. It was that simple.

Gunther turned away from the ledge and drifted back through the half-room. His eyes glossed over the stacks and stacks of papers everywhere, and just as he reached the door, he did a double-take to a faded brown note tacked above a nearby desk.

He moved closer. It was a letter — one he had sent to Jens years ago. He stood stunned as a chill ran through him.

    2ⁿᵈ August, 1943

    Dear Jens,

    Oh my God. That's so awful. You were shot? I think my heart stopped when I read that. I guess I should have realized that if you were writing a letter, you're doing OK ... I can't imagine being shot. I'm not that strong; if I got shot, I'd probably just die outright. I'm really glad you're OK.

    I'm scheduled to go to Romania in October; I don't even know why. We're supposed to be taking trucks, but Martin says there might not be any left by then and we might have to walk —

Gunther stopped. He couldn't bring himself to read any further. He knew what was next: he would ask about what Jens was doing, complain about Heinz, and worry about how he would send and receive mail once making it to Romania. It was the last letter Gunther had sent to Jens. Jens' reply had never received one of its own; the one Gunther had written was in his jacket the day he was shot.

A tear dripped from his eye — the one Josef had removed. In the days since Gunther's escape, he had noticed something incredible: the eye had healed. He could even *see* out of it. Although he had been unable to coax himself into examining his reflection, it felt as though his eye was back to normal. It had come at a gruesome price, but most of his body was in startlingly good shape.

Gunther reached out to the letter with a shaking hand. Almost two years had passed since Jens' reply had reached Gunther, but Jens had never seen a response. It filled him with dread that Jens may have presumed Gunther no longer cared for him. As reasonable a conclusion as it may have been, it couldn't be further from the truth.

As he took hold of the tack to free it from the wall, a sudden harsh voice startled him, accompanied with the bright shine of a flashlight.

"Hey — what are you doing?"

Gunther slowly turned to the intruder. It was the

same girl from before. With his own flashlight in hand and pointed at her, he could make out her face as she could surely his. She was younger than Gunther by a few years, and in her free hand was a pistol, shaking with her terror.

"I'm German," Gunther replied, quietly.

"I—" The girl stifled a stammer and forced composure. "I didn't ask that."

Gunther looked at the letter, ignoring her, and plucked it from the wall. He scanned it again and then glanced to the girl.

"We need you outside," she ordered.

"Are you in charge here?" Gunther asked calmly.

"Of *you* I am," she insisted, gesturing to the insignia on her shoulder. Gunther looked her over, noticing now she was wearing a jacket much too large and with the markings of a Gruppenführer officer—a senior Schutzstaffel ranking.

"It's your duty as a German to join us in the defense of Munich."

Gunther stared through her. The girls' conviction was unobscured despite her fear.

"What do you suggest we do?" Gunther replied, eyes moving back to the letter. "You and I are going to stop America?"

"You and I are the future of Germany," she barked.

He couldn't bring himself to look at her. She really believed what she was saying, as though she couldn't think far enough ahead to know that the sun would soon rise, and with it, the American forces would surge through the streets. The girl would die before she gave up. Gunther turned to her.

"Give me that." He motioned to her coat.

"*Excuse* me?"

"You're gonna die—for nothing."

"I'll die for the Führer." Her hands were shaking even more now. "You're just a coward, like Sydney."

"Like *who*?" a third voice interrupted from the hallway.

The girl's head jerked to the interloper, along with the flashlight's beam. Gunther's followed as well, and the two lights soon illuminated a slender man standing in the door frame. He was somewhere in his late teens or early twenties and wore a plain white shirt with dark suspenders. "I thought I told you to go home."

The girl swallowed nervously; her zeal was beginning to waver under pressure. "I—I won't."

"Elisabeth—"

"Shut up, Sydney," she yelled.

While she was distracted, Gunther started toward her. She noticed immediately and spun her flashlight back. "Stay away."

"Elisabeth," the man shouted once more.

Now stricken with terror, she did the only thing she could think to do in reaction to Gunther's movement: her trembling hand pulled her gun's trigger.

With an echoing *BANG*, the bullet tore through Gunther's lower chest. He gasped and fell to the floor, dropping his flashlight.

"Elisabeth," the man screamed, rushing to her and wrestling the gun from her weak, paralyzed grip. The girl stood motionless, terrified of what she had done. With the gun secured, the man grabbed her shoulders and spun her to meet him eye-to-eye.

"Listen to me," he shouted. "It's over. This isn't a game and you can't do anymore good fighting."

"I just—"

"Give me that damn thing." He grabbed the collar of the jacket, pulling it backward and sliding it from her shoulders. She wanted to resist, but couldn't manage. The man worked it off her and flung it toward the chasm at the end of the room; the Nazi uniform fell into the darkness and rubble below.

"Get out of here, now." He pushed her toward the door. She hesitated, still terrified from the shot she'd fired, but with another shove from the man, the girl, at last, relented and fled. Her panicked breaths entwined with her echoing footsteps as she hurried down the stairs and away from the scene.

"Are you okay, kid?" the man asked urgently, reaching for the flashlight.

"Uughh," Gunther grumbled, fighting to sit up, "I'm... fine."

"Whoa, fuck—" The man gasped as he shined the light on Gunther's torso; the bloodstain on his collar was clearly visible. "You're not fine."

"It's old," Gunther replied, struggling to his feet.

The man adjusted the flashlight to illuminate all of Gunther. The bullet hole in his shirt from the girl's shot had little more than a tiny red circle around it—it had hardly bled at all.

Gunther finished standing up. When he'd been shot, his fist had involuntarily clenched and crumpled the letter in his hand. He tried to flatten it, ignoring the man beside him until, after a moment of silence, the man's voice whispered like he was seeing a ghost.

"... Gunther?"

Gunther's hands slowed to a stop. He registered the voice as somehow distantly familiar. He looked over at the man, invisible behind the glare of the flashlight. There was silence for what could have been a full minute before the man spoke again with an indescribable emotion in his voice.

"Gunther...."

Gunther's mind was frozen. He couldn't let himself believe what his heart was hoping, and yet his lips began to move. "Jens?"

Silence arose once more; this one even greater than the previous pause. The man slowly turned the flashlight to his own face, showing himself to Gunther, and it was him—it was Jens. He had six additional years on him since when he was just a gawky fourteen-year-old, but he was still the same. He turned the light back on Gunther, who looked down, unable to hide shame at his appearance. He could only imagine what Jens must think of him: a pale, sick, battered shell of a human being. He hadn't in his wildest dreams really expected to find Jens here.

The stunned silence continued until Jens broke it. "Are you okay?"

Gunther could say nothing. Jens took a step toward him. "Gunther?"

He couldn't move. He stood in the beam of light, staring down at the floor. The urge he felt to run toward Jens and grab him was suppressed by a feeling of defeat. Silence hung between them until Jens' arms suddenly wrapped about Gunther's whole frame. It was hard to tell what was happening.

"I'm so happy to see you," Jens whispered.

Gunther failed to move. All he could do was tremble as Jens continued to squeeze him. When his grip at last loosened, he bent his head to the side, trying to make contact with Gunther's averted eyes. "Gunther?"

He could neither move nor speak. The thoughts and feelings in Gunther's mind formed a deafening cacophony; the elation he felt at the sight of Jens seemed impossible, irreconcilable with all that he'd been through. He hadn't been sure it was in him to feel joy at anything, and he knew for a fact he no longer bore any resemblance—physically or otherwise—to the boy Jens had once known.

Concerned, Jens touched Gunther's face. Jens' warm fingers felt like fire on Gunther's icy flesh, and the inverse was no doubt true for Jens; he immediately jerked his hand away. "Holy shit, you're freezing."

Gunther's heart—such as it was—dropped with Jens' recoil. He could hardly be described as human any longer, and would undoubtedly soon face Jens' rejection.

Jens cradled Gunther's face in his hands. He stared Gunther straight in the eyes. Jens seemed to be past the initial shock of Gunther's temperature; perhaps it was only concern, not disgust.

"Gunther, talk to me," he begged. "Are you okay? Are you hurt?"

There was another long pause, but Gunther at last let a word escape his lips, "No."

"'No' what? Are you okay?"

"I don't know."

Gunther now knew this was a bad idea. He had only sealed his own pathetic fate by coming here and subjecting Jens to his ghastly transformation.

"I just wanted to see you," he paused, "one last

time—"

"I've wa—what?" Jens asked, not sure if he had heard correctly when they spoke over each other. "Are you kidding me?" He let his hands drift down from Gunther's cheeks to his shoulders, "I'm not letting you go *anywhere*," and moved in to hug Gunther once more.

Gunther stood wrapped in Jens' arms, and somehow, still shaking, managed, in time, to press his hands against Jens' back.

Jens comforted him. "Everything's okay...."

There was silence as they stood together deep in their own thoughts. In time, Jens spoke once more. "I missed you."

"I...." Gunther swallowed; he knew now there was nothing to stop impending flow of tears that had welled in his eyes. "I missed you, too."

Jens pulled back, his hands returning to Gunther's shoulders. He took a long look at his friend's face, and Gunther expected the worst at Jens' continued examination.

"You look good," Jens smiled, brushing a strand of blonde hair from Gunther's eyes. Gunther cringed on the inside, still waiting for Jens to discover the hideousness that felt so strong beneath his skin it seemed it *must* be apparent from the outside. As Jens moved the strand of hair, something *did* catch his attention. He furrowed his brow. "Is your eye okay?"

Gunther's instinct was to turn away, but he stopped, realizing the eye that held Jens' interest was not the one Josef had operated on; it was the one that had been fine. Jens glanced to the other, but didn't seem the least bit concerned with it. Gunther remembered Josef saying something about his eyes being red, and when a mirror had been forced upon him, he had witnessed it himself: deep red hues had replaced the bright blue eyes he remembered as his own. One of those red eyes had been removed. He had yet to see what had taken its place.

Jens quickly noticed Gunther's discomfort and dismissed his own curiosity. "Gunther," he lowered his hands to take one of his, "we have to get out of here."

He didn't move.

"Gunther?" Jens pulled his friend gently forward, toward himself and the exit.

Gunther slowly brought his eyes to Jens' and hesitantly spoke. "I can't."

"What do you mean you can't?" With the same charisma he'd once used to thwart playground bullies, Jens gently commanded him, "Come on."

"I can't go with you." His hands hung limp in Jens'.

"That's ridiculous. What are you talking about?"

Gunther's voice grew weaker each moment. "Just go."

Jens watched him, and let a sympathetic smile creep across his face as he shook his head and shrugged. "No," he replied, embracing Gunther once more.

"I don't know what's happened to me." Gunther shook his head. "I'm some kind of monster."

"Yeah," Jens sighed. "You and me both." He turned so his cheek rested on Gunther's forehead. Through one of the nearby windows, a Swastika banner hung from a flagpole, flowing and flapping in the night's breeze. Jens watched it and continued, "You, me, and a whole nation of desperate idiots who cheered for Adolf Hitler. We all could have fought this," he looked down at Gunther, "but the best I ever did was roll my eyes and wait for it all to end."

That wasn't Gunther's point. He tried to find the words to explain what he meant. "I can't say 'no.' I'm not even human. I've killed four people...."

"Yeah?" Jens sounded unmoved. "Want to know what I've done?"

Gunther looked up at him, completely unable to hide the hurt on his face.

Jens reached out a hand to him. "Gunther, I'm—"

He slid away from Jens' touch and cut him off. "How can you fucking mock me?"

"I'm not—" Jens struggled to find the right thing to say. "I'm sorry." He reached out to his friend once more, and despite Gunther recoiling farther, Jens ignored the resistance and moved in close enough to wrap him in his arms.

"I'm sorry." He bent his head to look into Gunther's eyes again. "Gunther, do you really think there's something you could tell me that would make me think ill of you?"

Through his grief, Gunther considered what he could possibly say to Jens, or how he would begin to explain what he had become. He felt like a creature from folklore, with an infinite capacity for injury, possibly even possessing immortality. Fear and terror were words that fell far short of what he felt at the touch of wood or the sight of his own reflection. He had listened to Luther die because a beam of sunlight had frightened him. In the week since Gunther's escape, he had bitten and drained the life of four men; blood siphoned straight from the living was the only thing that cured him of a reluctant thirst. How could Jens believe—or respect—any of it?

Jens smirked and touched Gunther's cheek again, still ignoring the bitter temperature of his icy, pale flesh. "What are you afraid of?" Jens asked.

"Everything."

Jens let his hand fall and took hold of Gunther's fingers. "Yeah, me too." He pulled Gunther's hand to his chest and looked deep into Gunther's eyes. "Everything except you."

It almost brought a smile to Gunther's pained face. Some part of him knew he could tell Jens the truth, and in the same cool, collected way as always, Jens would—at worst—ask a few questions before simply accepting it all. He'd believe anything Gunther said.

"I trust you." Jens smiled, verifying that thought.

Gunther remained paralyzed, however calming Jens' voice was. He had forgotten in their many years apart just how overwhelming a presence Jens was to him. Gunther's already-stiff body tensed as his friend's arms wrapped around him once more, but this time, it wasn't from fear; it was from a feeling muddled deep beneath all his others: he was happy. The thrill he felt in knowing Jens still cared for him had surfaced and obscured the grief that had gripped him.

For the first time in his life, he admitted to himself what he felt. He liked Jens in a way unlike anyone else, and for all his new fears, it no longer scared him to think it. The fear of rejection was nothing when weighed against what he felt at the sight of the sun, and the world that Gunther had always known—where his desire was for the wickedest sin—was buried beneath the rubble around them.

It was a distant memory, but he could picture one particular summer night in his bed beside Luther. Luther had spent the day with his own crowd, including a very pretty girl, and Gunther had been left alone with Jens to talk about pop music and traveling the world. As they wandered the streets, Jens conveniently turned before they reached the disturbing poster at the corner store, and the detour brought them to an orchard on the edge of town. There, as they sat on a hillside watching the sun disappear, Gunther knew even as a ten-year-old that something was wrong with what he was feeling. At the time, there wasn't a word for it, and that brought him to ask Luther.

His brother was quiet. As they lay in the dark, Gunther could feel the seriousness in the silence. Luther was stern in his eventual reply, though his tone betrayed concern. "Don't ever talk about that again, Gunther."

Luther, second only to Jens, would have been the most likely to understand him, but the exposed secret took their relationship from one of normal brotherhood to something cold and hostile. It was that very night that a shift began. Jens noticed it too—the narrowed eyes and subtle aggression that Luther now showed them. It persisted for months—right up until the evening dinner where Luther had angrily spat a word Gunther only knew to mean something really, *really* bad: "Schwul."

He wasn't supposed to feel what he felt, but while direct and terse verbiage in the pamphlets and posters violently rebuked the hideous crime of homosexuality, that was never what Gunther had seen himself as. A homosexual, as he understood it, was a godless, hedonistic, indiscriminant fornicator bereft of all morality, but just like the Jewish caricatures, it had all been a lie.

Maybe it wasn't normal, but nothing about him *was* any longer. Jens' rolling eyes dismissing the convictions others were willing to die for had always resonated more with Gunther than any pamphlet or speech from the Führer.

That was that, then. He was astounded by his own clarity.

Gunther swallowed nervously, but found the strength to open his mouth. "Jens, I...."

Something had happened while he had been lost in thought; Jens had moved closer, and suddenly Gunther's parted lips found themselves making contact with his friend's. Although the two of them both froze for a moment, a soft leading movement of Jens' mouth turned it into a genuine kiss.

A feeling surged through Gunther that might have been — under different circumstances — mistaken for a palpitating heartbeat. His cold skin felt weightless as Jens slowly pulled an inch away.

"Sorry." Jens grinned with his devious, ever-present charm, but his confidence faltered for the first time in Gunther's memory.

"... It's okay." His voice was trembling.

Jens grinned again and brought his lips back to Gunther's. The feeling, though it sent his mind racing, was enough to dissolve the last of his panicked thoughts about where they were, the circumstances around them, and even what he had become. The two stood wrapped together, able to ignore the ravaged office and crumbling city — able, in some way, to let their minds drift away from the past.

Chapter 8

An unexpected knock came from the door.

Aurelio brought his eye to the peep hole, where an unexpected face stared expectantly back at him. He unlatched the locks and pulled the door inward, exposing his sparsely furnished living room to the cold, hazy December afternoon. The snow from the weekend's storm clung weakly to the grass in a delicate film, unlikely to last another day.

"Good afternoon, sir. My name's Officer Wilson with the Kent Police Department. We're notifying everyone in the neighborhood of an Amber alert issued yesterday for two local teenagers." He handed Aurelio two photocopied sheets of paper, one bearing a girl's image and description and the other a boy's.

Aurelio gave it a glance. "Oh, okay." He nodded, looking it over.

"Hannah Knotts and David Boylan. Both went missing a few days ago," he explained. "Look familiar to you at all?"

Aurelio shook his head, sympathetically. "Nope."

"Well, we're asking everybody in the community to keep an eye out and to please call the number on that flyer if you see or hear anything."

"Of course, yeah, I will." Aurelio shifted in the doorway, expecting the conversation to end.

"… You look familiar." Officer Wilson stopped him. Aurelio looked back, unsure, before remembering the face at the same moment Officer Wilson remembered *his*.

"Oh, right, the other night in the car."

"Oh, yeah." Aurelio chuckled, trying to remain friendly despite remembering the hefty fine the Officer had left him with.

"You get that ticket paid for yet?"

"No, sir. Soon though." Aurelio smiled, uncomfortably.

"You remember to take care of that."

"I will."

Aurelio moved to shut the door as Officer Wilson turned to leave, but then the Officer stopped and glanced back at him. "By the way, if you don't mind," he pried, "how do you know that girl and her brother?"

"Uh…." Aurelio wasn't sure what to say.

"The girl you were with the other night?"

"Uh, they're just friends of mine." Aurelio shrugged, unsure of what Officer Wilson really wanted or why he was asking.

"How long you known 'em?"

"I guess like, a little over a year?"

"You ever noticed anything strange about them?"

Inside the house, Stam sat perched on Aurelio's bed. Through the bedroom door, she could hear Aurelio's side of the conversation.

"Not really. No. Why?"

"It was before I met either of them."

"No, don't think so."

"Sure, I will."

"Yeah."

"Okay, thanks. You too."

She heard the door shut, and then leaned down slowly to pull a blanket away from where it had been stuffed into the space under the bedroom door. Unlike at home, Aurelio's had a small gap beneath it which easily let in light.

The door opened. Aurelio stood in the doorway and shrugged, "So." He chuckled nervously. "*That* was weird."

Stam looked at him.

"That cop who pulled me over the other night just showed up... asking about some kids that are missing." He flashed the flyer at her. "You know 'em? It says they go to Saint Elia's."

Stam's eyes lingered on the images of a smiling girl and a grinning boy before she asked, "Why did he come here?"

"He's talking to everyone in the neighborhood." Aurelio shrugged. "Oh well, you want anything to drink?"

Stam's gaze followed the flyer as Aurelio's hand lowered, but at last, she glanced up to him. "I'm fine, thank you."

"Okay, well, you can start the movie back up." He turned to head down the hallway. "Be right back."

Stam reached for a remote, plucking it carefully from the wooden surface of a nightstand. She pulled the blankets of Aurelio's bed closer, swaddling herself tightly as she leaned back against a pile of half a dozen mismatched pillows. It wasn't the first time she had been in the room. Now and then there was reason to visit Aurelio in his modest duplex apartment, and his humble bedroom filled with collectibles and film memorabilia was always intriguing to her. A few DVDs strewn about the floor surrounded a brand-new player still beside its box, countless film posters lined the walls, and a VHS-filled shelf stood tall in the corner beside a huge flat television that dwarfed the dusty box in Ashley's living room. On the screen, a flickering face with its mouth agape stared at Stam.

She pressed the "play" button, bringing life back to the wheelchair-bound man in dark sunglasses. He went on to explain in a nasally-toned German accent to someone off-camera a plan for the survival of the human race after nuclear war.

Stam scooted over, welcoming Aurelio back to the bed when he reappeared in the room holding a glass of water. He sat down carefully, keeping a thoughtful distance from Stam, and quickly busied himself with taking a drink. Stam, closer to the wall, took a brief look at a few pinned-up Polaroid photographs of Aurelio and Ashley together. One was from a Halloween party at Saint Elia's — Aurelio had been a pirate, complete with Sydney on his shoulder, and Ashley had pulled off a flawless Dracula. There were pictures of Stam too, turned face-down on the nightstand as politely requested of Aurelio before she would enter the room.

"I don't know why you don't like these," Aurelio remarked as he picked up the removed photos after noticing her examining the wall. "You look really good. Remember when we went to Cedar Point that one night?" He offered a larger photo to Stam — it was one of all three of them together, taken during a roller coaster ride as they plummeted downward.

Stam's head jerked away while her hand rose involuntarily. She stared at the wall and away from the photo.

"Oh, come *on*. You're so ridiculous."

"I remember," she assured him, keeping her focus on the television screen, which was now repeatedly showing footage of mushroom clouds.

* * *

Ashley lay flat on his back on the floor, sunk down into the deep carpet beneath him. Nearby, from the arm of the couch, came the only sounds in the room: those of Sydney, who was comfortably roosted and occasionally croaking a word in his sleep.

He had so many *things*. His record collection alone was massive, but over the years, he had also accumulated a tremendous supply of miscellaneous junk — much of which he had no use for whatsoever — and it only made the notion of leaving the house even more daunting.

He peeled himself from the floor and made his way to his feet. Standing straight, he looked around the room, taking it all in and reaching back with his mind to pluck what few memories he had of his earliest years there.

It was a sweltering summer night in 1981, he remembered, when he came upon the little home nestled in the quiet northern Ohio town. The past seventy-two hours had been spent on the road and in hotels, fleeing the filth and grime of his old home in Manhattan. He was willing, at the time, to give up the liberality of the people and the liberty of nightlife for something — anything — less oppressive and busy. Back then, his neighborhood had been poor and on the fringe of town, in every way the opposite of New York City. He'd paid in cash, all up front, to the family selling the house. It had belonged to an old woman who had been long-since diagnosed with Alzheimer's disease and had moved in with her daughter across town. She'd insisted upon saying goodbye to her house and Ashley politely indulged her before beginning the long process of removing all of the exposed wood inside and boarding up the windows.

Only a few days later, however, the woman returned, knocking on the brand new door and crying out desperately to be let in. With the sunlight outside, Ashley could do nothing to assist her save calling the family to pick her up from the stoop.

It happened again, and then *again*. Each time, he heard her begging to be let in to her own house, and each time, it wounded him further that he couldn't will himself to unlock the door for her, to let her see it once more.

The last time it occurred, it was a cold late-autumn afternoon and a violent rainstorm had overtaken the town. Still, even obscured by the clouds, the outside light was too frightening to be overcome — more frightening than the wails of the old woman. He listened to her for almost half an hour until the daughter arrived to take her home.

Nine days later, her obituary was in the news. She had died from pneumonia. Ashley never heard from the family again.

In the twenty years since, he too had grown attached to the house and felt as badly as ever about the woman. He knew all too well what she had felt and was especially reminded of it now. He wondered how long it would take before things spiraled completely out of control. It had all started with an idiot preteen girl's game of keep-away, and would likely end in disaster.

There was a knock at the door.

"Braawwkkk... Hello...." Sydney murmured in a sleepy haze.

Ashley glanced to his cell phone:

5:39 p.m.

He took a breath before moving to the door, somehow knowing who would be on the other side. He opened it, and there on the stoop was an unpleasantly familiar face.

"Evening, Mr. Miller." Officer Wilson smiled.

Ashley had lost patience with the man the first time he visited and had yet to restock it. It showed clearly as he let out a grumble in response to the greeting.

Officer Wilson sighed. "Something wrong?" He placed his hands on his hips, irritated. "Why are you being so hostile with me?"

"What do you want?" Ashley asked, neglecting to hide his contempt.

The officer sighed again and held out a flyer. "We're looking for these kids. They've been missing since Thursday night. The two of 'em were last seen during a concert at Saint Elia's." He moved it closer to Ashley, hoping he would take it. "Have you seen either of them?"

Ashley pulled his glare from the Officer and down to the flyer. There was little reaction on his face. "What makes you think I would have?"

"They're classmates of your sister's, so maybe—"

"She's homeschooled."

"Pardon?"

"She goes to *church* at Saint Elia's. They're not her classmates."

Officer Wilson thought the information over, and responded skeptically, "*You* homeschool her?"

"Well, to a degree." Ashley raised an eyebrow, seeing if Officer Wilson caught the joke. He did not, and Ashley continued, "She's very bright. She takes care of herself."

This gave Officer Wilson some pause. "Uh-huh... well, yes, she does seem bright, but awfully quiet, don't you think?"

"She's okay. She gets lonely now and then — it's hard to be on your own."

"And what about you?"

"Me?"

"You said your mother passed away — that's got to be hard even for somebody your age."

"... I imagine it's difficult no matter how old you are."

"Yeah," Officer Wilson agreed. "So it's got to be tough on her."

"Like I said, she does okay."

"You know, that reminds me — you're nineteen, right?"

"That's what I said."

"So you were sixteen when your mother passed away? Whose custody were you in until you turned eighteen?"

Ashley frowned. He had an answer prepared, but was reluctant to give it. "My uncle, Manfred. Manfred Müller."

Officer Wilson removed a notepad and pen from his jacket. "Would you mind if I contacted him?"

"By all means."

When Ashley made no further offer of information, Officer Wilson shrugged and asked expectantly, "Phone number? Address?"

Ashley reached for and took the notepad. He scribbled something down and handed it back to the officer.

He read it. "New York City?"

"You should be advised that he doesn't speak much English."

Officer Wilson sighed. "Ashley, is this a real address?"

"Yes."

"Well, I hope so, for your sake," he replied, obviously annoyed as he pocketed the notepad. "How's your sister doing, by the way?"

"Much better now."

"That's good. Would you mind if I asked her about the missing students?"

"She's out right now — at a friend's house."

"Ah, well, would you mind if I came in?"

"Yes."

"And why's that, Mr. Miller?" Officer Wilson folded his arms while also cocking his head to see past Ashley and into the house.

Ashley stepped outside onto the porch, pushing the door to his home shut behind him. He did little to obscure that it was a hostile gesture, but eventually cut the awkward silence. "I'll let you know if I hear anything about those kids."

The two now stood on the small stone stoop in the bitter chill of the winter evening. Ashley's house and yard were dark, unlike most in the neighborhood, which had been decorated with bright lights for the impending Christmas holidays.

Officer Wilson shook his head. "Ashley...."

Ashley ignored him, stepping past him and onto the stone path leading to the road. It didn't take long for tremors to overtake his body in the cold, but he remained standing, staring wistfully down the quiet street before looking back at his own small house. Officer Wilson watched him from the stoop, and with a sigh, eventually moved toward his cruiser. He opened the passenger door and dropped his spare flyers onto the car seat before shutting it. He glanced at Ashley, who was still staring up at the home.

"Promise me you'll talk to your sister," he instructed. "These kids' parents are inconsolable. Imagine if it was your sister who was missing."

Ashley continued staring. He had no discernible reaction to the officer's plea.

* * *

Who is this?" Gunther asked Jens of the voice escaping the mouth of their record player.

"Mm?" Jens asked, lazily adjusting his face from where it was buried against Gunther's chest. He gave him a gentle squeeze. "Nat King Cole."

Gunther nodded, not surprised, and recognized the voice now that Jens had identified the singer.

The two had holed-up in Germany for a short time until seeking refuge in England. With the help of false identities, they found a home in a small rural town... for a time. Gunther's sloppy murders forced them to flee from one place to another until a technique was refined. Finally settling into a town called Aylesbury outside of London, they were free to build a happy life together in peaceful isolation. Jens had taken a late night job with a record company in the city, and while he slept during the daylight hours, Gunther busied himself preparing elaborate meals and organizing his lover's fledgling record collection. In time, the memories of their brutal adolescence were banished by a quaint, domestic bliss.

The interior of their Victorian era townhome was typical of the 1950s and sat inconspicuously amongst the others of their neighborhood, save for its lack of windows. The walls in their dim bedroom were adorned with promotional posters for the groups and singers Jens admired, photographs of places they had been or aspired to visit, and boxes containing those contents of Jens' record collection which had yet to find their way to the meticulously categorized shelves in their living room.

As much as they both loved their home, there had been recent rumblings of a plan to move, this time to America. Jens' aunt had emigrated to New York City before the war, and given his adoration of American singers, following in his family's stead only seemed natural.

The pair listened to the song in silence for a time, but Jens soon squeezed Gunther once more, murmuring something.

"What?" Gunther asked, briefly patting a messy patch of Jens' hair.

"I had a dream about you," Jens yawned, "or *us*, I guess...."

"Yeah?"

Jens yawned again, stretching and lifting away from Gunther only to scoot closer, gracing his neck with a few lazy, fluttered kisses.

"It was supposedly the future, the year two-thousand or something of the sort."

Gunther smiled at Jens' sleepy voice, through which now only the faintest hint of a German accent surfaced through his new Londoner's accent.

"Nobody had flying cars or space rockets or anything like that, though." He kissed Gunther again. "Kind of dull on that side of things, but you an' I were still together...."

Gunther waited to hear if there was any more.

Jens looked up at him. "That's all."

He laughed. "That was your whole dream?"

"Yup." Jens smirked. "You'll still love me in the year two-thousand, you think?" he asked, unusually sheepish. "When I'm even older and fatter and greyer?" He patted his ever-so-slightly thinning hair. Now in his thirties, Jens had begun to show the subtlest signs of age.

"You'll be in your seventies," Gunther started to answer, "though, so will I."

"I'll be a withered old man." He laughed. "Though I definitely got the better half of the deal here," he remarked, caressing Gunther's smooth, wrinkle-free, pale face which was unchanged after a decade and a half. "'Cause I get to look at you."

"I disagree." Gunther smiled, assuringly, returning the gesture to his lover's face. "You're still beautiful. It's too bad I only love you for your looks."

"Typical guy." Jens laughed as he pulled himself up to climb out of the bed, only to be caught by Gunther, whose intentions were instantly clear when he brought his face to Jens'. It took several lip-locked minutes before Jens was able to pull away.

"... I've gotta go to work," he insisted half-heartedly.

"Mmhmm," Gunther replied, unrelenting in the attention he paid his lover's lips, face, and neck. Reluctant though he seemed, Jens resisted sufficiently to slide out of bed. His hand was immediately caught by Gunther, who slid out with him. Both standing, Gunther kissed him once more and whispered, "I love you, Sydney."

"I love you, too," said Jens.

Gunther was in the kitchen, speedily preparing a simple breakfast of eggs and toast. His hands moved skillfully about the cupboards and drawers, as though it was an art he'd been born to craft.

Jens soon appeared, buttoning a fresh shirt and—as Gunther poured a bowl of oats—began scanning the walls of the living room for a particular record.

"Oh, you know, I forgot—in my dream last night, we had a parrot."

"A parrot?" Gunther raised an eyebrow. "Were we pirates?"

"Don't think so, but you know that actually seems like the perfect pet for you." Jens laughed. "One of those macaws or whatever that live for a really long time. Certainly sounds like a better option than a tortoise or something."

Gunther rolled his eyes, with a smile, as he plopped a plate onto the table. "Just eat your breakfast."

"Think about it." Jens continued, seeming to give up on making any selection from his records. "If we bought a parrot today, he'd still be *around* in the year two-thousand."

"What would either of us want a parrot for?"

Jens shrugged. "It *was* only a dream, but now it's got me thinking about the future...."

Gunther removed two pieces of bread from their toaster and brought them to the table, and at the same time, took a seat beside Jens, who continued, "I've never been so excited about life." A smile formed on Gunther's face in response while Jens went on, "I'm sure it sounds a bit maudlin, but," he said, placing a hand on Gunther's leg, "I'm real happy. In the old days, it seemed—a bit too often—like I might never get out of that awful pigsty of a country or find a way to be free. I hardly ever dreamed life could be like this. Not really, anyway."

"That was a long time ago..." Gunther reminded him, but then added, "... and neither did I."

Jens picked up a piece of toast, and careful not to drop the slightest crumb, took a slow bite while Gunther examined a series of dates and times scribbled on a sheet of paper.

"Someday," Jens eventually said once his mouth was no longer full, "we should take a trip way up north—way up there—where the sun doesn't rise for weeks at a time."

Gunther smiled. "Is this before or after we're going on vacation to Egypt, Brazil, New York City, Japan—?"

"Oh, there's no particular order." Jens shrugged. "I'm not that old and grey yet." He leaned close to Gunther, speaking in a hushed tone punctuated by a few more kisses. "Did I mention that I love you?"

"You may have." Gunther chuckled.

"In case I didn't...." He kissed Gunther once more on his icy lips. "I love you, Ashley."

* * *

Stam sat cross-legged on the floor with VHS cases scattered around her. Her eyes were fixated on the screen, where a blurry figure moved through a fuzzy void. Trebly, hissing music tracks by a group she recognized but could not name played through the speakers; it was the only sound in the film or the bedroom until it was interrupted by a ringing telephone. Aurelio lay sleeping nearby with an arm dangling off the side of the bed, but with the third ring of his phone, he stirred and began to fumble for it.

He opened it. "... Hello?" His voice betrayed his current state.

"... No, it's okay. What's up?" He wearily looked over to Stam, who smiled and turned back to the television. "Yeah, sure... uh...."

He looked to a nearby clock:

8:14 p.m.

"… Yeah, I could come by."

"… No, it's no problem. I'll see you soon."

He clasped the phone shut and sat looking around as though shocked he had fallen asleep. He rubbed his face.

"Man, sorry…."

"Hmm?"

"When did I fall asleep?"

"Three hours ago."

"Ugh, sorry," he apologized again.

"It's okay." Stam shrugged, looking back to the television.

Aurelio climbed to his feet. "I hate when that happens."

"Most people sleep," Stam replied.

Aurelio chuckled as he scanned the floor for something, and then glanced at the television screen. "Oh man, you're watching this? I don't even know why I own this." Aurelio gave the screen a disgusted look before spotting his shoes, which he hastily tossed on. "I can't stand Andy Warhol."

"This is strange," Stam agreed.

"Yeah, that's Edie Sedgwick, though—the girl we were talking about the other day." He picked up his phone and wallet. "There really is a resemblance—I mean, you're a lot younger…."

He watched with Stam as the unfocused blob continued to drift about. She couldn't really make out what the woman looked like at all.

"So, Ashley just asked me if I would bring your box over there…."

She was motionless for a short time before turning to Aurelio. She said nothing, but her face suggested acceptance—no real objection.

"Do you mind?" he asked, curious about her silence.

"… It doesn't matter," she answered cryptically as she took hold of the metal case beside her and offered it to him. "It's his, not mine."

He nodded. He wasn't really sure what to say. He knew what was in the case—he had asked about it a long time ago—and it wasn't anything interesting. Why she bothered to carry it around, or why Ashley would want it right now, he couldn't say, and had it been Ashley's only request, he might have declined.

"He also asked me if I could watch Sydney. You just wanna stay here?"

Stam eventually replied, "I probably should," and turned back to the film. In the background was another song, by the same group as before, which she recognized from Sydney's collection.

* * *

"Good evening, friends. This is Horace Batchelor at the microphone, the inventor of the famous Infra-Draw method for the Treble Chance. I have, myself, with my own coupon entries, won one-thousand and twelve first Treble Chance top dividends, and my ingenious method can help you to win also. Don't send—"

"Oh please," Gunther scoffed, leaning forward, switching off the car radio.

"Don't send any money," Jens started up, carrying on the now-silenced advertisement, "just send your name and address to Horace Batchelor, Department One, Keynsham, spelt K-E-Y-N-S-H—"

"Ugh," Gunther moaned in mock exasperation as he tried to ignore Jens and get back into a newspaper he had been reading.

Jens let out a chortling laugh and glanced to him before taking a hand away from the wheel and placing it palm-up on Gunther's thigh. Gunther took hold of it, smiling as he kept reading. They sat, saying nothing, listening only to the sound of the rumbling engine as the car bounced along the dirt road.

"All right," Gunther leaned up once more, switching the radio back on, "I know you like the Deep River Boys."

The advertisement was over and had been replaced by a trio of male voices singing their adaptation of a rock-and-roll tune.

Jens groaned, looking at the radio. "Covering Elvis Presley? Really? Show some class, boys."

"Hmm," Gunther murmured, re-engrossed in his paper.

Jens began to fiddle with the radio dial. Static hissed in and out, as did an evening news broadcast, and then more static, before Jens settled on the original station. The same song continued, and agitated, he shut it off. He glanced at Gunther, who glanced knowingly at him.

"You know," Jens chuckled, bringing his attention back to the road. "When I feel blue in the night...."

Gunther smirked. "Oh yeah, that's not inconsiderate."

Jens continued, "And I need you to hold me tight...." He touched Gunther's shoulder while his voice began to more and more closely mimic the tune of a song by the Everly Brothers. "... Whenever I want you, all I have to do is dream. Dream, dream dream —"

Gunther shook his head, pretending to ignore Jens' singing, but he only sang louder, keeping a close eye on him. "I can make you mine, taste your lips of wine, any time — night or day.... Only trouble is, gee whiz...."

Gunther began to mouth the song, silently, along with Jens. "I'm dreamin' my life away...."

He caught sight of Jens' gleeful smile and reluctantly joined him. "I need you so, that I could die—"

"Not funny," Gunther called, feigning offense before continuing, "I love you so, and that is why... whenever I want you, all I have to do is dream...."

It was late before the pair found themselves at their destination: a non-descript night club in the middle of a dark and dreary London. The streets were bare but for men shamefully skulking from one bar to another. Gunther shuddered as he shut the car door and stepped out.

"Nothing like Soho to bring you down," he grumbled as he observed a young woman flagging down passersby beneath a flickering motel sign. "Such a miserable pla —"

Jens' fingers on Gunther's cheek silenced him. Before he knew it, his head was turned to his friend and their lips met.

"Thanks for coming with me," Jens whispered, lips still on Gunther's. He resumed the kiss, but Gunther soon pulled away.

"Stop." He looked around nervously before glancing back at Jens. "... Not here."

"What's gonna happen?" He shook his head before moving back in for another kiss. Gunther resisted the urge to resist.

Nazi Germany was a distant memory to all, but even in an enlightened, freedom-loving London, hatred for what was only natural — the most human part of Gunther — lived on. For this reason, Gunther and Jens' affection was displayed subtly, at best, in the presence of others. With only the rarest of lamentations, they had both grown accustomed to a secret relationship; in the interest of maintaining a social life, they maintained the ruse even in the company of their closest friends. It was a moment of weakness on both their parts that brought their lips together, and Gunther finally had to pull away again. "Okay, okay...."

He looked knowingly at Jens, who just grinned, "Okay," and then shot a glance around them in search of any on-lookers. Once certain they were safe, Jens turned and started toward a nearby nightclub, only to stop after a few steps upon realizing his companion hadn't followed.

"Ashley?"

Gunther was standing in place, with one hand held to his stomach, failing to suppress a sick and familiar feeling.

"Oh...." A troubled look crossed Jens' face.

"I'll be fine." Gunther winced before pretending to ignore the pain. He started after Jens.

"Ashley, don't —"

"It's okay," Gunther reiterated.

Jens sighed, easily detecting the lie. He'd reached out to Gunther's shoulders to stop him when the door of the nightclub swung open, letting a roar of revelry spill out into the street. The sound stopped Jens from moving in any closer to his ailing friend.

"Sydney, ol' chap." a voice called. It was clear — to Gunther, anyway — that Jens wanted to ignore him, but felt an obligation to respond.

Jens glanced over. "Evening, gents." His voice feigned excitement despite his focus on Gunther.

Gunther smiled weakly. "It's okay," he said again.

"Ash—"

Jens was cut off by the sudden clasping of a hand on his shoulder and the same voice urging him again. "Come on then, Sydney." The well-dressed, grinning twenty-something beckoned. "Alexis Korner is up next."

"In a moment," Jens assured him, turning back to Gunther.

Gunther shook his head. "I'll be fine. I'll meet up with you later."

"But—" Jens began.

"What's the matter there, Ashley?" The well-dressed man, now flanked by another, was eyeing him.

"Nothing. Just feeling ill." Gunther forced a half-smile and then turned to Jens. "Just go, have a good time." He swallowed. "I'll be back."

The gritty streets of Soho only grew seedier as the night dragged on. The scurrying men sank deeper into the shadows, increasingly loathe to be seen as they snuck about.

Gunther was among them. He had learned over the years that an unattended teenage boy, such as he appeared, elicited a great deal of unwanted attention at this time of night, in this part of town. He hated London, and in an ideal world would have spent the night comfortably at home, but even if it meant coming to the city, he was always happy to join Jens on his trips to see singers and performers. Afterward, they'd go out dancing, which he genuinely enjoyed. Even after thirteen years of freedom, Jens was Gunther's greatest and only passion, but it was still enough to keep him content.

There were nights like this, however, which marred an otherwise happy life. He had been fighting it for days, but a familiar sickening feeling was now winning its war against his will. On average, it was every ten days or so that death reached for him from inside, but refusing indulgence was not enough for him to perish. The feeling simply swelled toward greater and greater agony.

There was only one clear, simple, and ugly cure: the blood of a living victim. It was a medicine needed to squelch an ill pulsation in his body. Although he did not *crave* blood as one would food, Gunther likened it to hunger, a sensation he'd not felt in thirteen years. That was the best way to explain it to Jens.

Now here he was, wandering the streets in search of some derelict soul. When he was finished, he would obscure the whole event with the skill and precision of over a decade's experience. It was beyond ugly, but even if death were an option, he couldn't be sure he'd give up Jens. Every kiss was still elating, and each word Jens spoke still held him captive; it was enough to get him through any given day, and as the years passed, killing became easier. The unbearable emotional toll of the countless lives he had ended since 1945 was soothed by Jens, whose love allowed Gunther to take things one day at a time, and suffer the guilt of one murder at a time.

Gunther checked his watch:

12:23 a.m.

He had been out for two hours now; Jens would be worried. Gunther was naïve enough now and then to attempt to overcome his reluctant addiction, and had wandered the streets deep in thought in an attempt to distract himself. However, not unlike willing himself to step into the sunlight or examine his own reflection, it always proved impossible. Giving in, he set his sights on an unsightly drunkard passed out in a heap of rubbish.

Jens nervously glanced to his watch:

12:46 a.m.

He took a short sip from a glass in his hand as he looked around the room; he was detached from the whirlwind of activity around him. A loud skiffle tune played, seducing dozens of teens and twenty-somethings into a dancing frenzy.

He sat the drink down and looked at his watch once more:

12:47 a.m.

"Hey, Sydney, lighten up." A man slapped him on his back. "You look down tonight."

Jens was quiet. "It's nothing." He glanced at his watch again:

12:47 a.m.

The man threw his arm around Jens and pulled him toward a nearby cluster of dancers, all laughing and bouncing together.

"Hey," one asked Jens, "what did you think of Korner earlier?"

Jens' attention was unfocused, but he offered a reply. "Korner is brilliant. He's going to turn the blues upside-down."

"You still movin' to the 'States?" another asked.

"Planning on it," he replied, looking at his watch yet again:

12:48 a.m.

A cold hand clasped his wrist, covering the time. Attached to it was Gunther, flashing a charming smile in a fashion he had learned from Jens.

Jens smiled back as his concerns dissolved.

"Hey, Sydney," a girl in quintessential Mod-style called out over the clamor. "Who's your friend?"

"Oh, I'm sorry. This is Ashley, my nephew."

"Yeah?" She grinned. "You want a purple heart?" She started to fish in her pocket for something.

"Oh man, you must not know Ashley." A boy next to them laughed as he pulled a cigarette from his mouth. He threw his arm around Gunther and patted his shoulder.

"Yeah," a girl interjected. "Ash can go all night."

Jens stifled a chuckle and Gunther discretely smacked him in the arm.

"Syd and Ash are into clean living," the boy with the cigarette called out over the music. "Don't even smoke." He offered the cigarette, which was still in his hand, to Jens.

Jens politely held up a hand. "No thanks."

"It's just *Drinamyl*," the girl insisted. "It's safe."

"Believe me," Jens said, grinning, taking another sip

of his drink, "he doesn't need it. He could dance 'til the sun comes up."

Gunther rolled his eyes at Jens.

"Yeah?" The girl took hold of Gunther's arm. "Let's go, then." She pulled him out to the thick of the dance floor and began to show off her moves. Gunther moved with her, slowly. She took hold of his hands and then, shocked, dropped them. "Whoa, you're freezing." she said over the music, grinning.

"Sorry." Gunther laughed, rubbing his hands together before shrugging and stepping up the pace of his dance to match the girl's.

Jens watched them from the sidelines, smiling.

"So you're really going, eh, Sydney?" the boy with the cigarette interrupted him.

Jens was quiet. "Yeah."

"We're gonna miss you guys, you know."

"It's the right thing, I think." Jens smiled, looking over at Gunther who was now in full swing, tearing up the dance floor with several girls.

"You got family there, right?"

"My auntie and her son—my cousin, Manfred."

"You're lucky, ol' boy." The boy laughed. "America's where all the good tunes are at."

"Britain will catch up." Jens shrugged.

"Think so?"

"Give it five years—it'll get there."

"What makes you so sure?"

"Mods and Rockers." Jens set his drink down, shaking his head. "It bloody well can't get worse."

The boy laughed, snuffing out his cigarette. "Might be onto something there." He looked out to the dance floor and then nudged Jens. "Hey, let's not let Ash get all the girls, huh?"

"Sure." Jens, in his own time, followed the boy out into the sea of bouncing bodies. Gunther soon took note, and shimmied to his friend's side.

The night pressed on, and Gunther indeed did outlast his amphetamine-fueled fellow dancers. The girl who had originally challenged him shook her head in amazement as Gunther moved, sweatlessly, into his fourth straight hour of wild oscillations. Jens chuckled at the look on her face; he himself had long since given up and retreated to the bar where he had found conversation with an aspiring record producer.

"Hey Ash. Need a drink?" someone called to him.

A beet-red girl struggling to stick it out to the final beat of a song stumbled to a stop.

"Nope." Gunther gracefully spun to a halt. A few onlookers cheered his performance.

"Come on, Ash."

"Yeah, it's on us."

He plopped down in a free seat next the gasping girl. "No thanks."

The girl leaned in coyly. "So, where're you from?"

"Here in London," he lied. "You?"

"Manchester, originally." She fluffed her hair.

Jens, nearby, smirked and looked at his watch: 4:51 a.m.

He yawned, rubbing his face, and turned to Gunther. "Hey, Ashley, my boy."

Gunther looked over attentively.

"Time to get you home. Your mum is going to have it out with me."

"Aww...." Gunther feigned frustration as he stood up. The girl joined him.

"You gonna be around next week?"

"Definitely." Gunther gave a suave nod to the girl—something he had no doubt picked up from Jens—before looking to where he now stood by the door, watching impatiently. Gunther glanced to the girl again. "Gotta go."

Outside, the grimy night from earlier had transformed into something even darker and stranger. From the alleyways and crevices of the sinister buildings—where previously prostitutes had descended like vultures upon each stumbling, wayward drunk—now only the occasional rat dared to dart. In the last few minutes, a cool mist in the air had coalesced into a gentle rain.

During their first few steps on the wet concrete, the pair said nothing, until, as their sideways glances to one another connected, they both laughed.

"She was all over you," Jens teased him.

"Yeah? Well, how about you and that boy?" Gunther shot back.

"I think I'm the wrong gender for 'im."

"Well, she was the wrong *person* for me," Gunther wittily retorted.

"Hey." Jens stopped him, planting a kiss square on his lips. Against his best judgment, Gunther reciprocated. Then it happened again, and again.

"I've got an idea," Jens whispered, forehead against Gunther's.

"Yeah?"

"Let's forget going home and just stay here tonight."

"Yeah?" Gunther raised his eyebrows suggestively.

"Yeah: the seedy Soho motel treatment."

"You're such a romantic." Gunther chuckled.

"Part of my irresistible charm." Jens smiled, lowering his hands to Gunther's. He held them briefly as they started to walk, but soon let go as they passed onto a better-lit—albeit empty—street. As the rain grew heavier, Gunther made his way to the first motel in sight while Jens made a quick stop at their car.

The room Gunther secured was on the backside of the building, the best that they could get in terms of seclusion. Nearly every detail of the room lived up to expectations: it was debatable if the room had *ever* been cleaned. The aura of the last transient boarder—who by now was probably back on the streets—still hung heavy in the air. A small section of wall was missing by one of the beds; the pair could only imagine what might be hiding in the black void. A single flickering light bulb sat in a dangling ceiling fixture casting eerie shadows across the room. The setting was made complete by a rusted tub in a small bathroom with what Gunther hoped was just murky water pooled in the cracked ceramic basin.

"It's perfect." Gunther laughed as he pulled away from the bathroom, totally aghast at the severity of the room's decline as he glanced to Jens in the doorway.

"Wow, you nailed this one...." Jens trailed off as he looked around.

"I don't know what you're talking about." Gunther picked up a pillow, half-expecting to find something under it. "This is high-class right here."

On a wobbling table, Jens set down a pile of wooden boards he had fetched from the car.

"Come on," Gunther called, throwing the pillow at his lover.

"Yeah, yeah, hold on." Jens chuckled as he picked up a board and held it over the one and only grime-covered window. He grumbled as he judged the size of it, "They don't have a complete wall and yet we get a bay window?"

"Oh, it's not that big," Gunther insisted.

"You wanna do it?" Jens feigned irritation and offered a hammer and a wooden board to Gunther.

"No, thanks." Gunther smiled.

"Are you *sure?*" Jens wiggled the board at Gunther and then moved closer and began to exaggerate a scary voice, "Whooo.... I'm going to get you. I'm a spooky piece of evil lumber. So scary."

He brought it to within inches of Gunther's face. It was met by Gunther's unenthused stare.

"Sorry." Jens laughed as he lowered it. He moved to the window and began to nail the board across the glass, shutting away the outside world. He worked quickly and had gotten nearly three quarters of the window covered before an angry hand began to rap against their door.

"Hey, what the fuck you doing in there? Knock it off."

Gunther shrugged at Jens, who kept on going.

The rapping at the door sounded again. "Hey!"

Jens finished and stepped away from the window, now totally barricaded, and admired his handiwork.

"You better shut the fuck up." The man at the door relented with the end of the noise. He grumbled angrily as he stormed away.

"Fuckin' bastards."

Gunther looked around for an alternative to towels; the only viable option appeared to be the single blanket on the bed, which he pulled off slowly, worried again about what he might find below. With the blanket in hand, he moved to the door and stuffed it into the crack, eliminating any chance of light shining through. As he stood up, he found himself immediately trapped by Jens' arms wrapped around him from behind. Jens rested his head on Gunther's shoulder, landing a kiss just below his ear, ignoring the small bandage on his neck. "Hey."

"Hey." Gunther smiled.

Gunther and Jens had had a busy week getting their various affairs in order and stocking up on boxes in which to pack up the contents of their humble home. Jens had sold their car and already closed a deal on their house. All that remained was to wait.

"You can come in," Jens, as he stepped in through the front door, informed Gunther who followed close behind.

The living room was immaculate as ever, though it was indisputable that Jens' record collection had outgrown the space, and they had already agreed that only some — not all — would be able to follow them to the United States. The rest, Jens figured he would leave to his local friends for safe-keeping. He wasn't thrilled about the idea, but it was a necessary concession.

Gunther's mood all day had been wistful; he suspected it was because of the impending move and the daunting task ahead of building a new life in a new city. Jens had been the same way too, probably for similar reasons. Gunther looked over at his lover who now, approaching his mid-thirties, wore reading glasses when he examined the mail; his hairline had begun to recede, and his skin was just slightly less firm than it once was, but to Gunther, he was still beyond beautiful.

Jens eventually realized he was being watched. "What?" He smiled.

Gunther only smiled back, saying nothing as the

telephone began to ring. Jens, who was closer, reached over. "Hello?"

He listened to someone on the other end. "Oh yeah? You got 'em?" There was a pause. "Sure, we can come by right now—you're gonna be up for a bit, I imagine? ... Okay. See you, mate. Cheers."

He hung up and nodded at Gunther. "Tickets."

"Yeah?" Gunther answered.

"Yup. Pete says they came in this afternoon." He moved a stack of telegrams from his lap and, upon standing, plucked his coat from a rack by the door. "Coming with?"

"'Course." Gunther smiled. His coat was still on, and he quickly followed Jens out the door. The earth outside was wet from a storm the previous night, but the night sky above them was clear and cloudless. He checked his watch:

8:41 p.m.

Jens took hold of Gunther's raised hand, and after shooting a brief glance around them, moved his lips close, kissing him. "... I love you."

"I love you too."

* * *

Ashley had set himself to the task of packing up his living room. Nearly all its contents were now tucked away into cardboard boxes. The exceptions were the largest items of furniture and most of the records which would, he figured, be safest if just left in their milk crates during transportation. Sydney, nestled in Ashley's lap, murmured softly as Ashley stroked his soft blue feathers. Sitting around them were the last few unpacked items: the record player, a yellowed newspaper, and some scattered photographs.

The room was now foreign and unwelcoming. With each trinket he pulled from a shelf and each small item sealed in a cardboard cube, the home became less his own. He hated the feeling more now than he ever had in all his previous moves; this *was* his home and soon—already, even—it would be no longer. One day, his memories of it would fade to dust.

The doorbell rang.

Instantly, a look of some consternation spread across Ashley's brow; he had nearly forgotten that he even *had* a doorbell, considering how seldom it was used. Agitated by the noise, Sydney puffed up and tried to sink his head into his torso. Before heading to the door, Ashley moved the bird onto the only small space on the couch that was not a host to piles of boxes. He grumbled, dreading who he might see on his porch; it wasn't going to be Aurelio, whom he was expecting, but who knew full well to knock in an agreed-upon manner. There was only one person it might be, and he was hardly in the mood to put up with the chubby police officer right now.

It was Sister Carroll.

Ashley's eyebrow rose suspiciously at the unexpected visitor standing on his stoop. "Yes?"

"Hi, Ashley." Sister Carroll flashed her weak, ever-hopeful smile. "Is this a bad time? Do you have a minute?"

His eyes drifted away from Sister Carroll as he took a breath. "Sure," he replied, less than convincingly, as he pushed the door wider and stepped aside. As Sister Carroll entered, she immediately took notice of the piles and piles of boxes.

"Are you going somewhere?" she asked with clear concern.

"Afraid so," Ashley answered as he moved his feet carefully through the maze. "Seems to be the best thing for us."

Sister Carroll stood in the open doorway, taking in what she saw around her. Eventually Ashley glanced her way, and it moved her to step inside and shut the door.

"I had no idea." Sister Carroll said meekly.

"Nor did I, until recently," he replied, dragging his hand across a box top.

"When are you leaving?"

"Soon."

She was quiet as she collected her thoughts. "How is Stam taking it?"

Ashley cracked a half smile. "She's prepared for it. She'll be okay."

"Is she home right now?"

"Sorry." Ashley shook his head. "She's out...." He trailed off as though he might have been thinking about saying something more.

"Out," Sister Carroll pried, making a suggestion, "with your parents?"

Ashley sighed, and reached out to the pale, faded wallpaper, unchanged and still clinging since the 1970s. He took another moment to himself before turning to her. "What did you want to talk about?"

Sister Carroll's face was pained. She seemed unsure how to begin, and pursed her lips as she looked around the room.

"Would you like to sit?" Ashley gestured, offering the room and any box to her.

She smiled. "I suppose I could." She carefully placed herself onto a small stool that was sitting out, unpacked. "Why are you moving? Where are you going?"

"This town just isn't the right place for us anymore, I guess, but I brought it on myself. And as for *where*—I don't know yet."

"You don't know?"

He moved closer, taking a seat on the floor next to his record player and not too far from Sister Carroll's feet. "Somewhere—nowhere. It doesn't much matter, really."

Sister Carroll puzzled on this, more acclimated than most to Ashley's cryptic manner; she had, after all, had to endure something similar from Stam for the last two years. She accepted it and noted, "You really don't sound too happy about it."

Ashley was quiet.

"Ashley?"

He was still hesitant. "This is my home."

Sister Carroll nodded. "Moving can be hard," she began, but was unsure where to go with it.

Ashley picked up the conversation for her, "A lot of things are." he looked up at her. "That's just life, huh?"

"Life can be very hard, yes," she agreed, clearly

thinking on something. "Very hard...."

There was silence between them for a moment, but Ashley eventually spoke up, "What was it you wanted?"

"Oh." Sister Carroll shook her head. "I, it's nothing, I guess. I shouldn't have even come by."

"What is it?" he asked.

"I just—I worry so much about Stam. I moved to a new town when I was about her age, and I certainly didn't feel like I fit in."

Ashley nodded, listening.

"Things were really tough for my family at the time. My older sister had gone missing a few years before—that really devastated my family—and I had a lot of trouble making friends, talking to people, fitting in... you know? I wasn't super pretty or popular or even all that normal. I felt awkward at home, at school—no matter where I went...."

Ashley continued taking in her story.

"When it came to my sister, I just kept wondering if I did something wrong...." She resisted a tear in her eye. "If I could have done something to stop whatever happened...."

Ashley was quiet, but spoke as his thoughts remained far away. "Feeling powerless to help someone you love is unbearable."

Sister Carroll nodded sadly. "I suppose you know what I mean."

Ashley added, "It's also why you're so upset about Hannah and David."

She was surprised by how blunt a remark it was, but nodded. "It's been, wow, I guess over thirty years now, and I was just a little girl then, but it still hurts to think that I could have done something differently."

Ashley nodded and Sister Carroll continued.

"If Hannah and David were having trouble—problems at school or at home—why didn't they feel like they could talk to me? What could I have done to help more? Was Hannah under too much pressure at the choir concert? Or what if something did happen to them? Maybe I should have kept a closer eye on them...."

"You shouldn't beat yourself up about it," Ashley replied.

"I know—I know that, but it's hard, you know? And then I think about Stam: she really is a sweet girl. I don't want her to feel like... like she doesn't belong. And I don't want her to be unsafe."

"Stam appreciates you," Ashley assured her. "She isn't the best at showing it, but if she didn't like you, or if you ever wronged her... you'd know."

Sister Carroll nodded. "Maybe...."

"She's not your average introvert. Goodness knows I have a hard enough time getting through to her myself—it's not just you, believe me. You've done a good job."

Sister Carroll smiled, wiping her eye once more. "Well, I... I appreciate that."

Ashley stood up from the floor. "How old are you?"

It was a strange question, but with hesitation, she answered, "Forty-three."

"So... 1958?"

"That's right." She nodded. "I'm an old lady, huh?"

"Mm." Ashley moved to a pile of milk crates filled with albums, "What kind of music were you into when you were younger?"

"... You really wanna know?" she challenged him.

"I already do," he answered. "I just want you to say it."

"Is that so?" She chuckled. "You think you know me that well?"

"Yes." He moved one particular crate, uncovering another, which he then paged through before taking hold of a record. "Well?" He looked over to her, expectantly.

She shook her head. "I was into a lot of sixties rock." She shrugged. "You know—the Kinks, the Who...."

Ashley waited for her to continue.

"... Velvet Underground," she added.

Ashley plucked up an album already in between his fingers and brought it to her.

"Oh, wow."

Still in its original shrink wrapping, with a small hand-written tag indicating a price of three dollars, was an eponymous LP by the aforementioned band.

"Where did you get this?"

"I don't know," Ashley replied, looking around. "You get to a certain point with all this stuff and it's impossible to remember how you came into possession of *this* album or *that* single."

"This is amazing. My sister and I used to listen to this all the time when it first came out." She turned it over. "This is a first edition and everything?"

"Yeah."

"Wow." She looked it over a while longer, before offering it back to him carefully. "Well, goodness, I don't want to mess it up—"

"Keep it." Ashley held up his hand.

"Oh, I couldn't—"

"Think of it as a Christmas gift. The joke, if you will, around here, is that all this music belongs to Sydney...."

They both looked over to the snoozing bird. Sister Carroll smiled.

"... And I can't imagine that Sydney would have—" Ashley paused, rephrasing, "would enjoy the Velvet Underground."

"What does he like?" Sister Carroll asked, humoring the notion.

Ashley thought on it for a bit. "That's a matter of some speculation, I suppose. I've always assumed he would like the Beatles."

"You think so?" Sister Carroll laughed.

"It's just a guess. Actually, he probably would have preferred Herman's Hermits, but as I said," he looked away from the bird and back to Sister Carroll, with a shrug, "who really knows? Music changed a lot in the early sixties."

"Hmm," was Sister Carroll's reply. She was finding it difficult to totally follow Ashley's thoughts. He briefly made eye contact, realizing that he had lost her during his wistful musings.

"Anyway." Ashley motioned back to the record in Sister Carroll's hands. "Please, keep it. Tomorrow is my birthday, and I have too many things already. Somebody ought to get a gift."

"Ashley, really?" She lit up. "Happy birthday. How old will you be?"

"Seventy-four."

Sister Carroll laughed. "Yeah? You act like it sometimes." She smiled. "You've got a very wise, old soul, as they say. Stam is lucky to have a brother like you."

Ashley considered the comment. "The girls at the school are lucky too," he nodded, "that they have *you*."

She looked down. "Maybe."

"Don't blame yourself about Hannah and David. I think you know as well as I — some things are beyond our influence, no matter how much we think we should have been able to change them."

"Hmm." She thought about it. "Hindsight is twenty-twenty, huh?"

Ashley shook his head. "… No, it's not." He let his hand rest on the aging newspaper article he had yet to pack away. The grizzly scene in the photograph on the front page was the same as always: the face of the man in the dirt was as obscured as ever. "I wish it was."

There was silence between them until Sister Carroll moved to stand up. "Well," she held Ashley's gift carefully, "I suppose I should be going. I really just only meant to stop by quickly — there's a candlelight vigil for David and Hannah tonight."

Ashley nodded to her. She looked over the record in her hands once more. "Thank you so much." She looked at him. "This really is a special gift."

"Will you listen to it?" he asked.

"Gosh, it's still sealed up. This must be a collector's item or something by now."

Ashley shook his head. "It might be." He shrugged. "But I used to know a fellow — a World War two vet — who used to say that there are very, *very* few things that remain the same forever. A recorded song is one of those things."

Sister Carroll thought about it as Ashley continued, "He was in Munich, Germany at the end of the war — the air raid sirens were wailing all around. He was terrified. He was sure he was going to die, but to escape from it all, he put on an old Bing Crosby record from his childhood. For a few short moments as it played, he felt safe—timeless and happy." He smiled at Sister Carroll. "I can't say that these songs have such a profound effect on *me*, but maybe it'll be true for *you*. That's worth more than money."

The story seemed to move her tremendously—far more than Ashley expected. Sister Carroll was deep in thought, and suddenly, she wiped a tear from her eye. "You're very sweet." She looked down at the album. "My sister used to love this record. Her favorite song was at the very end: 'After Hours.' She went missing just a few months after it came out, and back then, I used to listen to it when I was thinking about her, but I haven't in ages.…"

"Do you have something to play it on?" Ashley glanced to his record player.

"Oh, Ashley, I couldn't—"

"Here." He picked it up, offering it to her. "It's thirty years old and still works as well as the day I bought it. One less thing for me to have to pack."

Ashley seemed set on the choice, and so, Sister Carroll put up no more resistance. "… Thank you very much. I hardly know what to say."

Ashley shrugged before he moved to the front door. He opened it, stepping out onto the stoop which was just now beginning to collect a thin film of snow. Sister Carroll soon joined, gazing with him out across the yard and quiet street.

"This feels more like my birthday than yours." She held her gifts tightly under her coat.

He smiled. "If only time worked that way."

Chapter 9

Jens held two tickets as he and Gunther left a small farm house and started back toward home.

"So," Jens glanced to Gunther, "how do you want to spend our last three weeks in England?"

"Mm, I don't know."

"Me neither." Jens chuckled. "I almost wish we were leaving tonight...."

He offered the tickets to Gunther, who looked them over before sticking them into his thick coat's pocket.

An unsettling feeling came over Gunther as he gazed out over the plains around them. It was a grim night, for some reason conjuring his darker feelings to mind. Nervously, he took hold of Jens' hand and kissed it. He also examined his wrist watch.

2:27 a.m.

The two drifted along a narrow dirt road dividing two desolate moors. A broken sign lay in the dirt: *Aylesbury – 6 km.*

Their arms were draped softly across one another's shoulders while their hands tenderly entwined. It wasn't the most efficient way of walking, but their travel time had been precisely calculated.

"Are you scared?" Gunther eventually asked. His bright eyes looked up at Jens.

"Of going to America?" Jens replied, still watching ahead. "Are you?"

"I'm afraid of a lot of things," said Gunther, "but I guess that isn't one of them."

Jens smiled. "I'm not afraid of *anything* when I'm with you."

Gunther laughed. "That's a rubbish answer. I knew you'd say that."

"Because you know it's true?" Jens leaned in to kiss Gunther's forehead. Gunther leaned in to kiss back and caught Jens' lips. They slowed to a stop while they indulged in the moment; their fingers untangled they moved to embrace one another. Jens eyes closed— Gunther's did not.

Jens brought his hand up let his fingers slide through the soft, short blonde hair of his lover.

Seconds passed.

"Oh *shit*," called out a shocked voice.

Gunther's eyes turned away from Jens' face to see a boy—maybe nineteen years old—standing stunned a short ways down the road. The lovers' mouths broke apart as they turned to face the interloper.

"Did you just fuckin' see what I saw?" the boy asked to another whom had appeared from behind a tree.

He was buttoning up his pants. "No, mate, what'sat?"

"It's a couple o'queers," barked another boy, sitting on a nearby fence.

Jens was unenthused as the boy from the fence hopped down to join the others—he was shorter and looked considerably meaner.

"Did you see 'em kiss?"

"You're fuckin' sick, you know'at?" the short boy said, sneering.

"Your friend just peed on a tree," Jens replied, calmly. "If anyone's couth is suspect—it's yours."

"Shut up, queer."

Jens shrugged, "Just back off," and moved forward, attempting to side-step the abrasive gang. The taller reached out an arm to block him.

"Don't touch him," Gunther commanded, pulling the gang's attention to him.

The short boy scoffed, "What're you gonna do 'bout it?" and took a few steps toward Gunther.

Gunther shook his head. "Just leave us alone. We didn't mean anything—"

"You a Kraut?" the boy demanded.

"What?"

"You look like a fuckin' Kraut to me."

Gunther's mind had already raced to a worst-case scenario and what he might have to do if things continued to escalate. Inside, he shuddered at how violent a solution he had jumped to.

"You're a fuckin' Kraut, aren't you?" he reiterated his suspicion and shoved Gunther, causing him to take a step back.

"Leave him alone." Jens started toward them, only to have his arm caught by the taller boy. Jens quickly shook free and forcefully shoved him away before continuing toward the short boy in front of Gunther, whom he grabbed by the collar and tossed aside. Now, however, the third boy was approaching with a rotten wood fence post in hand which he swung like a bat toward Gunther's head. Forced by his uncontrollable instincts and dread, he made no attempt to deflect it and simply dove to the ground, leaving Jens' arm wide open to take the hit.

From the ground, Gunther immediately recovered and hurried to his feet—too late to avoid a harsh kick to his side from the short boy which sent him back down.

Jens had only been slightly fazed and was already wrestling the wooden post away from the third boy when suddenly, a strong kick from the taller boy landed against his back, toppling him forward and to the ground.

Gunther latched himself onto the leg of the short boy, preventing another attack, and with fury brimming, grabbed his knee with every ounce of his strength and snapped the joint. The short boy screamed as he fell to the ground. Gunther scrambled to his feet, quickly met again by the third boy with the fence post. He swung it again, and Gunther had no choice but to stumble backward. The taller boy easily took advantage of his distraction and grabbed hold of him, allowing the third boy a free shot, which he took, jamming the splintery post into Gunther's stomach.

He screamed—not from the pain, which paled in comparison to a thousand things he had endured in the past, but as the wood tore into his shirt and skin and incapacitated him with terror. He flailed wildly against his captor so forcefully that he did at last break away, but not in time to avoid another strike from the fence post; this one bashed against his head, split his scalp and knocked him to the dirt.

By now, Jens had begun to recover, but was too late to totally defend against a sudden attack from the tallest boy, who jammed his foot into Jens' face, and cast him against a rickety farm fence on the side of the road which collapsed under him. He struggled to free himself from the twisted heap, but stopped as the third boy swung his bludgeoning weapon downward.

Gunther began to crawl, pushing through his injuries, only to be halted as a foot from one of the boys—who, was unclear—crushed his face.

He lay face down in the dirt, eyes ever wide.

* * *

Ashley had returned to his seat on the carpet. Tenderly, he picked up one of the photographs he had left unpacked, and placed his thumb over his own image standing beside a young girl. There was another of himself, Aurelio and Stam together at the midnight premiere of some movie he couldn't remember.

Soon a knock came from the front door; it was a familiar one.

"*Brawwwkk... Aure....*" Sydney cooed quietly.

Ashley let out a breath. "Come—" he cleared his throat, realizing how quiet he was, "come in."

The door opened and there stood Aurelio. "Hey, Ash—" He stopped, shocked by the state of the now hardly-familiar house with all of its comforts tucked invisibly away into boxes. "Whoa...."

Ashley looked over to him, flashing a sad smile, as Aurelio stood in place looking all around.

"... What's going on?" he asked, still taken aback.

"Stam and I are moving," Ashley answered bluntly, seeing no other option.

Aurelio was stunned. "Moving?"

"Afraid so," he replied, climbing to his feet. "But the decision has been made."

"But why? Where?"

"I don't know where yet. As for why," he shook his head, "it's complicated." He knew his terseness was unkind, but found it difficult to explain much further, and knew that Aurelio rarely pressed him.

"... Huh." Aurelio didn't know what to say. There remained a heavy air and awkwardness between them until Ashley spoke up again.

"I'm sorry about the other evening." He changed the subject. "It's no excuse, but I was stressed out—I was an asshole."

"It's okay—"

"It's not." Ashley cut him off. "I don't deserve all that you do for me. I'm not such a great guy."

"Whatever. You really helped me out—I'd probably be on the streets if it weren't for you."

"You'd just be working at a different convenience store if it weren't for m—"

"No way," Aurelio interrupted. "I'd live on the streets before going back to that."

Ashley smiled.

"I owe you a lot." Aurelio shrugged. "So, whatever I can do...."

"I've already asked too much."

"Watching Sydney?" Aurelio laughed. "Yeah, *way* too much."

"And Stam," he reminded him.

"Yeah, that's really hard work." Aurelio offered

Stam's metal case to Ashley, who took it after some hesitation.

"Thanks." He set it down on top of a nearby box and began gathering Sydney's things, but eventually made idle conversation. "What have you and Stam been up to?"

"What do you think?" He laughed again. "Movies — she never gets bored of them."

"I guess you're a good match."

"I guess so…." Aurelio trailed off, thinking. He was staring down at the ground, falling deeper into thought until he made a glance over to Ashley, who had been watching for some time. He was smiling. He knew what was on his friend's mind, and it caused Aurelio to look away, nervously.

"You should take a chance." Ashley handed him Sydney's travel cage.

"… Take a chance?"

"Sure," Ashley replied. "If something can't kill you, what's the use in being afraid of it?"

When Aurelio said nothing in response, Ashley continued, "Do something you're afraid of — go to Los Angeles or New York like you always talk about."

"Oh." Aurelio furrowed his brow. "Well, maybe I could do it."

"You thought I was talking about Stam?" Ashley picked up Sydney gingerly. "You never know — I fantasized about my first love for a long time… a *long* time. Finally throwing caution to the wind was just about the only thing I ever did right in my life."

Aurelio was very quiet. He had grown pale and swallowed nervously. "I — "

"Don't worry," Ashley assured him. "It's not that obvious — I've just had a lot of time to observe the little things."

Aurelio remained silent.

"You like her. I understand why that might be a bit…" he searched for the right word, "… unsettling for you."

"I mean, I — I *like* her, but she's only — "

"Don't deny it for my sake. Or yours, for that matter."

Ashley, with Sydney nestled into the crook of his arm, reached out to Aurelio's shoulder. "There are a lot of monsters in this world, but you're not one of them. There's a lot less wrong with what you're feeling than you think."

Aurelio remained pale and mute.

"You're afraid because of what others' eyes see — because of what they would believe to be true and have no reason to question." He rephrased it, "You're afraid — not that there is necessarily something wrong with you — but of how others would see you if they knew how you felt about her." Reading his friend's discomfort, Ashley stopped, and asked very earnestly, "Do you mind if I confess something?"

Aurelio shook his head very slightly.

"My first and only love is a thirty-three year old man."

"… Huh?" was all Aurelio managed to respond.

"He loved me, too," Ashley continued. "It was a beautiful thing from the inside, but if somebody had seen us as we appeared? A teenage boy and a middle-aged man?"

Aurelio seemed to be about to respond, but Ashley wound up going on, "You know — albeit perhaps not as well as I — that your feelings toward Stam are hardly inappropriate. You shouldn't be ashamed of not being ashamed."

Ashley handed Sydney to him. Unable to respond — like a child caught misbehaving — Aurelio avoided eye contact as he received the bird.

"My love said to me many times," Ashley added, "that a life spent fleeing from fear is wasted. I've been meaning to tell you for a while, though I hadn't seen a way to not make you uncomfortable."

Aurelio indeed seemed to feel that way, and Ashley quietly sighed before adding, "Just in case this is my last chance to say it… you should stop being afraid."

* * *

"Fuckin' queer."

From the corner of his vision, Gunther saw one of the boys deliver another brutal kick to Jens, whom still lay twisted against the collapsing fence. The short boy was still clutching his own injured knee, and the tallest had come to his aid.

"You alright, mate?"

"Wanker broke my fuckin' leg," he wailed.

The tall boy reached out, "Let me see it—" and then jerked to a stop. The short boy looked up: clenched onto the throat of his friend were Gunther's teeth—so tightly they nearly tore right through. It was so forceful and quick that stunned horror was the only reaction from the tall boy before Gunther, adept with his technique, pulled away and let him fall to the ground, dead.

Terrified, the short boy scrambled away. Gunther flew right past him toward the boy looming over Jens, who had already been startled by Gunther's resurgence. The boy was hardly able to do more than brace himself before Gunther was upon him, toppling him backward. In a flash, Gunther's mouth had latched onto the boy; he flailed and fought, pounding his fist against the deep fracture in Gunther's skull and kicking with both legs. It was futile. Within seconds, he fell lifeless and the fight came to an end.

Gunther dropped to Jens' side and turned him over. "Sydney!"

His bloodied and bruised face wore no expression. As Gunther's whole body trembled he was unable to discern any movements from his friend.

"*Sydney!*" He screamed.

His own pain made it difficult to focus, but there was little, if any, life in his lover. Gunther's head spun as it flooded with a thousand terrified thoughts. He didn't know what to do.

"No… no, no, no…."

A panicked choice was made. Frantically, he pulled Jens close and sank his teeth into his warm neck. His mouth remained there for only a second, but in those moments, a more conscious realization struck him of what he was trying to do.

He didn't care. He couldn't lose Jens, no matter what it took.

Draining very little blood, he pulled away, remembering, through his terror, the interruption that had stopped his own demise in Romania.

"Sydney!"

There was no response.

"Sydney!" He bit down once more, hyperventilating, and peeled back one of Jens' eyelids; it fell shut as he let go.

He took his mouth away again. "Sydney!"

He clutched Jens' body, squeezing desperately.

"Sydney!"

* * *

Ashley was alone now. With Sydney gone, Sister Carroll's unexpected visit over, and Stam still away at Aurelio's, there remained no one left to distract him.

Outside on the street was a rented truck which he would soon have to load, but he felt little desire to begin the process. He felt little desire for anything.

Perhaps he wouldn't even bother, after all.

He took hold of the ammunition case. The padlock's rusted metal loop had long since fused in place, and looking at the mechanism, it seemed unlikely that the key—wherever Stam was keeping it these days—would even work it any longer. Staring through the case, his mind drifted at once further away and yet ever closer to the contents. Minutes passed before he stood and moved to an unsealed box nearby, from inside which he unearthed a pair of heavy bolt cutters which he brought back to the metal ammunition case. He positioned the tool's bladed mouth onto the thin metal lock loop.

"We're old men now, you know." He looked at a small, folded note beside his ancient newspaper. "I should just admit it. Give up." He shook his head. "How depraved can one person be?"

He considered his own words, and then clasped his hands—with them, the blades of the bolt cutters pinched through the ammunition case's lock. It creaked and cracked as it spit flakes of rust.

With more care than necessary, Ashley gently worked it off and set the rotted lock aside. Afterward, he let his hand rest upon the folded note.

"... Happy birthday, Luther."

* * *

Snow had begun to fall earlier in the night, and now, as Aurelio returned back home, it had begun to thinly coat the sleepy suburban streets. Sydney had puffed up in the short, cold walk to the car, but now seemed cozy and comfortable in the heated interior.

Aurelio's thoughts remained stuck on what Ashley had said earlier. He was hesitant even to think about Stam — as though doing so might make it even truer and betray his feelings to others than just his best friend. He had never done anything bad in his life, and yet, he felt now like some sort of criminal, kept safe only so long as Ashley remained quiet.

He drove carefully through the dark, empty neighborhoods, and then slowed as he came upon a large gathering outside Saint Elia's Academy for Girls. Dozens — perhaps hundreds — of cars surrounded a candle-wielding mass of heavily-bundled teenagers that had assembled outside the school. At their center, illuminated in a shrine of candles, were two enlarged photographs of a teenage boy and girl Aurelio had seen once before on the flyer he received earlier. He frowned, sympathetically, and pressed onward, only to stop as he saw a police officer in an orange vest hold out his hand.

Somehow, it caused his heart to race — as though the officer might read his mind and see in his face what Ashley had — but he had no choice but to comply and roll down the window as the man approached, shining a bright flashlight into his eyes.

"Evening," the officer greeted him. "You know you've got a headlight out? You looked like a cycl—oh, it's you again."

Through the harsh light, Aurelio couldn't make him out, but the voice was enough at this point. "Oh, uh, hi...."

Officer Wilson, who had readied a flyer, lowered it. "You get that ticket taken care of yet?"

"No sir, not yet." Aurelio recounted that it had only been earlier that day that he had been asked the same question.

"I've been seeing a lot of you lately, huh?"

Somehow, the notion made him more nervous. "... Yeah, I guess so."

Officer Wilson continued to look the interior of the car over, before noticing Sydney in the passenger's seat. His brow furrowed. "Is that...?"

"Huh?" Aurelio looked at him, confused.

"... Nothing." Officer Wilson was quiet, as though drawing connections in his head. He glanced to Sister Carroll, who stood only a few yards away talking to a group of parents, and then looked back to Aurelio. "You make sure you get that headlight fixed and that ticket paid, okay?"

"... Yes, sir."

Officer Wilson left the window and headed into the sea of teenagers and parents. Aurelio puzzled on their interaction as he raised his foot from the brake and continued down the snow-dusted street. Behind him, he could see Officer Wilson flag down Sister Carroll.

With no further incident, Aurelio pulled to a stop in the driveway outside his humble home. His half of the duplex was now one of the few places on the block not yet decorated for Christmas. The previous year, Ashley had come by to help, but he had seemed so stressed lately that Aurelio thought it best not to suggest it.

The shock of Ashley calling out his feelings was enough to prevent it from sinking in that he and Stam were *moving*. That's what he had said: they were leaving. To where? How far away? Would he see them again? And he forgot to wish Ashley a happy birthday. He was a mess.

With a sleepy Sydney in hand, Aurelio entered the house and then his bedroom. There was Stam, under the sheets, engrossed in another film.

"Hey. Brought you a friend."

Stam smiled as Aurelio approached and offered Sydney to her. She took him, carefully, and held the bird in her lap while Aurelio stood awkwardly, still wearing his coat, as if he were some sort of intruder in his own home.

"Can I get you anything?" he asked Stam, realizing that he had been standing motionless in thought for almost a full minute.

"I'm alright," was Stam's predictable reply.

"Okay," Aurelio swallowed, "I'm gonna—I don't know—uh, get some popcorn."

* * *

"*Sydney....*"

Gunther had latched tightly onto his lover, bawling and howling into his chest. His mind raced in short, blurry circles.

For how long they lay there was unclear. He could neither move nor think.

And then he felt something.

It was faint at first, but it was there. It was a feeling he remembered.

"No... no...." Gunther cringed, averting his eyes westward and away from the pale glow of the morning light that was beginning to creep from the horizon.

Gasping, crying, and still wrapped around Jens, he began to crawl—just inches at a time.

The terror, however, continued to well up inside of him and steadily replaced all else. Shelter became his only concern, but there was none. Panicking all over again, he pulled himself into his coat, cowering like a frightened animal. Writhing in a frenzied, chaotic fear, he tried to put whatever he could between himself and the sky. He flattened himself against the earth, coiled against Jens' body, trying desperately to sink away.

There he remained, panting, unable to acknowledge the sound of an approaching truck which screeched to a stop nearby.

"*Oh my God….*"

"*Lord in Heaven, what happened here?*"

"*… Oh Jesus….*"

Gunther still was gasping, but the sound was weak. He squirmed again, still trying to somehow distance himself from the sun's encroaching rays. Disoriented as he was, he could hardly assign meaning to the words he could hear.

"*Hey.*"

"*Oh my God…. Hey!*"

Gunther felt something touch his arm. Furious and scared, he tried to flail and resist, only to sink his face back into Jens' chest.

"Son," the voice called. "Can you hear me, son?"

Gunther gurgled an unintelligible reply as two arms took hold of him. He was powerless to fight, but squirmed, terrified as his body was hauled upward. Unable to shut, his wet eyes captured the first mortifying morning sunlight they had in years, illuminating Jens' lifeless form, face-down in the dirt.

* * *

Ashley's hand now rested on the edge of the ammunition case, ready to raise the top and expose the contents.

"I've never wanted to hurt anyone—not one day in my life. Not for all these years." He eyed his fragile, yellowed newspaper. "What would *you* have me do?"

He sat in silence.

"… We should all be dead—if not now, then soon."

He pulled the lid of the ammunition case open and stared at it through the sound of the groaning hinges. After giving the contents a quick look, he reached out to the newspaper. In the photo was the back of a man drenched in blood and sunlight. With tears welled in his eyes, Ashley set it down and turned back to the ammunition case's exposed contents. He reached in, slowly, and pulled out a dirty cigarette butt, giving it a look of disapproval before flicking it across the room.

"I don't want to live this way —"

His was interrupted by a loud rapping at the door.

"Ashley Miller," a voice called out.

He had little reaction, not as though he had expected it, but as though it was so absurd and ill-timed that *of course* it would have happened.

He drew a breath. "That's not even my name."

There was another aggressive knock.

He sighed quietly and stood. He slid the ammunition case away with his foot, top still open, letting it mingle in with the other boxes, and then started toward the door.

"Ashley Miller," the voice called again.

His eyes narrowed as he reached out to the knob. With one last deep breath, he swung the door open and was met by Officer Wilson and another unfamiliar policeman.

"You planning on going somewhere, Mr. Miller?" Officer Wilson made no hesitations this time.

"No." He shrugged. "Why ever do you ask?"

The two officers glanced into the box-filled living room, then to the rented moving truck parked down at the street in front of the house, and then back to Ashley, expectantly.

"Oh, *that*...." Ashley half-heartedly feigned consideration of the matter.

"One more chance, kid." Officer Wilson's voice had become aggressive. "You've been nothing but evasive with me, and it needs to stop *right now*."

"Really?"

"You and your sister were at Saint Elia's the night that Hannah and David disappeared."

"Were we?"

Officer Wilson ignored him. "Why did you leave that little bit of information out when I talked to you this afternoon?"

"I didn't think it was relevant."

"Did you also not think it was relevant that Hannah was *here in this house* the day before they went missing from the school? And that your sister and David had met up at the church that night?"

"Those events would only be relevant if Stam and I kidnapped those two, which I assure you, we did not."

"You think you're real funny, huh?" Officer Wilson folded his arms. "This is grounds enough to arrest you on obstruction, you know." Ashley had no response, and so the officer shook his head. "Where's your sister?"

"You mean Stam?"

"Yes, *your sister*, Ashley." His patience had thinned.

"She's away — visiting friends."

"What friends?"

"She didn't say."

"Ashley." Officer Wilson was very serious.

No response.

"You're laughing right now, sure, but things are about to get a lot more real, *real* fast, kid."

"I'm not laughing," Ashley replied.

Frustration showing, Officer Wilson glanced to his cohort, who began to ready a pair of handcuffs.

"One more chance: where's your sister? And what were you doing at the school that night?"

Ashley's head hung wearily. He turned away, looking into his hardly-familiar home and taking it in.

Officer Wilson let out an angry sigh. "You're under arrest for obstruction of a police officer," he began. "You have the right to remain silent — anything you say can and will be used — "

"Policemen actually say that?" Ashley furrowed his brow, looking back to them.

" — against you. You have the right to an attorney; if you can't afford — "

"Is this the first time you've ever said this to somebody other than your reflection in the mirror?"

" — one, then one will be provided to you." Officer Wilson shook his head disapprovingly at Ashley. "Look, I don't want to have to use these — " He motioned to the cuffs in his partner's hand.

"Don't you? I think you've been waiting for this chance for years: something more exciting than another rolling stop or broken headlight to liven up your career."

"You're not as funny as you think—"

Ashley threw his hands out, limply and side by side, offering them to Officer Wilson. "Come on." He smiled.

* * *

"Who is that?"

"Who?"

"That one."

"Oh," Aurelio popped a piece of popcorn into his mouth, "that's James Dean."

"And her?" Stam asked as a woman appeared on the screen.

"Natalie Wood."

Stam winced subtly, from habit, as a sun-soaked scene graced the screen. Her hand, which had been idly stroking Sydney's feathers, tensed but soon returned to normal.

"You know," Aurelio offered, still suppressing a strange apprehension, "we can do something else if you're bored. You don't have to watch my weird old movies all night."

"I don't mind."

Aurelio was always endeared by Stam's contented demeanor. Attempting to keep a conversation going, he asked, "I guess you're used to it with Ash, huh?"

"Hmm?"

"Ash—well, I mean, *Sydney's*—music and stuff. We're both a little old-fashioned."

"I like most things," Stam replied. "Ashley is more particular—he's never really enjoyed movies."

"Yeah." Aurelio remembered this, and then mused, "I wonder what he thinks about me wanting to act and stuff."

"I think he admires it." Stam's eyes glanced down to Sydney. "He admires aspiration."

"Yeah...." He knew this to be true as well. "What about you? Do you think I'm dumb for wanting to do it?"

"No," Stam replied.

"You sure?" Aurelio had expected that response, but

was still hoping for something more.

"I don't know anything about actors." She glanced up to see James Dean again. "It must be difficult."

"Well, anymore, you've got to know the right people, live in the right place, go to the right auditions...."

Stam listened.

"I guess that's why I want to go to LA." He paused. "Speaking of moving, why didn't you tell me about you and Ash leaving?"

"He made his decision?"

"... You mean you didn't *know*? He just packed everything up without even *asking* you?"

"It's his house. He faced a difficult decision. I would have been surprised no matter what he chose to do."

"He's got the whole place packed up...."

Stam remained quiet, thinking.

"You don't sound like you're going to miss it here very much."

"No," she considered, "I don't know that I will."

It disheartened him. "You don't care where you go, either?"

"No."

That was even more disheartening. Eventually, after a few minutes of silence, Aurelio spoke up, "I mean, maybe now that you guys are moving away, I could too. I dunno—do you ever miss New York?"

"No," Stam replied again.

She was being difficult to talk to—terse, even by Stam's standards.

"I'd miss things about Ohio," said Aurelio. "But I guess the thing I'd miss most is *you*... and Ash. So, if you guys won't be here anyway, maybe I could do it. It just always seemed so daunting, but Ash doesn't think so."

He offered a piece of popcorn to Sydney who, though tired, wearily took the snack with his beak and gobbled it down.

"Ashley can endure a lot. Nothing is daunting to him." Stam responded.

"... Yeah, I guess so. He's tougher than me."

Silence had taken over between them for a while afterward. Stam found it hard to focus on the television as much as she had been previously, and took a break to re-examine the photographs on the wall. She reflected on the events of the last two years which, to her, were quite recent.

"Hey, Stam," Aurelio finally asked, prompting her to turn away from the photos. He continued, "I know this is weird, but," his discomfort showed, "is there anyone you like?"

"I like Ashley."

"Well, okay." He chuckled nervously. "But, anyone who isn't family? Is there anybody you," he hesitated to stress the word, "… *like?*"

"You mean romantically?" she asked, not looking away from the wall.

"… Yeah," Aurelio answered after she offered nothing else.

"No."

"Oh." He shrugged, carefully obscuring disappointment. "I was just wondering."

Silence resumed, and Stam eventually glanced back to the television; on screen now was a young male who had first appeared while Aurelio was out.

"Who is that?" she asked.

"Umm," he took hold of the case for the tape and read over the back for a moment, "Sal Mineo."

"He looks familiar—from one of Sydney's album covers." As she thought about it, she caught sight of Aurelio's clock:

12:03 a.m.

"May I use the phone?" she asked.

Aurelio reached for and offered it to her while suddenly, on the television screen, gunfire sounded and Sal Mineo's character fell to the ground, shot dead by a police officer.

Stam turned back to it and analyzed the scene intently, very off-put. "Why'd they shoot him?"

"He had a gun—they didn't know it was empty."

"That's reason to kill somebody?"

"Self-defense," Aurelio shrugged again, "I guess."

She watched grief poor from James Dean at the sight of his friend, and shifted uncomfortably before beginning to dial a number.

* * *

Gunther's naked body lay on a cold metal table. His open eyes stared up at a dim, uncovered light bulb dangling from the ceiling. He was motionless despite the activity and two voices carrying on around him. One was a police officer, the other some sort of doctor.

"Little freak killed all three of 'em."

A page of a newspaper was passed over his head from one man's hands to another's.

"You said he bit 'em — like a vampire — right?"

The men's accents were even thicker than the one Gunther had forged over the last decade.

"Right — he's got the teeth for it, that's for sure." The doctor pulled Gunther's lips apart, showing off his sharp fangs. "See 'at?"

"He's a fuckin' Kraut. Wouldn't be shocked if he had horns too."

He passed the newspaper back across, and the doctor — a gaunt middle-aged man with thick-brimmed glasses — leaned down and looked into Gunther's eyes.

"Can those big eyes see *this* from Hell?" He held the paper, on which was a picture, in front of Gunther's empty gaze. It was a gruesome scene of a man lying face-down in the dirt. "You're a fuckin' murderer is what you are."

"The kid who ID'ed 'em said he just came outta nowhere."

"Right, and that kid too — they said he ain't gonna be walking on his own anymore. It's lookin' pretty bad."

"Fuckin' Nazi trash. Wish he hadn't bought it before they brought him in." The police officer drew a gun and pointed it, lazily, at Gunther. "Been a long time since I got to shoot a Kraut."

"Ain't much good to shoot him now." The doctor chuckled.

"Right, right...." The police officer put the gun back into its holster, which he then slid off himself before removing his hat and stepping away from the table. "I gotta use the toilet."

"Enjoy that. I just got to put *this* piece of shit in the freezer."

The police officer disappeared from the room. Around Gunther were the sounds of some tools clicking and clanking as the doctor gathered them up. Before long, his silhouette passed between Gunther and the light once more. The doctor cocked his head, staring into Gunther's wide open eyes.

"Those really are something...."

He shook his head and then pried Gunther's lips apart once more, looking at the teeth. He ran his finger down one of the fangs.

In a nearby washroom, the police officer dried his hands on a rag before heading back out into a hallway. There, he noticed his belt was still unbuckled and began to fiddle with it, only to stop when a scream rang out.

Shocked, he looked up. "Ben?"

The scream went on.

"Ben!" He hurried to a nearby set of double doors and threw them open. Inside the room, he saw Gunther standing upright, as ghastly and pale as the corpse he had just been, with the doctor's hand—still attached to the doctor—held in his teeth.

"Holy shit."

The doctor continued screaming, trying to pull away, as his free hand swung and struck Gunther's face repeatedly. Still, it wasn't enough to break the hold he had taken.

Speechless with horror, the police officer scrambled toward a chair where his holster and gun had been left, but as he neared them, Gunther moved, bringing the doctor with him, to grab the weapon first; he immediately aimed at the officer, who stopped and threw up his hands.

"Shit—listen, please—"

A shot rang out and a bullet ripped through the

police officer's leg, sending him to the ground.

"Oh, fuck. Jesus," the doctor pled.

The doctor's aggression was waning. Gunther had chewed at this point into the space between his thumb and index finger and had not relented for even a moment. The police officer, meanwhile, crawled for the door. A second gunshot rang out, causing him to wince in terror before he realized he hadn't been the target. Gunther dropped the doctor's body to the floor behind him.

Panicked, the police officer began to push against the door, and just as he began to make it into the hallway, screaming for help, he felt two icy hands grasp his leg and pull him back inside.

A ticking clock was the only sound. The hands on its face sat directly upon one another:

12:00 a.m.

Gunther sat on the floor, still naked but for a splattered coat of blood spread from his chin, down his chest. On the floor was the newspaper bearing Jens' photograph, and at the top of the page, the words "Vampire Slay" headlined a story that described four friends being attacked by a violent stranger: an illegal German immigrant who died in the hospital shortly after being identified by the only survivor of the assault. Victims, the story explained, were brutalized and bitten by the deranged youth playing out a sick fantasy.

1:00 a.m.

2:00 a.m.

The hours wore by as he remained where he had been left, paralyzed not by any mysterious force, but by nothing more than grief. It was so natural—so human—compared to so many feelings, and yet, he felt it to a degree that was anything but. He trembled with his quavering breaths.

… 3:00 a.m.

His mind was empty. He wasn't as scared now as he was in the sun, his pain was not enough to deprive him of clarity, his reluctant thirst was satiated, and yet, he had never been more helpless.

Still shivering, he raised his head. Across from him was a wall of drawers. He worked his way to his feet and began to drift toward a target. There was a tag on the handle:

Unindentified – 06/07/1958

Gunther took hold of it with shivering, blood-soaked fingers which seemed to give him pause. Tears fell from his eyes as his face contorted with anguish. He looked up to the ceiling as he pulled out the drawer.

In time, he brought his eyes to the slab he had exposed. On top was a covered body.

He could only tremble and shake. Jens had kept Gunther sane as he marched toward death, consoled him as he lay dying, and offered hope as he endured something that could only be described as hell. All those years ago, no matter what happened, there was Jens: the *hope* that he would one day see the boy he loved again.

"… What do want me to do?" Gunther's raspy voice whispered through short, tearful gasps.

"What *can* I do?"

He collapsed forward, burying his face into Jens' covered chest and holding his arms around the body that even to *him* felt cold.

"… I can't."

"Sydney… I can't…."

In one hand, he still held the police officer's gun, which he slowly dragged toward himself and brought to his forehead.

"There's always a way out…." he remembered his friend's childhood wisdom from the day they stood in the infirmary during military training and Jens expounded on the opportunities the future held. He told Gunther to do what he wanted in life, and not worry about what it meant to anyone else. *"You shouldn't ever do anything you don't want to do. Nobody can make you. If things get too bad, there's always a way out."*

It may have been true once, but not anymore.

The gun fired.

Gunther's head jerked backward; it took the rest of his body with it, and slammed him against the wall of drawers, but within in seconds, he stirred and coughed a horrible, gurgling cough. Still crying, he brought a hand to Jens' slab and pulled himself upward. He clutched hold of the sheet over his friend and pulled on it, exposing Jens' battered face.

Gunther only winced more and sunk further into despair. He brought the gun again to his temple… and fired.

It shred his face and toppled him onto Jens' body.

There, unable to do anything more than whimper, he remained.

* * *

Ashley and four officers now stood in his cramped living room.

"I don't know much about law, but don't you nee—"

"Cut the attitude, Ashley," Officer Wilson snapped. "Where's your sister?"

"She's fine. What does it have to do with me?"

"Guys, it looks clean," an officer called, stepping into the scene from down the hall. "We got nothin'."

"Well, Ashley?"

"Hmm?" He shrugged.

"You're only digging yourself deeper." Officer Wilson scowled. "Why can't you tell me where she is?"

"I'm really confused." Ashley turned directly to him. "You're not making any sense to me—do you think I had something to do with Hannah and David? Is that why you're here?"

"You're the one who just said that—not me."

"… Are you just so bored with your life that you've concocted some magnificent story in your head about the weird pale kid in the windowless house on the edge of town? Do you think my sister isn't truly such, but some victim of a bizarre cult-inducing charisma?"

"Do you remember what I said, Ashley?" he answered calmly.

"Look at me." Ashley was stern. "What do you think I am? A kidnapper? A *murderer*? How wild are you going to let your imagination run before I'm exotic enough to validate the decades you've wasted serving as nothing but a minor inconvenience to people who want nothing more than to drive the streets in peace?"

Officer Wilson seemed unfazed by Ashley's outburst, and reiterated, "Anything you say can be used against—"

"You said I'm under arrest for obstruction of an officer. That's unbelievably vague."

"'Vauge' doesn't even begin to describe the answers I've been getting from y—"

Interrupting him, Ashley lashed out, "You had nothing better to do with your time than to run the license plates of *legally* parked cars all night?"

The increasing aggravation in his tone prompted a perplexed look to spread across Officer Wilson's face as he waited for Ashley to continue.

He sighed. "It's strange, really, how things start." Ashley bit his lip. "One day everything is normal, and then some common nuisance cascades into disaster. This wasn't how I wanted things to turn out, you know?"

Then a sound rang out: Ashley's recognizable ringtone emanated from a small pile of his personal belongings sitting on a box top. Officer Wilson reached down and took hold of it, looking at the name on the screen: Aurelio.

"Huh, well, look here." He showed the screen to Ashley and then analyzed it himself once again. "Answer this."

"You know," Ashley watched him, "we got off on the wrong foot, but really, I didn't have much of a problem with you. I just don't understand what you have against me."

"We're only having trouble here because you can't seem to answer my questions or offer me any respect."

"I didn't say I *respected* you," Ashley replied, before adding in a somber tone, "respect for authority is dangerous."

Officer Wilson sighed and looked the phone over before pressing a button to accept the call. He then quickly located a speaker feature and held the phone out to

Ashley, gesturing for him to talk.

Ashley took a slow breath, frustrated with the situation, and only reluctantly did he finally open his mouth. "Hello?"

"Hello. Who is Sal Mineo?"

Officer Wilson recognized Stam's voice. His eyes widened as he looked to the other officers. He cocked his head to the phone and nodded excitedly.

Ashley was taken aback. "Uh, I'm not really sure...."

"Don't you have a record by him?"

"Do I?" Something seemed to click. "Oh yeah, I do, actually—there was one that Sydney liked called 'Keep Movin' and he released another one called, uh..." he struggled to think of it, "... 'Make Believe Baby,' I think. Why do you ask?"

"He's in a movie we're watching. He just looked familiar."

Officer Wilson had already approached his companions with an air of authoritative self-satisfaction in finding his suspicions had been correct: she was with Aurelio, and soon, they would find her.

"... Okay." Ashley glanced around at his captors as they listened in. "Is that all you needed?"

"I wanted to wish you a happy birthday, so...."

Ashley smirked, looking at the time-display on the phone which indicated it was just past midnight.

"... Happy birthday."

"Thanks, Stam," he replied. "I'll talk to you later."

"Okay. Goodbye."

"Bye."

The call ended and Officer Wilson, after giving it a quick glance, sat the phone down and then looked expectantly over to Ashley.

"See? She's just watching movies over at her friend's."

"With that Aurelio kid, huh?" he asked, folding his arms. "What's the story on him, anyway? He's been awfully suspicious too."

"Everything looks suspicious to you," Ashley grumbled.

"Ashley." Officer Wilson was very serious. "If your

friend is helping you evade our investigation and hiding your sister, *he's* going to get wrapped up in this mess you've made." He added, firmly, "Do you want that?"

"No," Ashley replied.

"Well, we're going over there now," Officer Wilson declared, taking hold of Ashley's arm and walking him out of the house. The others followed them out into the cold night.

* * *

The movies continued; on the screen was a man at a tearoom, smiling and flirting with an aloof waitress. Stam now lay at the foot of the bed, watching intently, while up by the pillows, Aurelio quietly snored. Before long, the scene changed — the protagonist now waited in a crowded station, and the volume was sufficient to rile Aurelio. He rubbed his eyes while realizing that he had dozed off yet again. He looked at the time:

12:13 a.m.

He then glanced at the screen, wincing from the brightness of the black-and-white film as he tried to determine what movie had been started.

"You're watching this?" He sat up straight. "This is my favorite movie."

"Is it?" Stam asked, not taking her eyes from the screen.

"Two of the greatest actors ever," he yawned. "Leslie Howard and Bette Davis."

Stam continued to watch, holding a sleeping Sydney in her arms.

* * *

A vacant delirium had been Gunther's only guide in however long had passed. Even less than as a prisoner in a dirt cell could he grasp a thing such as time, and the pain was no less now than it had been the day Jens was taken. The day Jens was killed.

Gunther had been robbed of his youth — of *growing*

up. He had been robbed of life, of growing old and even *death*.... And now robbed of Jens.

Thirteen of his years—however many there were in total—lived only in memory, doomed to fade with each passing day until they, too, found oblivion.

His time with Jens had been but a brief foray into happiness—into something that made everything else endurable, and with its end, each moment seemed impossibly thick. The future, brutally indefinite, was black and intangible. Where his next footstep would lead was an impossible prediction.

The house had been descended upon by the police and media, but even if it had been left alone and his home untouched, what would he find there? Only more fleeting memories.

And so his footsteps led him away. In his wake he left dead anyone in the wrong place at the wrong time. The concern he once gave to kill only the immoral and ill had been dismissed; he couldn't care now who *anyone* was.

He drifted like a ghost in a direction he only truly realized as his foot touched down on a platform. Behind him, a nervous railroad conductor pulled shut the door, eying him and betraying a sense of relief at his departure. With a hoarse whistle, a train Gunther could hardly recall boarding began to crawl away, leaving him, the lone exiting passenger at a darkened station. He stood stiff, draped in a mud-stained, ill-fitting suit jacket that had at some point found its way to his shoulders. The seams had frayed and the dirty clothes he wore beneath were thin and ragged. In mismatched shoes, his feet brought him down a few rickety steps to a dusty earth road stretching through a humble village. A small sign above spelled out the quiet town's name: *Vişeu de Sus*, and beneath it, *Maramures, România*.

* * *

The same two characters that had met in the tearoom were still on the screen, but one—the girl played by Bette Davis—was screaming furiously at Leslie Howard. As the woman took hold of a plate and threw it across the room, she suddenly froze; Stam's finger rested on the "pause" button of the remote. She glanced to Aurelio, who had been drifting in and out of sleep for most of the film, and with her brow furrowed, said, "I don't understand...."

"Huh?" He looked over. "What?"

"Why does Leslie continue being so nice to somebody who treats him so poorly?"

Aurelio had to think for a moment, to be sure of what she was asking, but then chuckled. "Well, that's kind of the point of the story. Philip — Leslie's character — is in love with her. He can't really help it."

"Why would anyone love someone like that?" She raised an eyebrow.

He laughed. "Like I said: that's the point."

Stam remained unclear — it showed on her face. Aurelio pursed his lips before explaining further, "It's sort of about how people become *bonded* to other people, even when they really don't want to be."

"What is it you like about it so much?"

"I dunno." He shrugged. "I guess it just *says something* that makes sense to me. I mean, it's about unrequited love, but *more* than just that...."

He looked over to Stam, who seemed to understand the words, but at the same time, wasn't sure what he was saying.

"Like, I felt like Philip a lot when I was working at the convenience store and these groups of girls would come in and pretend to flirt with me while their friends tried to steal candy and stuff. Just stupid things like that. The way Mildred uses Philip just *resonates* with me, I guess."

She nodded, accepting it. It reminded her of something Ashley once said about music.

"Also, he has all this trouble with school." He shrugged. "I know *all* about that...."

"How so?"

"Just the fact that people tell him he can't be an artist — he just gives up. Then he struggles with medical school and everything and can't afford it. I could never afford to go to school in the first place—not that I even wanted to...."

Stam listened, watching him.

"... I mean, I kind of wanted to go take acting classes, but mostly I was just so happy to be out of high school. Then my parents kicked me out, and then I even lost my stupid job." He shook his head, realizing he had been rambling. "Man, I'm pathetic, huh?"

"I don't think so," Stam replied.

"This movie kind of makes me feel old." He sighed. "I first watched it when I was like twelve or something, and Leslie Howard made me want to be an actor. Now I'm almost twenty—everybody I went to high school with is halfway through college and, well, you just heard how much I've done with my life. Maybe my parents were right...."

"You're not old," Stam interjected as Aurelio seemed to trail off.

"Feels that way." He offered a strangely sad smile. "Especially when I'm around you."

"Ashley says the average American male lives seventy four years these days," she replied. "You've still got—"

Aurelio chuckled. "Yeah, yeah—I know." He began to extract himself from beneath the covers and moved to the bed's edge. "But I'm not getting any younger, and I guess... I guess I'm just afraid of too much."

"What are you afraid of?" Stam asked, sitting up. She now was right beside him, and it seemed to give Aurelio some pause.

"... I dunno. *Everything?*"

"Such as?" Stam dismissed the hyperbole.

"I don't know—it's more than just being afraid of failure or rejection. I feel like," he tried to find the right way to explain, "like it's not okay for me to admit what I want...."

"Why not?"

"Well, with acting, when I told my parents that's what I wanted to do and it was all I'd consider going to college for, well—you know how that went over...."

Stam nodded.

"I feel like that about other things," he added.

"Other things?"

He said nothing more, looking away. Stam, knowing she had been heard, did not repeat herself, but continued to watch him. Silence persisted until, with agonizing hesitance, Aurelio looked over to her and swallowed nervously. "Okay, like… would you be totally creeped out if I said… that I liked you?"

Stam had little reaction at all.

"… Maybe *romantically*," he added, clarifying via earlier terminology.

She was hardly as appalled as Aurelio had anticipated. She opened her mouth to respond when suddenly a loud rapping on the front door of the duplex could be heard. Aurelio glanced to the clock:

1:03 a.m.

"What the hell?" He gave a confused glance to Stam, who shrugged. The air still hung heavy from his confession, but as the rapping failed to relent and only grew in intensity, he had to address it. He stood up and moved into the hallway, where he could immediately see red and blue flashing lights shining in through his windows.

"Oh, *come on*…."

The angry rapping began once more, and as he opened the door, Officer Wilson was revealed.

"Evening, son," he greeted Aurelio. "Hi there, sweetie," he added upon seeing Stam behind him.

Chapter **10**

Gunther continued through the quiet town. He couldn't cite a thought—any conscious decision—to come to this place, but a hopeless motivation existing somewhere outside of his own mind had made it to be. With no grave to lie in and no home to haunt, it seemed the only place to go.

The modest homes and narrow streets around him slept soundly; neither a light nor a soul intruded upon the dark and silence. Gunther, too, resembled little more than a shadow as he passed through the thick of town and out to where the tightly clustered buildings thinned. Before long, the town itself dwindled to a peppering of barns and open fields, and soon those dissolved to an expanse of wilderness. The roads degraded from stone, to dirt, to nothing.

There was a river he recalled from the days he had spent marching away his youth—it loomed now as a wall to the west. He had learned years ago that among his many afflictions was also the inability to cross over running water; like entering a home uninvited, to will himself past his reluctance was *impossible*. The placid flow of the river sent short pangs of terror down his spine as he eyed it from his path. He followed it for a time, before veering east into the dense woods he only distantly remembered. When they had marched there so long ago, they had moved almost blindly through the forests of northern Romania with little more than the Carpathatian Mountains as a compass; all Gunther knew to do was head east.

He stumbled as he walked, hiding his hands as he pulled his jacket up and over his face. He shuddered with each limb that smacked across his humble shield and each twig that snapped below his feet as he traipsed through gnarled branches.

How long the night had worn before there was a clearing, he couldn't say. Ramshackle houses huddled together there in a nameless heap, but he knew where he was. Fading away in the darkest corners of his memory were a curious boy, a frightened girl, gunfire, rage, theft, rape and murder — all buried beneath a swath of blackened earth to be forgotten. The homes now were more silent than those of before, as though untouched — as though still empty — with the same open eyes in the same bleached photographs staring from the mantle, forever, into the lives they'd lost.

And as he had twice before, he put the town to his back and moved on, letting it sink away into the darkness.

Blind and terrified, he pushed on through the trees; his body shivered as wet morning dew began to coat the world around him. Before long, his protective jacket, sleeves and arms grew damp and soggy. Dirt from his grimy, unwashed face began to drip into his eyes and the rough, raw gashes in his cheeks still unhealed from where he had sent bullets through his skull.

After innumerable hours, he felt the woods disperse. He could hear a sound, and pulled the jacket from his head, ready to face the running stream that lay before him.

The serene and otherworldly clearing was a place not so far — physically — from civilization, but somehow in a world all its own. It was as though there were no farther place from Germany or Poland or England or America—no farther place, even, from the surrounding Romania. It was a lonely realm, unsuitable to hosting life, existing now only in paralyzed isolation.

Gunther raised his foot to pass over the withered creek, but no different from any other: it stopped him. The sight of the tepid running water sickened him, forcing his recoil.

It was the edge of the Earth; he could go no farther.

Furious, he stepped back, took a deep breath, and then—with all the anger and courage he possessed—threw himself toward the invisible wall. He flew at it, only to feel his convictions dissolved by terror; in mid-jump, he retreated, collapsing and scrambling backward more urgently than he had once in this same spot fled from advancing Soviet soldiers. Dirt and rocks were kicked away as he clawed and clutched hold of the ground. He lay where he was with his filthy, distorted visage—still unhealed from his hopeless attempts of suicide—staring upward, while the moonless sky threatened at any moment to alight with the glow of the rising sun.

A short time passed before his defeat was interrupted by another unique sound: a quiet metal jangle, awakened by—yet nearly inaudible beneath—a whispering gust of wind.

His body remained where it had dropped, but his eyes—wearily seeking the source of the sound—soon pulled his head in its direction. As it came into focus, he twisted and righted himself. He could see it now: a rotten wood post bent halfway to the ground. He struggled to his feet and approached the decaying monument, knowing already what it was. At its base lay another piece of moss-coated wood, from which a short length of moldy, blackened twine connected it to the standing post. Dangling—tangled and woven in with the crumbed cross' remnants—was a rusted chain.

Gunther gently took hold of it and let his dark fingers slide to its end, to a thin piece of metal—the letters on which had long since become indecipherable beneath corrosion, mold and rust. Only one marking could still be made out: a two-letter code—an abbreviation for "*Rotten-führer.*"

A short distance below Gunther, still buried in the dirt, was the body they had left that day. In fifteen years, Martin had remained undisturbed, embraced forever by a simple death.

Gunther stood up slowly, letting the cold metal slip from his grasp. In the distance, just as he had seen all those years ago, loomed the mysterious church steeple just beyond a hill. He moved toward it. With each step, more became visible, until its full silhouette was exposed. It was a squat building—looking as though it could hardly contain more than a single room—covered by a steep roof stretching many times the height of the walls. In the darkness, he could make out little else in the area but another dilapidated grave a few feet ahead.

Then there was another.

… And another.

There were still more as he began to let his eyes search for them throughout the clearing. Soon the count could only have been in the hundreds; a sea of wooden crosses in various states of decay stretched from where he stood all the way to the distant forest walls.

His heart—or whatever had replaced it—sank. He could feel a human fear taking hold that if ever there were a place on earth that should not exist and no one should find: this was it.

His breaths grew short. There was a palpable sense of despair—of loneliness and loss—that drifted in the air and through his ragged form. The thought had already occurred to him maybe it was just a dream; he may have finally lost his mind and was at last descending into complete delusion, but as always, no matter how great a haze overcame him, some part of his mind remained alive and alert, uninterruptable and painfully aware of reality. The hope that his mind may have just simply been playing tricks was silenced by a voice inside whispering that *this* was Hell. There was nowhere lower—nothing further from the light of joy, a fictitious God, or hope.

He wanted to run—never return—and forget that he

had ever laid eyes on such a place. He didn't want to know what might lurk inside the strange church, and just as he moved to turn away, his eyes caught a dim light from its window. Fear gripped him again: had the light been there before? It resembled the glow of an old oil lamp, and whether it had been there all along or not, its lifetime was short and would have had to have been recently lit.

Someone else was here.

He felt a childlike terror that grappled with his sense of reason: he was immortal, and as such, there was nothing on earth worth being afraid of. He had already met and endured the worst of fates.

With a breath, he forced himself to continue approaching the church. It was maybe thirty feet away now, and with the aid of the oil lamp's glow, he could see a unique quality to the structure: it was wooden—*entirely* wooden.

He froze. Again, his mind fell into a chaotic whirlwind of urges to flee fighting against logic. His imagination of what this could be and why it was here spiraled uncontrollably. In the fifteen years since the day he became whatever he had become, he had spent little time strongly considering the implications and reality of what Dr. Mengele had referred to as his "condition." At first, it was because he was hard-pressed to string two thoughts together amid the pain of his injuries and the doctor's experiments, but later—with only a limited understanding of his nature—he had travelled to Munich, where Jens had hardly posed a single question. As their years together went on, Gunther came to understand his own nuances, but had never felt the need to worry about the *how* and the *why*. When it seemed he might, Jens was quick to offer a distraction in the way he had always come to Gunther's aid. The effect of his absence had already manifested in the form of Gunther's delirious journey and racing thoughts.

He took a deep breath where he stood staring down the foreboding structure. What was indistinguishable from logic or a complete lack thereof indecisively prevailed, and his mouth opened, "Hello?"

The sound of his own voice chilled him. There was no response.

"Hello?" he tried again.

He looked around once more and then noticed something he had missed while distracted by his thoughts: houses standing together in a small gathering not far beyond the church. With continuing trepidation, Gunther moved toward them, only to stop when he saw that where should have been the main road of the little village, the disjointed graveyard had continued to sprawl; rotten crosses were scattered about in no discernible pattern with some even standing in doorways. The homes themselves were broken, abandoned and ancient — little more than just small, dilapidated husks — and as Gunther's eyes continued to search the area, he began to note an unusual detritus amongst the ruins: what little equipment and other signs of daily life left were antiquated — far older than anything Gunther had ever seen outside a museum. The town was long since derelict and dead, undisturbed in a number of years he couldn't venture to estimate, and yet nearby, the light in the church remained.

Held back a few feet by a narrow porch lining the building's perimeter, he had come as close as he could to the window of the church where the lamp sat. He took another breath and called out again, "Is anyone there?"

He managed to get the question out clearly, but his voice faltered as he felt an encroaching sense of terror: the familiar companionship of the sun. He averted his eyes from the east, shivering and letting a short gasp escape through gritted teeth. He regained his composure enough to speak, but could not stave off panic.

"Hello?" he screamed. "Anyone?"

He scurried over to where warped wooden steps stood forebodingly between himself and the door.

"Ist jemand hier?" he tried German, knowing no Romanian.

He winced again, and with no other choice, carefully started up the stairs; he shivered with each urgent footstep until he arrived at the door. In lieu of knocking, he aggressively kicked it. He winced with each blow. "Somebody, please!"

His fear only grew as the sky, imperceptibly to anyone else, brightened. His kicks soon changed in intent, growing more violent, and with little resistance one of the thick double doors gave way as it broke from its hinge. As it fell, Gunther scrambled backward. Once it had settled, he moved toward the entrance, only to find it still as inaccessible as before. To enter unwelcomed was impossible.

"Please," he howled into the dark room before him, unable to make out anything inside.

With still no answer, terror pulled him back and his head began to jerk as he searched for somewhere else to hide. He toppled down the stairs and fell to the ground, scrambling toward any form of shelter. His only option seemed to be the abandoned village, however insufficient the crumbling homes may have been to block the sun. He crawled for them urgently, and then saw something unique: a strange stone structure built into a hill, like a tiny mausoleum. With little ability to think, he diverted toward it and grasped the handle of its thin iron door; he threw it open and exposed the black interior. Without indulging in his reluctance, he launched himself into the crypt. His hands immediately fumbled to shut the door behind him; they pulled it close with a hideous creak.

He sat in the dank cell slowly regaining his composure, though it was not without difficulty given no sight to expose what horrors might be lurking in wait. His eyes darted about, seeing nothing but pitch darkness—even the edges of door itself had been fashioned in such a way as to block out any and all stray light. His functional senses struggled to discern what his eyes could not; his ears noted nothing but his own panting breaths, and beneath himself he could feel a dirt floor. There was also a smell: it was subtle, but still harsh and rotten.

He didn't want to know. He held his nose while his mind raced through every possible sickening scenario, but as seconds, minutes and more passed, he soon calmed down enough to shift from the uncomfortable position he had dropped into upon entering. As he did so, his foot tapped against something which clanked loudly. It startled him at first, but he soon grasped for it upon realizing it had only been a glass bottle. He felt it in the darkness and took a smell from its lip, immediately wincing. Whatever was inside was rancid and had solidified, and was the source of the stench in the room. Nervously, he continued to move around and discovered a few more bottles littered about. His hand then passed onto something larger and made of metal; he fumbled with it before determining it was some sort of lamp not unlike the one he had seen in the window of the church. The overpowering stench in the cell had been whale oil — long since spoiled. He breathed an unpleasant sigh of relief and continued to apprehensively explore the tomb. He determined it was maybe four or five feet across, slightly shorter in height than himself, and maybe seven feet deep. There were several thick wool blankets on the ground, and sitting on top of them was a small, hard-covered book. There was also some sort of small metal object around the same size of the lamp, with a small glass dome on one side. In the back was a small key, and upon turning it, a quiet ticking sound indicated that he had found a clock.

Having examined every corner, he now sat, waiting, only able to guess at what time it might be and how much longer he would have to remain there counting the passing ticks.

At least an hour had gone by before, outside, very abruptly, he heard a nervous voice call out, *"Tu eşti Stam?"*

Shocked, Gunther hardly believed what he had heard, and hurried to the door to listen.

"Este cineva acolo?" There was a pause. "Stam?"

Gunther hesitated, not wanting to answer. By now, the sun would be well over the treetops, and there was little he could do to hold the door if the man outside chose to open it.

Knuckles rapped against the iron and the voice tried one more time, "Alo?"

At last, words squeaked from Gunther's mouth,

"Hello."

"*Este cineva acolo? Stam?*"

"Don't open the door," Gunther shouted, knowing his words had no power.

"*Ce faci aici înăuntru? Tu eşti Stam?*"

"I don't speak Romani. I'm sor—" He felt the door shake. "Stop," he screamed. "Please!"

A sliver of light crept in, and with it, Gunther dove to the ground and buried his face beneath the blankets, "Stop, stop, stop!" he cried. "Please!"

Through Gunther's howls, the man gasped, "*Oh, Dumnezeule, fie-ţi milă,*" and slammed the door. As Gunther's panting subsided, he could hear the man mumble to himself outside, "*Ce ai făcut? Stam, ce ai făcut...?*"

Gunther crawled out from under the blankets, and continued listening to the worried murmurs. When he spoke again, it froze Gunther.

"... Gunther?"

It was a name he hadn't heard in years—a name that he had tried to forget. Terrified all over again, he replied, "Yes—I'm Gunther."

The man said nothing else. After a minute or so had passed, Gunther tried again, "I'm Gunther."

It was a lie, as far as he was concerned. *Gunther* was an ugly thing from the past. In escaping Germany, the new name he had adopted put to death what he had once been and been through. He had hoped to never hear it again.

"Hello?" Gunther called, having received no reply.

Minutes passed—then hours. The man outside had fled.

Gunther sank back to the dirt floor. As he did so, his hand came to rest upon something cold: a chip of metal he had disturbed when diving beneath the blankets. He felt it over, soon determining what it was, and nervously clutched it as he waited out the day.

When at long last he had the assurance that night must have fallen, he approached the door. He had been second-guessing himself for hours now, reassessing and evaluating his estimations. He had been in the cell since sunrise; then maybe an hour passed before the man arrived. Since then, he had counted fifteen hours, and had now stalled by *at least* two more. Still, without complete certainty, facing the fear in all of its severity seemed impossible.

With much hesitation and with the wool blankets covering him, he kicked the iron door. With the same piercing creak from earlier, it flew open. Outside, Gunther could hear the same haunting silence he had the night before, and slowly, he lifted a tiny corner of the blanket. When that proved safe, he lifted more, and more, until he could read the face of the clock by the ambient glow of the night:

7:21

Quickly, he noted it was inaccurate, since it had been unwound for who knew how long. Still, the lack of light was bearable, and slowly, he worked his way out from the blankets and took with him the little book he had found. He looked around the landscape, unchanged since the night before, and over to the church where tonight the light was extinguished. He moved quietly to the door. It had been moved from where he had kicked it down; somebody had in fact already begun to repair it.

He examined the book in his hands. It was small, but thick, and the pages were made of a fibrous material unlike any modern paper he had ever handled. It was a well-preserved little journal, but even in the darkness, he could tell it was *tremendously* old.

He opened to the first page. As expected, it was illegible, but not only because of the language: the scribbled text inside was blocky and huge, resembling that of a child's penmanship. As he paged through, he began to encounter lists of numbers, and before long, he concluded they must be dates. The first, which he struggled to read due to the handwriting, was *14/4/1791*, and beside it was some kind of notation. While the first few pages covering 1791 were nearly impossible to read, the pages of 1792 saw an improvement and were filled with large sections of what looked like writing practice: the same word repeated over and over and over until perfected. After another two years, the practicing seemed to end, and in each subsequent entry, a near identical pattern emerged: a date, the phrase, *"Azi am ucis,"* a name, and then the ending, *"Sper ca Dumnezeu să mă ierte."*

As the entries progressed, the handwriting shrank and became more refined until, by entries in 1796, it had become flawless. Also interspersed — quite rarely — throughout the journal were dated entries that resembled those of a diary. Gunther's sinking feeling returned as he began to form suspicions on what he had found. Typically, there were around sixty dated entries each year: much more at the beginning, and slightly fewer by the 1800s.

Eventually, toward the very back of the book, he noticed where a loose piece of paper had been stuck in between two pages. He carefully unfolded it, but stopped dead as he discovered what it was:

30, November, 1943
Dear Jens,

It was the letter that had been in Gunther's jacket when he was shot. His hands shook as he looked the letter over; it only contained a short introduction. He could no longer remember why he hadn't finished it, or why it was written on such a small scrap of paper, and he could not bear to read its contents.

Slowly, he examined the list of dates on the open page of the journal. The first followed the normal format:

14/10/1943 — Azi am ucis Ana. Sper ca Dumnezeu să mă ierte.

Then afterward, to an unusual degree, many had no name associated — just a second phrase in addition to the one that repeated throughout.

23/10/1943 - Azi am ucis un om. Nu ştiu cum îl cheamă. Sper ca Dumnezeu să mă ierte.
30/10/1943 - Azi am ucis un om. Nu ştiu cum îl cheamă.

Sper ca Dumnezeu să mă ierte.
7/11/1943 - Azi am ucis un om. Nu ştiu cum îl cheamă.
Sper ca Dumnezeu să mă ierte.
13/11/1943 - Azi am ucis un om. Nu ştiu cum îl cheamă.
Sper ca Dumnezeu să mă ierte.
21/11/1943 - Azi am ucis un om. Nu ştiu cum îl cheamă.
Sper ca Dumnezeu să mă ierte.

Then suddenly, as seemed to happen on occasion, there was a spike in the frequency of entries. The first contained an unusually long comment:

29/11/1943 - Azi m-a împuşcat cineva. Am pierdut mult sânge, aşa că am omorât doi oameni. Nu ştiu cum îi cheamă.
30/11/1943 - Azi am ucis un om. Nu ştiu cum îl cheamă.
Sper ca Dumnezeu să mă ierte.

And then there it was, date and all—the very last entry in the book that had spanned 150 years:

1/12/1943 - Azi i-am făcut ceva groaznic unui băiat pe nume Gunther.

He swallowed. The language conveyed little to him, and the specifics were obscured, but the ultimate message contained in the entries was clear. *December 1st, 1943* was the day he had met his fate, and beside it was his name. The phrase which preceded it was unique within the journal, and below it all was a short block of text unlike any other.

Beyond it, the rest of the book was blank.

Trembling, he sat on the earth and let his eyes drift about the field of crosses with the same sinking grief he had felt the night before. In his jacket, he remembered, he had pocketed the small metal disc he had found after disturbing the blankets in mausoleum. He pulled it out, hands shaking, and it was what he had suspected: another dog tag, just like Martin's. He had long since forgotten his own military service number—the tag might easily have been anyone's — but in his beatless heart, he knew what he had found.

A warm summer wind blew past, rattling the distant trees while Gunther remained in place, unable to think or move.

* * *

25/12/1792 — killed woman
3/1/1792 — killed man
11/1/1792 — killed man
18/1/1792 — killed Mihai Nistor
22/1/1792:
me me me me me me me me
it it it it it
is is is is is is
and and and and and
the the the the the the
Stam Stam Stam Stam Stam Stam Stam Stam Stam Stam
Stam Stam
name name name name name
my name ~~it~~ *stam*
my name is stam. my name is stam. my name is stam.
25/1/1792 — killed Iona. God ~~forgev fer~~ *forgev me*
2/2/1792 — killed ~~man~~ *a man. God forgev me*
8/2/1792:
a man
a woman
a a a a a
~~forgev~~ *forgive forgive forgive forgive forgive*
~~ples ples ples ples plees plees plees plees~~
~~plees plese plees plees~~ *pleese pleese pleese*
8/2/1792 — killed a man. God pleese forgive me
9/2/1792:
please please please please please please please please
14/2/1792 — killed Aron Ovidiu. God please forgive me.
16/2/1792:
~~wil wil wil~~ *will will will will will will will*
~~tody~~ *today today today today today*
20/2/1792 — today i killed Vasile. i hope God will forgive

me.

27/2/1792 – today i killed a woman. i hope God will forgive me.

3/3/1792:

Today Today Today Today
that that that that that
do do do
not not not do not do not
him him him his his his his
her her her her her

4/3/1792 – Today I killed Catalin Banciu. I hope that God will forgive me.

10/3/1792 – Today I killed Muruna. I hope that God will forgive me.

16/3/1792 – Today I killed Boian Antonescu. I hope that God will forgive me.

23/3/1792 – Today I killed Costin Munteanu. I hope that God will forgive me.

1/3/1793 – Today I killed a woman. I do not know her name. I hope that God will forgive me.

1/3/1793:

~~ded~~ deAd dead dead dead dead dead
sun sun sun sun sun sun light light light
~~scard scard scard~~ scared scared scared
wood wood wood wood wood wood wood wood wood wood
dead dead ~~deadth deth deth deth~~ deAth death death
blood blood blood
~~strem strem strem strem streem streem~~
streAM stream steam
hurts hurts hurts hurts
die die die die die
father Father Father Father Father
bury bury ~~buryd buryed buryed buryed~~ buried buried
alive alive alive alive alive alive alive
unburied

Chapter *11*

"What can you tell me about your friend Ashley?"

A bright light shone in Aurelio's eyes from a desk lamp, eliminating his ability to read the expressions of the two men opposite him. The scene evoked a shocking cliché—something he had seen in at least a dozen crime dramas. The interviewer's voice was gentle, to the point of carrying some condescension, but regardless of the tone, it did little to calm Aurelio's nerves.

Reading his distress, Officer Wilson's voice spoke, "It's okay, son—you're not in trouble, understand?"

Aurelio nodded, unwavering in his apprehension, and unable to really answer the question. "What do you want to know?"

"Anything at all," the interviewer replied. "You'll agree with us that he's a unique character, wouldn't you? We just want to get your take on him and verify some things."

"It's all very standard procedure," Officer Wilson assured him. "You're not going to get him in trouble, either."

"That's right," the interviewer agreed before looking

over a few notes. "So, when did you meet Ashley?"

"It was like, two years ago —"

"What month?"

"Uh, the summer, I guess. Probably June or July?"

"How did you meet him?"

"I was working at the Value-Mart over by Kent Shopping Center."

"But you became friends. When was the first time you saw him outside of work?"

"It was around last Christmas, I think. He came by right when I was getting off early and he gave me a ride home since I didn't have a car back then. I invited them in and we played video games and stuff."

"*Them*? Was his sister there, too?"

Aurelio's nervousness increased again. "Uh, yeah."

"When was the next time you saw them?"

"I usually just saw both of them together during my shift. I usually worked all night and they were always busy during the day."

"You've touched on an interesting point." The interviewer leaned forward in his seat. "Have you ever noticed anything *strange* about that?"

Aurelio shrugged; he hadn't really often thought about it. He was so used to a nocturnal schedule from work and sleeping the days away that it had never posed much of a conflict as far as making any plans together. It had occurred to him maybe once or twice that there was something curious about how Stam and Ashley went about their lives seemingly entirely at night, but he could just about say the same for himself.

"Nothing strange at all?" the interviewer asked. "Have you ever seen Ashley or Stam out during the day?"

"Uh, I guess probably not. Maybe once or twice, but I mean, I'm not really sure."

"Think carefully," he instructed. "Has it ever seemed like maybe Ashley was avoiding something? Or hiding? Like he didn't want to be seen?"

"Not really." Aurelio shrugged. "But he's kind of shy. He keeps to himself."

"Mmhmm." He nodded. "Have you ever noticed

anything else strange — *anything at all* — about him?"

Aurelio was unsure how to answer. "Like... what?"

"Anything."

"Uh, I guess it's kind of weird that he lives alone with no parents, but his parents passed away —"

"Do you know when, precisely, that happened?"

"His mom died just before we met at the store — he's never really talked about his dad."

"So you never met their parents?"

"No."

"How does Ashley survive? Do you know what he does for a living?"

"He said his parents left him money."

"So then, what does he do with all of that free time?"

Aurelio wasn't sure how to answer. "Collects records, I guess."

"You don't think that's weird?"

"Not really. I mean, everybody's different — I wouldn't judge him for —"

"I'm not saying *judge*, Aurelio. What I mean to ask is: do you think there's anything at all wrong in his life? Do you think he's a normal kid?"

"He's a little unusual, I guess, but not in any *bad* ways...."

The interviewer looked at something on the table before changing gears once more. "Was Stam usually around when you two hung out?"

Mention of her name gave him pause again, but he tried not to show it. "Usually — unless she was at work."

"Have you ever seen her without Ashley around?"

He could feel his heart rate increasing. His mind started to race, but he continued to hide it. "Not very much. I mean, a few times, maybe."

"And nothing was different when Ashley wasn't around?"

He felt flushed, unsure what the interviewer may have been getting at.

"Aurelio?" he asked again.

"No," Aurelio said, forcing confidence.

The interviewer seemed to notice the shift. "Are you

sure about that?"

"Like... different *how*?"

"You tell me."

He shrugged helplessly, unable come up with an answer. "I don't know."

The interviewer let out a breath which came close to resembling a sigh, and offered Aurelio some guidance, "What sorts of things do you and Ashley do when you hang out?"

"Uh, we went to Cedar Point after I lost my job." He calmed a bit. "We take walks sometimes, we've been to a few parties—"

"You went to an amusement park?" the interviewer asked. "All three of you?"

"Yeah."

"During the day?"

"No, actually. It was like a late-night thing they had."

"Mm. What about when you and Stam have been alone? What do you do?"

Aurelio swallowed. "Just hang out, I guess."

"Do you ever go anywhere?"

"Not usually—she likes to watch movies most of the time."

"You don't think it's strange that she doesn't act like normal girls?"

"... What do you mean?"

"Well, girls Stam's age are usually interested in, oh, *fashion* and *boys* and hanging out at the mall—normal teenage girl things."

"I dunno—she's just not into that stuff."

"Any idea why?"

Aurelio shrugged helplessly again. It wasn't nearly as strange to him as it was to them, but he wasn't about to say how narrow-minded he thought they were being. "She just isn't."

"So she's just a normal girl to you?"

"Yeah, I guess so," he lied. He hadn't said she was normal.

* * *

8/3/1793 – Today I killed Isabela Ursu. I hope that God will forgive me.
10/3/1793:
Father wants me to write more **doarec** *(?) it is bad to forget things. He said to write about death. There was no noise. I could not see. I was very scared. Father told me it was like being dead. I do not* **înțelege** *(?) dead. You can not stop being dead but I think I did. Father said (asked?) me what* **sa întâmplat** *(?) do not know. Maybe* **cred nimic** *(?)* **doarec** *(?) I was dead but dead is forever. (?) I was wooden (?) and bad. He said I was buried and people I killed. I do not believe (?) I was not dead* **înainte de** *(?) it was a bad thing. It is bad that I am alive. (?)*
14/3/1793 – Today I killed Antonela. I hope that God will forgive me.
22/3/1793 – Today I killed Rozalia Enăsoni. I hope that God will forgive me.
29/3/1793 – Today I killed Olga Pîrcă. I hope that God will forgive me.

There were three obstacles working against Gunther as he sat hunched over a table in a grungy hotel room examining the bizarre journal. First: he had only been able to obtain a Romanian-English dictionary, and however fluent his English had become, it was still his second language. Second: the diction used throughout the journal was antiquated, rife with archaic terms and phrasings. Third—in the early portions, anyway—it was filled with spelling errors and illegible handwriting. Given all those factors, the task of translating the entries was arduous.

He sat back to take a brief break, and glanced to a clock:

6:11 p.m.

He could hardly read it; blocky text swirled about in his head and at this point, letters and numbers all looked alike. He had been holed up in the room all afternoon trying to decipher the first few pages. It became, not unexpectedly, an immediate obsession to uncover just what kind of monstrosity might have lived in the awful little crypt in the midst of those antiquated ruins. It seemed impossible—and yet somehow undoubtedly true—that the journal belonged to the pale-skinned ghoul whom he had so fleetingly glanced while he lay dying in the snow. Gunther hated what he had become, but it had hardly occurred to him to hate the beast itself for what she had done to him. With Jens' death, he had sunk into a wrathful despair kept at bay only by a competing sense of apathy and enduring helplessness. His desire to end everything remained as strong as it had been the night in the morgue over Jens' body, but he had yet to find a way. At the same time, he could feel a rage sufficient that, given the chance, he would destroy—at any cost—the creature that brought this fate upon him.

All he could hope now was that somewhere within the pages of the journal he may find something—anything—to give him guidance.

> *11/6/1793 – Today I killed Stefan. I hope that God will forgive me.*
> *19/6/1793 – Today I killed Petru Cernea. I hope that God will forgive me.*
> *26/6/1793 – Today I killed Lia. I hope that God will forgive me.*
> *28/6/1793:*
> *I have to write about death. It was not like death though. Father said that forgetting is the same as death.* <u>Am fost în</u> *(?) the wood box for many years. (A) year is a long time. I did not think then.* <u>Totul</u> (Everything? All?) *was the same* <u>pintru totdeana</u> (forever?) *but then it was not. There was nothing. It is hard to write about* <u>nimic</u> (anything? nothing?)
> *I do not know many words.*
> *I think there was a sound. Again again again.*
> *I could not talk.*
> *there was sun and it was bad. More bad than wood and the same.*
> *Father says* <u>expirenţă</u> (experience?) *is to live.*
> *Then I was alive.*
> *2/7/1793 – Today I killed Ema. I hope that God will forgive*

me.

9/7/1793 — Today I killed Dorina Mihăilescu. I hope that God will forgive me.

* * *

In front of Aurelio were a half-eaten cheeseburger and a few soggy fries on a waxy fast food wrapper. He had been left alone.

He took a nervous sip from a small soda as he glanced at a clock:

7:48 a.m.

Despite his several naps the day before, the hours he had spent in the room at this point being questioned were beginning to wear on him. He wondered if it really was like all those crime dramas where people found themselves deliriously coerced into confessions after spending forty hours locked up and badgered by police. What could they want from him? They kept making strange inquiries about his friends, and even in offering the complete truth, there was nothing shocking or terrible he could say about Ashley or Stam. They had always been unusual — maybe even strange — but they were who they were, and he liked them. He had never once had reason to think ill of either one.

Was he missing something? He couldn't comprehend what the police might have wanted him to say. It felt like a parent trying to guilt confessions from a naughty child: *"you and I both know what happened."*

... But he didn't know. He had no idea what he was doing here.

The door opened. Officer Wilson stepped into the room with a large cardboard box in hand and plopped it onto the table.

Aurelio's eyes had become fairly adjusted to the bright light in his face, and beyond it, he could see Officer Wilson begin to dig through the box. He at last produced a paper which he sat upon the table between them.

"Did Ashley ever tell you his mother's name?" He made no hesitations in resuming the questioning.

Aurelio furrowed his brow, thought back, and drew a blank. "I don't think so."

"When I first talked to him about his car, he told us his mother's name was Stam; I had forgotten that by the time we learned his sister's name was *also* Stam."

Aurelio nodded, listening.

"There is no record anywhere in this state of anyone named Stam Miller. However, there *is* a cell phone registered under that name, which we found in Ashley's car."

Aurelio nodded again, not sure what he was getting at.

"What there *is,* is *this.*" He pushed the paper toward Aurelio.

He looked it over. It was a legal document: the deed to Ashley's house, he determined as he examined the information. It didn't look that strange to him.

"Right there." Officer Wilson pointed to an early paragraph.

This indenture of sale made on the 13th day of July, 1981, between Edith Tucker, hereinafter known as THE VENDOR (which expression shall include wherever applicable heirs, executors, legal representatives and assigns) and Ashley Miller, hereinafter known as THE PURCHASER...

Aurelio wasn't sure what he was supposed to take away from it.

"And there's this."

He handed another, somewhat less complicated document to Aurelio. This one was a bank statement—from 1982, once again in the name of *Ashley Miller.*

"Okay...?" Aurelio still failed to follow Officer Wilson.

"And this." Officer Wilson removed a much, *much* older, yellowing document from the box. There was a section of it obscured by paper held on by crackled, dry tape. It was an Immigration Certificate dated from 1959, on which the name *Ashley Miller* appeared once more, indicating a move from Aylesbury, England to New York City.

"Read along here, out loud, if you could." Officer Wilson pointed to another section on the certificate.

Aurelio, still confused, did as he was instructed, "Uh, name: Ashley Miller, aged sixteen, color: white, fair complexion, blond hair." He paused before reading the next line. "Color of eyes: blue and red."

Officer Wilson watched Aurelio's face for a reaction. It wasn't a big one; he was a little perplexed, but really, what could he make of what he just read?

"We just spent the last half hour on the phone with U.S. Immigration, and what you've got there is one hundred percent genuine, unlike his bogus driver license."

Aurelio still had no response to offer.

"The evidence points pretty strongly to identity theft, son." Officer Wilson wore a very serious look. "What we want to find out is why somebody Ashley—though that's likely not his real name—why somebody Ashley's age would feel the need to lie about who he is."

Aurelio shook his head, still not ready to really believe it, and murmured, "I don't know...."

"We think this *Ashley Miller* might at least be his relative," Officer Wilson pointed to a corner where the crusted tape had already been peeled up slightly, "take a look under there."

Aurelio again did as he was told and delicately pulled up the edge to expose the covered section of the certificate. There, in faded sepia, in a forty-year-old photograph, was the unmistakable face of his friend.

* * *

The bright light of a camera flashbulb erupted in Gunther's unblinking eyes, forcing him to wince and rub them as he moved away from the backdrop against which he had been posed.

"Thank you very much, Mr. Miller," a woman said as he took a small piece of paper from her and moved onward through a mass of people and outside to a busy seaport. He pocketed the paper and then produced a ticket. As he walked along the wooden piers, paying special attention to his footing, he began to search for where his own ship might be.

In his time since leaving Romania, he had agonized over whether to fulfill his end of Jens' dream and depart for America. With nowhere to go, and the same directionless haze possessing him, running away ultimately seemed the only possibility. Herded with hundreds of others—all families and couples—he found his way to the windowless coach-class cabin where two beds had been reserved. Once alone, he shut his door and sank to the floor—fighting back the latest wave of tears—and waited for the journey to end.

* * *

8/1/1794 — Today I killed Teo Petrescu. I hope that God will forgive me.
15/1/1794 — Today I killed Nic Petrescu. I hope that God will forgive me.
17/1/1794:
The Father wants me to continue writing about death, and also about life. He says my writing before is not very clear. It is hard to be clear about things when they are so confusing. But I will try.
I was in total darkness for a very long time. I do not know how long. The Father said it was at least 80 years, which is a very long time. That is why I forgot things. It was also quiet and there were no sounds at all. The coffin was made of wood and it was very bad and scary but I did not know why. I still do not know why. I felt very sick and very bad. The church and trees and houses and many things are made of wood also and I do not like touching them.
I did not know what days and time were when I was in the coffin. I was there and then I was not.
First there were sounds like scratching and then thumps. Then there was the light of the sun. The sun is very bad and it hurts and is scary. The Father says that the sun does not scare other people.

There was a man and he took me out of the sun. I still did not have thoughts. I did not know what people were. We were in a dark room and he tied me up. He talked to me but I did not know the words. I did not know what words were. Then he touched me. He did it a lot.

The Father says that death is forever. I do not understand forever. I was buried like the dead people, but I was not dead. If I was dead, I would have to be dead forever. But forever cannot end. But I have not been alive very long. The Father said that I was taken out of the coffin in 1778. Then i was out and very sick for 7 years. Then he made me bite a woman and I stopped feeling sick and bad. I got away. Then I bit more people and killed them. All I knew was to stay away from wood and the sun. When the sun came up I would scream and cry. The man dug a hole and made a stone room for me to hide in. When the sun was up he would talk to me so I learned words. Now I know a lot of words but there are still more.

The man said his name was Father Tepes. He said he was sorry about the things he did to me. He told me about God. God is good. God is what makes everything. Even bad things. But there are more good things than bad things. He said when people die they go to Heaven and live forever. So when you die you still live. I asked if this is what happened to me but he said it was not. I do not understand. He said that killing people is very bad. But Heaven is a good place and that is where they go. I do not understand.

23/1/1794 – Today I killed Sanda Grigorescu. I hope that God will forgive me.

29/1/1794 – Today I killed Ramona Bălan. I hope that God will forgive me.

6/2/1794 – Today I killed Silviu. I hope that God will forgive me.

* * *

For days, Gunther had been in bed, painstakingly translating what had been — thus far — the longest of the entries. His technique had improved, as had the diction itself, while the subject matter remained disconcerting and yet strangely resonant. The simplistic descriptions of fear and confusion were just as — and in some ways *more* — articulate than anything he could say about his own feelings at times. He felt a sliver of sympathy for the author of the journal. The horrific list of lives they had extinguished — when weighed against however many he himself had — lost its punch. He flipped through the journal, taking note of how many years were covered, and with some quick math, deduced that inside were at least seven thousand names. *Seven thousand* murders.

It failed to move him.

With each beggar, businessman and drunk that he killed, it had become easier, and with Jens' murder, the last trace of any respect he had for life had disappeared. He knew it was terrible, on some level, but what did that matter? Whoever penned these entries seemed to resent the life they were living for many of the reasons Gunther did his own, but this understanding was the limit of his sympathy; it was hard to say whether or not the author possessed any genuine remorse. They had made the observation that killing was bad, but Gunther was hard-pressed to believe they knew what *bad* was. His hatred remained cemented; if the monster who brought this all upon him was indeed the author of these entries — he still had found no way to forgive.

Flying past one hundred and fifty years, he flipped to the last page of the journal, reading it once more:

1/12/1943 - Azi i-am făcut ceva groaznic unui băiat pe nume Gunther.

His translation produced: *Today I did something terrible to a boy named Gunther.*

It read with the same tepidity as every other line: the same dry, unmoving tone — even after a century and a half. He then began to work through the entry below his name. Within half an hour, he had uncovered the first two sentences:

I have extinguished the light in thousands of eyes, ending lives young and old and taking more than has ever been my right to take. What I am due, I cannot say, but know that God shall grant.

Gunther glanced at the clock:
4:43 a.m.

He rubbed his face and set aside the dictionary, his pen, and the sheets of scrap paper on which his translations were scribbled. Feeling cramped, he stood up from the bed and had to awkwardly avoid the wooden frame as he stretched. The door to his cabin remained unopened for half the week and he had yet to walk the decks above or see the ocean around him. Wearily, he pocketed the journal to keep it safe.

Not unlike the train to Romania, he could hardly recount what had brought him here. Romania itself was already a distant dream; the only way he could prove the delirious trip had occurred at all was the journal stuffed in his coat. That was how everything was now: one disjointed experience hardly leading to another. Each day felt impossibly far from the last, but there he was, adrift at sea.

He found his way to the main deck and over to a railing where he could see a deep-red sliver of moon slipping beneath the horizon. The night sky was indistinguishable from the black water beneath him. In all of its nothingness, it was still beautiful, and all he could think was how he wished he might share it with Jens.

He looked around the deck. It was late—or early, depending—and the only sign of any life was a young couple, arm in arm, staring out to sea.

That was what he should have had. Their romance would need to be kept a bit more obscured, but to simply have Jens by his side would have been beyond bliss.

He took his eyes from the couple; they made him sick. There was a time he would have possessed selfless appreciation for their happiness, but now he could feel only resentment. He had become someone he'd never imagined being; he loathed the both of them. He loathed *everyone*. He was beyond simply feeling pitifully sorry for himself; he wanted everyone to suffer as he had and not blindly live out their lives unaware of what grief *really* was. Did those two, in their stupid, youthful naivety know *anything* about the world they lived in? Did they have any grasp on what happened in Europe only fifteen years earlier? Did they know what Nazis were? Would they care? *Could* they care about anyone or anything that wasn't exactly like them? Could they imagine—for even a moment—what it might be like to be somebody else?

Nobody, Gunther thought, could fathom what it was like to walk the earth, perpetually awake, unable even to blink, slowly forgetting the taste of food and the warmth of the sun, with the only thing more horrifying than the memory of watching your own twin brother die being the realization that that awful memory was disappearing. He had been unable to save Luther, unable to save Jens, and had spent the last decade inflicting death upon the innocent…. Yet to those entwined lovers, his plight meant nothing more than what the suffering of the Romani villagers meant to the Einsatzgruppen.

He took his unsavory disgust with him as he moved down the length of the ship and away from the couple. Before long, he had reached the stern. Down below he could see the choppy wake of the vessel as it propelled him toward a new continent and away from all he had ever known. Second only to the feeling of Jens' embrace, he wished that the journey could take him farther than just the breadth of the ocean—that it could take him infinitely far from the past and when he reached his destination, he would be rid of himself and his life.

He wished, for the thousandth time, death.

* * *

Aurelio blinked harshly as he read the face of the clock:

4:58 p.m.

His hand feebly reached for a cup of coffee which had long since grown cold. He debated whether or not to indulge, not sure if he even wanted any more of it. Gripped with an increasing disorientation, he made no decision, and sat motionless, letting minutes pass — what had seemed like minutes, anyway, until he looked up and saw an unchanged face staring back:

4:58 p.m.

He had been left in the room for at least two hours, and it had been expected of him to somehow rest in the stiff plastic chair. He felt his pulse quicken each time footsteps outside passed by his door, and hoped that they were at last coming to tell him: "*You're free to go. We're done with you now. It was all a big misunderstanding and everything's just fine.*" but after the twentieth time or so, the excitement had faded such that when the door knob turned, he hardly noticed at all.

"Aurelio?" Officer Wilson called to him from the doorway.

"… Yeah?"

Officer Wilson appeared to be on the verge of posing a question, but chose instead to step inside and shut the door behind himself. He approached Aurelio, instead of taking a seat across the table, and knelt down so as to join his eye-level. "Listen to me," he began, with an unusual sense of focused concern elevated beyond his standard state. "If you care about Stam *or* Ashley, I need you to be honest with me…."

Aurelio was unsure what the officer could be getting at this time. He shrugged, helpless but expectant.

Officer Wilson took a deep breath. "Stam just confessed to *murder.*"

Aurelio was taken aback. The seriousness of Officer Wilson's tone juxtaposed against the absurdity of Stam actually hurting *anyone* almost made Aurelio laugh out loud, and he would have, had he not been as uncomfortable as he was. Instead, he managed to squeak out, in a tone of disbelief, "Murder?"

"Of Hannah Knotts," Officer Wilson clarified and waited for it to sink in.

There was such intensity in the officer's face that it seemed he must have whole-heartedly believed the lie or — as was Aurelio's second thought — was completely over-acting. Inside, his mind had grown a bit hyper amid his sleep-deprived haze, and it raced, reflecting on television scenes. Was this the part where the Officer would approach him, candidly offering him a sympathetic ear and the opportunity to help his friends if only he cooperated? Was it the pivotal moment where he would be tricked by the phony confession? He could picture it in a dozen films from every type of policeman: "*Your friends already spilled their guts. You'd better talk now, kid.*"

He didn't know what to say, and Officer Wilson was forced to continue, "Listen, Aurelio — the best thing you can do for your friends is tell me the truth."

He still had no idea what this "truth" was that Officer Wilson kept alluding to, but at last, the man shed some light on the matter, "Stam volunteers at Saint Elia's, as you know, which is where Hannah went to school *and* disappeared from." He reached up onto the table, sliding around the scattered documents they had examined earlier before taking hold of a photograph which he offered to Aurelio. It was Hannah.

"Did you ever meet anyone from Saint Elia's Academy? Anyone that Stam volunteered with or worked for? Any of the students?"

Aurelio shook his head, "I really don't—" and suddenly paused. "Actually, I did meet a lady. She came over one—"

And then it hit him.

He gave the photo a hard look — much harder than he had given to the flyer he received days ago — and his head began to feel light. There *had* been a girl who came by Ashley's house with the woman. It was such an ancillary event, he had thought, and he hadn't paid her any mind, especially with everything else going on that day. And the more he thought about it, could that boy — David — have been... *David?*

"Aurelio?" Officer Wilson asked, detecting his change.

The girl in the picture was nondescript: a dime-a-dozen bleach blonde that couldn't have been bothered to give one look to Aurelio in high school. The kind that would scurry about the Mini-Mart snickering as they worked up the courage to try out their fake IDs on him, and unless he wanted to endure their bitter, scornful disgust, he'd have to pretend to be fooled.

"Aurelio?" Officer Wilson asked again.

What could he say? It may have been her, but what did that matter? It was definitely suspicious, but why was he even thinking about this? Stam didn't *kill* anyone. She was probably locked up in a small room like his, just as scared as him—though she didn't scare easily—and had been coerced into some kind of crazy confession, just like in the movies.

But that, too, didn't seem like Stam.

Aurelio swallowed. "I really don't know."

"Are you *sure?*"

"I just don't know—I really don't think I've seen her before." He indulged Officer Wilson in continuing to study the photo, but he grew more nervous with each moment that he looked at the girl's face.

Officer Wilson sighed and said nothing, waiting to see if his disappointment elicited anything else from Aurelio. When it didn't, he stood up. "Well," he took the photo from Aurelio's hands, "I don't know what we're going to do then, kid…." He took a few steps toward him. "Do you know why she would confess to something like this?"

"No." Aurelio shook his head. It was true: he didn't know.

Officer Wilson thought some more, took a breath, and then turned to speak more directly to him. "Hannah Knotts wasn't murdered. She and David either ran away or were kidnapped—and I'm thinking the former."

Aurelio's eyebrow rose, surprised by him.

"When you think about everything else that's been going on with those two though, Aurelio," he shook his head, "something's not right—an emotionally healthy preteen girl doesn't confess to killing somebody, especially when they didn't. There's no evidence of a murder."

Aurelio took it in. Officer Wilson was on the same page as him, after all. But what did he want, then? He was still looking for Aurelio to expose some dark secret about

Ashley and Stam, and there wasn't one that he could.

Officer Wilson continued to move about, uncomfortably. "Stam said she killed her at the school. She said that she hid the body and we'll never find it." He shook his head. "It's just *horrible* to hear something like that from a child."

Aurelio pictured Stam, in her flat tone, saying those words, cold and dispassionately. Maybe it was how tired he was, but again, it almost made him laugh. It was so ridiculous — but serious too. He knew that you couldn't just *say* things like that to the police. He could see Ashley expressing snide contempt to the officers — maybe some of that had rubbed off on Stam. That was what *really* worried him now.

"Could I see her?"

Officer Wilson furrowed his brow and thought on it. Something was holding him back, but before he replied, a voice crackled through his radio, "Wilson? You there? Has anyone seen that girl?"

His look of perplexity increased, and he popped the radio from his belt and spoke into the transmitter, "She was in the break room." He waited for a response.

"Break room is empty," the voice crackled again. "Anyone else see her?"

Only silence came through on the receiver.

With further concern crossing his brow, Officer Wilson moved to the door and shot out into the hallway. Unsure of what to do, Aurelio remained seated until his own concerns stirred him sufficiently for him to glance up to the clock:

5:22 p.m.

He stood, and then paced around the room. Had they been talking about Stam? What was going on? He wavered for a few minutes more before he made a choice and, with a breath, pulled open the door and stuck his head out into the hallway.

It was empty.

Cautiously, he stepped outside and looked down the way he had been brought in. There was a small sign on the wall pointing to the break room, and with trepidation, he started toward it. He had only taken a few steps before an enraged voice shook him, pulling his attention down another hall.

"What the hell do you mean, you *lost* her?"

"Calm down, just calm dow—"

"Shut up. Just shut up, you fat sack of crap. You think you can just barge into our fucking lives like this?"

The furious voice was familiar. Alarmed, Aurelio rushed toward the scene, only to screech to a stop when a chair came smashing through the window of an interrogation room a few feet before him.

"Ashley, just calm down—right *now*." It was Officer Wilson's voice pleading.

"You lost my sister, asshole. Don't tell me to calm down."

"Ashley, you're really making a big mis—Ashley. *Ashley*. Stop!"

Another chair came flying through the already-shattered window. Terrified, Aurelio hurried ahead to where he could see the struggle. Though Ashley's hands were still cuffed, his violent outburst had been enough to prompt Officer Wilson to ready a small canister of pepper spray.

"All we fucking wanted was to be left alone."

"Ash," Aurelio called out, horrified.

Ashley's eyes caught Aurelio's, and Officer Wilson, too, was surprised and glanced to him. Something flashed in Ashley's expression, but it was unreadable to Aurelio.

"Get the hell out of here," Ashley growled.

"Ash—" Aurelio protested, only to be interrupted by Officer Wilson.

"Son, step away," he instructed him, before pulling out his radio and putting his mouth to it. "Listen, I need some help down here—"

Ashley cut his transmission short by shoving a table, with his foot, toward Officer Wilson, forcing him to dodge. Immediately following, Ashley lunged at him, only to have his shoulders grasped by the officer's hands. Continuing the assault, he began to kick furiously at Officer Wilson's shins and legs, backing him up against the table.

Aurelio called out again, "Ash, stop."

It had no effect. Officer Wilson struggled to shove him away, but Ashley would not relent.

"Ash," Aurelio cried once more, suddenly noticing another officer sprinting down the hallway toward them. "Ash—stop it!"

The officer thrust Aurelio aside, but was unable to enter the room from where the table now blocked the door and was held fast by Officer Wilson and Ashley's weight. Alarmed, the officer drew a taser and called out to Ashley, "Get off him."

He had no reaction, and his violent strikes against Officer Wilson grew in fury.

"Ash," Aurelio shouted again, to no effect as the officer discharged his weapon. In a flash, the electrified probes lodged into Ashley's skin and immediately dropped him to the ground. In less than an instant, heralded by Ashley's horrendous scream, all fell quiet save for the harsh breaths entwined with his convulsing spasms on the floor.

* * *

Minutes had passed while Gunther watched the water churning in the ship's trail. He could only manage another day—two, at best—without blood, and the last thin thread of his compassion and humanity was unwinding; he didn't want to kill a derelict, or a drunk. He wanted to destroy those lovers. He *hated* them.

Was this something that girl thought about as she prowled snowy battlefields in search of the injured? Was there an element of decency that possessed her to seek out those already on the precipice of death?

He removed the journal from his coat and examined the ruddy leather cover. He thought about the people he had killed; there had been hundreds, and within a few years, it might reach the thousands. He couldn't imagine writing their names in such rapid succession. The author of this book, it seemed, lived a life defined only by the death she caused.

On a random page, he took note of a date: 4/8/1861. From there, he skimmed forward, from one year to the next, until 1873, where he encountered a small entry that broke the repetition of murders. In twelve years, the author had nothing to say, made no observation—no account of her own life—and simply killed. Killed, killed, *killed*.

She didn't sleep. There were no days and nights, and age meant nothing. Murder, itself, was her clock.

It was becoming Gunther's, as well. Was his fate that he would simply devolve into nothing more than a slavering, undying beast? He looked at the girl's writing once more: every entry—even the earliest—ended with a plea to God.

Did that help her, somehow? Did it make things easier? How could it? Gunther had already figured God out: he was either a myth or the Devil.

Gunther was thirty-one now—still in the guise of a teenage boy. He would remain that way indefinitely, it seemed, and the journal had only verified the suspicions he had formed long ago: that death might elude him forever. He had expressed that fear to Jens at one time, and somehow, Jens assuaged it. Even as Jens grew older—with his first grey hairs taking root—he convinced Gunther never to worry. Perhaps Jens had a plan. If ever there was somebody who would magically know all the answers, it was him.

They had hypothesized, at some point, about potentially afflicting Jens with the condition so that they might both live forever and so on. Abstractly, it was a romantic idea, but neither deemed it wise, in the end.

He remembered Jens' words: *"There's always a way out...."*

There wasn't now.

If Mengele had been unsuccessful in ending his life, and two bullets to the head had done no better, what *could* kill him? A naïve thought crossed Gunther's mind that he might leap into the ocean and waste away at sea. But he knew, inside, that it would fail. If his translation of the journal had been correct, the girl had written of being in a *wooden coffin for eighty years*....

Naturally, such an interment would kill a man within days—perhaps hours, if there were no air. If he were in that position, he'd flail, in terror, from the wood, but would be met in all six directions by more of the same. Gunther knew—when not directly faced with it—that fearing wood was absurd, and yet as he considered what it would be like to be trapped in such a box, it sent a shiver down his spine. After a few days, he would grow weak, needing blood; that need would continue until he dissolved into the pitiful mess he had been in Mengele's captivity.

Eighty years....

It would be enough, he figured, to strip *anyone* of their humanity. Whatever life she had lived before then might have simply disappeared. Perhaps the girl *was* as simple as he imagined: an unthinking killer failing even after a century and a half of self-reflection to grasp what it really meant to end seven thousand lives.

Her story was sympathetic, but *she* was not.

The same could be said of himself.

Gunther shuddered, reeling in his mind from where it had begun to wander. He could picture the sun, somewhere just beneath the horizon, scattering light into the sky which raced, already, across the ocean and through the clouds to where it could soon descend upon him. With a breath, he worked the journal back into his pocket and took a last look out to the sea before turning away.

To his shock, his eyes met with those of a figure behind him.

… It was her.

The sight was beyond what he could believe. It couldn't be real: he must have finally gone mad.

The girl wore a blank face, and stood motionless, absorbing a sigh that had shaken her.

Neither could speak.

This moment, more than any before, sent Gunther's emotions ablaze. There were no words; it was all beyond grief, fury or terror. She was there—really there—right in front of him. Her meek and frail figure was the vessel of an ageless nightmare. Behind her pale face, hidden by colorless hair, was the wickedest evil.

He remembered her looming above him; he remembered fingers colder than snow caressing his cheeks, the careful way she held him, her tiny nose pressing against his flesh, the pain of her teeth.... And here she was, on the deck of a ship, a thousand miles from any place either had ever known as home. It didn't occur to him to wonder *how* she may have found him or what she might want. She was here, somehow, and it was all he could realize before his thoughts had dissolved as they were now so quick to do.

"Gunther?" Her sweet, wispy voice spoke as though it had not in years.

She was tiny in both height and frame. In one hand she held a thick metal suitcase, unwieldy for a girl so weak and ethereal. He studied her while his mind descended into chaos, recalling a day so long ago in which both life and death were ripped from his hands. He remembered being nothing more than another dead soldier, and in terror, accepting his fate. He remembered Mengele's sinister grin, Luther's delirious pleas, and Jens' disfigured face. He remembered the first man he killed, the second, the third, and each subsequent victim with fading distinction. He remembered, in an instant, his whole unnaturally-lengthened life and all the despair brought to him by what he had become—by what this girl had done. All of that—all of it—was because of this thing standing before him, and before he knew what was happening, he was upon her, immediately forcing her tiny body to the wall. His hands found their way to her throat, grasping with fury beyond his own strength as he slammed her head once, twice, three times, again and again, into the steel behind her.

She could hardly react. Her weak resistance was immediately put down by the force of Gunther's rage, and her painful cries were stunted with each strike. The suitcase dropped from her hand as her skinny arms struggled to cover against his blows.

Gunther had snapped. He had no control at this point. His hands continued bashing anywhere they could with unfocused savagery. He could feel her skull crumble—the cracking of a cheekbone, the shattering of her jaw—as he pounded her face into grotesque distortion. Before long, the two had slumped to the ground, and beneath Gunther's fists he could feel ribs cave and her collarbone snap. Relentlessly, he continued for as long as his muscles would allow, and for minutes, every ounce of his strength poured into his ferocious attack. He may have been screaming—he felt like he must have been—but he wasn't sure. If he *had* been, it had devolved into crying.

With each rise of his clenched fist, the drop began to slow. He had beaten the limp ragdoll beneath him for minutes now, and his hands could do little more than lift and drop into her collapsed chest. He fell forward, into her, bawling against her jagged face, while she lay silent and immobile beneath him.

He couldn't say how long had passed before the girl let out a gurgling croak. Exhausted and drained, Gunther couldn't react as the girl slowly struggled to shift beneath him. She barely looked human now, with her face and torso almost shredded to pieces. Whimpering amid the sound of gasps straining to escape a crushed throat, she still tried to move, but not to fight back. Instead, she was reaching; her trembling arm was crawling toward the metal suitcase which, Gunther observed as he twisted his limp head, was not a suitcase, but a metal ammunition crate not unlike ones he had seen in the war. It was old and rusted, and as he examined it while her fingers crept toward it, he could make out the faded symbol of a tiny Iron Eagle with a Swastika in its claws.

Once she had worked the handle of the case into her feeble grasp, Gunther took hold of her wrist and stopped her hand. She then said something—or tried—to no effect, as Gunther grasped the case. The girl did her best to wrestle it back from him as she continued trying to speak.

What words did escape her bloodied, split lips were Romanian; illegible.

The girl was unable overcome Gunther's strength. Upon ripping the case from her hands, Gunther bashed her face with its bottom once, twice, *three times*, until, with the fourth hit, it slipped from his grip and tumbled from the girls face. It rolled a few feet away, and only stopped as it hit the railing of the ship.

Her gurgling voice pled, *"Ai nevoie – "*

Gunther's attacks continued, silencing her, but his short burst of strength soon depleted for a second time. With a few final weak drops of his unclenching fist, he collapsed against her once more, and this time, rolled off onto his back beside her.

At some point, the journal had fallen from Gunther's pocket and onto the deck nearby. The girl seemed to notice it, but her attention still reverted to the ammunition case. Again her hand, and now her unpinned body, began to creep toward it, but Gunther clutched her hair and pulled her back. She gasped as he restrained her, "Ai nevoie… de asta –"

"Shut up," Gunther screamed, shaking her again.

Still, with what seemed the last of her strength, the girl writhed from Gunther's weakened grip and got one hand – then the other – onto the case. Furious, Gunther shoved his body weight toward her and slammed her battered figure into the railing; it forced the case – along with her twisted forearms – between the bars. She held on desperately, but as Gunther pulled her violently back toward him, the case at last slipped away and dropped down the side of the ship. Horror spread across what was left of the girl's face as she watched it.

"Oh, Dumnezeule… ce ai făcut?" her voice choked. She stared out at the water before Gunther, now on his knees, grabbed onto her bruised shoulders and spun her to face him.

"Ce ai făcut…."

"Shut up. Shut up," Gunther howled, shaking her against the railing before slumping against her in grief. His tear-filled eyes pressed against the girl's shirt, and under his breath, he began to mumble, "Why me...?"

The girl said nothing; her attention was still held by the ocean which had swallowed the heavy metal case.

"... Why *me?*"

His face remained buried against the girl's limp frame and she made no movements until Gunther's grip began to loosen. His hands dropped; there was nothing more he could do. He couldn't kill her, but it was his only impulse: destroy her. *Somehow,* destroy her.

The only sound was that of Gunther's gasping hyperventilation. Finally, the girl brought her eyes back from the sea and looked down at her attacker before, with sudden force, she cast her knee to Gunther's throat, buckling him backward with a hideous gag. Free, she stumbled with her shattered body to the absolute stern of the ship. Her head hung limp from a broken spine as she stared out into the darkness.

Gunther wrestled back his composure, and holding his throat, turned to watch her. She placed a crooked hand onto the railing, and then a foot. Gunther's eyes widened at what she was about to do.

"Stop," he cried, struggling to his feet and lurching toward her.

He was too late.

With only the briefest look back, the girl launched herself head-first into the sea.

"Stop!" He slammed against the railing, only catching sight of her as she disappeared into the foamy wake below. Thoughts racing and panic-stricken, he watched for her as the seconds passed. Still overcome with irrational hatred, he began to climb the railing. She was going to escape; she had been right there in front of him and now she was going to *escape.* He wanted to leap, and yet he found himself held back—not by the near limitless list of reasons he shouldn't cast himself into the middle of the North Atlantic ocean—but because he realized that, upon the sun's rising, he would be unable to hide. He did his best to ignore the fear and force the jump, but could not.

He fought against the invisible restraint for minutes until, still without sight of the girl, he sank back and

dropped to the deck. The event had been beyond surreal—
despite the small splatters of blood on his fists and shirt,
he still debated in his mind whether it had truly occurred.

As suddenly as the girl had appeared—she had gone.

Chapter 12

A set of double doors flew inward as a gurney burst into a bright hospital hallway. Atop it was Ashley, eyes staring vacantly upward with no reaction to any sight around him. On his mouth he wore a respirator. Two paramedics at his side were quickly joined by a doctor.

"Patient is a taser victim—went into cardiac arrest. No luck with the on-board defibrillator."

"White male, late teens; no identification."

The trio shot medical jargon back and forth as they discussed his condition further. They wheeled him toward a small room while Officer Wilson hurried behind, frantic and flushed, only catching a brief glimpse of the gurney as it disappeared.

"Clear," a doctor called out as he placed the thick electrodes of a defibrillator on Ashley's bare chest. He shook as the machine sent a shock through his body, and an EKG monitor blared the high-pitched sound—familiar to anyone—as a marker of death.

"Clear."

Officer Wilson came to a stop outside the room. His face had a few small bruises and bumps—nothing he had yet bothered to address. Nurses swarmed about the pale boy, but Officer Wilson could read their hope fading, and it took only minutes before one of the men shook his head in an obvious sign of defeat. Officer Wilson's eyes widened; he couldn't believe it. The whole thing had transpired so quickly; just minutes ago, Ashley had been upon him, and now... this.

A doctor noticed the injuries and grave look on Officer Wilson's face. "Did you see what happened?"

Officer Wilson could hardly force a reply. The scene just played over and over in his head: after the radio call and Stam's sudden disappearance, he had gone to check with Ashley. The interaction quickly became heated; Ashley seemed to notice right away that something was wrong, and before Officer Wilson knew what was happening, it became violent. The boy had lashed out—furious about his sister—and the other officer had only done what seemed necessary. Of course, it was common knowledge that there were rare instances of tasers being deadly, but it all felt so sudden. One moment, Ashley was there—and now he just lay motionless.

Officer Wilson slid past the doctor—ignoring the question—and into the room. His stomach churned as the doctor reached to silence the cry of the heart monitor and glanced to a clock:

5:56 p.m.

With a sigh, the doctor looked down at Ashley's wide-eyed face.

"Time of death: five fifty six," he said in a somber tone before turning away. Once he had, his eyes met Officer Wilson's. "Can I help you?" he asked, his tone aiming for an appropriate tone.

Officer Wilson only shook his head. His eyes remained on Ashley.

"Officer?" the doctor asked, taking notice of a split lip likely to need stitches.

* * *

Aurelio was sitting at a different table from before, frantically penning a statement about what he had seen. His hand raced—though not as quickly as his worried thoughts—as he tried to finish. There was a crowd of officers milling about; most of them appeared to be doing nothing at all, but now and then a question would find its way to Aurelio.

"Does that boy have any history of violent behavior?"

"… No," he would mumble, trying to push past the distractions.

"What do you think made him assault Officer Wilson like that?"

"I don't know."

"When was the last time he did something like this?"

"He hasn't," Aurelio grumbled, answering the question, rephrased for at least the fourth time.

He dropped the pen and offered his written account of the events to the officer before him as though turning in a test. The officer looked it over, seeming to scrutinize each word.

"Mmhmm." He paused. "Hmm."

Aurelio looked around. Opposite a window into the hall, he could see two men speaking to the officer who had fired the taser. Officer Wilson had hurried to the hospital with Ashley after he failed to recover from the electrical shock.

"Can I get out of here?" Aurelio's timidity was waning after such a long interment and having seen his friend in such a dire state.

"In a minute, in a minute…. What do you mean by this, here?" He pointed to the page. "Can you clarify?"

* * *

Officer Wilson had taken a seat at Ashley's bedside. His face rested in his palms, but the wheels of his mind spun. He felt responsible—like he had somehow just orphaned that poor little girl. The police hadn't yet drawn any conclusions; they had been looking at Ashley as potentially some sort of kidnapper, but was that really what had happened? He and Stam looked nothing alike, but there could be explanations for it—maybe it really was just a small, broken family struggling to get by. Maybe he'd been wrong all along.

"Ashley...." He sighed. "I'm sorry. This shouldn't have happened this way."

There was a sheet across Ashley's face, but Officer Wilson still couldn't erase the image from his head of the boy lying there, dead, yet with a look as alive as he had ever had.

"I know you were upset—maybe you were right to be." He sighed again as he stood up. One of Ashley's thin arms was stuck out from beneath the sheet, and gingerly, Officer Wilson reached out to touch it. "I'm sorry—" he cut himself off, recoiling sharply in shock at how cold to the touch the boy's pale flesh had already become. It was a horrifying chill, and it only served to make him feel worse.

"... I'm sorry, son."

* * *

Had it only been a dream? It seemed impossible that it could have been anything else.

How had she found him?

Gunther agonized for the rest of the journey on the matter. Maybe she had seen the newspaper, and read the sensationalist "Vampire Slay" headline and set out in her search—but could she even read English?

Gunther's tracks had been well-covered. He had never officially emigrated from Germany; his British citizenship coalesced slowly in the disorganized wake of the war. The names *Ashley* and *Gunther* never once crossed paths on any documentation, and yet, somehow, she had found him. Perhaps a decade and a half was sufficient to track *anyone* down.

Had she left in pursuit of him the very first night? His entry, after all, was the last in the...

... the journal!

Gunther shot up from the bed in his cabin. He felt the pocket where it had been — at some point in his blind fury, it had fallen out. The girl disappeared into the water, and he himself had been too weak — too scared — to follow. He had slumped against the ship's railing, deliriously waiting out the night until he knew the sun's arrival to be imminent. Then, careful to avoid the cruise's early-risers, he stumbled to his cabin. He had just left the journal behind.

Urgently, he eyed the clock:

12:11 p.m.

It would be hours before he could head upstairs. He sank against the wall, knowing full well that somebody would have already found the book kicking about on the busy decks above. He could only hope it might be turned in — ideally to somebody who couldn't read Romanian.

With a sigh, he stood up from the bed, looking hopelessly at the pile of translation materials. He had only scribed the first few of the dozen or so entries, and now, he might never see the rest. He felt like a fool. He *was* a fool.

Five days passed, and despite ceaseless pleas to crew and passengers alike and countless searches of the small section of the stern, the journal was gone. The one hint he had — the one account of an experience like his — was no more.

He thought about why he had gone to Romania to begin with. He had been so hopeless with loss that it seemed the only thing he could do. It was a far less than conscious choice, and he still was unsure what he had hoped to discover. Perhaps he wanted to find the girl or even a whole secret society of people like himself. It had been a fruitless endeavor, regardless, and now was even more so. He had no idea why he attacked her, when he could have tried speaking, and he didn't even know why he was going to America.

He couldn't account any longer for his actions; nothing he did seemed as though it contained purpose or reason. It was just like his other afflictions: he couldn't say *why* the sun terrified him, or wood, or the gentle flow of a stream. He couldn't say why he did the things he did or why he felt what he felt, and little of it, anymore, seemed to exist in any semblance of harmony with his own desire to simply — quietly — disappear.

Those thoughts followed him through the afternoon and into the evening, through the United States' border and through their customs and a brief physical inspection. It stayed with him along a short ferry ride, and several blocks of aimless walking through a dense city he had never possessed any personal desire to see. It had been Jens' dream to come here, and it was Gunther's dream to simply follow him.

He came to a stop on a street corner that reminded him of so many from London. New York City, it seemed, had a similar personality: it was grimy and dirty, with trash piled in great mountains stretching endlessly in every direction. Flickering neon signs seemed as though they had been designed with the flaw in mind; rats appeared as comfortable on the sidewalk as anywhere else; there seemed to always be a wailing siren in the distance, and what few *human* creatures he had seen about made the whores and drunks of London's Soho look aristocratic. He couldn't imagine anything happening *anywhere* in the neighborhood without a taint of criminality to it. It wasn't too far from what he had expected, but the seedy underbelly of the inner city had no appeal without Jens there to see it.

"Hey boy," a raspy voice hissed. "You got a cigarette?"

Gunther made no effort to reply — not even with a look — to whoever had asked. Instead, he wandered up the street to take in the sights. Now and then he would be eyed with suspicion or — though he couldn't be sure — flagged down by figures in the shadows. At one point, his eyes passed over a wraith of a woman standing in a doorway, wearing high stiletto heels and a red bandana tied about her neck.

Idly, his hand reached into a pocket to produce the

name and address of Agnes Müller—Jens' aunt. He wasn't
sure there was any real reason to find her. What would he
tell her? All he could say was that he was a friend of her
nephew's and that, oh—by the way—her nephew was
dead. Gunther would likely be nothing but an unpleasant
nuisance to her. It wasn't as though he'd ask for anything,
but he'd still be an unexpected guest, and Gunther himself
never cared for those.

As he walked, he soon came upon a song; Gunther
winced in response to lyrics he had once heard from an
album in Jens' collection. It was coming from a radio
seated on a chair outside a small record store. This version
was newer, with a piano in the background and a voice
that, while he did recognize, he couldn't pin down. The
singer sang of the sun and its lucky lot in life—it had
nothing to do, after all, but roll about Heaven all day.

He had done his best to avoid contemporary music,
but tried even harder to stay away from those old songs of
Jens'; they did nothing to soothe him and merely
reminded him of what he no longer had.

Jens once made the observation about pop music,
"Doesn't it sound like they're singing about you, sometimes?"

Gunther's reply was that popular music was
supposed to be accessible, so it probably sounded that
way to most people.

"No, no," Jens had replied. *"I mean about* you. *There are
all these songs about dreaming and closing your eyes and the
sun in the sky and lonely nights and dying. It's sort of...
strange."*

"Wouldn't that mean they're singing explicitly not
about me? Mocking me, perhaps?" Gunther laughed.

*"Well, a song doesn't necessarily need to be about you to
be... about you. It's not like Bing Crosby singing about
wrapping troubles in dreams had much, specifically, to do with
growing up in Nazi Germany."*

In stopping to think, he had waited out the remainder
of the song. As it drew to a close, a small girl—maybe
seven years old—who had stopped beside Gunther shot
him a bashful grin as she reached down to pick up the
radio. She waited with him until the final beat, at which

point, sheepishly, she unplugged and coiled the cord before hurrying back inside.

After another minute or so, once his mind had wandered back from where it had gone, Gunther departed. His thoughts remained on Jens; in some slight way, the song had brought him back to one of those nights together. For a fleeting moment, he could remember — more vividly than ever — the feeling in the air when Jens was beside him while a record played in the living room.

It wasn't particularly far to Agnes Müller's, and within the hour, he found himself staring down a tall, dark building. It was old — like everything else in lower Manhattan — and most of the windows were boarded up. It looked more or less abandoned. He confirmed the address with the paper, looking back and forth between the two several times. He supposed, though, it wasn't beyond the realm of possibility that he had written the address incorrectly in the first place.

Hesitantly, he picked up a loose brick he found on the stoop, and entered into a dank hallway lit only by a single, dim bulb shining down from the second floor.

Gunther checked the apartment number — it was 3A — and he moved down the hall in search of it, past two other units, until he found it tucked away at the very back of the building. He stood there at the door as several minutes passed. With the brick still in hand, he felt reluctant to reach out and knock. Had he come all this way — thousands of miles and several decades — only to come right back to the past? It seemed more likely he would find things that haunted him than anything else, and yet, with a deep breath and little in the way of intentions, he rapped on the door.

Nothing.

He tried again. Still nothing.

With one final try, and its apparent failure, he turned away, defeated until a voice called out from inside, *"Whaddya want?"*

Gunther swallowed. It had been a man's voice that called out.

"Uh—I was looking for Frau Müller."

There was silence again for a minute, but the door creaked open. From behind it, two eyes peered with suspicion up at Gunther.

"Who are you?" the eyes asked as they evaluated him.

"My name is Ashley. I'm a friend of Sy—er, Jens'."

The eyes narrowed as they continued to size him up.

"Who is it?" a woman's voice called from inside the room.

"Some kid." The eyes glanced away toward the other voice. "Says he's Jens' friend."

The eyes disappeared as somebody else approached the door. This time it was a woman. "Oh, really?"

"Frau Müller?" Gunther asked.

"Yes? Who's asking?"

"Well, you don't know me. I'm a friend of Jens'—"

"Yes, yes." She seemed oddly pleased—unlike the man had been. "What can I do for you?"

He wasn't sure what he had really wanted from her. "I, uh—well, what I mean is…."

"He's just some bum," the man's voice hissed before the door began to shove shut.

"Wait," Gunther cried, sticking his foot in between the door and the wooden frame. His shoe was all that protected him from its touch. "Do you, uh," his mind worked quickly, and his mouth blurted out the first thing it could think of, "do you have a photo of Jens anywhere?"

The woman looked at him with increasing skepticism. "What?"

"A photograph—do you have one of him?"

She shook her head. "What for?"

"*Mutter,*" the earlier eyes, which were now only a voice, commanded quietly, "*sprechen Sie nicht mit diesem Wahnsinnigen.*"

After prolonged disuse, Gunther's German had grown a bit rusty, but he could tell what was being said, and replied, "*Manfred, Ich möchte Ihnen nicht zur Last fallen.*"

He could detect hesitation at first, but the eyes

replied, *"Ach ja? Warum schwinden Sie dann nicht von hier?"*

Gunther quickly cobbled together another lie, expanding on what he had already asked. "The American INS won't let him in without one. A photo is all I'm asking for."

There was hesitation once more, and the door slammed shut. Gunther heard chains unlatching and a voice protesting, *"Mutter — Mutter! Lass ihn nicht rein — stopp!"*

The door swung inward, and Gunther could now, much more clearly, make out the two occupants of the apartment. Frau Müller was a squat woman, short and wide; she was in her mid-fifties, though she had aged well from Gunther's *very* distant memories of her. They had met maybe once or twice, and he was certain she'd have no recollection of him at all.

Her son, Manfred, did not look as well. He was Jens' age — somewhere in his early thirties — but the right side of his face and neck had severe scarring. He watched Gunther from a seat in a wheelchair, which he was bound to due to having no legs below his mid-thighs. He bore little resemblance any longer to the boy Gunther had met on a few occasions as a child.

"You say Jens is stuck at immigration?" Frau Müller asked.

"Yeah—" Gunther began to reply.

"That's ridiculous," Manfred spat. "Mum, if they need a picture of Jens, they'll need a *recent* picture of Jens."

"I'll take any photo you have." Gunther stuck to the lie. "I don't know what they need it for."

If Frau Müller had any suspicions of her own, she neglected them as she produced a small photo album from underneath a coffee table. "I might have a photo from when he was just a boy...."

"Mum," Manfred cried again, before grabbing a baseball bat leaning by the door. "He's got a fuckin' brick." He started to swing the bat at Gunther, who tossed the brick away as he jumped back to evade the attack.

"Manfred—" Gunther began.

"How do you even know my name?" Manfred

growled.

"I told you — I'm a friend of your cousin's. He's talked about you."

"I ain't seen that faggot in twenty years," Manfred barked, gesturing angrily with the bat.

"So what?" Gunther shrugged, now backed against the wall opposite the apartment's door. Manfred had placed himself square in the entrance.

"So what's he's doin' talking about me?"

"I don't know." Gunther shrugged. "You're his cousin — he's mentioned you."

"Hey," a fourth voice now inserted itself into the conversation — it came from down the hallway outside the apartment, from a gaunt man with a heavy Ukrainian accent. "Shut up with the fucking noise." He then noticed the bat in Manfred's hand. "There some kind of problem here?"

Gunther glanced to Manfred, who growled, "Damn right there's a problem. This fucking guy just — "

"There's no problem, Mr. Pavlenko," Frau Müller called, sticking her head out from inside the apartment and nodding to the man. "Manfred," she took hold of his wheelchair, "you come in here this instant."

The man had approached and was standing by the door. He took a quick look into the apartment before turning to examine Gunther. "Who are you?"

"What's it matter?" Gunther replied, antagonistically.

"Ashley," Frau Müller interrupted. "Why don't you come in for a bit?"

Surprised, Gunther accepted the invitation, but in his attempt to push past Mr. Pavlenko, he was blocked. "You listen to me," the man snarled. "You fuck around in here: I fuck you up — understand?"

Gunther responded with a raised eyebrow and a tone lacking in sincerity, "Sure," before stepping past the man and into the apartment.

Frau Müller took hold of the doorframe and smiled at the man. "I'm sorry about the noise, Mr. Pavlenko."

With a grumble, the man shook his head and angrily marched away, back down the hallway. With him gone,

Frau Müller shut the door and set to work latching an elaborate series of locks while Gunther stood awkwardly, a few feet behind her, with the baseball-bat-armed Manfred still staring him down.

"So you're a friend of Jens' from Britain?" Frau Müller asked, finishing with the door and moving back to the photo album she had retrieved.

"Yes, ma'am." Gunther nodded.

"Is he still there?"

"Yeah." He struggled to keep his lie—which was already painful—as cohesive as possible. "He was held up at immigration by the British. I think it has something to do with his German citizenship."

"Of course," Manfred interjected. "The kid's a fucking Nazi *and* a faggot—they ought to string him up with the rest."

"Manfred." Frau Müller was shocked. "Your language."

Gunther shifted uncomfortably, trying to divert the conversation. "Did you have any photos?"

"Not in this one," she replied, sitting the first album aside as she reached for another. "We didn't have a camera back then. Times were tough—that's why we came to America in the first place...."

"We came to America because fuckin' Hindenburg gave Germany to Adolf Hitler," Manfred grumbled; his displeasure with the whole present situation was still palpable as he kept his eyes on Gunther.

"Manfred, please, honey...." She looked over to him. "Nobody wants to ta—"

"It's because of people like Jens that people like *me* had to go fight an' lose their goddamn legs," Manfred rambled. "The Nips and the Krauts both—"

"Aren't *you* a Kraut?" Gunther challenged him.

"Please—" Frau Müller tried to interject.

"I'm no fucking *Kraut*." Manfred swung the bat again, though he was too far to actually make contact with Gunther. "I'm pure one-hundred-percent American." His hand fumbled into a shirt pocket. "You see this?" He produced a small medal. "I lost my legs fightin' the Nips over Tarawa."

Gunther nodded. "I'm sorry—you're right—"

He tried to apologize, but Manfred continued, "You limeys don't have a clue. How old are you? Sixteen?" He eyed Gunther with tremendous suspicion and judgment. "Your buddy Jens was in the *Hitlerjugend*—you even know what that was?"

"Yes, sir." Gunther nodded, forcing himself to be polite.

"Manfred, honey—"

Gunther interrupted Frau Müller to continue, "*Everyone* was in the Hitler Youth."

"That's right," Manfred spat before folding his arms angrily. He seemed somehow content with this resolution to the argument.

"I think this is one," Frau Müller called out as she pulled a photo from under a plastic sheet. "Isn't that him, there?"

Gunther hurried over. He hadn't seen Jens' face in months, and... it wasn't him.

"I don't think so." Gunther half-heartedly studied it, not wanting to be rude. The photo was of a few very young children in front of a house from their hometown, but there was nobody that he remembered.

"Oh, darn," she replied, sticking the photo back into the album. "I thought for sure he was in here somewhere." She offered the album to Gunther. "Why don't you take a look?"

He took it and sat down beside Frau Müller on a murky green couch. He examined his surroundings; the room was very dark, lit only by a floor lamp in the corner, and the only window was tinted and buried beneath plants. The décor, in general, had not been addressed or updated in any way since the late '40s. The condition of the room suggested that the present times were not being very kind to the mother-son pair.

Gunther wearily began searching through the album. Inside, there were indeed memories: a few of the houses from his youth were visible, and he couldn't quite be sure—having not seen him in almost twenty years—but

there was a man who may very well have been his own
father in one of the pictures. There was one of Frau Müller
with her sister — Jens' mother — and another toward the
very end of the Fischers: his Jewish neighbors that had one
day vanished.

While he paged through the album, Frau Müller
climbed to her feet and put a hand on Manfred's shoulder.
She watched Gunther for a bit, and before too long, asked,
"Do you have somewhere to stay?"

Manfred interjected, "Mum, no —"

"I have a hotel room downtown," Gunther lied, eyes
not leaving the album.

"Jens sent a telegram, oh — it must have been back in
February or March — and said he'd be moving here
sometime in the summer. We talked to Mr. Pavlenko
about him renting a room here in the building — the space
next door is still open, I think."

"Well, I appreciate the idea." He clasped the photo
album shut, unsuccessful in his search. "I'm sure I'll find
something."

"I haven't heard from Jens since then," Frau Müller
observed. "Did he say when he would be coming?"

Gunther was quiet. His composure was wavering,
but managed to hold as he replied, "Well — I guess it's all
just immigration trouble...."

"So ridiculous," Frau Müller grumbled. "If a grown
man wants to move to another country, he should be
allowed."

Gunther looked over to Manfred, expecting him to
protest this, but he seemed to be preoccupied with angrily
murmuring to himself.

Gunther climbed to his feet. "I suppose I should go."

"Already?" Frau Müller seemed genuinely
disheartened. "Are you sure you wouldn't like to stay for
supper?"

This started Manfred up again. "We can't afford food
as it is, mum —"

"Manfred —" she began.

"It's fine," Gunther interrupted both of them. "I'm
really not hungry either way." He approached the door

and placed his hand on the knob.

"Please tell Jens," Frau Müller called to Gunther, "that we'd like to hear from him."

Gunther was quiet as he pulled the door open. "I will." He glanced to the two of them; Frau Müller's fragility was an unnerving compliment to Manfred's scowling face and the bat in his hands. "Take care."

As he set out into the hall, he suspected that it would be in the best interest of his own sanity to never see either of them again, but as he passed by the next apartment— 2A—he noticed that the door was opened and Mr. Pavlenko was moving a few boxes around. What Frau Müller had said struck him now, as he realized that this could have been his home with Jens had things not gone as they did. Gunther knew that Jens had been in touch with her, and it would only have made sense that they move in next door, at least for a while.

"What you looking at?" Mr. Pavlenko snarled at Gunther, whose eyes remained focused on the dingy room.

He studied it a bit longer, noticing that there were no windows, and in the swift, irresponsible manner with which he made all decisions anymore asked, "How much for this place?"

* * *

Officer Wilson gently touched his cheek where a nurse had just finished applying a bandage. She offered a hand mirror in which he examined his face; embroidered into it were some fresh stitches by his mouth.

He nodded, "Thanks," and offered it back.

His guilt about Ashley continued to eat away at him—the whole thing was so cruel and terrible. He struggled to think what he would tell the boy's sister when she turned up. She was clearly already disturbed; she had confessed to a murder that couldn't have possibly occurred. There simply wasn't any evidence to support it. Her confession stemmed only from stress—or perhaps irritation — which was what her tone conveyed when she spat out the lie: *"I killed Hannah Knotts."*

They'd have to tell her *something*, though.

Officer Wilson stopped at a door. It had been closed, though the lights remained on. On the opposite side, Ashley lay in bed, lifeless. Even if his wildest, most unspeakable suspicions about the boy had been true, he couldn't believe that this was the way things should be; he was dead because of the search for some missing teenagers, and as much as his imagination once let him think it — and as weird as the kid had been — it seemed less likely than ever that Ashley had played the slightest role. Through the window he could see a doctor who periodically checked beneath the sheet and spoke to a nurse who, clipboard in hand, took notes on his dictation. He wasn't sure why he felt the urge to enter once more, but hesitantly, he pushed the door open and knocked as he stepped inside.

"Yes?" The doctor looked up.

Officer Wilson didn't know precisely what to say. In some odd manner, he felt like Ashley had somehow become his responsibility; the boy had no parents, after all.

"Officer Wilson, right?" The doctor approached, offering his hand. Wearily, Officer Wilson took it, indulging in the shake.

"I'm Doctor Dawson. Pleasure to meet you."

Officer Wilson could feign little interest in exchanging formalities. His hand fell, lazily, as soon as the doctor's powerful, professionally-rehearsed grip loosened. Officer Wilson kept his attention focused on Ashley, struck once again by what had transpired.

"He was someone you knew?" Doctor Dawson asked when he noticed the officer's mournful expression.

"Not well," he answered, in time.

Doctor Dawson chose not to press the matter, and left Officer Wilson to be alone while he himself went back to his work. He peered beneath the sheet on Ashley and, after making a quick observation, glanced to the nurse. "Give us a second."

She obliged and left the room, but only after shooting

back a flirtatious glance to which the doctor smirked in reply. The doctor watched Officer Wilson for a minute or so before speaking again, "Does he have any family here?"

Officer Wilson shook his head, irritated with the questions. "No."

"Doctor Dawson?" Another young nurse poked her head into the room. As she noticed Officer Wilson, she hesitated. "Oh, I'm sorry to bother you —"

"It's fine." The doctor headed to the door and politely walked out with her onto the other side of the window.

Officer Wilson took a final look at the sheet and the boy beneath. He could think of nothing more to say than he already had, and offered the same sentiment he had before, "I'm sorry."

"*Me too.*"

Officer Wilson froze, shocked speechless by the voice. Ashley's limp arm reached up, pulling the blanket away and exposing his face which, though still filled with its normal, lifeless pallor, wore a small smile. His eyes which quickly sought out Officer Wilson's — they were an easy target at the moment.

"H — h — how...?" Officer Wilson stammered, stumbling back and knocking into a small table.

"I'm sorry," Ashley replied quietly, looking ashamed. "About this little charade, in part, but also about some of the things I said...."

Officer Wilson still had not recovered and was unable to utter a word as he watched.

"I haven't really been fair to you." Ashley shrugged. "So, I'm sorry."

Officer Wilson shook his head in disbelief; he had regained enough composure to be irritated with Ashley. He already knew that the boy hadn't been unconscious at any point and had acted out this whole thing.

"Look, Officer," Ashley began. "The more I think about it —"

"Oh my God!" Doctor Dawson stood paralyzed in the doorway with a third nurse at his side.

"You were just doing your job — who am I to criticize it, really?" Ashley looked over to Doctor Dawson, but his words continued to be for Officer Wilson. "If I thought *you* were bad, just think how I'm going to feel about *this* idiot."

Doctor Dawson didn't seem to notice the jab. He, like Officer Wilson, was still reeling from the resurrection. It took him time to find enough clarity to turn to the nurse. "Go fetch his charts."

Ashley adjusted himself and sat up. He eyed Doctor Dawson, who had moved to the side of the bed, pager in hand, typing something frantically.

"How are you feeling?" the doctor asked, looking up from the device.

"Okay, I suppose," Ashley replied unenthusiastically.

He glanced back to Officer Wilson, who swallowed, murmuring, "You're a real fucking bastard."

"Yeah, that's fair—" Ashley swatted at Doctor Dawson's hands, annoyed as they brought a stethoscope to his chest. "*Excuse* me."

"You were pronounced dead almost an hour ago. I just want—"

Ashley ignored him and turned back to Officer Wilson. "I should have handled all of this better. I've been a bit stressed out lately...."

"You were faking," Officer Wilson grumbled, "that *whole* time?"

Doctor Dawson interjected, "You can't fake cardiac arrest—"

"I was," Ashley replied, cutting him off. "I'm sorry."

"Why?" Officer Wilson growled, not hiding his anger.

"Honestly? I... just wanted some time to myself. Some time to make some decisions."

Officer Wilson shook his head. "You're really fucking crazy, you know that?"

Doctor Dawson's beeper sounded, prompting him to check it. Whatever he read seemed to frustrate him. "Dammit." He looked over to where the nurse was had just returned with a clipboard that he quickly snatched and began examining.

"Again, that's fair." Ashley sighed. "I probably am."

"Ashley—is that British?"

"Sure."

"Well, Ashley, it says your heart stopped at five thirty-one—"

"I'm sure it says all sorts of things."

"May I please examine you? I'll be quick."

"Why don't you go get me something to eat?" Ashley asked, shooting him an agitated look.

Doctor Dawson hesitated. "Of course—what would you like?"

"Fruit."

He smiled, "Sure," and turned to the nurse. "Could you bring some up?"

As she departed the room, Ashley turned back to Officer Wilson, who was still scowling with disapproval.

"Any sign of Stam?" Ashley asked.

Officer Wilson was fighting a dozen urges to storm out of the room while taking back every apology and reconsideration, but as he continued to think about it, what he had thought before was still likely true. Now, at least, he could get the answers, and nothing—not even Ashley's contempt—would stop him. "No," he replied.

"She'll turn up." Ashley sighed before examining Officer Wilson's bruised face. "I really am sorry—I hope I didn't hurt you too badly."

"I'm fine." His response was terse. Ashley's reaction to Stam's disappearance really *was* an act. All that proved, though, was that the kid was an asshole and still knew *something*—some secret—of which he was reveling in his possession. "Do you know where your sister would have gone?"

"She's not really my sister," he replied calmly, staring at the ceiling above. "Just an old friend—well, no, *friend* isn't the right word...."

Officer Wilson sighed, knowing that the boy again was starting a convoluted riddle. The tone carried enough weight to silence Ashley. "Dammit, Ashley," he growled. "I don't care—I just don't care anymore." He approached him, threateningly. "Just tell me where she would have gone."

Ashley was quiet. His eyes remained on the ceiling as

he formed his thoughts, but a sudden distraction came in the form of the nurse's return. She had two small fruit cups, one of which she offered to Ashley. He took it, graciously, "Thank you," and then watched Doctor Dawson examine what couldn't possibly be a very informative medical chart.

At some point, the doctor's eyes lifted—just for a split second—to the nurse's behind as she bent over to dig in the bottom drawer of a nearby cabinet for a spoon.

Ashley had made an unforgiving assessment of Doctor Dawson quite quickly when it had just been him, under the sheet, with the doctor and a nurse in the room. He didn't like doctors.

The nurse handed a plastic spoon to Ashley.

"Thanks."

"Ashley?" Officer Wilson's agitation was still showing as he pushed for an answer.

Ashley fiddled with the fruit cup in his hand. "I don't know."

Officer Wilson laughed, disgusted. "You really are something." He stood up angrily. "Just when I want to feel bad for you, you just keep pulling the same bullshit. You *do* know; you know *everything*, don't you?"

Ashley was quiet.

"What do you *want?*" Officer Wilson demanded.

"… I want to be left alone. I want to go home."

Doctor Dawson interjected, "Well Ashley, you just recovered from a very serious condition. I think it would be in all our best interests for you to stay here, at least through the night—"

"At this rate, the only place you're going is back to the station." Officer Wilson pointed to the bandage on his face.

Ashley sighed, looking over the fruit cup yet again for nearly a minute before thinking of something. "Officer Wilson—how many days ago did Hannah and David go missing?"

He didn't bother looking at Ashley. "… About six days now."

"That's it?" He was disheartened. The last few days

had crawled. "I suppose it makes no difference, but, I really am sorry."

"Ashley," Officer Wilson's started to shout, "If you were *sorry*, you'd tell me the truth. If you were *sorry*, you'd stop being such a weird little jerk. You'd let the fucking doctor do his job and check you out. You'd *answer* me."

Ashley winced a bit, partially from the volume, but also as a gut reaction to the thought of a doctor poking and prodding him. He glanced to Doctor Dawson, who in one hand held a stethoscope he wanted desperately to use. In time, Ashley looked back to Officer Wilson, and with a voice—quiet and submissive—asked, "So, I've got two choices then. Go with you, or..." he shot a glance to Doctor Dawson, "... with him?"

Officer Wilson shook his head. "Ashley, if you could just stop your stupid act for just two seconds—" he cut himself off, and began to storm away. He'd had enough, but stopped himself as he reached the doorway.

He had an idea.

With a deep breath, he turned to Ashley. "Okay." He took a few steps back toward the bed. "How about this...."

Both Ashley and the doctor listened.

"You stay here, get yourself checked out, *talk* to the doctors—none of this crazy bullshit—and I'll make you a deal."

"What's that?"

"I *was* unfair to you—not as unfair as you seem to think, but maybe I could have done things differently."

Ashley waited for him to make his point.

"So you stay here, get yourself looked at, and we'll forget about this whole assault thing."

A look of some skepticism crossed Ashley's face. "What do you mean?"

"You know what's going to happen if you leave here now? You're going to be arrested, held for another twenty-four hours, arraigned, then indicted, for the assault of a police officer—a bit heavier than that obstruction charge—and Ashley," he paused, "you're gonna go to jail."

Ashley's skepticism remained. He had already known what Officer Wilson explained; he knew that there was no quick or easy way out of this situation. He had been exploring the more violent solutions for quite a while, but he wanted to believe that *somehow* there was still a way to end it all peacefully. Returning home was a lost cause at this point; the peaceful anonymity of nearly two decades was over, but what would happen next—and how smooth a transition it would be—would depend on what happened now.

"Stam will turn up." Ashley repeated from before as he sighed and pulled the sheets down to expose his chest for Doctor Dawson. "She always does."

* * *

Aurelio stepped into his house. He could feel something odd in the air. Things were changing far more rapidly than he desired; maybe it was just the events in the police station, but for the first time—as he looked around—Ashley's suggestion that he move away and pursue his silly dreams seemed more reasonable—more *necessary*—than ever. It shocked him that he was still here, in the town of his birth, feeling in no way at home.

Maybe it *was* the stress of the day's events, or maybe he was just getting old, or maybe it was that his two best friends—his only friends—were in a terrible mess, but the strange feeling stayed with him as he moved through the living room and into a tiny kitchen. He saw a photograph of himself, Stam and Ashley together on the fridge—it was the one he had taken the night they heard about Ashley's car. He hadn't paid much mind to the look on Ashley's face previously, but it caught his attention now: his eyes betrayed a terrible weariness—an overwhelming sense of burden and stress without merit even after the disappearance of his car and the unexpected guests from Saint Elia's.

Aurelio sighed as he stripped off his shoes and socks. Growing up he had, with regularity, faced some—from subtle to severe—element of disapproval for who he was and what he wanted from life. Ashley, he could tell, knew something of that feeling too. Ashley had always been calm and reserved, seemingly content to spend his teen years not unlike how Aurelio imagined an elderly man might languish in old age, with his heart trapped in another place and time.

Aurelio knew his friends were strange, but he himself had always been too; his interests seldom meshed with those of the majority, and it didn't help that he was one of maybe three or four Hispanic students in his high school. There was never a niche for him to fit in to; even in the handful of theatre acting programs he had been involved with, he was hard-pressed to find any friends. Ashley and Stam were similar; he was relatively sure that Ashley didn't even have any other friends, and regardless of how beautiful Stam was, it had come as a tremendous shock that a boy had asked her to a school dance.

Ashley and Stam were hardly troubled by their private lives and seemed at peace with their reclusion, but Aurelio himself had always sort of longed for more company. Once—and he realized as the words fell from his mouth that it was unbelievably awkward—he had pointed out to Stam that she was the first girl he'd ever had in his bed. It was just one of many awkward remarks he'd made to her, he thought, as he considered his earlier confession. Every time he thought about it, he felt light-headed. He was almost twenty but he knew he had feelings for a girl who was only barely a teenager. She must think of him as a creep.

He stopped. Even that brief consideration made him ill with embarrassment. He could only imagine what people would think of him if they knew of his desires. But then there was Ashley; Ashley had somehow figured it out, despite Aurelio's attempts to hide it, and even more strangely, had been accepting—even encouraging—of him. It didn't seem right that he should.

He was unclear on much of Ashley's past, even catching little contradictions and oddities in what he had heard, but he never pried, since to him, Ashley—and Stam—were simply who they were, needing no explanation. He knew Ashley felt the same about him. It wasn't disinterest: it was *acceptance*, one of life's great rarities.

He shook his head, wrestling himself away from his wandering concerns. There were other things to worry about right now: Stam was missing somewhere and Ashley was in the hospital. It was ridiculous. How this had all happened still mystified him.

One of the last things Officer Wilson had said was that Ashley may have been committing identity theft, which was absurd. Still, something had been eating at Ashley in the last few weeks — Aurelio could tell — and it had now culminated in his assaulting a police officer. It was a bad situation.

He departed the kitchen, heading for the bedroom, when a knock echoed from the front door.

"Really?" His nerves tensed. He wondered if the police had decided there was reason to come for him after all, but tried to calm himself, knowing they probably just had more odd questions about Ashley.

"Don't they know what a telephone is?" he murmured to himself as he pulled the door inward, revealing Stam.

"Hello," she greeted him.

"Stam?" His surprise was apparent. "Where have you been?"

"The house," she replied. "May I come in?" she asked — not as an idle courtesy, as it often appeared to Aurelio — but as if, this time, there was a chance he might deny her.

"Of course." He checked outside as though the police may be right behind. Stam remained quiet as Aurelio, satisfied they were safe, shut the door and turned to her. In her silence, it became Aurelio's burden to speak first. "You're okay?"

Typically, a question such as that would be met with an assertive one-word affirmation of her unfazed condition, but this time, there was unusual reservation in her reply.

"Aurelio." She spoke softly, without looking in his direction, as she adjusted the metal case in her arms.

"… Yeah?" he asked. For the first time he could recall,

Stam seemed to be having difficulty — perhaps even trepidation — about saying what she wanted to say. It was a strange moment, and in the silence before her words, he let his imagination take a frightened flight.

"Are you afraid of me?" she at last asked.

It wasn't what he was expecting in the least.

"What?" He looked at her, totally perplexed, and his tone made clear his bafflement. "*No*."

She reassessed her words. "Perhaps that's not the best way to put it. Are you afraid of how you feel about me?"

If ever there had been something that made his blood run cold, it was *that* comment. He did is best to feign innocence. "W-what do you mean?"

"It is a fault of mine that I can be so terse — but right now, I don't know what is going to happen, and I may not have another chance."

Aurelio couldn't tell what she meant by all of that.

She continued, "I've tried hard for a long time to understand how and why people feel about others the way they do, because I don't often see things the way everyone else does."

Aurelio swallowed, and not sure if it was the right thing to say, replied, "That's what's always made you special — to me, anyway."

"Is that what it is?"

He chuckled, feeling slightly more at ease in reaction to the very Stam-like comment. "It's more than *that*," he tried to assure her. There were girls — goodness knows, they had been plentiful in high school — who could only be satisfied by a bulleted list of all their appealing qualities, but in Stam's case, she asked from true curiosity, and whatever Aurelio answered, she would accept. "There's a lot to like about you — I can't really imagine how you're not swarmed by guys...."

"Can't you?" Stam asked, knowing full well that she was strange enough to put off most people. She knew Aurelio could see it too, and yet, she knew he wasn't lying.

"Well I guess, maybe not every guy would see your appeal. I mean, most guys are, you know, pretty awful."

"Ashley says you shouldn't make sweeping judgments like that." Stam reflected on a similar comment Ashley once rescinded.

"Yeah, well, Ashley didn't go to public school." Aurelio laughed. "Trust me, Stam...."

She said nothing.

Aurelio was still nervous. He knew he had to follow-up on his earlier admission. "Look, about the other night—if it was weird, what I said about, you know, liking you...."

"It wasn't."

It was a shock—he only ever in his wildest fantasies imagined anything but the most horrified reaction to the confession he'd made.

"So it's okay?" he asked, timidly.

"Is there a reason it wouldn't be?"

He didn't want to offer one. "... I don't know."

Stam seemed content with that non-resolution to the matter. Silence took over between them briefly, until, in a strangely shifted tone, she said, "Listen—Ashley does not want to give up what he has here. The home he's made and the memories it helps him hold are all that he has—but it's unavoidable now. I've never feared losing things, as he has, because there is nothing I want to remember."

"... What do you mean?"

"To Ashley, there is nothing more important than remembering the past. He clutches hold to it, desperately, with a weakening grip," she replied. "But to me, the past is something I only wish I could forget sooner."

Aurelio opened his mouth to speak, but Stam continued, "Still, I hold onto it—just the same as him. It is important to remember where you've been and what you've done, even if it's horrible.... Even if *you're* horrible."

"What are you talking about?" Aurelio asked, disturbed by her grim melancholy. He tried to deduce her meaning, and countered it, "*You're* not *horrible*."

She smiled again, but not because she believed him. She didn't know *why* she was smiling.

"Listen, Stam—if you know everything about a

person, it's easy to find things wrong with them. There's something wrong with everyone. Someone really introspective like you is likely to find a flaw or two, but I know at least *some* things about you, and, well—I like you."

Stam was quiet for a while. "Whether I'm horrible or not," she replied, not noticing Aurelio's disappointment that she hadn't reacted more to his last words, "is not really a matter for debate. I was prepared to give up everything without a look back, but... I know I'll miss you."

Aurelio was about to ask what she meant by that when she started to move in toward him. It must have taken several seconds, but Stam's face and lips pressed close to his, and it was so swift and sudden that he could hardly process what had happened. Stam's pale lips were as smooth and cold as ice—unlike anything he'd ever felt before. His fears and self-doubt, though likely to return in time, dissolved from his mind which could do nothing more than enjoy the soft feeling.

She flattened her feet back to the floor from where she had been standing tip-toed, and pulled away from the kiss. Her gaze first was on Aurelio's lips, but then moved to meet his eyes. He looked dazed, in such a way that she could no longer be assured her action had been proper.

"Was that what you wanted?"

Aurelio could hardly speak. "Uh, I—I, uh—" He at least managed to nod before a huge and embarrassingly absurd grin spread across his face, "Y-yeah." He then thought about the implication of her question. "I mean, uh, you wanted to, too—right?"

That was a stupid question: Stam wouldn't have done something like that if she didn't want to. It was the sort of thing she wouldn't even respond to—

"Yes," she replied, unexpectedly.

"Cool," he responded, uncooly, not sure what else to say.

She adjusted the metal case in her arms, which had been compressed between their bodies during the kiss.

She glanced to a clock in Aurelio's kitchen:

3:59 a.m.

Only a few short hours remained between her and sunrise. She had hoped it wouldn't be so, but her next movement would need to wait. She turned to Aurelio, lost in a state of paralysis, and checked on him once more. "Are you sure you're okay?"

"Y-yeah—I just," the grin was still on his face, "really wasn't expecting that."

"I'm sorry—" Stam began, but Aurelio quickly silenced it as he took hold of her.

"No, no, no, don't be sorry. I really, really liked it."

"I'm glad."

Aurelio might have eventually said something else were he not so disoriented, but before then, Stam asked, "May I stay here today?"

Aurelio stumbled through his continued speechlessness, "S—sure. I mean, yeah, of course." He let his hands fall from her shoulders.

She smiled again, though her thoughts and voice remained strangely far away. "Thank you."

Chapter **13**

"It's happening," a voice proclaimed. "It's finally happening."

"What is?" Gunther asked as he lifted a ladle from a pot on the stove to give it a whiff; a soup he had been crafting all afternoon was nearing perfection. The voice had come from Manfred who, at present, was seated inches from the small television in the living room.

"Kennedy's gonna drop the bomb."

"That so?" Gunther pulled open a cabinet to retrieve some bowls and utensils.

"Right on those Commies' fuckin' heads."

"Uh-huh," Gunther replied, idly.

The front door of the apartment began to unlock. Manfred could hear it, despite his fixation on the television screen, and glanced over to see the knob of the first lock turn.

"Dammit, Ashley," he called out upon realizing that neither of the door's two thick security chains had been latched. "I told you to lock up."

The second lock turned, and Frau Müller entered.

"We're dead now, you know," he shouted to

Gunther. "We just got robbed and killed by some street gangs because you left the door open."

Gunther rolled his eyes before picking up a tray where he had placed a bowl of soup. He hurried it out to Manfred, who didn't even notice the offering, being already drawn back into the television.

"In eighteen years of peace and good faith this generation of Germans has earned the right to be free, including the right to unite their families and their nation in lasting peace with goodwill to all people...."

Gunther watched as President Kennedy delivered a speech; it didn't sound much like an announcement of nuclear war.

"Where is he?" Gunther asked.

Manfred said nothing, still too deeply absorbed.

"So let me ask you as I close, to lift your eyes beyond the dangers of today, to the hopes of tomorrow, beyond the freedom merely of this city of Berlin, or your country of Germany, to the advance of freedom everywhere, beyond the wall to the day of peace with justice, beyond yourselves and ourselves to all mankind."

"I don't think he's dropping the bomb, Manfred," Gunther pointed out, prompting Manfred to growl.

"He fucked up the Bay of Pigs—that wouldn't have happened with Eisenhower, I'll tell you that." He noticed the bowl of soup being offered to him and took it before continuing, "It's his fault the fuckin' Commies took over Cuba. Damn Soviets think we're a bunch of cowards."

Gunther had already headed back to the kitchen. "I thought that whole thing resolved."

"Oh-ho-ho," Manfred laughed. "You *would* think that, wouldn't you?"

Gunther couldn't be sure what that was intended to mean; he watched the evening news just as frequently as Manfred. Of course, he didn't pay much attention to it, and Manfred had subscribed to a political magazine— which often sent him into furious rants—so perhaps he was, indeed, more in-touch with the world's state of affairs than Gunther.

"I think it's nice that the President is in Berlin," Frau

Müller interjected. "That whole mess is absolutely horrible—"

Manfred interrupted her, "Oh sure. Yeah, *talk* is gonna stop the Reds." He gestured angrily at the television with the soup spoon. "I ain't got legs—that's why I didn't fight in Korea. What's your excuse?"

Frau Müller answered for Kennedy, "He was in World War two, Manfred, in the Pacific, just like—"

"He's still got legs," Manfred growled.

Gunther handed a bowl of soup to Frau Müller, who had now removed her coat and taken a seat on the couch. She mouthed thanks to him, not wanting to interrupt Manfred during his ramblings. Gunther nodded and turned to watch the remainder of the speech.

"They're applauding this idiot?" Manfred was shocked. "We aren't gonna be free men much longer with people like this running the show. This man is a disgrace. What kind of idiot would appoint Ed Murrow—*Ed Murrow!*—to be the head of the USIA?"

"I'm going to head out." Gunther excused himself as he started toward the door.

"Oh Ashley, you have to have some of your soup, too," Frau Müller insisted. "It's very good."

"I did already," he lied, knowing Manfred wouldn't possibly have noticed. "Thank you."

Upon safely escaping from the room, he stepped one door down, to what had become *his* home. In the years since his acquisition of the space, he had made several improvements: carpet had replaced the hardwood floors and the fixtures had all been upgraded to metal ones. The overhaul had taken months, and much frustration stemmed from his inability to make easy trips to the corner hardware store; clever evasion of the sun had to be employed in order to purchase supplies. There were numerous shops and stores he had never seen open, with their hours ending by five or six in the afternoon, and he had yet to open a bank account. The world, it seemed, was only interested in functioning while he was imprisoned indoors. Even if he had desired to move out of the room and forge for himself a more legitimate life of *voting* and *paying taxes* and *getting a job,* he couldn't; it was impossible to do anything of the sort and it only served to nurture his growing disaffection with the civilized world.

Continuously, it occurred to him that he really could use a friend — someone other than Manfred for obvious reasons — to help him with these sorts of things. There were times during the process that the difficulties served as a harsh reminder of Jens being gone, but then, *everything* in life seemed to be.

In his own room there was no television. He did possess a radio — something he had only acquired recently during a city-wide newspaper strike. There had always continued to be something unsettling about the radio to him ever since those last days in Poland, when he had listened to a near-constant stream of desperate broadcasts. At any moment, he expected an announcer to break in over the program to say something terrible, and given the absurd situation between the United States and the Soviet Union, such an expectation was not unfounded.

In the years after the war, he and Jens spent very little time reflecting on or listening to the news and observing the aftermath of Berlin's occupation, but Gunther was at least somewhat aware of the tensions that formed between the eastern and western world in subsequent years. What Mengele and so many others had said about there no longer being a Germany had yet to be proven *or* disproven. The country was divided in two, which was a far cry from anything anyone had expected back then, but there was still a *place* called Germany. What the Nazis and their supporters aspired toward was gone, and the economic hardship remained — supplanted, in many ways — by something far worse. Jens once said he felt no sympathy for the German people; they had sat by and watched — just the way he did — and they all deserved whatever misfortune came to them.

"*What's going to happen,*" Jens explained, "*is years are going to pass, and people will dismiss the sins in their conscience. But the passage of time doesn't absolve anyone of anything.*"

Gunther challenged this, citing that they were only kids back then, and that his attitude was very unforgiving.

"Our choice, most realistically, was to be a part of the Nazis or die." Jens rephrased it, *"Die, or deserve to die; that's really an unnaturally cruel position for a nation to put its own people into. Even a child knows the difference between right and wrong. Everyone knew. I knew."*

Somewhere toward the end of the conversation, Jens made a final point: *"If people don't accept their own failures and flaws, rejecting anything that they don't like while vilifying the leader they once praised — what will become of us all? If the Cold War fails to remain such, then there really won't be a Germany, and there won't be much of anything else either. Adolf Hitler may have a hand in the end of the world after all."*

When Gunther was young, it had struck him on more than one occasion that it was strange to distrust anyone simply for a conflicting ideology or way of life. Germany's assertion that anything non-German was subversive and bad was mystifying enough, but the present split between Capitalism and Communism was even *stranger*. It occurred to him he might say something to Manfred to that effect, but he elected to stay silent since it didn't matter to him one bit either way. He found nothing compelling in any of it anymore. He didn't care what happened to the world.

He lay in bed, occasionally hearing Manfred yelling about something through the thin walls. His bed was very nice — an improvement from any other in his life — but he'd return to a sleeping bag on the dirt if he could, just for a night, have the feeling of Jens' arms around him.

When they were first reunited, Jens' arms were much like his own in terms of general shape and size. As the lovers aged, Jens' body was the only one to change, and yet, it somehow went unnoticed by Gunther. What he loved about Jens was ageless, and would have remained even once they were forty, fifty, sixty, seventy, *eighty* — if he had lived that long.

Gunther found the future difficult to imagine. Jens had always insisted that the future was the best thing about today: being able to look forward to and *make* a better tomorrow was one of life's greatest joys. Jens hated himself for his role in the war, and in no way had ever forgiven *or* forgotten, but despite it, the future was his own and he never shied from embracing it. When Gunther would make grim observations about his apparent immortality and the fact that one day, no matter how long Jens lived, there would come a time when they were apart, Jens would steal Gunther's attention with a kiss. Jens always maintained that there was *probably* a way for Gunther to die, and it was *probably* simple.

"You'll have time to figure it out when I'm gone." Jens laughed, jokingly adding, *"Won't be any reason to live after that, right?"*

It was funnier at the time; neither had expected the day to come so soon. Jens arms, just like Gunther's, would age no more, and they would never again find their way around him. He grasped hold to the memory of Jens' arms, wishing he could feel them again, and with each wish, the memory faded further. That alone was his greatest fear: that when he was fifty, sixty, seventy, *eighty* — he may not remember at all.

Wearily, he reached to the radio and switched it on. A guitar and vocals crackled through its speaker — a tune from the newest teen sensation, The Beatles, played for the eighth time that day.

Certain lows of the past still stung vividly in his mind. Though these, too, faded, he would happily suffer again through the anguish of death and spend another year — a hundred, even — in Mengele's clutches, if it meant he could again know and never forget Jens' touch, or voice, or face.

* * *

It had been a rough night.

The latest of Ashley's troubles began as Doctor Dawson had touched the stethoscope to his chest, checking and rechecking for a beating heart. Then he tried a different stethoscope. Then he examined his pulse, put his ear to his chest, and hooked up the EKG monitor once more—all with no results. After that, he shooed the nurse and Officer Wilson from the room and—very seriously—asked Ashley if he knew what was going on.

"Your heart isn't beating...."

Doctor Dawson's astonishment rivaled Ashley's own the day that *he* had realized that fact. He had so long ago accepted it as reality that the doctor's reaction seemed trivial to him; he didn't have a heartbeat, Stam didn't have a heartbeat—why should *anyone* have a heartbeat, really? In turn, Ashley's somewhat blasé response to the news only drove Doctor Dawson's curiosity further. After he took a half hour break—to collect his thoughts Ashley supposed—he returned with a long list of questions: presumably all the questions he could think of that would be prompted by the discovery of a man living with no heart. He started to ask them, but couldn't get through very many before simply making his own shocked observations:

"... If your heart isn't working, then your body isn't circulating oxygen."

"... And your lymphatic system wouldn't function."

"... I mean, your cells shouldn't even.... You—you shouldn't be able to...."

He paced around crazily. At some points, he would struggle to calm himself down. At other points, he would repeatedly inform Ashley of the severity—the uniqueness—of his condition. At first it was worrisome, but as the night wore on and he realized the young doctor apparently had no intentions of running off and turning the discovery into some kind of national news story—not yet, in any case—Ashley calmed down some. He did his best to nurture Doctor Dawson's reactions, keeping him in the room, prodding and asking questions, rather than letting him run free to tell the world.

Ashley glanced to a clock:

5:58 a.m.

About half an hour earlier he had been moved into a windowless room at his request. It was in the Intensive Care Unit, and he had a single roommate who, thus far, had been asleep. Doctor Dawson explained that his shift was ending and politely requested that Ashley remain in the room until he returned the following evening. He would be back to just make a few more observations and — assuming that he really was healthy — he would be free to go.

It was a crassly transparent lie. Ashley had had all night to expand upon the story in his head about the doctor, and what seemed the most likely reality was that he somehow expected to shock the medical world with his discovery of this mysterious anomaly. He would keep Ashley as long as he deemed necessary to prepare a grand unveiling of this fascinating creature that would shake to its very foundations our modern perceptions of clinical death. Each of Doctor Dawson's actions only seemed to corroborate that suspicion.

A few minutes passed and Doctor Dawson made a final appearance; he quietly opened the door so as not to disturb Ashley's neighbor, and approached the bedside.

"I'm off now," he explained. "You need anything before I go?"

Ashley had been feigning some level of respect and obscuring his complete disdain for the man; it would make things slightly easier for the time being. Once a fresh night rolled around, he would politely — or not so politely, if it came to that — excuse himself from the hospital and be done with all of this. There was no sense in making things any more difficult.

"No, I think I'll be fine." He grinned a grin as fake as the doctor's.

With his departure, and the sound of the door closing behind the doctor, Ashley let his eyes come to rest on the ceiling. He thought about Officer Wilson's response to how long it had been since Hannah's disappearance — six days — which meant that within another day or two there would be that unmistakable shift between feeling *fine* and beginning to notice his one, solitary need. At present, he was alone with a potential victim — a sleeping old man — and with nearly fifty years of experience, he had perfected the art of obscuring any evidence, even in a difficult scenario such as this one....

But he wouldn't do it; he stayed away from the elderly. Save for the lowest of lows in his life, the idea of harming the frail or weak sickened him. In their shaken voices and sagging eyes, he could see his true self; the way that age should have him appear.

His thoughts were poised to embark on a dangerous path of introspection which he needn't be traveling. In desperation, Ashley took hold of a television remote control and turned to a muted news program where a reporter covered the morning traffic and weather.

* * *

"Have you heard this one?" a girl's voice asked as she excitedly held up an LP.

"Yeah."

"What about," she produced another, "this one?"

"Yep," Gunther replied, giving a brief glance to the cover. He was digging quickly, but carefully, through each lettered section in the record store. He was only three quarters of the way through the alphabet and the store had closed five minutes prior. The girl, however, didn't seem to mind, and appeared happy to stay late in an effort to stump her customer.

"Okay, *this* one?"

"You never give up, do you?" He smiled before shaking his head. "I've heard them all, Marie."

"But you're telling me you don't know the Beatles?"

Gunther rolled his eyes. "I know who the Beatles *are*," he moved onto the next letter, "but as I said, anything after 1958—"

"So you don't know Del Shannon?" Marie excitedly offered him another record.

"No."

"You've got to listen to him," she insisted as she forced the record into his hands. Reluctantly, Gunther accepted it.

"Fine, fine...." He moved on to the 'W' section and made a selection.

"The Weavers?" Marie laughed, not with condescension, but shock.

She was about to add something when Gunther interrupted, "It's just to get on my cousin Manfred's nerves; Pete Seeger was on the blacklist in *Red Channels* in the fifties."

"You sure know a lot about musicians."

He chuckled, skimming quickly through the final letters of the alphabet. "It's not by choice, I assure you."

This, in turn, made her laugh as well. He shot her a smile before gesturing to the clock:

9:09 p.m.

"Sorry to keep you here." He handed her his small pile of albums. "Thanks for staying open."

"It's no trouble—not for you." She blushed and made an addendum, "I mean, for such a great customer, that is."

"I appreciate it very much."

As they reached the counter, Marie sat down the pile of LPs and began to total their cost. Without looking up, she asked, "How is that record player you bought working out?"

"Great—thanks. It's a lot better than my old one."

"It's top-of-the-line. It'll still be working thirty years from now." She patted a record player—just like one Gunther had recently purchased—which was sitting beside her.

Gunther smiled and then glanced over to a television where footage of men in spacesuits was being shown.

"In less than twenty four hours, the crew of the Apollo 11 Lunar Module—Commander Neil Armstrong, and Lunar Module Pilot Edwin 'Buzz' Aldrin—will touch down on the surface of the moon—"

"Isn't it exciting?" Marie asked, noticing what he was watching.

"I guess so." Gunther shrugged, keeping his eyes on the screen, but paying little attention to it as one hand stayed pressed against his own stomach.

Marie stopped on one of the albums. "What's this one? 'In Other Words?'"

Gunther glanced to it and chuckled. "It's very appropriate for the occasion." He took it from her. "This is the original title of 'Fly me to the Moon.' It's on Kaye Ballard's and some of the other early recordings."

"That *is* appropriate," she laughed.

"You should get this one, too," a small girl's voice spoke up, catching both Gunther and Marie's attention. Behind the counter, Marie's little sister stood offering an album to them.

"Oh, Carrie...." Marie rolled her eyes.

"It's good," she insisted.

"Let me see." He took it from her.

"It *is* a good record," Marie conceded as Gunther looked it over. "We've been listening to it for months now, but it's too modern for you, I bet."

"Just a bit." Gunther smiled and set it down next to his purchases onto a pile of rejections.

She finished calculating the last of his purchases, and then paused before announcing the total. Instead, she mentioned, as casually as she could, "You know, my daddy is having a party tomorrow afternoon to watch the moon landing...."

"Oh yeah?" he asked, trying not to sound painfully disinterested.

"Yeah," she said. "Maybe—I dunno—maybe you'd want to come over?" She tried hard to mask her own continued blushing.

"Marie," Carrie interjected, putting her hands on her own hips. "Daddy said—" She stopped abruptly, covering her own mouth.

"I can't," Gunther replied, pretending he hadn't noticed Carrie at all. "I've got to watch it with my cousin, you know? Things are kind of lonely for him right now."

"Aw, that's so sweet." Marie seemed completely enamored, despite the rejection of her invitation. "Well, maybe—maybe we could do something *tonight?*"

"Marie," Carrie shouted again, only to be ignored, save for a glance from Gunther.

"Ahh, I don't know.... I'm not really—"

"Oh, come on," she insisted. "I think we could still catch the last showing at the Waverly."

"I mean, movies aren't really my thing...."

She began to take the hint, "Oh," and deflated, "well, I guess that's okay…."

Gunther sighed, quietly. It happened now and then—though quite rarely—that people sought to make a personal connection with him, but he was hardly shocked at this point by how little he desired it. He hadn't spent more than ten consecutive minutes with anyone but Manfred or Frau Müller—before she passed away—since Jens, but it seemed not to matter. He had been frequenting the record store whenever he was able for almost two years now, and Marie seemed to have taken a liking to him; she had even agreed to keep her father's shop open late on Saturdays during the summer just so Gunther could make it there. He had been worried for quite some time that this day would come.

"Sixteen dollars and thirty nine cents." She gave him the total for the pile of albums.

Gunther pursed his lips, hardly believing what he was saying and what it would inevitably mean. "You know," he reached into his pocket, searching for money, "maybe we could go, I guess…."

She looked at him, still with a look of dejection in her eyes.

He smiled. "We could go see a film."

"No, it's okay—" she started to respond, but he interrupted.

"I'd like to—I'm sorry. I get a little shy at times. I'm not very good with girls."

She remained suspicious. "Are you sure?"

"… Yeah." He nodded, producing two twenty dollar bills. He looked at them, and then, looked over at the pile of rejected albums. "I'll take those, too."

"Marie, you're not supposed to." Carrie tugged at her sister's skirt. "Daddy said—"

"Daddy doesn't know how to have fun." Marie hushed her with a smile, trying not to seem too annoyed.

"Can I come with?" she asked then.

"No, Carrie—"

"Why not?"

"Maybe next time," Gunther offered to her.

Carrie was clearly frustrated, but said nothing else as she examined him. She eventually seemed to take an interest in his face, and with the little tact that could be expected from a girl her age, she observed, "You've got weird eyes."

"Carrie," Marie scolded her. "That's so rude."

Gunther offered a half-smile in response.

"I've got to take Carrie home," Marie explained as she handed Gunther his change. "Want to meet here?"

He let out a short breath. "Sure."

* * *

Static quietly hissed from the television; Stam had remained in bed since the last film had ended, as moving would likely disturb Aurelio from his sleep. He had been very quiet, though perhaps more affectionate than usual, all day. Their single kiss, it seemed, elated him sufficiently that he needn't another. Instead, he had snuggled quite close to her for the duration of their morning film marathon, passing out halfway through something called "Frankenstein."

Stam wondered what people thought about while they slept. It had been explained to her once, long ago, that sleep was essentially an absence of sensory perception in which time itself flowed instantaneously. That, of course, came with the caveat that it wasn't exactly like flipping a switch: it was a slow, hazy process, sometimes resulting in dreams. Dreams required a lengthy explanation of their own, and when it was all over, Stam was unsure that she had any real grasp on the concepts at all. Prior to Aurelio, she had never watched anyone sleep for long—only briefly in the moments just before she killed certain victims.

She looked over to a clock:

5:11 p.m.

Aurelio's films always kept her nearly endlessly distracted; there was so much to see in them. First, there were the carefully composed visuals, and then the music which accompanied them, and the personalities of the characters and the things that happened to them. There were subtleties too, that she knew she was likely missing, especially when Aurelio had explained what "Citizen Kane" was about. In two hours — sometimes less — a story could be told that conveyed days, months or even *years* in the lives of people and worlds. Sometimes they were grounded in reality, and other times were entirely fictional. It was an interesting craft, and she could see why Aurelio desired to be a part of it, but she wondered how it would be possible to pretend you were someone you weren't. Stam only knew how to be herself — even the simple lies she offered Officer Wilson had taken much preparation. Then again, she knew that Aurelio had practiced long and hard to be a better actor; it was a skill one had to hone.

She looked down to where his arm was draped across her. Not far away, his face was nuzzled against her thick sweater sleeve, radiating a heat that she was used to only feeling from the skin of those about to die.

Long ago, in a time she now struggled to recall, she had been warned against divulging her nature to anyone, and until she met Aurelio, there had never been a reason to. She wondered what would happen if he knew the truth.

Perhaps she would ask Ashley.

Carefully, Stam reached into a bowl of popcorn left on the nightstand and plucked a single fluffy kernel up with her fingers which she then slid into a pocket:

5:13 p.m.

From another pocket, she produced a list of upcoming sunsets which she had removed from the fridge at their house; today's time was only minutes away.

It was curious to her that Ashley had elected to be taken to the hospital, but she supposed it may have made sense. Things had gotten to the point where a bloody, violent struggle might have been the only viable option for escape, resulting in far-reaching consequences. Ashley wanted it all to end in such a way that he could return to the life he had had: quiet and unknown. He didn't want police on his trail, or his face in the news.

… Or maybe he had no intentions of going forward at all.

Carefully, Stam extracted herself from the bed, leaving Aurelio to sleep the evening away.

It had been nearly a week since Hannah's death, and soon, a crippling desperation would take hold of Stam, forcing her to find a new life to take. It would surge through her in waves, with an intense *need* to make it stop cutting away at her rationality, and if that happened at the wrong time, it could be a serious problem.

She looked back to Aurelio and two thoughts formed: the first was obvious; she could kill him, but the second was strange—something she couldn't remember ever feeling before. This was a day that had come many times before; she couldn't pretend to be a young teenager forever, and eventually, questions would arise. Those questions would lead, inevitably, to disaster; it was an unavoidable consequence were someone to know what she was. As a result, her friendship with the boy would sever. Never before had she felt the slightest pang of sorrow at this; it was simply the way of the world. It was in her very nature to move on and forget; it was in everyone's, to some degree.

In hundreds of years—those she could recall—she had never missed *anyone*, and yet... she would miss Aurelio.

* * *

"Gosh, that was really depressing," Marie observed as she departed a theatre with Gunther.

"Yeah, it kind of was," Gunther agreed. He didn't venture to see movies often and certainly had little in the way of expectations about the film, "Easy Rider," before spending the last ninety four minutes with it. Much of the experience made him uncomfortable; it cemented his feeling that cinema was simply not for him.

"It was good, though," she continued. Gunther only smiled in response and then looked at his watch:

11:47 p.m.

"Are you sure you don't want something to eat" Marie asked. "You didn't have any popcorn."

"I'm okay," he lied. It wasn't food that he needed, but the pangs of his thirst had been flaring all evening, and though the film had distracted him on some small level, it became more and more taxing each moment to remain focused and lucid.

"You sure?"

"… Yeah," he answered. "Hey—don't you live that way?" He gestured in the direction opposite where they were headed.

"I thought we could walk by the river…." Her eyes and smile were hopeful.

Gunther had been detached from the situation—the date—from the start. He wasn't naïve, and he knew where it was headed and just how it would resolve. The last ember of humanity in him, he was sure, had been smothered out, and he listened to his own voice take things to their inevitable end. "Sure. That'd be fine."

They walked down a few streets that in no way were appropriate for a young girl to travel alone—even as a couple, it was a dubious course of action, but it only took a few minutes for the pair to reach the piers looking out toward New Jersey across the Hudson River. "Come on." She hurried onto one in particular: a long wooden deck extending dozens of yards out into the water. Gunther stopped in his tracks.

"What's wrong?" she asked, looking back.

There was nothing stopping him; his shoes were ample protection from the wood, and though he was unable to *cross* the river, he could at least venture the short way out. Still, he felt a certain apprehension. It was long enough to prompt Marie to hurry back to him, and much to his surprise, she took his hand.

"Whoa," she gasped. "You're so cold." It was a bit of a shock, given that she herself had been sweating all evening in the hot mid-July weather amplified by the city.

"Oh yeah." Gunther made no effort to sound interested. "Sorry."

To his surprise, she clasped both hands onto it. "We'll

have to warm you up, then." She giggled and tugged him out onto the pier. He followed, pulled along, until they made it to the very end where she let go and sat down, letting her legs dangle above the water. Cautiously, Gunther took a seat as well, keeping his knees to his chest. Up above them, the moon was a waxing crescent, and after a moment, Marie said, "It's so hard to believe—we're really going to the moon."

"... Yeah."

"I wonder if you had a real good telescope if you could see the space rocket."

"Not likely. It would have to be a *real* good one."

"Do you think in the future, people will live on the moon?" she asked, still looking up.

"... Maybe someday," Gunther replied. "The Vice President says we'll have a man on Mars by the year 2000."

"I'm sure we will by then, but I wonder *when* it'll happen."

Gunther couldn't offer anything more.

"How old will we be in 2000?" she asked, starting to do the math in her head.

"... Seventy-someth—" Gunther cut himself off. "Er... forties. Late-forties."

"Seventy!" she laughed. "Now *that's* old." She looked over at Gunther, who was staring into the black water beneath them.

"What do you think they'll find on the moon?" she asked, looking back up at it.

Gunther, who had not yet glanced upward once, only brought his gaze over to the city across the river. "Rocks?"

"Oh, come on." She smacked his arm, softly. "Don't you think it's exciting?"

"I suppose it is." He smiled. "I don't know what they'll find."

"I wonder what part they're landing on," she said. "Did you know that the dark side of the moon isn't really dark all the time? It's a bad name for it."

Gunther thought about it as Marie explained, "The dark side of the moon is just the side we don't see, but the sun lights it up just like the rest of the moon when the side we see is dark—it's not like the sun just stops."

"Oh yeah." Gunther nodded. "I guess that's true. Kind of like how it's always daylight *somewhere* on earth."

"Yeah." She laughed. "See? I know about more than just music."

Gunther chuckled and pulled his knees further into his chest, fighting the sick feeling within himself. Normally he was preemptive in dealing with his need, but he had passed on it in a rush to get to the record shop and *now* was paying for it.

His thoughts were suddenly interrupted by the feeling of Marie's head resting on his shoulder. He looked at her, turning his own head slightly.

"Ashley?" she asked, confidence fading from her voice. "Do you, um… do you like me?"

He winced a bit, out of her sight. He had been expecting something of the sort and it made him feel even more unpleasant than before for the same reasons he had neglected to end things sooner: he remembered Marie from when she was just a small child. He had crossed paths with her in 1959, the first time he passed the record shop, when she was only seven or eight years old. He had no personal connections in his new life—Manfred aside—and what few he made would end abruptly in their demise. Such was his disaffection anymore: everyone he met would be right to fear and loathe him. It all seemed quite appropriate, when he thought about it, but it wasn't scripted: he simply drifted now as a thoughtless killer making no distinctions. Always though, some part of him retained that sliver of lucidity that had haunted him for twenty-five years: the shred of a conscience that—though powerless to guide his actions—would ensure that guilt besieged him.

"You're a nice girl," he replied.

It wasn't a particularly satisfying answer and he knew it. He was surprised though, by her forwardness. It had been his understanding that it was well within a male's jurisdiction to ask questions such as those, but perhaps he had been too slow. It was, after all, rather unorthodox for a girl to ask out a boy in the first place.

"Would you... kiss me? If I asked?"

Gunther swallowed, uncomfortably, and held up his wrist so that Marie could see the time with him.

12:02 a.m.

"Maybe. But never on a Sunday."

Marie got the joke, and very quickly brought her lips to his neck, kissing him very lightly right beside a bandage on his throat.

Gunther's body tensed. A handful of victims in the past had fought back, and of those, a few had bitten him in frantic terror, but the last lips to have graced his flesh in affection had been Jens'. It was a feeling he could no longer remember, but still did not want replaced, and as the warmth of Marie's breath began to dissipate, disgust surged through him. Disgust for himself, toward her, toward everything in the last eleven years. He knew it now: this was his fate. He had sat by all evening, watching Marie craft her own destruction at his hands, and despite what she had done for him in the past, despite his memory of her as just a little girl, and despite the fact that she, of all people, seemed to genuinely *like* him, he would make no move to stop it.

He would kill her.

With hideous efficiency, her neck was held fast in his clenched jaw. There was a short spat of terrified flailing and tears before, as though nothing had happened at all, she was limp and silent.

Gunther remained on the pier as the moon made its way across the sky. He wasn't filled with regret, nor even the guilt he had anticipated; there was some self-loathing, to be sure, but not in the manner he'd once had. It was difficult for him to say what it was anymore.

Long ago, when he had arrived in Munich and reunited with Jens, his death toll was four. *Four people*. Four people's loves, hates and passions all extinguished because of his irrepressible urge. Jens, however, loved him all the same, and grew accustomed to what Gunther had to do no matter how many people died—but it was different then. By now, he had surely slain over a thousand, and *anyone* would see that he was a menace and a monster; Jens should too, but probably wouldn't. Perhaps it was because he saw Gunther's affliction for what it was: an affliction. It was an unnatural disease with only one apparent cure — death — which had been rendered impossible. Would Jens even be right anymore to see anything good in him? Gunther was just a boy. A strange boy — perhaps more burdened by constant introspection than many others — but he had been mostly unremarkable. The fate that befell him could have come upon anyone; that wretched creature in the woods could have chosen *anyone* else, and they too would have slowly morphed into this mess. Jens resented the Nazis, as any reasonable person would, but Gunther wasn't much different. He was a pitiful archetype — what anyone could be under similar circumstances — and whatever had once made him unique, he was certain, was gone.

In that sense, he had lost himself, and more importantly, had lost Jens.

* * *

"You think you could turn that down?" Manfred grumbled angrily to Gunther, who already had the volume respectably low on the record player he had brought to the kitchen while he prepared dinner. Annoyed, Gunther pulled the needle from the record, silencing Patti Page and appeasing Manfred. There was silence for a while, until eventually Manfred grumbled again, "That pipe isn't going to fix itself, you know."

"Do you want to eat or not?" Gunther shouted back, nearly chopping a plastic cutting board in half with a kitchen knife as he slammed it down.

"Jeez — what's wrong with *you?*" There came no reply, and after a while, Manfred followed up, "I'm just saying, with that Pavlenko gone — and good riddance, the Bolshevik dog — this ain't going to fix itself. It's your problem now."

Gunther ignored him. Manfred's abrasive manner was, in particular, an aggravation today — likely due to the residual stress of last night.

It was true that Mr. Pavlenko was dead; Gunther himself had killed him a few years prior and, not incidentally, managed to obtain ownership of the apartment building. It had been in such a dilapidated state that renting out the rooms was no option, and he didn't anticipate he would make a very good landlord anyway. All the same, he devoted the last half-decade to renovating the building, by himself, as he had done with his own room. It was a project: a distraction that kept him busy. As he worked, he listened to music, passing the days, months and years as he steadily made improvements to the rooms. From the outside, it simply appeared to be a generic, abandoned walk-up, but on the inside, it had become quite unique: there were fifteen units in the four-story building, and each of them—as well as the hallways—were carpeted. The windows had been fitted with light-proof shutters on the inside, and the heating system worked a bit *too* well.

"They're counting down," Manfred called out eventually, seemingly finished with making complaints against Gunther.

"How long?"

"Fifteen minutes," Manfred called back.

Gunther glanced to his watch:

3:02 p.m.

He hurried up with the rest of the dinner preparations and eventually headed into the room with Manfred, who was glued to the television screen, watching Walter Cronkite and Wally Schirra cover—despite being struck with silence—the impending moon landing.

Okay. You should have him now, Houston.

Eagle, we got you now. It's looking good. Over.

… Eagle?

The conversation between the astronauts and their mission command went back and forth while only a few observations here and there found their way from the mouths of the newscaster or his guest. On the screen, a large overlay showed the time until the landing: ten minutes and forty four seconds remained.

It wasn't very interesting.

Okay, rate of descent looks good.

Eagle, Houston. Everything's looking good here. Over.

Roger. Copy.

Eagle, Houston. After yaw-around, angles: S-band pitch, minus nine, yaw plus eighteen.

Copy.

"We did it." Manfred watched the counter decrease. "We beat those Reds to the moon."

"Mmhmm." Gunther picked up a newspaper and began to page through it.

"There ain't anything good in there," Manfred assured him. "Boring news day." He paused, "Actually, there was a thing on page twenty-something, I think, about some fuckin' Nazis. Some assholes in West Berlin defaced a prison memorial the other day—painted swastikas and shit all over it."

"Hmm...." He found the article and scanned through.

"You know they changed the laws there—they aren't trying Nazi war criminals anymore."

Gunther raised an eyebrow. "Why not?"

"Who knows. Hell, they're all living in America now anyway, just like the commies. You think outta all those scientists we got from Germany after the war that most of 'em didn't belong to Hitler? Hah."

"But why aren't they trying the ones they do find?"

"Eh, something to do with statues of limitations—and a lot of guys get off saying they were just 'following orders.'"

"That makes it okay?"

"That's the fuckin' Krauts for you," Manfred replied. "They don't even *want* to catch those guys. Nobody wants to. Remember when the Jews caught Eichmann way back when?"

"Who?"

"Adolf Eichmann—he was one of the big ones. It was right around when you started hanging around here."

"Huh."

"Anyway, it was this whole big fuckin' thing—they found him in Argentina and kidnapped him and there was this big argument between them and Israel. Since then they don't seem to want to try too hard. Took forever for them to get Franz Stangl, and nobody's even goin' after guys like Walter Rauff or Josef Mengele or —"

"Mengele?" He hadn't heard the name from someone else's lips in over twenty years. It sent a shiver through him. "Josef Mengele is dead. It was in the newspaper."

"You kidding me?" Manfred laughed. "Eichmann was dead in the newspaper, too — a lot of those guys were. A lot of 'em were captured and then escaped. Europe was such a mess back then — all you had to do was take a false name and nobody came looking for you."

"Where did you hear that?" Gunther's tone became very grim.

"What? About Josef Mengele? I dunno —"

"I'm serious."

"I don't fuckin' know. I think it was in some documentary at the end of the fifties when they caught Eichmann. Mengele and those guys were hiding in Argentina or Brazil or some backward place like that, but they never got 'em."

Gunther was very quiet.

Six plus twenty-five. Throttle down...

Okay. Looks like about eight-twenty...

...Six plus twenty-five. Throttle down.

Roger. Copy.

Six plus twenty-five.

Same alarm, and it appears to come up when we have a sixteen sixty-eight up.

Roger. Copy.

The program on the television continued, re-capturing Manfred's interest and leaving Gunther to sit alone with his thoughts.

When he was first reunited with Jens, he wanted nothing more than to forget all the things he had endured, and several months passed before he described to Jens the nature of his captivity and what had happened to Luther. At that point, they were still hiding out in the ashes of Munich, extremely limited in what information they could obtain, but Jens eventually managed to verify — through a few lingering connections — that the most of the German troops fleeing the camps in the region Gunther had been in were captured. More than one report came in from allied forces that Josef Mengele — who was on the short list of war criminals — was dead, and later on, it was in the newspaper.

Gunther himself had killed nearly two-dozen people at that point and was haunted, relentlessly, by each. If there had been one person he could have slain remorselessly, it would have been Doctor Mengele. If ever there was a man who deserved death, it was him. Gunther could hardly imagine him *still* alive.

Walter Cronkite spoke up as the screen showed footage of others watching the event.

"This is the international arrivals building; Kennedy Airport, with a big display board there.... This is Disneyland in California...."

The astronauts continued speaking:

At seven minutes, you're looking great to us, Eagle.

Okay. I'm still on Slew so we may tend to lose as we gradually pitch over. Let me try Auto again now and see what happens.

Roger.

Gunther remained frozen, lost in thought for minutes, until Manfred spoke up.

"This is it. Take that, Brezhnev." Manfred's eyes were gleaming as the countdown reappeared on the screen with twenty-two seconds remaining.

Gunther gave it a brief glance, and without a word, started toward the door.

"Hey," Manfred called. "Where are you going?"

"Out." He opened the door.

"What about dinner?"

With a slam, Gunther was gone.

Chapter 14

Saint Elia's church stared back at Stam as she examined it from across the lawn. It was not the first time she would say goodbye; a decade-and-a-half prior, before Sister Carroll or Deacon Boylan or anyone else had come to be employed there, Stam had volunteered for three years, cleaning and straightening through the nights. When her time ran out, she left to join a new church on the opposite side of town. Later, she joined another.

When the priests, deacons and nuns moved on with their lives and away from the parish, and there was no one to remember her, Stam returned as a fresh new face to offer her services. She had wondered how long they might live in Ashley's house before things changed. Now she had her answer, but how they would change, exactly, remained to be seen.

In her hand she carried the metal ammunition case, and once ready, used it to rap against the church's great double doors.

A minute or so passed with no answer, and so she tried again. This time, after a short delay, the door opened to reveal Hannah's friend, Sarah.

"Stam?" She was surprised.

"Hello." Her tone was flat as ever. "May I come in?"

"Uh, sure, I guess…." She nervously stepped aside.

Stam slid into the vestibule as the girl let the door fall shut behind her. The church was unusually quiet for the early evening; usually there were dozens of students around for after-school programs and other activities. It was a curious scene, and after a moment, she noticed Sarah had already hurried away down the hallway toward the annex, leaving her alone.

Stam moved into the nave, passing through the pews below the watchful eyes of stained glass saints until reaching the sanctuary. There, she stopped. It wasn't often anymore that she had questions for God, and yet she felt a compulsion pray. She knelt in silence with her gaze to the floor, reflecting on the unusual events of the past week, but didn't get far before a voice called out to her, "Stam?"

She remained in her position, recognizing the voice and well aware now that her time was short.

"Stam?" a different voice asked.

She stood, at her own pace, and turned to the two figures behind her.

"You're alright?" Officer Wilson stepped forward, stopping a few feet away as her eyes darted to his. The question needed no answer.

"Stam?" Sister Carroll, beside Officer Wilson, asked. "Is everything okay, honey?"

She looked at Sister Carroll. It took time for words to form. "I thought about what you said…."

Sister Carroll was taken aback by the sudden comment. "… What did I say?"

Stam scanned the saint-lined nave. "About talking to a person instead of God."

She nodded, remembering their exchange which, had it been anyone but Stam, would have been a very strange thing to abruptly conjure into to conversation.

"Where I come from, far away from here, you can see God. He is as real as the sky, and you can see Him there, just above the treetops. His voice is at best a whisper, but it is there as well."

Sister Carroll swallowed, put off, as she often was, by the way in which Stam spoke of such things. It wasn't a conversation she expected to be having right now, but she fulfilled her duties. "God is everywhere."

"He is," Stam replied. "But at certain places and times, He may be subtle. He hides."

She furrowed her brow. "When things seem that way, there are things you can do. Your brot—rather, *Ashley*—was talking about that with me just recently. I know things must seem very frightening and confusing right now, Stam, but—"

"Sister," she interrupted, and the nun silenced herself, waiting for Stam to speak. Stam looked back up to the saints; she knew each of their miracles, and had never once doubted their truth. She knew, however, that there were many things she might say to Sister Carroll which would not be believed. "May I tell you a story?"

"Well...." She glanced to Officer Wilson, who nodded approvingly. "Yes, I suppose. What about?"

Stam's unblinking eyes moved about the saints, and very clearly, as though it were a tale she'd rehearsed, said, "A long time ago, there was a girl who lived alone outside a small village. Her only friend was a priest who lived in a wooden church and taught her, with much difficulty, many things about life. In doing so, he exposed a secret: that the most important thing in the world was your own memory, for if you retained it, you could reflect on your actions. In reflection, you would learn compassion, and in learning compassion, you could approach God." Stam paused. "So the girl reached back, as far as she could to her earliest memories, and began to record her life...."

She glanced to Sister Carroll, who nodded, listening.

"One day, the priest died and another took his place. He preached to her the same gospel, teaching her further of God, and in doing so, exposed another secret: that the girl was cursed—doomed to live forever. At this time, she had been awake for forty years, and in that long stretch of sleeplessness, had committed countless sins. In living forever, she would never be judged. No matter how great her repentance, she would always sin again, and thusly push further from God." Stam paused again. "She knew that no living soul was denied God's judgment, and so sometimes, she wondered: was she already dead? And already judged?"

Both Sister Carroll and Officer Wilson listened intently.

"One day, the priest died and another took his place. He preached to her the same gospel, teaching her further of life, and in doing so, exposed another secret: that there was a way — and only one way — the girl might find eternal rest...." Stam hesitated. "And though the girl begged and pled, he would not tell her how. At this time, she had been awake for one hundred years, and her sins and remorse grew in tandem. The little village nearby was now empty, and for the girl to meet another living soul, she would travel miles and miles through a terrifying woods. She grew to resent the priests, for her sins could be ended if only they would give her an answer, and one day," Stam took a breath, "one day, in her anger, she killed the priest — but another took his place. He preached to her the same gospel, teaching her further of the world, and exposed the last secret: that for her to die...." Stam grew very quiet and brought the metal ammunition case close to her chest. "... For her to die, she need do nothing more than to sleep in the earth where her death began."

The unchanged look on the two listener's faces suggested neither totally understood, but both continued to pay attention.

"At this time, she had been awake for one hundred and fifty years, and her sins, each one meticulously numbered, drove her wild with regret. It was around that time that a world-wide war was leaving soldiers dead and dying near the girl's home. One of those soldiers was a boy, and through him, unwittingly, she committed the most wicked sin of all — a sin beyond all those of her past." Stam paused. "She spread her curse: the boy, like her, would live *forever*, committing sins *forever*." She swallowed. "She protected the earth in which his curse had been born — she knew that she must find and free him.

But her search took many years...."

Stam said nothing more, and so Sister Carroll asked, "Did she find him?"

"She did," Stam answered.

"And what happened?"

Stam shook her head. "That part doesn't matter," she answered. "My question is prefaced."

"What's your question?"

"Our religion, which I now know is but one of many, with a million interpretations across the world, teaches of fulfillment via closeness to God—to mimic Him is salvation."

"Sure." Sister Carroll nodded.

"What if you *cannot* mimic God? What if, in choosing life *or* death, your sin will persist?"

"Well—death is no one's choice to make, Stam, but in your story, the girl... I mean—it's true that everyone commits sin, but, God, if He created a girl like that, would have done so for a reason. No *curse*—as you called it—is insurmountable, even if it seems that way." She sighed. "But Stam, I'm just a nun, and what you're asking is really a theological question—the Father might have a better answer for you."

"There's no need. I only want to know what *you* think."

"Why *me?*" She smiled, despite her confusion.

"I don't know," Stam replied. "There have been a lot of things this week I've been unsure of."

"It has been *quite* a month so far, huh?"

Stam nodded. "You believe the girl in the story should live—don't you? She shouldn't let herself die."

"I wouldn't be much of a nun if I advocated suicide, would I?" she replied. "Not that I'm even a very good one."

"Why do you say that?" Stam asked.

Sister Carroll shook her head. "I think it's obvious—don't you?" She paused, and then added, "You know, there was something you said that made a great deal of sense to me the other day—you said something like: 'faith is not a means to an end.'"

She nodded, remembering.

"What made you realize that?" Sister Carroll asked, very seriously. "That's quite a revelation for someone your age."

"Liars."

"Liars?"

"There are a lot of people in the world whose convictions are founded on self-preservation and hate. They decide for themselves the truth and denounce that which may be at its odds."

Sister Carroll considered this while Stam continued, "Ashley does not believe in God—he has seen phenomenal cruelty and witnessed the worst of humanity, but his own eyes have never seen God."

Sister Carroll continued to listen.

"When he was young, he was taught of God, but only one perspective—one interpretation. A religion can only instill conviction or belief—not faith. God is the source of faith, and if He is silent, as He was in Germany, then one would be a fool to believe in Him. Ashley would be a fool."

"Germany?" Officer Wilson cocked his head, speaking up for the first time in a while.

Stam shook her head and ignored the inquiry. "He was taught from a very young age that he was a monster."

"What do you mean?" Sister Carroll sounded surprised. "A monster?"

"Ashley is gay," Stam replied. "More relevant than that, however, is that when he was very young, he loved a boy."

"That doesn't make someone a monster—" Sister Carroll began.

"One interpretation of God," said Stam. "What about the girl in the story I told you?"

"Of course not," she replied.

"Even if the girl's thousands of sins—each and every one—were murder?"

Sister Carroll considered it. "I mean—that would make her a very *cruel* person, I suppose, but still not an irredeemable soul if she truly sought absolution and oneness with God. You're giving a very extreme example, of course...."

"Everyone's life is extreme."

Sister Carroll thought about the remark. It seemed to make sense to her.

Stam turned to Officer Wilson. "You want me to go with you, don't you?"

"Well, Stam," he wore a serious expression, "you did sort of just disappear last night—nobody knew what happened to you. I came over to talk to Sister Carroll to see if she had seen you—"

"You need me to come back to the police station, right?"

Hesitantly, he nodded. "... I do, yes."

Stam turned back to the icons, giving them one last look. The church at Saint Elia's was especially beautiful; each church had its own appeal, but there was something special about this one. It was rare she felt nostalgia, and was surprised—not unlike how she had been with Aurelio earlier—by the unusual sensation as she realized she may not see the church again; the feeling even extended, in some way, to Sister Carroll.

Stam began to walk down the aisles of pews; Officer Wilson followed and Sister Carroll trailed behind. As they marched, Stam very discretely removed the now crumbled piece of Aurelio's popcorn she had hid in her sweater pocket.

The group reached the church doors, which Sister Carroll pushed and held open for Stam and the Officer.

"Thank you very much for everything, Sister." Officer Wilson nodded as he shook her hand.

"No trouble, sir. Thank *you*."

"Stam?" Officer Wilson asked, looking back into the vestibule to where Stam had fallen behind. She wore a curious expression on her face now and licked her lips as she approached the door after him. She stopped as she set foot onto the stoop out front and turned back to Sister Carroll.

"Sister." Her voice seemed oddly strained. "Ashley wanted me to ask you something...."

"Oh?" She raised a curious eyebrow.

"He wanted to know—" she suddenly looked very sick, "—do you remember what Marie looked like?"

"... My sister?" Sister Carroll was stunned to hear the name. "Um, yes—I have pictures of her."

Stam nodded. "I think that's what he wanted to know." She took a deep breath. "Sister.... I don't think—" her face twitched and contorted, "—I don't think you're a bad nun."

"Thank you, Stam, but...." She had already noticed there was something wrong with her. "Stam?"

"Stam?" Officer Wilson, too, noticed that she was trembling.

With no other warning, beyond a succession of rapid convulsions, Stam began to vomit. Blood by the pint burst from her throat and out onto the stone below in terrible, violent waves. The metal case dropped from her hands and rattled across the ground away from her.

"Oh my God," Sister Carroll gasped. "Stam!"

"Stam!" Officer Wilson took hold of her. She had collapsed to her knees; her outstretched hands were only barely able to lift her body from the pool of blood formed beneath her heaving face.

"W-What should we do?" Sister Carroll stammered, looking to Officer Wilson.

"Stam!" Officer Wilson still fought for her attention. "Stam!"

* * *

The old man beside Ashley in the hospital room had slept all day, not even once stirring. Ashley watched the clock change for what seemed like the thousandth time that day:

5:45 p.m.

With trepidation, he extracted himself from his hospital bed and crept toward the door. His apprehension about the present situation continued to be build; there was a doctor now who had documented several of his unique characteristics, and despite the fact that he appeared to be hoarding the discovery, such luck was unlikely to last. He passed by the sleeping patient and took hold of the door knob, with hesitation, as he glanced back to the television:

5:46 p.m.

Ashley had once speculated, during low times of his life, on what might happen if word of him got out—if the world at large knew of his existence. His affliction—his reality—was like so many others that had, at one time, been denied by the world due to being misunderstood or undesirable. In his youth, confusing, mysterious, and unpalatable mental disorders were simply ignored, and when it was not possible do so—when reality could not be denied—*hate* would arise. His nature, anomalous as it was, needed no clarification: there was nothing to be misunderstood about him and no argument to be made in his defense.

Stam once told him that in 1802, a mass of villagers armed in cliché fashion with pitchforks and torches came to kill her. They drove a wooden stake through her heart—a thought which still made Ashley's skin crawl—but when all their attempts had failed, the ones she didn't kill simply fled in terror.

He was unlikely to be so lucky. He imagined men in suits coming to take him away to a secret government facility like he was some sort of space alien. More unsettling than the idea of being whisked away by men in black, however, was a feeling reminiscent to that which he felt in his days with Doctor Mengele.

5:48 p.m.

Ashley had only barely begun to twist the knob of the door when it suddenly flung open, revealing Doctor Dawson.

"Hi there," the doctor greeted him. His tone was suspicious. "Where are *you* headed?"

Doctor Dawson had returned early; Ashley felt foolish having expected the doctor to have kept to his previous word and not returned until much later that evening. His eyes narrowed as he weighed his options: he could rush past Doctor Dawson, flee from the hospital and into the night, possibly — likely violently — obtain a car, figure out where the hell Stam had gone off to, where the hell his bird was, give up his record collection and what few other possessions he owned, and *hopefully* escape. A few months — or years — on the lam and they'd eventually forget about him.

"… Nowhere," Ashley grumbled, stepping aside.

"How are you feeling?" the doctor asked as he let the door shut behind himself.

Ashley wandered back toward the bed. Doctor Dawson had given his word that he would soon be released, but his word was worth nothing. Ashley would find little freedom until the young doctor's face was on every medical journal in the country, or at least, until his name was of some notoriety on his graduate school's campus.

"Not bad. Food's disappointing though."

"The nurses said you haven't had anything all day, and Mr. Wilson said you didn't eat anything at the station. Have you eaten *anything* other than that fruit cup?"

"You mean that?" Ashley glanced to the unopened cup by his bed.

A cross look spread on Doctor Dawson's face. "Yeah, *that*…. How long has it been since you've eaten anything?"

"… It *has* been a while," he replied, turning back to the doctor.

Chapter **15**

The weather in South America suited him; Gunther found he was able to comfortably wear little more than a long-sleeved sweater nine nights out of ten.

A long time had passed since he had stormed out of his home in New York City; he took only a few short days to make arrangements and put his affairs in order before his sole obsession became a Nazi doctor he had long presumed dead. He left Manfred with money, and — ignoring the man's insistence that he was a fool — left for Argentina. It was the same blind drive that had brought him to Romania a decade before.

It took ages for sanity to catch up to him, and as the days seamlessly morphed into years, it begged him to reconsider; he was on a manhunt, moving from town-to-town on a sometimes *monthly* basis in pursuit of a man whose death, if ever dealt, couldn't possibly soothe Gunther's weary soul. He was motivated — best as he could tell — by revenge; as much as he tried not to think about it, Doctor Mengele *cut out his brother's eye*. He sewed the twins together with the deranged hope that Gunther's strange immortality might bleed through and take hold in Luther….

As he researched Mengele, he was sickened to discover that their experience was far from unique, and amongst the doctor's countless fascinations was one particular fetish: twins. In part, Gunther blamed himself; he had spoken of Luther during a long string of questioning in which Mengele had been aiming to establish his medical history. There was no field of genetics back then, but the basics of inherited characteristics were apparent—*especially* to the Nazis. Their obsessions with racial purity had led to some curiosity regarding twins, and though it hardly seemed worth mentioning his brother to Mengele, he had done so anyway. The guilt never strayed far from Gunther's conscience, regardless of how easily the doctor might have discovered Luther through other means.

Gunther's latest home was a small adobe shack—just a single room—on the edge of a small town outside Asunción, Paraguay. The walls, coated in newspaper clippings in at least four languages, conjured to mind—not inaccurately—a madman's dungeon. Over four years, he had assembled articles, corresponded with Nazis, Nazi-hunters, and Israeli Mossad agents while following countless leads as he sought his target. It had been clear since his earliest days in South America, however, that Manfred had been right: local efforts to pursue war criminals were half-hearted, at best.

On a desk beside him was his record player. Music stores were few and far between—especially those with American or British names—but he had made a few acquisitions over the years. Bossa nova was on its way out, and the LPs were becoming progressively easier to find, casually passed off to junk stores and small markets. Through them, Gunther discovered Elza Soares and Astrud Gilberto. At the moment, Astrud's rendition of "I Had the Craziest Dream" filled the room.

Gunther plucked the needle from the record as he noticed the time on his watch:

7:12 p.m.

Also within reach was a small piece of paper, on which were scribbled the local sunset and sunrise times of the next several weeks. With a pen, Gunther scratched off an entry—*August 9, 1974 – 7:12 p.m.*—and then rose to his feet in an almost mechanical fashion, leaving a Spanish newspaper where it had been in front of him. A picture of Richard Nixon and Gerald Ford was linked to the cover story: *Richard Nixon dimite como presidente de los Estados Unidos de América.*

Gunther had taken to English with relative ease; he and Jens had studied it together and spoke it, exclusively, within months. After only a few years, their command of the language became more than fluent. Then there was Romanian, which he had aggressively translated and could now hardly remember a word of. Spanish, on the other hand, he had tried to be more methodical with: he began studying it fervently when he moved to Argentina and had become relatively adept, but since coming to Paraguay he had been forced to also take on the more obscure *Guaraní*. Learning two new tongues at once proved to be disorienting, but given his pallor and obviously foreign roots, he was usually met with patience as he stumbled through conversation.

The streets of the little village were quiet—they often were this time of night. The only sounds came from the occasional pack of children scurrying about the dirt roads, or groups of elderly men and women sitting outside, chatting in the evening cool. It was a poor town, but calm and happy, just outside of where the modern homes in the suburbs of Asunción began to dissolve into clusters of small adobe shacks and dirty wooden huts. Surrounding the area was thick forestation brimming with wildlife; it was an experience far-removed from New York City or anywhere else Gunther had ever lived. There was a secluded peace of which he quickly grew fond, but still could find no pleasure in, knowing the reasons he'd come.

That night, he had a new lead to follow: an engineer named Axel Werner who had worked with a man named Wolfgang Gerhard. *Gerhard* had been coming up quite frequently as of late, and in recent months, Gunther was certain that if the man himself was not Mengele, he was at least close to him. The engineer, Axel, had been questioned once before by Israeli authorities, but not about Mengele, according to records. Gunther suspected that a man who had already been interrogated once would be on the defensive — perhaps too much so to be useful — but he was still a concrete target.

He glanced to his watch:

8:22 p.m.

On his way home from work, Axel typically stopped in a pub not far from the factory where he was employed on the outskirts of a nearby town named Areguá. It was a convenient habit: Gunther supposed if the man was inebriated, he'd be all the easier to catch. For all the people Gunther had killed, he was not particularly strong; physically restraining a man was intimidating, but he needed Axel alive.

The pub was mostly empty, which seemed unusual for a Friday, but it worked to Gunther's advantage. Outside, he spotted Axel's car and then crept his way to a small window on building's side through which he could see a few employees from the factory gathered at the bar. Axel was sandwiched in with them. They were still ordering their first round from what Gunther could tell.

For over four years now, he had been on this chase, but had yet to come a long way from his earliest days in Argentina where he simply wandered the streets in search of anyone who looked like they might be German. Even once acquiring leads to pursue, it was a tiresome quest, full of dead-ends and defeat. Too often, he wondered what the point was — what the point of *anything* was. He could go back to New York and live out the rest of Manfred's days, eventually all alone in that empty apartment, stalking the city streets for new victims until the end of time…. Or he could do as he was, and perhaps, if he found Doctor Mengele, do some form of altruistic good for the world but putting the man to death.

He had to do something with his bleak eternity.

"*Brrawwwk….*"

"… *Rawwwbk.…*"

Through the breeze, Gunther could hear the sounds of a macaw; they were common, often chirping and clacking in the early morning not long after he settled indoors for the day. Their calls were like those of a rooster on a farm, announcing the sunrise and, to Gunther, serving as a sort of inverted alarm clock. The one he could hear wailing, however, sounded weak—perhaps hurt.

He glanced into the window, seeing Axel just beginning to nurse his first pint.

"*Brawww… awk.…*"

Gunther moved to the back of the building, toward the bird's cries, which were coming from a metal-fenced alleyway behind some nearby houses. As he approached, he could hear children's laughter—not the endearing sort, but a cruel jeering he knew well from his youth.

"¿Lo conseguiste?" a boy's voice called.

"Sí," came a response.

Gunther's eyes narrowed as he came upon the scene: a young blue-and-yellow macaw, just barely possessing full plumage and only recently fledged, was writhing in pain in the dirt. Nearby, a trio of boys sitting on a fence took turns throwing rocks at the injured bird. They continued to miss with their next few shots, and disgusted, Gunther turned to leave. He started back toward the pub, but then paused as he noticed a rock at his feet.…

One of the boys hopped down from the fence, armed with a stick which he extended at full arm's length, ready to jab the crying animal. With only inches to go, something struck the boy's stomach, buckling him to the ground.

"¡Ay!" he cried. "¿Qué fue eso?"

The other two immediately spotted Gunther. His apparent age was that of an older kid—a likely neighborhood antagonist to the boys.

"¡Qué demonios, hombre?" one called.

"¿Crees que es divertido ser un sociópata?" Gunther responded before picking up another rock. As he did, the first boy, recovering, threw the stick at Gunther's face. He winced as it bounced off his clothes and narrowly avoided his uncovered neck. Eyebrow raised, he threw the rock at the boy, hitting his chest and forcing a yelp—followed by tears.

"¡Qué demonios?" one of the other boys reiterated before throwing a rock at Gunther's arm.

Gunther quickly swept downward, plucking the rock up as it landed, and before both boys could hop down from their perch as they seemed to be intending, Gunther flung it right back, hitting the thrower in the cheek and toppling him backward, over the fence.

The third boy, now standing on the ground, began to call out, urgently, to anyone who might be nearby. "¡Ayuda!"

"Fuera de aquí," Gunther commanded, bluntly, as he picked up another rock.

"¿Estás bien?" the unharmed boy asked his friend who was struggling back to his feet.

"¡Fuera!" Gunther yelled, picking up a second rock, ready to throw both.

Frightened, the boys began to scurry off. Gunther helped them along with some extra motivation, throwing the rocks after them and narrowly missing their heads as he, himself, approached the battered bird. He knelt down beside it, trying to observe what had happened: its wing was broken, at least, and it was sufficiently disoriented that all it could appear to do was squirm and try to drive its beak and head into the ground.

"… Breeeek… breeee…."

Awkwardly, Gunther cupped his hands beneath the bird, which only struggled more at his touch, but was unable to escape. He looked it over; he didn't know anything about birds, but there was something about the poor creature that stirred an old emotion in him—not the fact that he was alone or suffering, as those feelings were still fresh to Gunther—but whatever it was, he supposed, would quickly be irrelevant, as it seemed unlikely the bird would recover. *He* certainly couldn't take care of it, but at the same time, he couldn't bring himself to just sit it back down on the road to die.

Against his better judgment, he started back toward the pub, bird in hand.

"*Brawweeekk....*"

* * *

Ashley was in a sterile, all-white room. There was a large machine nearby, as well as a window into a control station. Doctor Dawson had asked if he would be willing to undergo an MRI scan—it stood to reason that afterward, when the results came in, the doctor would be distracted, and that might offer him a decent chance to escape. Once he had vanished, the doctor would likely attempt to convince others of the existence of living man with no heartbeat; his only corroborative partner would be a small town police officer, and their evidence was tenuous, at best. A half-century-old immigration certificate and an MRI of a dead brain wouldn't take them far.

And of course, killing Doctor Dawson was still an option.

He wondered if perhaps he was being silly; the records in his collection were rare but replaceable, Stam was reasonably resourceful, and Sydney was probably safe.

It must have simply been out of habit that he still cared about making a clean escape when, just days prior, he had opened that old metal case and considered putting an end to things. Had Officer Wilson not appeared when he did, things might be *very* different right now.

… Or maybe they wouldn't. The option of death was only a speculative one. Stam had learned that the earth— the dirt—in which one's curse was first inflicted could be used to end their lives, but she had learned that only through legend; hearsay, passed via word-of-mouth, over several centuries, by a succession of priests with little incentive to speak a word of truth to her.

There was no proof—the only proof would be one of the two of them dying.

* * *

"We're almost there, Stam," Officer Wilson called to her, where she lay face down in the back seat of the cruiser. Her vomiting had continued for almost minutes, to a point at which Officer Wilson could have sworn more than a single person's worth of blood had been expelled. It was horrifying, but meanwhile, Stam continued to assure him with strange clarity, through labored panting, that she would be okay.

His car barreled into the emergency drop-off outside the hospital, and in a flash, he was out of his seat and helping Stam from the back. Though unable to walk, Stam grasped hold of her ammunition case, refusing to leave it behind as Officer Wilson whisked her into his arms and carried her into the lobby. All the way, Stam continued to gurgle and spit up tiny streams of stringy, half-clotted blood.

"Hey," he called as he rushed to the counter, "we need help."

"Oh, my—" the woman on duty gasped and reached for a phone.

Officer Wilson then spotted Doctor Dawson close by down a nearby hallway, checking a chart.

"Doctor Dawson," the officer called, heading toward him.

The doctor drew back, startled. "What's wrong? Who's that?"

"She's puking blood—a *lot* of it."

The doctor reached out to her forehead. "Whoa," he drew his hand back, "she's freezing—did she eat anything strange?" He reached for his stethoscope.

"I'm fine," Stam interrupted through a gargling cough.

"You don't sound fine," Doctor Dawson replied, placing the stethoscope to her chest, and after a silent pause, asked Officer Wilson very quietly. "Where are her parents?"

"... Ashley is as good as we've got there."

"Put me down," Stam commanded, weakly.

Doctor Dawson pulled over a gurney. "Lay her

down — we'll get her examined."

Stam writhed about, clutching her torso and gasping as she was rolled to a stop in a private room.

"How much would you say she threw up?"

"It was a lot," Officer Wilson stressed. "I mean, a *lot*."

Stam pushed herself up from the rolling bed. "I'm fine now. It was nothing."

"Stam, please—" Officer Wilson took her freezing hand as she tried to find the floor with one of her feet.

Doctor Dawson had moved to the door. He called out into the hallway, "I need a CVC—and a nurse."

"Where's Ashley?" Stam demanded as she wrestled her wrist from Officer Wilson's grip.

* * *

Ashley was patiently seated on the MRI scanner bed.

"Where are you from?"

"Oh, right around here—nowhere exciting."

"You go to school?"

An MRI tech was speaking through an intercom into the room, making idle conversation.

"Oh, no," he replied, with no intention of elucidating further. Now might be his chance to escape; what was the MRI tech going to do to stop him? He was about to stand up when, suddenly, Doctor Dawson reappeared on the other side of the window in the observation room—he looked harried.

"Okay, Ashley," he said through the intercom while the MRI tech began to type something. "Sorry to hold things up."

"You know I don't have medical insurance, right?" Ashley's eyebrow rose skeptically. "I have no intention what-so-ever of paying for *any* of this."

He laughed. "Of course, of course…. I understand, Ashley."

"Mm," he grumbled back.

"Go ahead and lay down for me."

Ashley complied, and the bed slab began to move, pulling him into the machine. It was only his head and uppermost torso that were inside—the rest of his body remained free.

"Everything okay, Ashley?" Doctor Dawson asked once it came to a stop.

"Just fine."

"Earplugs in?"

"Mmhmm."

"Okay, just a moment—this should be fairly quick. Try and be as absolutely still as you can."

Outside the room, Officer Wilson came to a stop. He could see Ashley through the glass and Doctor Dawson in the control room. Nothing seemed particularly out of the ordinary, but he remained frustrated by the doctor's complete preoccupation with the boy. Stam had been left in the care of a nurse, and after some pleading, Officer Wilson convinced her to stay put while he went to find Ashley for her.

The MRI machine's loud hum began. Even through the earplugs, it was quite a sound.

"You're doing just fine, Ashley," Doctor Dawson assured him through the intercom.

Ashley remained motionless, as instructed. It was a strange sensation being in a giant whirring tube and knowing that your brain was somehow being photographed. In truth, he had been a little curious about it. His internal organs always seemed improbable and mysterious to him, for obvious reasons....

His thoughts lurched to a stop.

He could feel something very odd in his lower chest, just outside the machine. It was warm—perhaps just the warmth that Doctor Dawson had mentioned, but it didn't feel quite right. It hurt, in fact, and was beginning to feel hot—almost like it was slicing at his stomach from the inside-out. He winced, no longer able to remain still, and as he did so, the muscles in his stomach flexed and made things worse. This wasn't normal.

"Doctor—" He began to speak, only to cut himself off as he realized what the problem might be.

"Something wrong?" asked Doctor Dawson. "Please don't talk unless—"

With a painful growl, Ashley buckled his body—his knees drew up and the top of his head smacked into the machine. He could feel something—skin, muscle; it wasn't clear—tear in his abdomen, and suddenly, a new sound— a loud rattling—filled the tube. With that, his growl became a scream.

"What the hell—" Officer Wilson drew back. From his vantage point, all he could see was Ashley thrashing, a sudden splatter of blood on the machine's walls, a growing red stain on the boy's shirt, and Doctor Dawson panicking in the control room.

* * *

"… *Brawwweeek….*"
"… *Eeerrrrrkk….*"
The macaw continued to cry with some frequency as a fat veterinarian with a cigarette in his mouth finished wrapping a bandage about his wing.

"Puede que no sea capaz de volar durante unos meses," the vet explained, placing the bird into a soft, wool-lined box Gunther had fashioned. "Fue buena idea mantenerlo fuera de la luz. Daña a los animales heridos cuando es intensa."

"Gracias, señor," Gunther replied as he placed a cloth over where the bird sat squawking unhappily.

He wasn't sure why he was devoting any effort at all to the creature, except for, perhaps, his memory of Jens once singing the praises of macaws. In idle passing, Jens had joked that they should one day adopt a long-lived macaw as a pet, and *that*, somehow, made Gunther unable to part with it. It helped the cause that the veterinarian adamantly pointed out that they would not be able to care for the bird, and it was *not* a wild animal—its behavior made clear it was somebody's pet. If it were released into the wild, it would likely not survive; the only humane course of action was to take it home.

Gunther entered his humble house and placed the box carefully in a dark corner of the room and left the now-silent bird to itself. He couldn't be certain, but when the veterinarian was describing what he could feed to the macaw, he was pretty sure he heard the word *"pollo"* in the list, which, according to his understanding of Spanish, meant *chicken*. He would have to read up on the animal's dietary options later, when he was done with Axel.

… Axel, at present, was tied to a metal folding chair, gagged, blindfolded, and dead; he had been there since the night before. He had given Gunther less than useful information about Wolfgang Gerhard, explaining that they did work together once upon a time, that he was *not*—upon comparison to a photograph—Josef Mengele, and that he lived somewhere in São Paulo, Brazil.

Unlike the bird, nothing in Axel's frightened eyes during their discussion had stirred much emotion in Gunther. His old self would have been repulsed by the idea of kidnapping somebody; he had long-since desensitized himself to quick, succinct murders, but not to the idea of inflicting prolonged terror upon someone. Upon finishing with the questioning around midnight, Gunther simply left Axel there to squirm all night, morning and afternoon. Just prior to his departure out the door to see the veterinarian, the engineer became the latest victim of his thirst.

It was ugly.

Gunther spent the remainder of the evening boxing possessions and preparing for his next move, only releasing Axel's body when it came time to pack up the chair.

* * *

"Graaagh," Ashley growled through a blood-coated respirator mask as he fought back against a small horde of doctors and nurses who had gathered around to subdue his violent flailing. It took a person on each limb to keep him down while a fifth drove a needle into Ashley's wrist.

"Why isn't he stopping?" another called, horrified

that their third injection of sedative painkillers had done nothing to slow the thrashing boy in the last fifteen minutes. It was a terrifying struggle just to get him to a gurney which they were now rolling toward a surgical theatre — Ashley fought all the way, swiping at faces and gurgling obscenities at his captors. Doctor Dawson was holding down one of Ashley's legs, and could see quite clearly the damage that had been done to him in the MRI: the lower part of Ashley's chest and down the side of his abdomen had been ripped and carved from the inside by small shards of iron. Shrapnel wasn't a consideration that he had taken during the hasty preparations for the brain scan; a shrapnel wound wasn't something that would have been logical to predict in a teenage boy, and Ashley himself had said nothing about it.

Panicked thoughts raced through the doctor's mind. He had messed up, and he knew it, and all he could do now was prepare an explanation for the reckless procedure. Of course, it wasn't *really* reckless: who'd ever heard of such a thing happening?

"The word 'magnet' is the name of the machine, for God's sake." Doctor Dawson mumbled to himself.

"Dawson, what the *hell* happened?" a doctor on one of Ashley's arms shouted over the growling and screaming.

Doctor Dawson had no chance to react before Ashley interrupted. "Get off of me," he hissed while thrashing with renewed vigor, jabbing an elbow into the chest of a nurse at his side. The nurse's grip weakened and Ashley's arm broke free, grabbing at the nearest doctor's collar. Pulling him downward, Ashley struggled to lift his upper half from the gurney and bring his teeth to the man's neck. He nearly reached it, only to be stunned by the pain of his shredded midsection; in his moment of weakness, he was restrained once more by another doctor. They had been fighting to get straps across his body for minutes now, but focused first on getting to the operating room.

Once there, the process of slipping Ashley's extremities under restraints began as a team of surgeons tried to peer through the crowd of doctors and nurses to see what they were up against. There were several spindly shards of iron, half-emerged all throughout his stomach. Nearby, a doctor held out a gloved hand, showing the surgeon a few samples that had been pulled clean out by the MRI.

"What was it?" the surgeon asked, looking them over.

"No idea...."

Officer Wilson watched from afar, recounting in his head how the events had unfolded. After Ashley lurched up from the MRI, it was quickly shut off and several doctors rushed in to his aid. The wounds were unlike anything he had ever seen: they had hardly bled on their own, but as Ashley jostled about, blood seeped from the cuts as though his body were nothing more than a hollow reservoir. He wondered if it had anything to do with what Doctor Dawson had observed: Ashley apparently had no heartbeat. Officer Wilson wasn't a doctor himself, but he knew as anyone did that such a thing was outside the scope of possibility—that such a person wouldn't even be *human*.... The idea was like something out of folklore or a horror film.

The day they had met, Ashley had joked about playing a vampire. It seemed appropriate for the fanged, sun-fearing, pale, parentless boy in a windowless house. The idea was all well and good, but as Doctor Dawson had pointed out: you couldn't fake *all* of Ashley's afflictions. There must be something he was missing. He hadn't gotten much sleep since the Hannah and David case had come up; maybe in his tired delirium there was something he wasn't seeing. A stolen car in an abandoned parking lot wasn't going to lead to the uprooting of a secret undead society in the suburbs of Kent, Ohio.

In time, the doctors would figure out what was wrong with Ashley *and* Stam—everything would resolve. At least, that was his hope up until this latest development; Ashley's condition was far worse than previously, and this time he wasn't faking anything.

Though they were met with tremendous resistance, the doctors tried to work a new respirator mask onto

Ashley's thrashing face. The whole event had been horrifying: Ashley's rage now—very much unlike his performance at the police station—was genuine. Ashley was *really* pissed off. Rightly so, in some respects—Doctor Dawson's motivations were suspect even to Officer Wilson at this point.

"We can't do anything unless he calms down," someone called out.

"Dawson." The agitated doctor turned back to him, reiterating an earlier question, "What's going on with this kid?"

Unsure what he could say, Doctor Dawson's gaze shot to a tray where the pieces of metal extracted from the MRI chamber and Ashley's body had been collected. Noticing Officer Wilson outside, plucked up the tray and hurried it out to the hall.

"Officer," he asked, displaying the metal to him, "do you have any idea what this could be?"

Officer Wilson examined them closely. The largest piece was a little under an inch in length—they were nothing more than thin, twisted little bits of a murky grey metal.

"Uhh...." Officer Wilson was puzzled. "I couldn't really say. It could be from a *bomb* or something, but wouldn't he have scars from an injury like that?"

"He should," Doctor Dawson agreed. "He said he never had any surger—"

He was cut off by a strange, audible rumble from somewhere beneath the floor. The ground trembled, and moments later, darkness fell upon them. Everyone— except Ashley, who was still thrashing about—was shocked into silence by the sudden tremor and black-out.

Doctor Dawson could only barely resolve Officer Wilson's face in the light of emergency lamps and exit signs, but he saw the man turn to look down the hallway from which he'd come. Almost inaudibly, the officer mouthed a name.

"... Stam."

Chapter **16**

Time now slipped through Gunther's hands like grains finer than sand. Memory fell with it, leaving him little more than his vengeful quest for a man who, by now, was surely too old and frail to be a threat to anyone.

Gunther glanced to a clock:

7:11 p.m.

On a sheet of paper beside him, he struck a line through the day's date and the sunrise time: *September 21, 1978 – 7:12 p.m.*

It had been *three years* since he had come to São Paulo on the advice of a German engineer in Paraguay he could no longer recall the name of — Axel, maybe? That sounded right. Axel had divulged that an ex-coworker named Wolfgang Gerhard lived in the city; Gunther's own research had determined that someone by the same name had both been questioned by Israeli agents *and* had been connected to at least one other Nazi war criminal in the region. By the time he figured out who Wolfgang Gerhard really was, the man had already disappeared from the country, but it had been verified that he was not Mengele.

Instead, there was a new name to pursue: Peter Hochbichlet, a friend of Gerhard's, who worked until 1974 for a married couple on a farm in Nova Europa, a town outside of São Paulo.

"¡Te Amo!"

By now, Peter Hochbichlet could be anywhere, but Gunther had at least located the married couple's home the previous evening and now waited for a fresh night in which to make his move. Hochbichlet was supposedly a German doctor, and his movements mirrored the few documented relocations of Mengele from Buenos Aires, to Paraguay, and now São Paulo.

"¡Te Amo!"

Gunther glanced over to his bird, who was balanced on a perch Gunther had constructed with old scrap metal and a broomstick. Until its acquisition, Gunther's various homes had always been kept painstakingly wood-free, but the bird had its needs — such as *food*. For the first time since his days with Manfred and Frau Müller, Gunther found himself shopping and even *cooking*. He had expected the bird to be nothing more than a nuisance, but curiously, the two grew attached in the months it took his wing to heal. The bird became a distraction — a source of focus to keep Gunther's mind from spiraling into places too dark — at least *most* of the time.

"Yo también te quiero, Sydney," Gunther replied.

Sydney gnawed on a wooden block which dangled from a string near the perch. He battled it forcefully for half a minute until, suddenly finished, he squawked loudly. Gunther watched the creature's arbitrary behavior: Sydney began side-stepping back and forth across the perch, briefly cleaned himself, flapped his wings, gnawed on the wood again, and then proclaimed, "*Know why!*"

"What?" Gunther asked, cocking his head to him.

"*Know why!*"

Gunther's brow lifted, amused. "Music, Sydney?"

"*Know why!*"

With a chuckle, Gunther stood up from his chair and removed a pile of newspapers from where they covered a milk crate full of records. He sought out one in particular, removed it from the sleeve, flipped it to the B-side and set it onto his player. With a crackle, a jangly guitar track started up.

"*Know why,*" Sydney chirped, head bobbing with the music.

Gunther smiled at the little bird's absurdity. Sydney seemed completely entranced by the melody; it was a bizarre sight, but one Gunther had seen before. In more ways than one, the bird brought an element of Jens' presence back to his life; he often learned lyrics and seemingly made musical requests. Gunther looked the record sleeve over: it was a single by some 60's band called Herman's Hermits, of which his own knowledge was very limited, but who seemed to be up Jens' alley.

"You're a good bird." Gunther turned back to the mess of articles and notes on his desk. On one, he had scribbled the address of Gitta and Geza Stammer—the farmers who employed Peter Hochbichlet. He plucked it up, along with a local map and a photograph of Mengele, and headed to the door.

"… Adiós, Sydney."

* * *

Extra emergency lighting had come on, and various machines could still be heard humming—kept alive by backup generators.

"What happened?" Officer Wilson asked someone at the counter in the lobby.

"We're not sure—they're checking it out now."

No sooner had she replied than a fire alarm sounded—a screeching wail and bright flashing light filled the hallways. It was startling, but no one seemed too concerned.

"Probably just from the outage," someone commented.

Officer Wilson turned to Doctor Dawson, who had come with him in search of Stam. She was not in the room where she'd been left. "Somebody needs to find that girl—*now.*"

"Any luck yet?" Doctor Dawson asked a nurse who had just returned from a search. She shook her head.

"I'm sure everything is fine—" Doctor Dawson glanced, eagerly, back in the direction of Ashley in the operating theater.

"Hey." Officer Wilson took his arm. "I'm serious."

The lobby had begun to fill with evacuees, and enough people were pushing against him and Doctor Dawson as they filed toward the exit that his grasp was broken.

"Hey," a janitor called as he looked up from a wall panel. Officer Wilson must have seemed like the person to report to. "It says the alarm started in the basement.

Officer Wilson looked around at the sea of confused staff and patients, who were still drifting idly toward the exit and wondering if this was a *real* emergency or not. It would be a little bit before the fire department arrived, and the hospital staff no doubt had their hands full already—hell, half a dozen of them were busy just dealing with Ashley.

"Where is it?" Officer Wilson asked.

The pair hurried to a stairway through the dark—but now very noisy—hall and began a descent downward, to a door which led into the electrical and boiler rooms.

A wall of heat hit them forcefully as the door opened. Inside, several electrical boxes and other equipment were engulfed in a blaze, spitting sparks and black smoke.

"Oh shit," the two gasped in tandem.

Officer Wilson turned to the man. "Get everyone out of here."

He did what he was told and hurried back up the stairs while Officer Wilson himself pushed into the room. The heat was intense—unlike anything he'd ever felt—and the fire itself, while not yet as massive as it *could* be, was intimidating in the claustrophobic cement basement.

"Hello?" he called, seeking anyone who might be injured. "Anyone there?"

It was hard to see—his eyes began to shut involuntarily as he averted his gaze from the flames. He could smell fuel of some sort in the air—it wasn't just an electrical fire—the scent was reminiscent of ordinary gasoline.

He hurried to the other side of the inferno—there was still enough room to move about without immediate danger of becoming trapped. It didn't look like there was anyone else in the room, and so, he turned to hurry back upstairs, but then something in the flames caught his eye. At first, he couldn't be sure, but then he knew what it was: the shattered remnants of the metal case Stam always carried. It had been blown to bits, almost as if….

He swallowed, deeply disturbed by what he was realizing.

… It was as though the case had been used as a bomb.

The hallways had devolved into a scene of some chaos. Firefighters had yet to arrive on the site, and the hospital staff was running wild, attempting to assist elderly and intensive-care patients to the exits. Doctor Dawson had found his way back to Ashley, who was being wheeled down the hall by one of the nurses.

"Here," the doctor offered, taking hold of the gurney. "I'll take him from here, thanks."

The nurse seemed more than happy to be relieved of the thrashing prisoner. Ashley's eyes quickly found Doctor Dawson, but went ignored. The pair continued moving down the hall until suddenly the whole building shook from another explosion—this one much more powerful than the last. Moments after, somebody screamed for help.

"Guys, we just lost the machines!"

Doctor Dawson and Ashley came to a stop as they ran into a sea of doctors who now were rushing to help in the ICU where back-up power had failed. Dialysis machines, respirators—everything—had ground to a halt.

"Dawson," somebody called. "Get over here."

Nervously—a bit dazed—Doctor Dawson was reluctant, but at last made a choice and, once assured that nobody was watching, pushed Ashley's gurney into a nearby room and shut the door, leaving him.

* * *

The puzzle was assembled: Peter Hochbichlet was *Josef Mengele*. It was a phony name, recently replaced by Wolfgang Gerhard. The *real* Wolfgang Gerhard had already left the country, but in his wake, Mengele had adopted the alias.

Gunther's encounter with the Stammer couple had been brief; Gitta quite readily spilled to him that the man in the photographs had lived with them until 1974 and now resided elsewhere in São Paulo with another family: the Bosserts. She claimed to have had no knowledge until shortly before that time that she was harboring a war criminal. Gunther felt no reason to debate her morality — or lack thereof — and left once he had the name he needed.

Over the next few weeks, he packed up his things and moved to a new home closer to the area of São Paulo which Gitta had mentioned, and by January, had begun his search for the Bosserts. He could feel now how close he was to finding the ghost from his past — his brutal captor and his brother's murderer. At the same time, he continued to wonder just what he would do once he found and killed Mengele — return to America? To what end? So he could live out the rest of his days — however infinitely they might go on — in pathetic isolation? The question had haunted him for years, but as always, he had to push it out of his mind. He could only take things one night at a time, and for the night, he had a mission.

Gunther sat in the backseat of a car, idly scanning a newspaper. There was nothing particularly newsworthy inside; the only thing which caught his attention was mention of a new optical disc technology for playing music. Gunther had failed to catch up with the modern era during the introduction of tape players many years prior, and suspected that this *new* media format would be just as unlikely to sway him.

He was waiting for his latest targets to emerge from a restaurant. The Austrian couple had taken some time to locate: this pair was number six on a list of nine different local families with the last name "Bossert," but he had a particularly strong feeling about them. They were older — enough so that they would have been around during the war. Wolfram Bossert, husband of Liselotte Bossert, was an engineer, just like Axel, and as Gunther now spied them heading out the door and toward their maroon Chevrolet Chevelle, he could see it in the couple's approaching faces — some ethereal quality that made it clear to him *these* were the ones. He knew it. He was *certain* of it.

They both got in — Wolfram assisted his wife into her seat and then moved to the driver's side. Once he had sat down, he slid the key into the ignition and began to pull away —

"Keep driving," Gunther instructed the couple, bringing his presence to their attention. Immediately, in horror, Wolfram slammed on the brakes, and Gunther reiterated his command, "I said keep driving, or you're both going to die *right now*."

"Who the hell *are* you?" Wolfram demanded, despite giving into the instruction.

"I," Gunther replied, leaning up between the couple, "am an old patient of Doctor Mengele's. You're going to take me to see him."

The man seemed unsure what to say — the shock of the unexpected passenger had yet to wane.

"Where is he?" Gunther asked forcefully.

"He— Josef Mengele is—" the man stammered, "— he's dead."

"Liar!" Gunther grabbed Wolfram's head, digging his nails into the man's face and blinding him as the car swerved — both Wolfram and Liselotte screamed until the car grazed the side of a telephone pole, but Wolfram had the presence of mind to slam the brake and stop it.

"Where *is* he?" Gunther shouted, moving his clenched hand from Wolfram's face to his throat.

"He's telling the truth," Liselotte cried. "He passed away last month."

Gunther continued to strangle Wolfram, turning to Liselotte now for answers. "Where?"

"We—were on vacation in Bertioga last month and he—he died—"

"How?"

Wolfram managed to wrestle Gunther's hand away and, grabbing at the door as Gunther fumbled to recapture him, managed to get it open and slip out. Gunther could see him hurrying to the other side to help his wife. Acting quickly, Gunther grabbed her with both hands—the car was still rolling since Wolfram had simply leapt out, and it was now heading down the wrong side of the street toward traffic.

"Dammit," Gunther grumbled, clutching Liselotte, who was now screaming in terror as Wolfram fought to open the door and rescue her. As the car began to pick up a tiny amount of speed and the oncoming cars took notice and slowed down, Gunther let go of the woman and thrust himself up into the driver's seat, connecting with the gas pedal just in time to raise the speed and break away from Wolfram while simultaneously making it too dangerous for Liselotte to leap out. She continued screaming, but was silenced as Gunther's fist flew, in a rage, at the old woman's face. She clutched her jaw and whimpered as Gunther wrestled the car back to the correct lane and drove with increasing speed.

"One more chance," Gunther warned her, continuing to drive faster and faster, with his hands poised to spin the car into the busy opposite lane.

"It's true," she whimpered through tears.

"How did he die?"

"He," she sniffled, "he d-drowned while we were swimming.... He had a stroke and—"

"Where is he now?" Gunther shouted. "Where is he buried?"

"Nossa Senhora do Rosario cemetery," she cried.

"Where did he live? With you?"

"He had a house," she whimpered. "It's—"

"How do we get there?"

"It's—it's on Estrada Alvare—"

"We're going there," Gunther cut her off. "Tell me how."

"But—"

"*Tell me*," he screamed so loudly that the car shook.

The uncomfortable drive took almost half an hour, until, along a dirt highway outside of the city, Liselotte told him to slow—that Mengele's house was just off the road and over a small hill. Gunther pulled the car to a stop and climbed out of the driver's seat, taking the keys and leaving Liselotte inside. She remained there, watching and perhaps waiting for Gunther's command, but he didn't make any. Instead, he marched up the hill toward a solitary yellow bungalow which was nestled into quiet obscurity behind a cluster of tropical forestation. It was painfully quaint. As a he moved farther, he heard Liselotte's door open, and shortly thereafter, her fleeing footsteps heading down the road, followed a minute or so later by her distant screams for help.

He didn't follow her. She no longer mattered. The lonely little home before him marked the end of a ten-year journey, and inside awaited a piece of the past.

The old woman had said that Mengele was dead. The words didn't exactly register. He had always considered the possibility that Mengele was no longer alive, but how could he let that influence his path? A decade's worth of research had made it quite evident that tremendous lengths were being taken to protect countless Nazis in the region. Falsifying the man's death hardly seemed unlikely, but then at the same time, it was believable—logical, even—that Mengele might be dead.

Somehow though, he couldn't believe it.

He found a small rock in the dirt which he leaned down to, took hold of, and brought to the wooden door, making three distinct knocks.

… There was no answer.

He tried once more, and then again—there was nothing.

If Mengele had truly died, and this was truly his home, there would be nothing to stop him from setting foot inside. He took a breath, then took a step back, preparing to kick the door down, when it suddenly swung open....

* * *

"Help," Officer Wilson called out. "Somebody!"

The momentary distraction that Stam's strange case had caused him was enough to trap Officer Wilson in the basement; the fire had spread to the hospital's diesel generator and caused something to explode, bringing down a mess of flaming rubble between himself and the door. It didn't yet look like the fuel reserves in the generator itself had ignited — that would probably be enough to incinerate the whole basement and him along with it.

He had to keep calm. That janitor, at least, knew he was down here, and the fire alarm had been sounding for almost twenty minutes at this point; the fire department would likely already be on the scene upstairs. The blaze itself was still isolated to one half of the room, and he had found a position as far away as possible and very low to the ground in which to wait, but still the heat was incredible.

His mind flashed with all the countless fire-training, fire-prevention, and fire-whatever-else sessions he had endured in his life. From grade school and into his career — none of it really conveyed the reality of such a predicament.

His mind began to jump about — panic was taking hold and he recognized it. He struggled to fight it by thinking about, of all things, Stam: had she really set this fire? *What kind of horrible person would do something like this — put hundreds of lives at risk?*

He wasn't sure, anymore, that he could blame some nebulous force in Ashley or Stam's life for their actions. As far as he was concerned, there comes a point — a point well before the one at which people start burning down hospitals — where your actions and choices in life are *your* responsibility. At Ashley's age — even Stam's age — right and wrong had been clear to him. They're clear to everybody, much as they might deny it for the sake of saving face. The more he thought about it, it seemed obvious: they weren't victims of some kind of parental abuse or neglect — they were just outright *sociopaths*. This was all a joke to them — another game.

For over a week now, he had wanted to believe that the two mysterious occupants of the little house could be explained, but there seemed no way to reconcile why a preteen girl would want to bomb a hospital.

Was Stam *that* afraid of losing Ashley? That wasn't likely; Stam wasn't the type to be scared. Vomiting gallons of blood didn't seem to faze her. She operated with cold, callous indifference to everyone, even though she knew it was wrong. If springing Ashley from the hospital was what she wanted, she'd make it happen, with no regard for *anyone* in the process.

Then he saw something — a fire hose. It was inside a red case on the wall nearby; it had been obscured by flames, but he had just caught a glimpse of it through the haze. He crawled toward it as quickly as he could, keeping far below the thick blanket of black smoke above him, until coming to a stop still far out of reach of the case. It was inaccessible — too close to the flames at this point.

Officer Wilson looked around frantically, in hopes there might be another in the room, but saw nothing of use. Coughing and forcing his stinging eyes to close, he struggled back to the opposite end of the room.

Was he going to die just because he was doing his job, and because he cared enough to worry about those two monsters?

Something in the room flared up, making the situation all the worse — he could feel a scorching heat from where it previously had been tame. He couldn't see much of what was happening — his eyes just remained on the door, hoping *someone* might appear.

Perhaps he hadn't taken things seriously enough; it seemed impossible that the pair had any involvement with Hannah and David, but what little evidence there was in the disappearance case that failed to support a runaway situation *did* point to Ashley and Stam. He'd never given real consideration to their guilt; while the two were suspicious for a thousand reasons, his only intent was to get to the bottom of things. But now, it seemed like it might be true: maybe they *did* kill Hannah and David.

… Very soon, Stam might likely kill *him*.

* * *

"You were a friend of Wolfgang's?" a woman asked, handing Gunther a cup of tea which he ignored and left her to place on a coffee table. Beside it was Gunther's photograph of Mengele, which he simply stared down at, looking right through it, as his thoughts churned in a thick, muddled mess.

"Something like that." Gunther's tone was empty and flat. His mind was far from where he actually was — it was stuck in cold isolation, laboriously reflecting on feelings he could not discern.

The woman explained that she was Josef's — *Wolfgang's* — housekeeper and that he had just recently passed away in a swimming accident. "It was February seventh. He was in Bertioga with the Bosserts — have you met them?"

"Yes."

"Wolfgang was a very solitary man — I'm sure you know. He didn't have a lot of friends…."

Gunther said nothing. He simply sat, unable to collect his thoughts well enough to respond, and the housekeeper carried on, "He's in a better place now, of course, but I still miss him, too…. He was a good man."

Gunther still made no effort to speak, and the woman's words meant nothing to him. The two might as well have been sitting in silence.

"I'm sure, though, that he'd want us to remember him fondly, and not just sit around mourning — right?"

Gunther raised his eyes and looked the woman over. She was somewhere in her thirties, Brazilian, and unmistakably very pretty. Maybe it wasn't Mengele, after all — Mengele had been a *Nazi*; he believed in racial hygiene and the supremacy of Aryans. It seemed against the man's core ideology to live in the company of this dark-skinned girl, and yet at the same time, as he searched his memory of the man, it seemed somehow plausible. All of this seemed that way—the little room was warm and inviting, the decorations were tasteful and pleasant, there was a squat writing desk in one corner and a huge shelf packed with books. There was also a tiny television atop a table by a big window through which—in the daytime—would no doubt stream more than enough light to drench the room in tropical sunshine. He could believe it of the man—that he put the past so far behind him as to forget it ever occurred. Sure, he may have lived a life on the run, but he had still lived a life.

"Ashley?"

He finally noticed that she was requesting his attention.

"... What?" he asked.

"I said: would you like me to leave you alone? It's alright if you stay here a bit."

Gunther took a breath and resumed staring at the ground through Mengele's photograph. He couldn't think clearly enough to answer.

"I've been sorting some of his things—old letters, stuff from over the years—even some of his old things from the war. It kind of helps me keep him around, in a way—makes him feel closer...." She took hold of a box sitting next to the chair where she sat. "I was going through this one earlier—it's from when he lived on a farm in Nova Europa about ten years ago—there are some pictures with the Stammer children and a few vacations...."

Gunther ignored her, but let his eyes drift to the pile of boxes. Most of them were labeled as being full of letters and diaries from recent years, but there was one which grabbed his attention. It said, quite plainly on the side: *"la guerra"*—the war. Gunther stood up and moved toward it, saying nothing to the housekeeper as he removed the few boxes sitting on top of his target. Once it was uncovered, he began to peel at tape which had kept it sealed for years.

"I hadn't really looked at that one yet," she explained. "He didn't really have much left over from the war—just a few old medical records and things. He was a doctor in the army."

Gunther continued to pay the woman no mind at all as he pulled the box top open and revealed its contents. It was mostly empty. It appeared to be nothing but pamphlets and procedure manuals — miscellanea of no particular relevance. He wasn't sure what he had expected to find — maybe some unmistakable link to the past which would tie up everything. But of course, there was nothing. After over thirty years, how could he have fooled himself into thinking it? Mengele was dead, and if he wasn't somehow, then he had at least escaped. Gunther couldn't do it anymore. He couldn't keep pursuing a ghost forever, with nothing to keep him going but the hope that three decades hadn't yet rendered the past irrelevant.

Jens was wrong; the past *didn't* matter. The past just dries up and disappears, vindicating evil and turning memory into nothing more than fantasy. Mengele was *a doctor in the army*; he was *a concentration camp torturer*; his name was *Josef* or *Peter* or *Wolfgang* or who knew what else. The Nazis were *categorically evil*; they were driven by *hatred*; they were driven by *fear*; the German people listened to Hitler because he was *charismatic*, because he was *loud*, because they had *no other options*... Was *everything* true? Was the past just some great canvas waiting to be repainted by whoever wanted to say whatever they wanted about anything? It didn't matter now, did it? All those things that Mengele did — who in the world even cared? Why punish anyone for anything? Why resent anything? Did that fucking brat Heinz ever look back once on the things he had said and done? Wasn't it all justified now because he was *only a kid*? Could Gunther just forget about the people he had killed? Was he justified in his apathy and disaffection?

When Gunther was growing up, he heard constantly about the *future*. The *future* of Germany — about how children are the *future*. It was the most important thing in the world: *preparing for the future*.

... But at some point, the future became nothing more

than the meaningless past. The only thing Gunther or anyone else was ever supposed to think about and prepare for became something of no worth to *anyone*. No one in the world seemed to consider the value of—even for a moment—pausing and *reflecting*. In never looking backward, one was immune to responsibility. If you hid long enough, obscured deep in the annals of history, time itself would absolve you. In that sense, Mengele wasn't a murderer: he was just a man now. Dead or alive, the years had washed away his sin. Josef Mengele had nothing to answer for: he was as virtuous as a saint.

It all made sense—Gunther wondered if he was perhaps the only person in the world who had *ever* felt compassion for anyone beyond the most transparent courtesy. He had obviously been wrong in doing so—the past became a prison as he directed his own life in pursuit of things which didn't exist. He had venerated Jens and vilified Mengele because of the things they had done in the past—the stupid, *irrelevant* past.

"Ashley?" The housekeeper's voice broke through his thoughts and into his ears. "Are you okay?"

He said nothing. He had gone through the entire box, and the picture it painted of Mengele was the same as the housekeeper's: a doctor who didn't bother hanging on to the silly old junk he accumulated in a long-forgotten war. Gunther took his hands out of the box and began to stand, stopping only as he noticed a folded-up piece of paper shoved in with all the other documents. He couldn't say what about it caught his attention, but knelt down to retrieve it. It was yellowed and delicate—threatening to disintegrate right in his hands—but carefully, he unfolded it and revealed the contents: it was a letter in an unfamiliar handwriting.

19th November, 1944
Dear Herr Mengele,

Thank you for the letter; I have been in the hospital myself for the last two weeks, but am due to be discharged tomorrow. I showed your documents to my Hauptsturmführer and he has granted me permission to travel out to Poland; I cannot say that I totally understand the situation, but I will make myself available for whatever you need.

In answer to your questions, no, I do not have any familiarity with the symptoms, nor do they affect me in any way that I know of.

I will be arriving in two weeks, which I hope will be sufficient for me to be of assistance. Until then, please do whatever you can for my brother.

Heil Hitler,
Luther Gruenwold

Chapter 17

Doctor Dawson crept nervously through the empty halls, avoiding the firefighters who were forcing their way into the basement nearby. Upon reaching the door he had been seeking, he stealthily opened it and slid in. The only illumination in the room came from an emergency spotlight which did little to make anything clear, but the doctor could *hear* Ashley's deep, quavering gasps. It was eerie being in a dark room with a creature like Ashley whom he hardly knew the limits of; the fury the boy had worn on his face earlier was enough to make Doctor Dawson's blood run cold, but he was left with no other option.

"Ashley?" he asked, creeping over to him.

The pained gasps continued, offering no response.

"Ashley?" he asked again, now only a few feet away. He could somewhat make out his face — eyes still open and staring at the floor. His breathing was slightly calmer now than it had been, which was at the same time comforting and a bit disturbing to Doctor Dawson. "Ashley, listen — I'm really sorry about this...."

Ashley only glanced to him—long enough to evidence displeasure—before looking down once more.

"I didn't know that would happen—in the MRI," he explained. "I—I thought I had made it clear, and... I just didn't think... I mean, *shrapnel* in somebody your age? I just—I'm really sorry...."

There was no reaction from Ashley.

"But anyone else probably could have *died* from that... or at least gone into shock. Everything about you is so... so," he struggled to find the right inoffensive word, "*unusual*...."

"You can stop," Ashley interrupted him with frightening clarity, through his own gasps. It was more than enough to stun Doctor Dawson. Ashley looked over to the doctor, still apparently unable to move. "I don't need you to explain yourself."

"But," Doctor Dawson was taken aback, but tried to continue on his original path, "you don't understand—somebody like you—you completely redefine just about everything about medicine—even *life* itself."

Ashley coughed, chuckled a bit, and was not amused. "Is that so?"

"Yeah," Doctor Dawson replied, almost encouragingly. "I mean, Ashley, all you need to be pronounced clinically *dead* is a lack of heartbeat, and you've got that down. That MRI we did—the few seconds of data showed that you had *no* blood flow *at all* to your brain."

"What does that mean?" Ashley asked, still struggling to control his breaths.

"I don't even *know*," Doctor Dawson shook his head, "but I got a little carried away...."

"In my mind," Ashley began before coughing again, "I imagined you a certain way. It wasn't very pretty."

"We both have a lot to learn about each other, right? I fucked things up, and I could lose my job over this...."

"Unless I help, right? Unless somebody proves you were justified?"

Doctor Dawson could discern his meaning and struggled to convince him otherwise. "I really didn't mean to put you through that—"

"I'm not mad about the MRI," Ashley responded. "I had long since forgotten about the shrapnel—honestly, I didn't even know it was *there*...."

"What could it be *from*?" Doctor Dawson asked, finding a moment to speak when Ashley hesitated.

"A grenade," Ashley replied, wincing as he began to shift.

"Ahh—Ashley, you really shouldn't be moving. That's why you're strapped—"

Ashley forced himself to sit up straight; the straps on his arms, chest and head had already been removed.

"—down...." Doctor Dawson finished his sentence, apprehensive now that Ashley was no longer bound.

With considerable strain, Ashley brought his legs from the gurney, dangling his feet from the edge. Doctor Dawson, nervously, began to take a few steps back, closer to the door. He placed his hand on the knob, ready to flee if things escalated.

Ashley stood, but in the same movement, his legs gave way and he collapsed. Stumbling forward, he caught himself against the wall with his shoulder. Through a painful wince, he turned so that his back could rest flat as his weak legs only barely kept him upright. He struggled to regain his breath sufficiently to speak. "The reason I don't like you... is because you're an asshole."

Doctor Dawson furrowed his brow at the insult, but nodded. "You're justified in feeling that way."

Ashley continued to breathe heavily and remained where he was against the wall. He said nothing more, and eventually, the doctor asked, "You were hit by grenade shrapnel?"

Ashley sighed. "A long time ago. Not very important in the grand scheme of things." He coughed. "But then, what *is*?"

"What do you mean, 'a long time ago?'"

"Look," he replied, dismissing it as his eyes rose to Doctor Dawson and he adjusted his slumped body. "You're like anyone else—maybe what you're doing right now is hardly worse than what any crappy doctor would do when presented with a supposed miracle medical case."

Doctor Dawson was unsure how to reply. Now that his eyes had adjusted to the dark a bit, he could see the large chunk of Ashley's bare torso riddled with jagged metal shards, from which tiny trails of blood had dripped down his side and begun to dry—it looked fake, somehow, like something out of a cheap horror movie. Still, he knew it was the real thing, and it seemed unlikely that *anyone* could survive an injury like it for very long.

"My eyes." Ashley pointed to them with two fingers. "They're always open. I can't even blink." He squinted his eyes, but try as he might, they never fully shut. "Can you imagine how much I see?"

"I, uh—I'm sure that you see a lot."

"I don't," Ashley replied. "There's really very little that is special about me, other than, perhaps, my circumstance." He tried to stand up from the wall, but with a stumble, had to catch himself on the edge of a hospital bed. Frustrated by his incapacity, he dropped his head down and was silent, seeming to abandon his cryptic speech. It was only after great hesitation that he finally said, "I could try and explain everything, but... it would only be for *my* sake. Words can't excuse murder."

"Murder?" Doctor Dawson couldn't follow his meaning, and after a brief pause, changed topics back to Ashley's condition. "Let me help you," he suggested, and though his initial step forward was apprehensive, he began to approach Ashley.

Ashley held up a hand for him to stop. "No." He struggled to his feet. This time, though marginally successful, he still needed one hand on the bed railing as a brace. "How would you *help* me?"

Doctor Dawson watched him; he was a pathetic sight. "Look, Ashley.... I know that there's something strange about you, but you're not invincible—we need to take care of your injuries before anything else."

Ashley's head hung once more and he smiled sadly to himself, "Yeah," before looking back up to Doctor Dawson with a profound sorrow in his eyes. "I hate this."

Doctor Dawson was about to ask what Ashley meant when a sudden noise by the door drew his attention away. As he turned toward it, before he saw anything, the force of a body slammed him forward, toward Ashley, who caught him.

"What the hell?" Doctor Dawson gasped, held sandwiched against Ashley by some small figure. In the darkness, he couldn't make out who or what it was, and as he resisted, twisting his head to get a better look at his attacker, he felt a sharp pinch in his throat—it rendered him unable to do anything but fight the attacker with his arms, and that too became impossible as Ashley took hold of his wrists to restrain him. He opened his mouth again to cry for help, when suddenly, he felt Ashley's face move in toward his neck on the opposite side, followed by a second sharp pain.

* * *

With a final spray of foam, the flames had been subdued sufficiently that firefighters could push into the basement.

"Anyone in here?" one called as they spread out.

"Oh man—do you see that?" Another pointed to the charred case sitting by the scorched generator and electrical boxes. It was obvious to anyone that the initial explosion had come from the twisted pile of metal. Cautiously, two of the firemen approached the case, and careful not to touch it, examined the outside. "It's like a tackle box or something," one pointed out.

"*Fuck*," somebody screamed from somewhere nearby. "Guys, we got somebody down here."

* * *

A cool breeze rolled across the grass, rippling tiny waves across a stream. It continued on through a serene, hazily moonlit valley, rustling the leaves of bamboo stalks before at last passing where Gunther stood beneath a gently swaying palm tree.

At his feet was a grave.

He had been standing for hours, quietly staring down at the plain stone marker set atop freshly disturbed dirt. What thoughts had run through his head—as was so often the case now—he couldn't say. He knew and felt too many things to decide on the words that would fall from his lips.

Doctor Josef Mengele was dead.

After everything—more than thirty long years since that day in Romania—it came down to this. His quest, like all things, met its end offering no answers—no closure— beyond just further proof of what he had long since feared was true and tonight finally knew: time could erase the past.

He spoke, unsure what his words would be.

"I was a fool...." His eyes drifted slowly to the false name on the headstone. "I let myself believe there was value in memory—that the suffering people endure *means* something." He shook his head. "I let myself believe that the crimes of yesterday matter today."

Slowly, carefully, he knelt down, placing both knees on the warm dirt. "Memory can't keep the past alive." He took a long, quavering breath. "Somehow, *I'm* still here. I've outlived everyone else from that time. I've outlived all its consequence. There's nothing left but *me*."

"You can destroy written records—you can *kill* people—but that alone can't erase history." He reached out to some mossy cover which had already grown over the birth date on the grave. "What does is *life*. In living life, you can choose to forget who you were and the things you've done... and make anything at all be the truth."

As the moss fell away, Gunther revealed an impossibly late year—probably that of Wolfgang Gerhard's and not Mengele's.

"You, me... Sydney... Luther. We were all the same— all part of an unforgivable evil—and we each obscured it in our own way. Luther died; Sydney saw the future as a haven in which to live a better life; you, I imagine, denied any wrongdoing; and me...." He shook his head again. "I don't even know what I did. All I know is I'm here. I'm the only one left."

Gunther placed his hand in the dirt. "I didn't come here to kill you—" he sighed, "—to deal your well-deserved death and avenge my brother." His fingers dragged across the earth, eventually forming into a fist. "I went to Romania to find that girl. I went to America for Sydney...."

There was a long pause.

"I just wanted to see you. I just wanted to show myself the past was real."

He sat against the marker and let his head rest against the cool stone as he stared up at the sky. As another gust of breeze washed over him, he noticed Luther's letter still in his hand, threatening to dissolve in the wind.

"All I really want is to die before I forget...."

He turned his eyes to the engraved letters beside his head.

"... But it's already too late."

* * *

"I'm gonna lay you down here, alright man?" assured a firefighter struggling to carry a very dazed and coughing Officer Wilson. "I'll go get help."

He placed him in a chair, and making eye contact, instructed him not to move. Officer Wilson managed to nod though his hacking cough before the firefighter hurried away toward the hospital lobby.

"Hey!"

He could hear him calling for help to the crowd of doctors outside.

"We got somebody in here. Bring a mask."

The hallways remained dark and silent, save for his coughing. He was still piecing together what had happened and where he was—his chest felt heavy and his throat burned with each breath. He had more or less passed out, but now, as his clarity returned, he remembered what he had seen in the basement. His thoughts returned to Stam and Ashley; by now they must have escaped....

Just as the thought crossed his mind, he heard a

distant sound echoing through the halls, like someone stumbling and knocking into something. Somehow, he *knew* who it was. Struggling, he lifted himself from the seat—it was nearly impossible to stand, but he would have to. One step at a time, he lurched toward the direction of the sound, still coughing and no doubt giving away his pursuit.

As he turned a corner, he saw an emergency exit door closing nearby.

He hurried onward, pushed on the crash bar, and stumbled past a stairwell and into a parking garage. Here, the electricity had remained on, and the bright orange glow of the lights was almost blinding. He looked around, in all directions, and at last—at the end of a long row of cars—he saw them.

"Ashley," he tried his best to scream through his hoarse, smoke-scorched throat.

Stam slowed at the sound of the man's voice. Her arms were wrapped about Ashley, who remained unable to stand without her support.

Officer Wilson hurried after the pair, still coughing violently as he began feeling for his gun. He drew it as he closed in on them.

Both Ashley and Stam wore drab, tired expressions. As Officer Wilson approached, he could see that both were still strained—physically and emotionally taxed from all that had happened. Half of Stam's face had been seared by fire—likely from the explosion she'd caused.

"Stam," Officer Wilson said with as much authority as his weak voice would allow. His pistol shook in his hand as he tried to think of something—anything at all—to add. There was something disarming about Ashley and Stam's pitiable state—they looked like two weak, downtrodden children huddled in each other's arms. Ashley, still panting quietly, had hastily applied bandages about the massive wound in his midsection. They were already blood-soaked, but his tired, pale face betrayed something far worse than just pain. Stam, too, burnt and bleeding, seemed taxed beyond what her own frail form could handle.

Officer Wilson likely looked similarly pathetic in his soot-smeared clothes, coughing repeatedly and hardly even able to wield his weapon. The three stood without exchange for what seemed like ages, until Ashley spoke, putting an end to the silent stalemate.

"Officer...."

"No, Ashley," Officer Wilson interrupted with as much force as he could. "I don't want to hear it. I don't want to hear another word."

Ashley obliged, said nothing else, and let his eyes drift from the officer.

"Stam." Officer Wilson looked to the girl. "What the hell were you thinking?"

She seemed unsure how to answer. In a way, her eyes suggested guilt, but it seemed unlikely to be real.

"... I hope no one was hurt," she replied quietly.

"You nearly *killed me*," he shouted back, angrily.

"You were there?" she asked.

"Stam." Officer Wilson remained forceful in his tone. "You tried to blow up a hospital."

"... That was not my intention."

Ashley interjected, "If this was anyone's fault, it was mine—"

"Shut up, Ashley. Just *shut up*." Officer Wilson coughed more as he yelled, this time wincing and stumbling from a sudden wave of faintness. He caught himself with one hand on the trunk of a car, and then held his free hand to his forehead.

"You need to find a doctor," Ashley observed.

"What did I just say?" he growled, struggling to raise the gun at the pair once again. Straining to stand, he pushed away from the car and slowly approached them, stopping only feet away. Their tired, sad eyes were on his, waiting for what he might do now.

Despite what he had said, Officer Wilson knew something to be true. He had resisted it, but now, as he stood with his gun aimed straight for Ashley's chest, there seemed no more denying it: their situation was untenable. He looked back and forth between them—first Stam and then Ashley—before shaking his head. "You won't come with me, will you?"

Ashley swallowed as his gaze fell to the pavement. He looked almost remorseful, in a way, as he brought his eyes back to Officer Wilson's and replied, "No."

Not surprised — defeated yet somehow liberated — he slowly nodded, accepting what he knew he couldn't change. He took a breath. "I guess that's it then." He let his arm and the gun fall to his side. "You win."

Ashley smiled sadly, thinking about the words, and then replied, "Officer." He waited to be told to shut up again. When he was not, he continued, "If you learned anything from Stam and I, forget it. You did everything right — well, as right as is reasonable. A little overzealous, but nobody's perfect."

Officer Wilson rose an eyebrow, unsure what Ashley meant.

"I greatly resented you — that much I'm sure is clear." He chuckled. "I thought to myself: why won't this idiot just leave us alone? Why can't he accept that there are strange people in the world who defy expectations? Why does he think just because we're *different* that there's something *wrong?*"

Officer Wilson swallowed, about to respond, when Ashley continued, "I have a lot of hang-ups about the past. Maybe I had every reason to react to you as I did — I don't know." He brought his eyes to Officer Wilson's. "I've never once thought my life was reasonable, but I somehow expected you to accept me."

"Hey!" the Firefighter's voice called out from a group which could see Officer Wilson from the opposite end of the garage.

"Point is," Ashley explained, "you had every right to look at me with suspicion and concern. You *shouldn't* have — as I wanted — left me alone. It was unreasonable of me to ask it, when I brought this all on myself."

Wincing as another wave of faintness came over him, Officer Wilson put his hand back to his forehead and stumbled forward, catching the only thing he could to stop from falling right into Ashley — Ashley's arm. Ashley tensed it, holding it stable, as the officer struggled to recover and stand up straight.

"Ashley," Officer Wilson struggled to say. "Hannah and David...?"

Ashley shook his head somberly, betraying an answer. As the firefighters continued their approach, he glanced to them, and then to Officer Wilson, helping him as best as he could.

"... A few days ago, I would have killed you if it came to it, and I wouldn't have looked back. I wouldn't be thinking about all this right now. I need to take a long look at why I let things get to this point."

With Stam's assistance, Ashley helped Officer Wilson to the hood of a nearby car where he took a seat, still recovering. Ashley then turned to the approaching firefighters.

"Maybe I'm not so self-reflective after all," Ashley mused. "I can't even look into mirrors...."

Chapter 18

Sydney roosted in the passenger's seat at Gunther's side, quietly rocking back and forth with the movements of the car. It had taken the bird some time to adjust to it, but he traveled well now, and aside from being painfully noisy at times, was a decent companion for a long drive. Caring for the creature — keeping him happy and well-fed — was Gunther's best distraction from the deep melancholy that had set in after the events of São Paulo.

Upon his return to their shack, he resigned himself to his fate of a slow deterioration, and wasted away on the cold stone floor with the intention of staying there forever. Even Sydney's complaints and nudges were not enough to rile him; the only thing which eventually pulled him outdoors was the need for blood, and after a week, it happened again, and again — just like always. He had debated for months whether he would return to New York — to the company of Manfred and the familiarity of the home he had fashioned in the old apartment building, but staying in South America seemed just as legitimate a course of action. Nothing he might do would matter; regardless of where he went, things would always be the same.

The seasons came and went for the rest of the year until, one night; a song worked its way into his head. It was an old tune he had heard sung by dozens of Jens' favorite artists, but he could no longer grasp its name. He could picture it, alphabetized amongst his meager stack of milk crates in New York, but simply *could not* recall the title. It was one of Jens' favorites, and somehow, despite Gunther's ugly revelations about the meaningless past, the fleeting hint of a melody teased and tempted him.

As the night continued, the song mingled with another, and then *another*. Bits of lyrics and brief whispers of the voices of Bing Crosby, Chet Baker, Frank Sinatra and others drifted in his mind. He peeled himself up from the ground, and somehow a decision was made, irrelevant as it was.

Three weeks later, a familiar — though augmented — skyline appeared on the dark horizon before him. He approached New York City with no more affection for it now than before — he could already imagine the stench of the streets, the endless mountains of garbage, and the gruff, rude people who stalked through the nights. Why anyone would ever elect to live in such a place remained — as it had since his first day there — beyond him.

He imagined he wouldn't stay. After all his time in the quiet isolation of his tiny homes in South America, he had grown quite accustomed to such a style of living. It was like how things used to be with Jens in England, and he had come to an important decision which finalized his choice in returning to the United States: he would hold on to what he could of the memory of the man he had loved. Maybe it didn't matter; it seemed inevitable that he'd wind up like that girl who made him this way — with nothing in life but murder — but to what other use would he put the remainder of his sanity?

There was so much he could scarcely recall from his life. Names, places, events — simple data, of course, he had as reasonable a knowledge of as would be expected — but there were countless feelings he had lost. Luther's letter, for all its sentiment, contained the words of someone he hadn't known since childhood; there was nothing written which could not have been said by *anyone* about their brother, and he knew there would come a day when he would remember nothing at all about his own identical twin—not even what he looked like.

Soon, Gunther and Sydney found themselves on the streets of Manhattan. Traffic had been surprisingly rough heading into the city—even beyond his expectations which had been prepped by the nightmarish conditions he'd witnessed ten years prior.

He glanced at the car radio's clock:

5:41 a.m.

Had it taken any longer, the impending sunrise would have become a very real threat. He was already feeling a pang of discomfort—not because he feared the sun, but because he knew he *would* when he *saw* it. On the dashboard was taped the familiar handwritten list of upcoming sunrises: today's was 7:02 a.m.

Nothing had changed. He was still the same wreck he'd been for as long as he could remember. His excursion to South America had proved pointless, just as it no doubt would have even if he had caught Mengele in time. Not one thing he'd done since Jens had died had any real point—he had taken nothing away from *any* of it, save perhaps Sydney, whose very name only proved Gunther's desperation.

"We're almost there, buddy."

"*Reeeeek….*"

Sydney's eyes slid open as he stretched and craned his neck.

"*Braawwwk!*"

He also then screamed for no apparent reason.

"… Thanks." Gunther winced.

They turned onto a narrow downtown street— Gunther could already see his building on the next corner and began to scan either side of the road for parking, with no luck. Eventually he began to pass by his apartment and, in dismay, screeched to a stop.

"What the…?"

Immediately, he threw the car door open and hopped out of his seat. From where he stood in the middle of the road, he could see that the building had been recently *re-renovated*. Gunther had specifically made the apartment to appear—from the outside—abandoned and uninhabitable, but had done a tremendous amount of work to the units themselves. Unlike everything else in the neighborhood, which was coated in layer after layer of graffiti, his old residence now looked brand new, as if… as if it *was* brand new.

Upon further inspection, he realized it wasn't his old building at all. All the others on the block were as he remembered, but his building was gone—replaced by something which only marginally resembled his old walk-up.

Stranger still, it had no windows at all.

"Manfred," he grumbled. Manfred could be anywhere—he might be dead for all Gunther knew. Angrily, not sure what he was thinking, he stormed toward the door of the new building and up the steps, onto the stoop, reached out his hand to the knob, and froze, unable to enter. He stood in place for a few minutes, holding the knob, overcome by another wave in an ever-rising tide of defeat.

"Of course," he mumbled to himself, quietly. He felt like a fool for expecting *anything* to have lasted ten whole years in his absence. All that work he had put into the apartments—he wondered if they were ever even used. He had done weeks of research, as well as massive work to the building's structure prior to his renovations; there was no reason the building would have needed to be torn down.

"Hey," a harsh voice called out behind him, accompanied by the sound of a car door slamming. He lazily glanced to it.

"This your car?" A traffic cop standing in the street gestured to the maroon Chevelle.

Gunther said nothing, ignoring the officer. He heard him grumble some sort of obscenity in response to the disrespect.

After another somber minute, giving up, Gunther slumped wearily down the steps and back to the street, where he sat down on the hood of the car, next to the officer who was in the middle of writing a ticket.

He glared at Gunther. "So, this *is* yours? You know you can't park in the middle of the street, kid."

Gunther said nothing. The traffic cop just shook his head, annoyed, and went on writing the ticket. "Whatever."

Gunther glanced to his watch:

6:19 a.m.

There wasn't much time—he'd have to find a hotel. He knew one a short drive away, assuming it was still there after ten years.

"I've only been here five minutes—where did you even *come* from?" Gunther glanced to the officer from his seat on the car hood. "Don't you have anything better to do at six in the morning than inconvenience people?"

The officer made the last pen stroke on the ticket and tore it off, holding a copy to Gunther. "Just doing my job, kid."

Gunther made no move to take the paper being offered him, and the officer sighed and let it go with a flick of his wrist before turning to leave. He had moved a few car-lengths away before Gunther noticed that the door he had heard shut was his own. The officer had closed it— presumably because it was blocking half the street—but in doing so, had locked Gunther's keys inside. He took a look at Sydney, who remained blissfully unaware of everything, half-asleep in the passenger's seat. Gunther's eyes narrowed as he tried the door, and soon, his head turned toward the officer.

Following him, Gunther glanced at his watch again:

6:22 a.m.

As Gunther was nearly upon him, the officer turned around and stopped, folding his arms. "What do you want?"

In his final footsteps, Gunther cast a quick sweeping glance around the area, and seeing no one, grabbed hold of the officer.

"*Rreeeerrk.*"

Sydney puffed up, annoyed, as Gunther tapped on the glass of the back window, trying to lure the bird away from the front of the car. It didn't seem to be working terribly well—Sydney only grew agitated by the sound and Gunther's confusing gestures.

He glanced to his watch:

6:36 a.m.

"Dammit," he grumbled, giving up and moving toward the front window. He maintained a close eye on Sydney, who was watching Gunther with a scowl of complete disapproval. Gunther then raised to the window a baton which he had relieved from the officer's possession, and with a breath, he slammed it forward, shattering the glass into a million tiny green-tinted blocks. Sydney's reaction was reasonable: furious, he flapped and hissed, and as Gunther reached in and opened the door, flew right out of the car.

"Sydney," Gunther screamed after the bird as it flew down the street. "*Sydney!*"

The bird settled on a third-story windowsill several doors down. He glared downward at Gunther with continuing irritation. Similar events had occurred in the past—it seemed to be in the temperamental nature of birds—and typically it was no big deal, but....

He glanced to his watch again:

6:39 a.m.

"Dammit, Sydney," he growled, looking back to his car. After another glance to the bird, he started toward the Chevelle, climbed inside, and sat down on his glass-covered seat. Once the engine was on, he rolled a few yards, taking a parking space which waited nearby, and got back out. He had no interest in being towed while he did what he was about to have to do.

He called to the bird once more, "Sydney," and again was met with haughty disregard.

With a sigh, he looked down at the trunk of the car, seriously considering that he might spend the day inside.

There had been plenty of other times in his life where his affliction forced him into pathetic situations, but this one seemed absurd.

He was about to call for Sydney once more, but then paused—he thought he had heard a voice from somewhere nearby. He glanced to the street, then up and down the sidewalk, until he saw a figure on the stoop of where once was his home....

... It couldn't be.

Gunther took a step away from the car, slowly, holding his eyes fixed to the girl who stood watching him.

"Gunther," she said his old name clearly.

He could only stare. On the deck of a ship, twenty years prior, Jens' death was fresh in Gunther's mind—that sorrow and despair merged with the disgust and resentment he felt for the girl, exploding into rage. That rage remained, reignited now by her appearance, but apathy had become an adversary to anything he might do. What he had said at Mengele's grave he believed to be true: the past didn't matter. Each passing day of his life had made it more painfully clear, and what was more: he couldn't kill her *anyway*.

The girl took a step forward, off the stoop and onto the top step, where she held out something Gunther had seen in her hands two decades ago: the old metal ammunition case.

"*Das ist für Sie,*" she said in poorly-skilled German.

Gunther could still do nothing. He remained paralyzed, able only to move his eyes to the case. By now, perhaps from falling into the ocean, it had rusted almost entirely through, but for its age and all it had endured, it had held together as if carefully protected. After a time, he swallowed nervously. "*Was ist das?*"

She seemed put off, unsure how to answer. Her brow furrowed and she tried again. "*Es gehört Ihnen. Ich habe es Ihnen abgenommen.*"

Her German remained weak. All she had said was that the box was his: "I took this from you."

"Ich will es nicht," he shook his head, *"das ist nur ein bedeutungsloses Ding aus der Vergangenheit."*

She failed to understand, and only tried offering it again, taking a few steps closer while Gunther stayed motionless.

"Braaaaawk."

Sydney swept down from his perch to somewhere on the opposite side of the street. Gunther only glanced to him before turning back to the girl—she was now removing a thin lace from her neck, on the end of which was a small key to a cheap padlock on the metal case.

"Acesta este pământul unde a inceput moartea ta," she explained energetically, in Romanian, as she offered both to him. *"Cu acest pământ vei putea muri — "*

"Shut up," he replied, shaking his head. "I don't understand what you're saying."

It was clear she wanted him to open the case, but to what end? What the hell could be so important that she would spend forty years on his trail—even leap out to sea from a cruise ship—to save it?

With a sigh, he reached out his hand for the key, but now, *she* seemed reluctant.

"Well?" Gunther asked, holding out his other hand to take the case itself.

Her lips began to move as she seemed to want to give some sort of instruction or warning—but she stopped, knowing there was no way to convey it, and took the final step forward to transfer the items to Gunther. The case was heavy—completely full. Slowly, he knelt down to the ground and brought the key to the lock—it was rusted and tight, but with some force, he managed to twist it, and with a good tug, brought the padlock away from the case. The lid itself was fused shut from disuse, but again, with some force, he was able to break it apart and reveal the contents.

His face was blank, and after staring at it for a short time, his eyes rose to the girl.

"Dirt?" he asked, flatly.

"Das ist damit Sie sterben können," she replied in German.

He was very quiet. "It is so you can die," was the direct translation of her words.

"… What?" he asked in a very small voice.

"Das ist damit Sie sterben können," she reiterated, annunciating better.

He looked down at the contents: it was dirt. Regular dirt. It had a sort of musty odor, and had solidified and dried into one large chunk in the bottom of the case.

"What do you mean?" He looked up at her when she failed to respond. "It's *dirt*."

"Cu acest pământ vei pu —" she started to answer.

"I don't understand," Gunther said from his crouched position.

The girl was quiet, and repeated her earlier words, "Das ist damit Sie sterben können."

"With a box of dirt?" Gunther growled, shoving it away. The girl tensed as the box scraped along the pavement, but made no move to retrieve it.

"Ich habe es Ihnen abgenommen."

"Shut up," he yelled again as his temper began to rise. The more the girl evidenced her inability to be reasonable — her strange lack of humanity — it only reminded him of what she had done to him.

It was *her* fault.

"*Nu ştiu cum să-ţi explic —*" she began speaking again, and Gunther felt something snap inside.

He reached out and grabbed hold of her collar. "This is all *your* fucking fault." He glanced to the box and then back to her. "What am I supposed to do with a bunch of dirt? *Eat* it?"

"*Lasă-mă.*"

"You had twenty goddamn years to learn my language and all you can say is: 'this is for you; it's so you can die?'"

"Lasă-mă," she said again, placing her hand on his wrist. She attempted to push his hands away, which only made Gunther's fists clench tighter. "*Nu are rost să ne batem —*"

Gunther took a step, still holding her collar, and dragged the girl before throwing her against the steps of the building. In the process, his foot kicked the case, knocking it over.

"*Oprește-te,*" she cried, as a few solidified chunks of dirt tumbled from the case and onto the sidewalk.

"Why the *hell* couldn't you just kill me?" he screamed at the girl where she lay struggling to climb back to her feet.

"*Es tut mir leid...*" she apologized, seeming to offer the last of her limited German vocabulary.

"... You're sorry?" He swallowed, shaking his head. "You don't even know what that means." His voice trembled as his head dropped. "Writing it in a book seven thousand times doesn't make it any truer." He looked up at her—the girl's attention seemed to be off him and focused on the case, just as it had the night they met on the ship. Gunther noticed, and it only enraged him further— he grabbed her, pulling her up. "Look at me," he screamed. "You didn't take a box of dirt from me. You took my life—my own death—*everything.*"

Once again, the girl resisted his clutch—this time more forcefully—and was successful in breaking away. She held her open-palmed hands out to him in a sign that there was no reason to act as he was, and said again, "Nu are rost să ne batem."

Furious, Gunther glanced down to the metal case and gave it a hard kick.

"Oprește-te," the girl screamed as the case rattled several across the pavement, spilled half its contents, and then eventually hit the wall of the building. As Gunther returned his eyes to the girl, she slammed into him, tumbling him aside as she hurried to the box. Immediately, she began to scrape the chunks of dried dirt up in her hands and drop them back in the case right along with whatever detritus existed on the grimy city sidewalks.

"It's *dirt,*" he yelled again, grabbing the girl and pulling her away from her task. This time, she fought back and flailed out of Gunther's grasp.

"Lasă-mă," she yelled back and then gestured to the case. "Das ist damit Sie sterben können."

"What the hell would you even *care* about me dying?" he screamed back. "Is it guilt? Do you even know what that *is*?"

She ignored him and moved again for the case, which pushed Gunther completely over the edge. He lunged at the girl, who seemed to expect it, and the two grappled before Gunther overpowered her frail arms. He shoved her against the wall of the building, where first, she stumbled over the case—further spreading its contents across the pavement—before she smacked head-first against the brick. The shock dropped her to the ground. It took her a moment to recover, and wincing, she put her hand to her forehead as she struggled back to her feet.

Gunther moved in, stepping on and grinding a wad of the dirt into the ground as he grabbed her shoulders once more and pulled her up. "What do you exp—"

The girl landed a forceful punch into Gunther's stomach—it wasn't terribly strong, but was enough to silence him as he buckled from it, and he had no time to recover before the girl's hand grabbed at and dug her fingernails into his face. Growling, Gunther flung an arm at her, but she managed to block it somewhat, and raising her small leg, she drove her foot into his thigh, pushing him back. As Gunther stumbled, he treaded across more of the dirt before stabilizing himself.

"*Vă rugăm,*" she seemed to command him. "*Cu acest pământ vei —* "

Gunther lunged back at her, grabbing her collar and thrusting her back into the wall. The force of the collision cracked her head against the brick, and when it was over, she failed to fight back. Instead, she struggled to raise one arm. Gunther was about to stop her until he realized her intentions—she wore a watch and seemed to be seeking the time.

Gunther glanced at his own:

6:58 a.m.

"*Nu avem timp de asta,*" she said, looking up into his eyes.

She weakly gestured to the sky. "*Soarele.*"

It was clear what she meant. It finally gave Gunther

pause. The girl, as had been obvious from her living quarters and the entries in her journal, suffered from the same insurmountable fear of the sun. It wasn't a shock to him—he hadn't *forgotten*—but the reality was that they had only four minutes remaining until a brutal, otherworldly fear would cripple them, rendering conflict, conversation—any interaction at all—completely impossible.

"*Braaawwwk!*" Sydney called from somewhere nearby, but there was no time left to look for him now.

The car trunk would be his only choice. His nervousness toward the impending sunrise rose—he knew how great his fear would be and what an awful sensation he would endure, and it was enough to make him no longer care about the girl. He pulled back from her, cautiously, but kept his hands at her throat. She remained where she was, making no move of resistance, with an empty gaze pointed at the ground.

At last, she looked up to him and said very quietly, "*Nu vrei să mori…?*"

Gunther shook his head in disappointment—defeat— whatever it was—and was about to let her go when he suddenly read something in her expression. It was the first real change he had seen in her face beyond her lips moving to speak. She looked alarmed—enough that Gunther turned about to see what it was….

A flock of pigeons had formed across the road at the feet of an old woman casting dried breadcrumbs to the ground, and the most tedious, absurd and obscure of all Gunther's nuances gripped him. He shoved the girl away and started toward the birds with increasing speed until reaching the scene. "Stop," he commanded the old woman with as much force as he had inside. It was enough to startle her *and* the dozen birds around them. Understandably disturbed, the old woman drew back as Gunther dropped to the ground and began plucking up the beads of grain. Sydney was there too—a bright blue accent amongst the blob of grey feathers.

Within seconds, the girl had joined them, stuck in the same ridiculous task as Gunther. The pigeons seemed annoyed by pair, but not enough to stop their feeding. It was pathetic—like all his other inescapable traits. He was crawling on the streets of the city amongst a flock of winged vermin, snatching up bread alongside the wicked creature that plunged him into a forty-year nightmare. There, too, was the clueless macaw he had found while on a deranged spree of vengeance. Not one thing in life—the desire to escape Mengele, save Luther, save Jens, and not even his meeting with the girl—was enough to obscure his curse. All things in life would be cast aside so he might flee the sun, drink blood or capture grain.

This is how it would *always* be.

A sick sensation crept up through both his body and mind—one of unbearable familiarity. The sky remained black to his eyes, but he could feel the fear of the light as it welled up inside. Panic washed over him like a wave—he gathered the bread as quickly as he could, growing ever more terrified.

"*Reeerwwwwk*," Sydney hissed at the pigeons, sending several scattering away.

Gunther glanced to the girl, who trembled now, affected in all the same ways as him. Her fear of the sun, her inability to walk away from their inane task, and even two dots on her neck—she was the same as him.

Gunther caught the time on his watch:

7:08 a.m.

He winced horribly, unable to contain a groan as he collapsed to the ground. Almost in tandem, the girl, too, fell. They continued seeking the bread, one piece at a time, as the pain and terror became worse and worse. Their bodies writhed with conflicting urges: stay, hide, stay, hide, *stay, hide*....

Gunther's eyes often shot to the girl, who herself continuously gazed back across the street, refusing even now to let the ammunition case leave her sight. Gunther's mind raced and wandered as he tried to decipher her words and insistence that a *box of dirt* would kill him.

He had craved death for decades, and however true it was that if he had died that day in Romania, he would never have had those thirteen years with Jens, what he had lost in his long life outweighed what he had gained. When he lay dying in the snow-powdered forest, there was vividness to his memory of Jens—his face, his voice, and even how his hands felt the one or two times they'd touched—but now there was nothing, and for that reason, his hate for the girl remained. After *seven thousand* victims, she elected, only then, to have the compassion to seek out dying soldiers, and in doing so, she found *him*....

That was when it all began.

He could feel his mind slowing—conscious thought escaping him as his terror swelled. No doubt the girl hadn't meant for all this to happen; she meant to kill him that night forty years ago, but what did her intention matter? What did *anything* matter?

He could hardly move any longer—the clash between two exclusionary needs paralyzed all but his weak, trembling grasps for the last of the bread. The girl was in the same state, wincing, with tears escaping her pained red eyes.

Gunther was crying too. It was the last thing he noticed as his thoughts faded into a static haze.

There remained one grain left. He reached for it. The girl reached for it. And as their hands nearly touched, Sydney snapped it from between them, raising his head and displaying his throat as he gleefully swallowed. With that, like two unchained beasts, both Gunther and the girl crawled in frantic desperation back across the street— Gunther toward the car and the girl toward the sidewalk. Sydney watched with curiosity, bobbing his head as he wandered after them.

Coughing, growling, groaning—Gunther batted at the trunk of the car pathetically, seemingly unaware that it required a key. He couldn't see the girl, but before long, he heard a metallic scraping from her direction. As he dropped to the ground, he caught a glimpse of her painfully contorted form, writhing on the pavement; with a weak grip, she was clutching to the metal case with the last of her strength as she inched toward the stoop of the apartment building. Much of the dirt still remained on the walk, but she seemed to be saving what she could.

Gunther strained, unable to move farther than a few feet. As he struggled to crawl, he tried to hide each part of himself using his own body—an arm would hide beneath his torso, until his torso tried to hide beneath an arm, until a moment later, his face needed shielding. He was a tangled mess with no direction to go.

The girl fought her way up the steps, agonizing with each tiny movement until she reached the door. She pawed at it, helplessly fumbling higher and higher until grasping the knob which, as she pulled downward, caused the door to creak inward. Her body fell against it, landing halfway into a hall.

Gunther caught a single glimpse of her as he continued to thrash and twist about the pavement. He tried to watch, but he was still trying to crawl to no place in particular—just *anywhere. Anywhere away from the sun.*

A fleeting thought passed his clouded mind as he saw the girl: she could go inside.

The girl struggled to force the rest of herself through the door, and as she finally made it, the case caught on the frame. She could let go, recoil inside and shove the door shut—but, she didn't. She held on somehow.

Gunther could hear her shout something, but what, he couldn't be sure.

"Komm rein."

The short phrase came again. It was German: an invitation.

Had she learned it just for him?

With the last of his strength, Gunther crawled forward, placing one hand, then his elbow, onto the first step as he started for the door.

Chapter *19*

Stam and Ashley entered an empty, no-longer-familiar living room.

The carefully packed boxes had been peeled open by investigators—many had been left with their contents spilt out on the floor.

Sydney, disturbed from a nap on the couch, looked up to them lazily before reburying his head.

"Feels longer than it's been," Ashley mused as his eyes examined the corners of the room. Still reliant on Stam's aid, he hobbled with her inside and let the door fall shut behind them. She brought Ashley to the couch, where he could lean against the arm.

"It does," she replied to his thought after taking a look of her own around the room. She had been there only hours before to bring Sydney to safety, and yet, she understood Ashley's meaning.

She headed to the kitchen while Ashley remained where he was and took in the room. He watched Sydney for a short time; he was subtly puffing up with each breath in his sleep. He then glanced to Stam, who was digging through and removing assorted junk that had been stuffed into a cupboard.

"Hey—what happened with Aurelio?"

"He's home," Stam answered. "I think he'll be safe."

"... What about the two of you?"

Stam slowed at her task. She was quiet, almost as if bearing a hint of modesty.

"Stam?" he asked, showing heightened curiosity.

"I kissed him," she at last replied.

Ashley's eyes widened. "*You* kissed *him*, or *he* kissed—"

"I kissed *him*," she answered.

He chuckled. "Wow...."

Silence took over between them as Stam uncovered what she had earlier hidden—a metal toolbox of no particular significance which used to be in the garage. Stam brought it from the cupboard, out of the kitchen and back into the living room, where she awaited what Ashley might say. He looked it over, knowing what it was, and let his gaze drift away; his eyes passed Stam's and landed on Sydney once more. He remained quiet for several minutes.

"Stam," he said finally, his voice now very different from before. "You know you don't have to do any of this. You don't have to go with me."

"... *Are* you going anywhere?"

"I don't know." He reached for the toolbox, which Stam handed off to him. He looked it over carefully before letting his hand rest on top. With his eyes still upon it, he added, "Now does seem as good a time as any to die. Where would I even go now if I didn't?"

Stam said nothing, but after a pause, Ashley continued, "I guess what I meant to suggest was you shouldn't feel so attached to me. Maybe you and Aurelio could... I don't know...."

He looked to Stam's face—it was blank but for the hint of a raised eyebrow.

"... You don't think so?" Ashley asked, surprised.

"It seems unlikely."

"That's not what I meant," he shot back. "A lot of things are *unlikely*—but what do you *want*?"

"I think you may be seeing more than is really there," she replied.

"Stam...." Ashley looked her in the eyes. "In twenty years, you've never sought anyone's company—you never even *liked* anyone, much less decided to kiss them, and I'm of the general impression it had never happened *before* we met, either. Am I right?"

"... I suppose."

Ashley shrugged. "All I was saying was that you should *think* about what you want."

She nodded, but remained skeptical.

Ashley continued after a moment, "Everything you and I do—the way we live our lives—it's all about avoiding fears." He looked around the room. "I tried to make this house as normal as I could, but I mean—come on—it has fake windows."

"I'm so tired of everything," he added after a sigh. "I've been tired for longer than I can remember." He glanced to her. "Longer than I've known you."

Stam was still quiet as Ashley placed a hand on his stomach. "I thought about something earlier...." He winced, taking hold of a tiny shard of shrapnel which protruded from his midsection. He looked down at it. "Where do you think *you'd* be right now if this grenade hadn't gone off fifty eight years ago?"

"... Dead," she answered after a time.

He nodded. There was much of Stam's past in Romania he didn't fully understand, but he did know that she possessed her own means of death just like his, and had put eternal rest on hold so that she could find him.

"All week," Ashley continued, "I've just been thinking about how I want this to be over—how I want my peaceful, lonely anonymity back." He shook his head. "I don't really deserve it. Just because I want it, it doesn't mean it should be mine—that policeman shouldn't have let us go." He looked down to Sydney, then to the shard in his own stomach again. "The only thing I really deserve is death—as a punishment, yeah, but as a *reward*, too. After all this time, I've earned the right to die, haven't I?"

Stam started to say something, but Ashley cut her off,

anticipating her response.

"Whether God agrees or not, *I* believe everyone has the right to choose death, no matter their circumstances. If you asked me back in 1980 whether or not I'd willfully remain on this earth another twenty-one years, I would have laughed...."

Stam continued to listen.

"I've killed over a thousand people since then, and I have nothing at all to show for it." Ashley lifted the toolbox and looked it over, "I kept living all these years, even after you gave me this, I guess, because I'm greedy."

"Greedy?" Stam asked.

"... Before I met you, I kept living because of a curse—because it was *impossible* to die. Then you gave me this dirt." He paused. "I wanted to understand it. I wanted to understand you, and there was also the fear that the first ray of hope I'd ever been given would prove false. I couldn't shake the feeling that those priests had lied to you—they had every reason to—and how could it really be that the solution was something as simple as dirt? Lying in the dirt in which my death began? If you were wrong, then I had *nothing*."

"That's not greed," Stam replied, but Ashley again spoke up.

"No, but I was lying to myself about all that. If there's one thing by which I'm undaunted, it's fear. It's not like what we feel when faced with sunlight."

Stam nodded, knowing that Ashley's will—much like hers—was inhumanly firm. Ashley took another look down at Sydney and reached one hand down to scoop him up. The bird murmured sleepily as Ashley brought him to his chest; he was careful to avoid the sharp protrusions from his torso. He offered the toolbox back to Stam, and she took it before stepping under Ashley's arm, helping him to stand.

Ashley took a long last look at the house, the stacks and stacks of records in milk crates, and the boxes strewn about the room. He took in and studied—for the first time in many years—the color of the aging 70's wallpaper, the texture of the deep shag carpet, the shape of the small room, and the chunky designs on the linoleum floor of the kitchen. He knew he'd forget it all someday, but he wanted to see them one final time.

Slowly — straining with each step — Ashley and Stam exited through the door and carefully made their way down the stoop and onto the walkway leading up from the street. Ashley turned back to examine the squat little house that had been his home for so long. Police tape stretched all about, and on the stoop laid a lock they had placed on the door after his arrest. For certain, it wouldn't be long before they returned.

The night sky above was clear and cold. Since the weekend snowstorm that canceled their bus and cemented Hannah and David's fate, the weather had remained calm and quiet, as if to mock Ashley somehow.

He brought his eyes down from the twinkling stars above and examined Sydney, who was puffed up in his arms and doing his best to endure the unseemly temperature.

"What do you think you'll do?" Stam asked.

"… I don't know." He took hold of Stam's arm for balance as he intentionally slipped from her support and dropped down on the cold, frosted grass. Once on the ground, he reached for the toolbox, which she handed him.

Stam watched him from where she stood.

"… I feared that it wouldn't work," Ashley continued his earlier thought, "but that wasn't what stopped me from trying." Still holding Sydney, he used his free hand to work open the clasps on the box. He opened it, revealing the dirt inside. Delicately, he let a finger drift across the dusty surface and trace a tiny line before stopping.

"I've had a long life — or an average one, at least — and if Sydney were still alive, or Luther, they'd both be near death themselves… and so would I. No matter what, we'd all end up losing each other."

Stam listened.

"I've spent a normal man's lifetime with nothing to show for it. I've done nothing but cause harm to people."

He smiled at Stam, sadly. "I don't think it's any sillier that you could like Aurelio than I could still be pathetically in love with a man less than half my age who died over forty years ago."

"What does that have to do with greed?" Stam asked, still awaiting an answer.

He looked back down at the dirt, and then to the bird, who remained inflated like a balloon.

"When I came back from Brazil, the truth had hit me at last." He swallowed, pausing to brush a small tear from his eye. "My memory meant nothing. I'd forgotten everything about the man I had loved. That was 1980, and Sydney died in 1958—after those twenty-two years, I couldn't remember a thing about him; his voice, how his skin felt, how he smelled—even what he looked like. I couldn't accept that."

Stam nodded.

I hold on to *my* life because...." He lowered his head and wiped away another tear. "Because, I think to myself, that if I can just live *one more day*, then just maybe... *maybe* I'll remember his face."

Stam thought about it. It was sad, even to her, to imagine such an attachment to something that was lost. Nothing in her own life had ever been worth as much.

"I'm a monster, when it comes right down to it." Ashley sighed. "I've spent two decades killing more and more people so I could cling to a ghost. I'd live another twenty years this way if it meant I could hear his voice just once more.... So much for compassion, huh?"

Stam considered this. She supposed he was probably right in that—at the expense of thousands of people—he had pursued a selfish desire. At a glance, no matter her understanding of Ashley's situation, it seemed inarguable. But at the same time, she knew the guilt, in the end, rested with her. He was *her* accident.

"I have a confession, too." said Stam. Ashley failed to look up yet, but she knew he was listening. "I don't want you to die."

At that, Ashley looked up at her. "Why not?" he asked, surprised.

She was quiet, and seemed unsure what to say before responding, "I don't have a reason."

He thought about that reply. It was vague; it was blunt—what one could always expect from Stam—and it was enough that a small smile crossed Ashley's face. "I suppose you don't need one." His smile slowly faded as his eyes returned to the toolbox and dirt.

"Back when we met, I know I said some cruel things—and blamed you for a lot."

"You were right to do so." Stam shrugged.

"Maybe." Ashley nodded. "But I also could thank you. I don't much remember them anymore, but those thirteen years in England with Sydney...." He glanced to his bird; Sydney had just shifted in his arms. "I know I was happy, and at the time, it made up for *everything* else. It wasn't you who killed him." He sighed. "After he died, *time* stole his memory."

Ashley was quiet for a long time before adding, "I think about all this every single day, in one way or another, and I knew I was tired of it, but.... It's funny that a towed car was what opened my eyes."

"It started with Hannah," Stam corrected him. "She took the dirt. I shouldn't have been as careless as I was."

"Oh yeah." Ashley nodded, though not agreeing with Stam's claim of fault. "That's right—but it might still be for the best." He looked down to the ground once more. "How long was I going to keep this up, Stam?"

"For as long as you needed."

Ashley smiled again, almost laughing. It had been a week filled with many strange remarks from Stam, whose cold and relentless stoicism had never left room for a response such as the one she'd just given.

"*Rreeeerrk,*" Sydney grumbled, squirming in Ashley's arm before looking up at him.

"I guess we've got to get you out of this weather." Ashley scratched the bird on his throat.

"*¡Te Amo!*" Sydney chirped before burying his face in Ashley's arm.

Ashley sighed quietly as he turned his eyes back to the box of dirt where his hand was now resting half-submerged.

"How did that girl get her hands on the case, anyway?" he asked.

"… I was checking the time and she took it. She and her friends were tossing it around and refused to return it."

Ashley nodded, expecting as much. He said nothing for a bit, and then mused out loud, "Sydney used to say that he deserved to die for the things he'd done—maybe he was right." He shook his head. "Sydney, Josef, my brother, me—we were all *Nazis*, after all."

He took a deep breath.

"I've seen people who believed that youth—and the passage of time—would absolve them of sin. I've seen people who think that it's somehow within their rights as human beings to be cruel—people who believe that we possess the freedom to *hate* others."

Stam continued listening.

"But we don't. Nothing can give you that right. No religion, no government—nothing." He shook his head. "To be hateful or cruel is to renounce your humanity. It's true of *anyone*, at *any* age."

He examined where his fist remained buried in the dirt.

"I'm not sure how God sees it, Stam, but I think *some* people deserve to die."

Epilogue

28/11/1943 - Today I killed a man. I do not know his name. I hope God will forgive me.

29/11/1943 - Today I lost a lot of blood when someone shot me, and thus, I killed two people. I do not know their names. I hope God will forgive me.

30/11/1943 - Today I killed a man. I do not know his name. I hope God will forgive me.

1/12/1943 - Today I did something terrible to a boy named Gunther.

I have extinguished the light in thousands of eyes, ending lives young and old and taking more than has ever been my right to take. What I am due, I cannot say, but know that God shall grant.

I was once warned of a terrible power — that it is within my curse that I may spread it to others. Now it has happened: I saw eyes that I have made like mine. Death, I have always spread, but never once stolen.

I came upon a boy from a place called Germany. He had only moments left.

I must try to remember his face, thick blonde hair, and two blue eyes turned red. On his person was a letter containing his name: Gunther, and one of an addressee: Jens.

This alone is what I have with which to seek him. I must return to him what I took, and spare him from a life like mine.
This is the greatest of my sins....
... I hope that God forgives me.

* * *

Somewhere, at some time, a girl's hand peeled back the plastic wrapping of an album while her two eyes scanned the cover. Soon, that hand reached out to the needle of a player, nudging it down to where vinyl now spun.

Music filled the room, whisking her away to a time when she and her sister sat huddled together, absorbing the sounds of their new favorite album. Those evenings together, she was certain, were bliss.

As she listened, a thought crossed her mind of a blue-and-red-eyed boy who seemed now to have never existed. His face vanished as another feeling—perhaps just a childish musing or hopeless nostalgia—struck her: the music around her was etched in a spinning disc, and would remain there whether one played the record or not. Whether she or her sister—wherever she was—remembered the songs or not.

The same, she figured, was true of herself: she was a record. If she ever forgot what she felt in that moment—whether it was a sweltering summer in 1969, an icy winter in 2001, or any day in between—her own fleeting memory was not what mattered. What had *been* would always *be*, and in some odd way, it was a comforting thought.

The last song of the album played, and as the vinyl spun, there was no such thing as time.

<u>Acknowledgements</u>

Tremendous thanks go to Anna Sears, Cassaundra Eck, Jenx Byron, Janet Jongebloed, Anon Adderlan, Dylan & Melissa McKay, Jeff Mach, Donna Lynch, Gavin Grant, Bastat, my brothers Byron & Leon, my mother Suzan & my father Steven.

Also to Aradia Schneider, Bernadette Klein, Lia Elena Perianu, Kasia Terrill, Maria Kuruskina & Andrea Montiel for their help with foreign language translation.

http://www.nicholaiconliff.com/

www.ingramcontent.com/pod-product-compliance
Lightning Source LLC
Chambersburg PA
CBHW050859250626
47155CB00001B/26